RECKONING
Rise of the Guardians

This book is a work of fiction. Names, characters, places, and incidents are a product of the author's imagination or are used fictitiously. Any resemblance to actual events, locales, or persons, living or dead, is coincidental.

Copyright © 2024 by Olivia Boothe
https://www.oliviaboothe.com

Cover Design by Trif Book Design
https://trifbookdesign.com

Editing by Silvia Curry
https://sites.google.com/view/silviasreadingcorner

RECKONING

RISE OF THE GUARDIANS

A HELL'S ANGEL NOVEL

BOOK 3

OLIVIA BOOTHE

Three Brothers Press

For all the women with hearts of fire… and for the silent sacrifices they carry—the ones that shape the world with quiet strength, yet remain forever unknown.

AUTHOR'S NOTE

Reckoning: Rise of the Guardians is a dark apocalyptic fantasy romance. This is book 3 of the Hell's Angel trilogy and cannot be read as a standalone novel. For the full reading experience, please check out:

Afterworld: Losing Salvation 0.5
A short prequel (Not required reading)
AVAILABLE FOR FREE
Click the link above or visit the author's website

Afterworld: Road to Redemption Book 1
(Required reading)
ALSO AVAILABLE ON KU

Descension: Knights of the Seraphim Book 2
(Required reading)
ALSO AVAILABLE ON KU

Content Warnings

Angels and demons, biblical lore, zombies, Four Horsemen of the Apocalypse, blood and gore, trauma, profanity, graphic violence, some explicit sexual content, animal in peril, mention of child abuse, and mention of rape.

Reader discretion is advised.

IF YOU BRING FORTH WHAT IS WITHIN YOU, WHAT YOU HAVE, WILL SAVE YOU.

IF YOU DON'T BRING FORTH WHAT IS WITHIN YOU, WHAT YOU DON'T BRING FORTH, WILL DESTROY YOU.

THE GOSPEL OF THOMAS

KATE JONES'S JOURNAL
YEAR 2033

Dear Luke,

I don't know if you'll ever read this letter, and I hope that, perhaps, you never have to. My fingers are shaking as I write, my eyes swollen with tears as I struggle to find the right words to say to you—my son, my baby. I barely had a chance to hold you before you were stolen from my arms, and I can't stop blaming myself every second of every day for not being able to do more to protect you.

I'm so, so, so sorry, my love. Sorry I wasn't strong enough. Sorry I couldn't fight harder. My heart is beyond broken. Heavy with the pain no mother should ever have to endure.

But I need you to know that I will not rest until I find you. There is no realm I will not scour and no demon I will not slay to bring you back home. If I must tear the Heavens down or break into Hell itself and rip off the Devil's wings. I promise you with every breath in my lungs and every drop of blood in my veins, the universe will know the true might of a mother's pain. Because there is absolutely nothing I won't do to get you back.

Love triumphs over hate, Luke. Always remember that.

Your Mom,
Kate

The Dark

Cell 532-14 / Prisoner 626

Wakey, wakey… the disembodied, menacing male voice that has tortured me since I was dumped in this hole slithers through the black void of my prison, making sure I am unable to find a gram of peace in the punishing still-quiet of this tomb.

Panic traces a sharp claw down my back. I thought I had managed to block away the nail-sharp trills of the words that spill from its non-existent lips. But hope is useless here. With my naked body still coiled in a fetal position, I jerk my head up from the stone-cold floor, my bones and muscles feeling like they are made of rusted metal, brittle yet stiff. My eyes strain against the unyielding darkness, trying to pierce through the nothingness that envelopes me. I'm unable to see anything, not in this depthless crepuscule.

Pointlessly praying that somehow, this time, I can shield myself from that all too familiar sinister voice, I curl back into myself and mumble infinitely, "He will not triumph. He will not beat me. He will not break me. He will not triumph. He will not beat me. He will not break me. He will not triumph. He will not beat me. He will not break me. He will not—"

Oh, Jax. But he's already broken you, darling.

Fear squeezes around my heart and my body trembles as I cover my ears. "No. No. No. Please let it stop. Please. Just for one day."

Come, now. We've been through this countless times, the voice taunts like a haunting echo resonating within the chambers of my mind.

"You're not here. You're not real. Not real. Not real…" I mutter almost incoherently, my voice dry and rough like sandpaper, unrecognizable even to myself.

I never leave, Jax. I'm always here with you. Eternally.

"Please. Just let me be. Let me suffer this sentence alone."

She's never coming for you. You know that, Jax. Because she's dead. They all are.

"Lies."

Are they? It's been decades. A century, even. It's over. Samael won. Your people lost.

I fix my gaze on the impossible darkness, hopelessly scanning the impenetrable gloom of my lightless prison. The stench of despair suffocates me. Jesus. A hundred years? It can't be. I refuse to believe I've been in this confinement for more than a lifetime. But how can I know? It feels like a day but also a thousand years. Time is torture down here. A chill penetrates my bones until I become one with the stone. A hundred years in this solitary confinement, in this crushing loneliness. How long has it been out *there*? Could it be everyone I love is gone? Am I truly alone? I want to cry, but my heart has forgotten how. Or maybe it doesn't believe in tears any more. Maybe it gave up.

You orchestrated this hapless end, yet you dwell in your misery. In your own mistakes. In every broken promise. In all the shattered dreams.

My mind wills my body to move, but the effort is taxing, and I struggle to breathe through each painful stretch until I am finally able to sit with my back against the damp, slick wall. I stare into the nothingness again, as if still believing this time I can summon a glimmer of light. As if this time, I will see its face—the face of my tormentor.

But there is only black down in this pit, only a hollow emptiness that sucks away at my spirit a little more each day. "I was deceived," I moan as I watch all my regrets roll out before me. "I was forced…"

Forced? Who held your hand when you pulled the trigger, Jax? When you killed that innocent man? When you offered his blood to your mother?

The memory plays out in front of me like a movie. No one held my hand.

Who held your hand when you lied, and cheated, and desecrated God's temple? Who, Jax? Who held your hand when you drank from your mother's cup and swore your allegiance to her—to us—only to shoot her in the head? You betrayed her. Betrayed your brothers and sisters.

I crumble into myself, unable to watch the images dance around my cell—accusing me, ridiculing me, condemning me.

Did you think your sins would go unpunished? That you could escape the consequences of your actions?

"I thought—"

You thought that a man like yourself deserved redemption? Love? A child? Your fate was to bring forth the end of days, Jax. Your fate was to kill—to lie, to destroy, to bring suffering to the world. Your fate was fulfilled. And now you lie in a pile of shit of your own making.

You're where you belong, Jax. No one is coming for you, especially not her. Kate was too good for you —you knew that from the first moment you laid eyes

**on her. You were the architect of her pain. You gave
her hope, only to take it away.**

"I never wanted to hurt her."

**What you wanted was to rewrite your destiny, Jax.
But there is no afterlife for you but this. Your
sentence is hunger; it's regrets and sadness and loneliness. Nothing more.**

A thick and choking weight settles over my chest. Closing
my eyes, I take a labored breath. "Am I *dead*?"

Does your heart beat, Jax? it asks, cold and steely, its
voice familiar yet not.

Why do I know that voice?

With trembling fingers, I touch my bare chest, feeling my
protruding ribs. I am nothing but bones covered in skin. I've
hungered and thirsted for so long, I think I've forgotten what
food is. It must be true, then. I am dead, and this is my
eternal damnation. To be in perpetual darkness. To forever
yearn for light. To ceaselessly beg for rest, knowing it will
never come.

Then… a sound, a feeling.

There it is, right under the sharp edges of my ribcage—a
thump.

Faces flash before me. Kate's brown eyes twinkle as her
loving smile stretches, making my chest swell. Luke's innocent
gaze and his sweet little coos fill me with warmth.

Something rumbles within me, and suddenly, I don't feel
so dead anymore. My heart remembers how to cry, and tears
pour down my face. My family's absence weighs on me
heavier than the iron chains bound around my ankles. I sob
into the abyss, but there is no solace here.

Oh, how I would give anything to hold them in my arms
again. To kiss Kate's lips, to smell the sweet musk of her skin.
To hold Luke's tiny hand, to run a finger down his button
nose. God, I miss them so much, every fiber of my existence
aches with such ferocity it crumples me back to the bitter cold

floor. I curl into myself, body shivering uncontrollably. There is no rest for me here. No sleep. No peace.

The rock beneath me is unforgiving, providing no comfort for my crippling bones. It is slick and carved with sharp grooves. My fingertips burn and ache, and I realize my nail beds are raw. The slimy substance beneath me is likely my own blood—evidence of my attempts to claw myself out of this hell.

But this is a hell with no escape, because God doesn't exist here. Hope doesn't exist here. Only silence. Only darkness. Only irrevocable pain.

Then why not embrace that darkness? Accept the gift and become one of them…

Them… The lost souls-turned-demons that claw at the walls from the other side. The dammed creatures who torture me with the promise of eternity in this hole. No. I can't become one of them. I *will* not. Teeth clattering, I whisper, "Kate. Luke. They will come for me."

Kate left you here to rot for eternity. And you were a mere blip in your son's life. Purely insignificant.

I shudder. "What do you want from me?"

I want you to remember, Jax.

"What else is there to remember? You've already shown me all my sins. You've already shown me why I belong here."

No, Jax. You are trapped here because you believe this is where you belong. His voice changes. There is softness. Love.

You are trapped here because you put yourself here. You crafted this prison, Jax. You put up these walls. You conjured this darkness. You conjured my voice. And you—only you—hold the key to leave.

"First you condemn me, then you weave false dreams of hope. Your cruelty is boundless."

Jax… it croons.

Why does his voice sound like my own? More tricks, more

lies. "Fucking leave me to this misery alone. *Leave.* I prefer the piercing silence over your wretched, nauseating voice."

Then… nothing. Not even the sound of my own breath. Good. My tormentor is gone.

But for how long?

I curl back into a tight fetal position, my body trembling violently from the bitter cold. I struggle to convince myself there is an end to this suffering. Hopelessness has burrowed itself deep into my marrow. It is a part of me, of my blood; it tells me the war is over. It assures me that all is lost. Humanity is a slave to a merciless king, and I am forgotten, left to dwell in this infinite, stifling darkness.

I pray for oblivion, for true death. *Please, let there be an end.* I don't want to exist anymore. Not without ever seeing Kate smile again. Not without ever looking into my son's blue eyes. Not without ever knowing who truly won the war.

But this is what Samael wants, isn't it? To feast on my anguish and desperation.

Kate wouldn't stand for this. Kate would slap me across the face and tell me to pick my sorry ass up off the ground. She'd tell me to fight, even when I believed the battle was over. *Fight for me,* she'd say. For Luke. For all of us.

I close my eyes and think about the day I met her. Of her strength. Her bravery. Of her stubborn heart and abundant love. Kate would never let herself perish here. Not if it was a day, a hundred years, or a thousand.

So, I cling to her strength and sink deep within myself. Her memory is all I have left, and I refuse to let go.

He will not triumph. He will not beat me. He will not break me. He will not triumph. He will not beat me. He will not break me. He will not triumph. He will not beat me. He will not break me.

PART I

Chapter One

KATE

Holding a flame-lit lantern, I climbed the spiral stone staircase up to the Nativity Tower of *La Sagrada Familia*. The small, iron-barred balcony windows jutting out from the façade every four to five steps provided a foreboding glimpse of Barcelona's once bustling streets, but on this moonless night, only darkness penetrated those windows, snuffing out any significant illumination.

The fragmented shadows cast by my flame flicked on the walls like an ominous ballet of dancing demons reaching up from the depths of Hell, their writhing bodies a taunting reminder that, even inside this church, we weren't safe. But nowhere was safe, not until we ended this war. Which was why I was ascending to the top of the tower—to formulate a plan out of this fucking mess.

Up I went, my thigh muscles burning with every step, chest tightening from the exertion. The Guardians said the entire staircase was close to five hundred steps. I didn't know how many steps I'd already climbed, but I'd been at this for at least fifteen minutes and prayed the end was near. Leaning against the wall for a brief second, I caught my breath as I stared up at the never-ending spiral.

Pre-end-of-the-world, the church had offered a working elevator to its visitors that brought them up, though they'd still have to descend the tower on foot. But even with their solar power, Amada's people couldn't keep the elevator running. It required maintenance that no one was skilled in, and using it had turned into a risk no one wished to take.

After two years of being without use, I wasn't about to take that risk, either.

It wasn't like I was a stranger to stairs. When the apocalypse hit and we no longer had electricity, my legs had quickly adapted to not having the luxury of elevators. Still, I wouldn't have minded a lift. These steps were extremely steep, had no railing, and were so narrow you had to climb in single file. If you suffered from claustrophobia, this would be your worst nightmare.

Thankfully, small, confined spaces didn't paralyze me. And at least I did have one companion.

Hank huffed down at me from his perch about fifteen steps ahead. "I'm coming, bud," I said, craning my neck so I could see him around the bend. "Mama ain't a spring chicken."

He wagged his tail as he waited for me to catch up.

Out of the six towers surrounding the cathedral, this was the only one built by Gaudi himself, and given he was married to his desire to craft his church with the focus on nature's connection to God, there were no light fixtures. His goal was to illuminate the space entirely by using natural light. Seemed Gaudi probably never considered visitors would be climbing in the dead of night on a densely shrouded night.

But apparently, this was also the tower with the best views of the city, hence why we were meeting up there.

My walkie crackled, the sound joining the eerie echoes of my boots. "Did you get lost?" Clint asked through the communication device.

I brought the walkie to my lips. "Funny. If you guys wanted me up so urgently, I happen to remember we have a magical teleporter who could've made this trip much easier."

But not safer, Mikha'el whispered into my mind. *Rifting humans comes with risks, for both of us. We need to conserve our power.*

Then you could've flown me up, so quit complaining about how long it's taking me to climb this damn tower.

This tower doesn't exactly have a landing platform. And I wasn't.

I sighed. The angel was right about not being able to just fly me up there. From what I'd recently learned, the structure had originally been designed to be a bell tower, not a tourist attraction. "You two done with the mind-talking thing? It's rude," Clint added through the walkie. "And don't believe a word he says, Kate. His wings have been rustling for the last ten minutes. It's kinda unnerving. Hank just got here, by the way, so you're close."

"I sure hope so because my knees are gonna give out on me soon."

Five minutes later, I finally made it to the top of the tower and lost the last of my breath the instant I took in the scene splayed right outside the viewing ports. I knew this fight wasn't going to be easy—that Samael wasn't going to take the most recent defeat lightly. He'd taken my son and Jax, but we still had the four stones. Without them, his vessel—Luke—would be useless to him. But he hadn't been cast out of Heaven for being weak and defenseless.

Samael was determined to win, which meant he was going to hit us with everything he had.

When I'd returned from my flight to the observatory with Mikha'el, we discovered the church had been surrounded by the largest horde of devoured I'd ever seen. Took every single person we had to barricade the church from the inside. After all the damage the main cathedral took, the only way to protect it from the undead was using wards, but all that power had drained Mikha'el and his small cadre of warrior angels.

They took turns putting up shields, but it was merely a temporary solution. Keeping *La Sagrada Familia* safe with wards was not sustainable.

We knew, sooner or later, Samael's army would find a crack.

And that's why Mikha'el and Clint had summoned me to the tower.

Tall bonfires had sprouted around the perimeter of the church, their spires reaching ten to twenty feet high. Without the actual bell, the tower was still extremely tight, and Mikha'el took up a decent amount of space, especially when he didn't spirit away his wings—even tucked, they were hard to ignore.

I eyed those impressive, beautiful brass-colored wings as I pushed past the black-armored warrior and headed toward the balcony. The archangel frowned at me but said nothing. His gold-rimmed eyes dimmed as his wings suddenly disappeared.

Clint handed me the binoculars he'd been using. "It's not looking good."

I scanned the plaza in front of the Nativity Façade and my lungs caved. Hundreds of devoured in different stages of decomposition pushed against the magical shields erected by Remiel and his twin sister, Cassael—Mikha'el's newly arrived lieutenant. Apparently, she'd recently managed to escape the revolt in Heaven and had decided to join our fight. If not to support the human cause, then in loyal service to her commander.

According to the archangel, Cassael had been one of his most trusted court spies, and it was she who infiltrated the Powers and informed Mikha'el of the rebellion taking root in Elysium. Rumor had spread in Heaven of a newly born Nephilim, the hybrid child Samael needed for his rebirth. While many had sided with Samael, pockets of resistance were growing, angels willing to stand with us.

But, according to Cassael, Khama'el, the Prime Judge for the Holy Council, had been summoned to Abaddon. He'd been the one to send the sicarii after me. Which meant Samael was coordinating an attack, not just with his unholy army, but we would likely have to fight against the sicarii again—and this time, it probably wouldn't be a small squadron.

My heart thumped louder as I scanned deeper into the darkened alleys. I struggled to form the words to describe the creatures spilling out from the shadows.

Clint nudged me with his shoulder. My stunned silence clearly told him what I'd spotted through the binoculars.

"I call them arachnodogs," he said, voice proud. "I know, not too original," he went on, "but the name fits. And Mikha'el seems to like it. Apparently, there's no angelic name for them because they shouldn't exist."

I turned to Mikha'el, but all he could do was shake his head as he crossed his muscled arms over his chest, trying to contain his anger, his disgust.

The demonic hybrids were in fact that: hellhounds with eight legs that crawled over buildings like giant spiders. A product of Samael's corrupted song of creation.

But that wasn't all that had climbed out of the depths of Hell. Three giant, gray-skinned humanoid creatures with no faces, but only ginormous maws, paraded in front of the church, massive cleavers scraping against the asphalt, sending sparks flying. The slicing shrieks from their blades made my skin crawl.

"Those are the Butchers," Clint said, "or as *los Guardianes* call them… *los Carniceros*."

I knew what they were, but until now, I hadn't seen one. Jax had briefly told me about the creature he and Mikha'el had fought while I'd been hiding inside that store's bathroom when we first rifted to Barcelona. He'd told me what Mikha'el had done to protect us, to buy us time. I'd seen the damage with my own eyes, seen the burns to his entire body.

He must have sensed my thoughts and shifted his golden gaze toward mine. I'd used my power until my heart faltered, but I'd healed those burns. Still, I could never thank him enough for his sacrifice.

His gaze glinted. *It was my duty to protect you. To protect Luke.*

Shaking my head, I put the binoculars back to my eyes. *Stop being so righteous all the time and accept the gratitude.*

He smiled. *And miss seeing you roll your eyes at me?*

I rolled them with extra flare. If an archangel could find humor amongst all this carnage, then maybe I could, too.

Unfortunately, the moment didn't last long. After a couple of more scans across the plaza, I finally spotted the true reason Clint and Mikha'el had summoned me to the tower. Humans were mingled among the hundreds of devoured—un-infected humans.

Devil's Army sect members.

And they were not only controlling the devoured, but they were also actively counter-attacking the wards with their own devil-magic. Whatever they were chanting, combined with the sigils they were tracing, chipped away at the golden shield. Reddish cracks where their power out-matched Remiel and Cassael's could be seen spider webbing across the protective dome, threatening to dissolve it.

The devoured were also supposed to be repelled by angels, but clearly, not even the presence of the two warriors was making much of a difference. The creatures kept pushing themselves against the wards, scorching their bodies to a crisp, all to break through the shield.

Dressed in golden-trimmed, body-tight armor, the two warrior angels knelt inside the dome, their wings and arms spread as they channeled their celestial energy to power the wards. "How much longer can they hold the shield?" I asked, my gaze trained on their trembling bodies.

"They are draining themselves of their power," Mikha'el said. "We have thirty minutes, maybe an hour, if I join them."

I eyed him. "If the shield cracks—"

"We will be too weak to fight."

My body shuddered. We were in too vulnerable of a position. And once the sicarii joined the Devil's Army…

I didn't even want to contemplate the outcome. The Guardians were skilled fighters, but without empyrean weapons or holy water, there was no way we'd outlast an attack of this magnitude. It wasn't even the devoured I feared; the hellhounds and the Butchers were a mere sample of what lurked in the shadows.

"The Guardians can cast simple protection wards but without holy water, their weapons will barely be able to nick the hide on those monsters," I said.

"I'm so sorry, Kate. I wish there was more I could offer. Imbuing water with the power of the Holy Spirit is a higher sphere ability. Last time I tried to invoke its power, I incinerated myself. God made it possible for your ordained priests to do it as a special gift."

I scoffed. Nothing pissed me off more than hearing about all the dumb rules we apparently had to follow blindly. "Of course. Why would God make things simple?"

"Kate…"

"Honestly, spare me the reproach. Feels like at every turn, there's always some stupid obstacle we can't tackle because of some arbitrary rule God imposed on your kind or mine. None of this makes any fucking sense. And don't start with the God has a plan shit. Because whatever that plan is, it's not helping my people right now."

"I… might have a plan," Clint chimed in, cutting the tension between us.

My brows pinched, and I placed the binoculars on the port's ledge. "Spill it," I said, hopeful the kid might have seen something I missed.

"There's a small group of Guardians who joined *La Sagrada Familia* when they got split up from their main party after their church was attacked by a horde, one controlled by who they claim is the sect's presbyter. These Guardians were a scion of the Eastern Guardians, who were stationed out of Saint Mary's Basilica, only a few blocks from here. They say there's a clergyman—well, they can't confirm if he survived the attack, but it might be our only chance at holy water, Kate."

I nodded toward the plaza. "Clint, there's no way out of this church, not through that horde."

His lips curled into a self-assured smirk—the smirk that usually meant he was about to reveal something absurd. The kid had proven to be an incredible asset in the war against the Horsemen of the apocalypse, not to mention he was an exceptional tracker. And with his newly minted empyrean steel bionic arm, the kid felt invincible. Which scared me shitless.

I also had a feeling what it was he was about to suggest—the city of labyrinths underneath Barcelona, full of tunnels and anti-aircraft shelters used during the Spanish Civil War in the early 1900s. I'd already experienced the hellish creatures that lived under the streets of New York City, and I had zero desire to send him into Barcelona's web of underground streets.

"There's no way I'm letting you go down there alone," I said.

"I already assembled a team of Guardians. They know their way around the tunnels and how to get to Saint Mary's. It's a simple mission, Kate. Let me do this. What else do we have to lose?"

"I can't lose you, kid. Not again."

His lips thinned, his boyish features hardening, those aquamarine eyes darkening to a moss-green, making him look much older than he was, wiser. God, I hated the idea of letting him go into those tunnels. When we were warding the church, we had to barricade the entrance into one of those tunnels located deep in the bowels of the church to keep the demons lurking down there from infiltrating the cathedral.

What lived down there was birthed from the darkest and most depraved nightmares known to humankind. "I can do this, Kate. I must. Without holy water, we might as well give up now."

"What if their priest is dead?"

"Then we'll figure something else out, but we can't stand around here, staring at our ugly faces." His gaze fixed on the horde, jaw muscles twitching. "Watch as those assholes break down the shield and overtake the church." Meeting my eyes, he said, "I can't stand idle, Kate. I was given a second chance to fight this war. Let me do my part, please."

I tried reading Mikha'el's mind, what he thought about Clint's suicide mission, hoping maybe he agreed with me, that sending the kid down there was a total mistake. He blocked me from reading his thoughts, but his gaze told me everything. "Fine," I said to the archangel, biting back tears. "But we need to buy Clint more time. Let me join Remi and Cass. I can give them my power to help them hold the wards."

The archangel shifted on his feet, and that thing he did to the shadows where everything seemed to deepen to an impossibly darker shade of black loomed around us. "No. You'll be defenseless if the shield cracks."

"We have no other choice," I snapped. "Without celestial energy, the shield will fall."

He rolled his shoulders, as if holding back his disapproval was taking every ounce of strength he possessed. Mikha'el was accustomed to calling the shots. As commander of God's Heavenly Army, he wasn't used to people telling him no or disobeying his orders, especially not a lowly human. "I don't like it," he gritted.

"You don't have to like my plan to execute it. The four of us can hold the shield up long enough to give Clint time to get to Saint Mary's and back… hopefully with enough holy water to burn through those fucking demons.” I then turned to Clint. “Take Chaz with you.”

“He’s more helpful here, Kate. I can handle myself.”

“Either he goes, or you don’t.”

Kid sucked in a deep breath, holding back his protest. Hands on his waist, he dropped his chin and nodded. “Yes, ma’am.”

When he looked up and met my gaze, I wrapped my arms around him and said, “You get your ass back here in one piece, you hear? Don’t you break my shepherd’s heart.”

Pulling from our hug, he gave me one of those silly smiles and ruffled Hank’s ears. “I wouldn’t dream of it.”

Chapter Two

CLINT

I ran down the spiral staircase two steps at a time, practically sprinting and almost flying off the stairs and face-planting several times, which would've been a comical end to my life: after surviving two years of the zombie apocalypse and an angel assassin, I'm killed by a dumbass fall—seriously comical.

But I really couldn't slow down. Even with Mikha'el and Kate helping to fortify the shield wall, I wasn't confident we could make it to Saint Mary's and back before the Devil's Army busted through. But I had to try. God damn it, I had to try. I'd promised it to Kate, and there was no way I was going to let her down.

Kate… she…

She reminded me of my late older sister, and perhaps a part of me felt like I owed this to Terri. Because it had been my inability to keep a promise that… Fuck. I almost lost my footing again. When I made it to the bottom, I leaned my back against the wall and took a long, calming breath.

Shit. Some days I ran on autopilot, just following orders and doing what was necessary to survive. Other days…

Other days, my past snuck up on me. Like moments earlier, when Kate had put her arms around me and told me to come back in one piece. The way she hugged me… the way I *felt* when she squeezed like she didn't want to let me go. I couldn't help but think of the last day I saw my sister alive. The memory still ripped me to shreds.

But I couldn't let that slow me down. I needed to shut down those haunting images and get my shit together. I took off running again toward the Guardians' main holding area, where everyone was gearing up for the attack. The clinking of swords, cocking guns, and clattering of voices choked the air. About sixty-something fighters were assembled in the small courtyard, and the rest of the civilians were barricaded inside the dormitories, the doors heavily warded.

I spotted Chaz across the way, leaning a shoulder against the tall apple tree, talking to Kelsey, one of the guardians from the Saint Mary's scion. I took a second to gather myself, patting down my shirt and pants, as if smoothing out a wrinkle or two made any type of difference when we were about to head into demon-infested tunnels.

For some reason, though, the girl made me nervous. Like real fucking nervous.

And it wasn't just because her blonde bouncy curls and radiant honey-colored eyes made her look like an angel sent straight from Heaven, but because she kicked demon ass like one. Since joining Father Ortega's church, I'd had the opportunity to fight alongside the anointed warriors, but besides Kate, I'd never seen anyone fight quite like her.

Every movement looked like a choreographed liquid dance of blades. After God called back the angels and took His empyrean weapons away from the Guardians, everyone was pretty much free to select their weapon of choice.

She'd chosen twin Katana swords, and they looked downright deadly and absurdly sexy strapped across her back. Dressed in the Guardians' typical black combat attire, she stood with her back to me, and despite being in a rush to get going, I couldn't control my gaze from traveling up her body.

Every piece of fabric hugged her curves in all the right places. I swallowed hard, my body feeling flushed in parts that were wholly inappropriate, and I had to shake the wicked thoughts invading my mind.

But the girl was beyond hot, and the idea of being in tight quarters with her both excited and terrified the shit out of me.

I'd done my best to sell this mission to Kate as if it was no big deal, but I'd seen what lived in those tunnels. Kelsey had been right there with me after the battle against Beleth, when we had to clear the church of the remaining demons and zombies. We were almost ambushed by a pack of night-crawlers and several of those Sin Ojos abominations.

But fighting those monsters wasn't the only reason this mission wasn't going to be easy. Whenever I was around this girl, I turned into a rambling idiot. And tonight, I needed to be at the top of my game. Problem was, she was one of only two Guardians who had volunteered to go on this suicide mission with me. And she was the only one familiar with the tunnels and how to get to Saint Mary's.

I had no choice.

She turned toward me as if she'd sensed my approach and flashed me one of her mind-obliterating smiles—those rosy, puckered lips awakening a flame inside my belly. I literally felt my heart drum faster within the walls of my chest. "Clint." Her voice was sweet and silky, her East Coast accent reminding me of back home. "Dude, I was just telling Chaz about the arachnodogs." She pulled out her military knife from her thigh holster and examined the blade, pressing the tip of her index finger against the sharp point. "Told him Mikha'el gave you naming rights. Lucky bastard," she added with a soft punch to my bicep.

"It's a lame name," I said, crossing my arms and feeling heat rise up the column of my neck.

Raising her brows, she said with a toothy grin, "Can't wait to slice up those eight-legged freaks."

Damn me. It was exactly the way she could talk about killing demons while still smiling, as if we were going for ice cream at the park, that had me feeling like I could fall stupidly in love with this girl. I returned her smile, trying my best to curl my lips into my usual charming smirk, but all they did was twitch like I was some fucking spaz.

Chaz breathed deeply, his black T-shirt stretching across his barrel of a chest. "Please tell me she's joking. Give me zombies. The damn Butchers. Even the fucking scorpion shits we saw in the sewers. But spider dogs? Nah, man, I can't do giant spiders. No fucking way."

"Well, big guy, unfortunately, you might have to face off with them sooner than anticipated."

He pushed off the tree trunk, shadows darkening his deep-set brown eyes.

"Boss lady is sending you with us into the tunnels, and we ain't got time to waste. Mikha'el and Kate are joining Remi and Cass to help fortify the shield wall, but that's only gonna buy us about an hour to get there and back. We gotta go. Now."

"Fuck. The thought of going back into those tunnels makes me want to shit myself, but if it's Kate's orders, I'll go grab my gear."

Kelsey tapped my shoulder. "I'll find Alex and meet you two at the tunnel entrance."

As Chaz and I hurried down the crypt stairs toward the subbasement of the church, he nonchalantly said, "She's cute."

A knot formed in my throat, but I tried to mask it with a cough. I quickly glanced behind us, then pretended to have no idea what he was talking about, though I knew exactly who he was referring to. The thought alone sent a spark of awareness down my spine.

"Who?" I asked, as if he was referring to someone *he* was interested in.

"Quit messing, man. I've seen the way you look at Kelsey."

"Dude," I said harshly. "Keep it down."

He paused on the staircase and put a hand on my shoulder, forcing me to look at him. "Look, I know I ain't nobody to tell you this, but just… don't get attached, okay?"

I smirked. "You getting jealous on me, big guy?"

He gripped his dog tags. "After losing Tavs, I realized there's no room for love in this world. All it does is cripple you. You don't love nobody, then there's no fear of losing them, know what I mean?"

"So, if I get munched by one of them spider dogs down there, you ain't gonna shed a tear?"

A grin split across his face as he shook his head and kept walking down the stairs. "You mention those fucking things again, and I'm leaving your ass behind."

After a short walk down a poorly lit hallway lined with broken-down pews and old religious statues with chipped paint, we came around a corner and my heart jolted. "You two princesses ready to roll?" Alex asked, twisting his overgrown black mustache, his Texan accent punctuated with a playful tone.

Next to the barricaded double doors that led to the tunnels, Kelsey leaned against a wall while she used her army knife to slice into an apple she'd plucked from the tree in the courtyard. Her red and yellow scarf was wrapped loosely around her neck. She popped a crisp slice into her mouth and crunched it down, a bit of juice coating her lips. "'Bout time you showed up."

I cocked my head. "How the hell did you make it down here before us?"

"We weren't jacking off," Alex said as he adjusted his rifle.

"Where's everyone else?" Chaz asked.

Kelsey flung the apple core into a back corner, then tightened her ponytail. "We're it, baby."

Chaz eyed me. "You said you'd assembled a *team*."

I shrugged, a sheepish smile curving on my lips as I pinched my fingers together. "Small team."

The big guy shook his head in disbelief, a groan rumbling through him. "We're gonna die. We're gonna fucking die."

We removed the pews that had been stacked against the double doors, then used a set of bolt cutters to cut through the lock and chains that had been looped through the handles. When we pulled the doors open, a cold and damp breeze breathed out of the opening, chilling my bones. A rank stench seeped out as well, and we were forced to cover the bottom of our faces with scarves.

The solar panels didn't feed power into the tunnels, so we would have to rely on flashlights to navigate through the winding passageways. The four of us stood at the entrance, backs tense, chests rising and falling with deep breaths. No one seemed eager to be the first to walk through. "Last chance to turn back," I said, knowing we were all thinking the same thing. We knew we would be going in there, but had no clue if any one of us would return—alive or dead.

Kelsey flicked the flashlight on her headband, then unsheathed her Katana swords from her back. "Stay quiet. We don't want to wake anything up." She took first man position as she was the most familiar with the layout of the labyrinthine corridors that snaked under the streets of Barcelona, her footsteps quick as she entered the tunnel.

I followed Kelsey as Chaz flicked the tactical light on his rifle and took third man position, and Alex took fourth. The tunnels were wide and stretched on endlessly, the echoes of our footsteps mingling with the muffled groans of the devoured clogging the streets above us. There were so many, you could feel the rumble of the horde's footsteps vibrating through the ground as they pushed on the shield wall.

Another reminder we were on borrowed time.

The air was thick with the reek of decay, rendering our makeshift masks useless. I lowered mine. If the miasma of rotting flesh was going to assault my nostrils whether I covered my face or not, I'd rather breathe more freely.

Kelsey kept a fast and even pace as she moved through the darkened passages, following a path that seemed more muscle memory than anything else, because down here, without proper lighting, there was no easy way to read any signs that pointed east, west, north, or south. I had to trust she knew exactly where she was going. We couldn't spare a single second down a wrong turn.

Our flashlights caught fast glimpses of blood smeared, yellow-tiled walls, rubble from places where either the ceiling or walls had collapsed, trash, dust-covered crates, and the real reason for the stench suffocating the air—mangled corpses and demon guts. I raised my scarf to my face again, trying to block the putrid smell that accosted my nose as we passed a heap of decomposing human bodies. A shiver skidded over the back of my neck. Someone else had been down here to have piled them up like that.

As we continued to amble forward, the loud crunch of cracking bone echoed down the dark tunnel behind us, star-tling Kelsey and me.

"Dude, watch where you're stepping," I said over my shoulder, thinking someone had stepped on a corpse.

"Wasn't me," Chaz said. "Probably Alex."

When the Texan didn't reply, we all turned around.

I don't think I ever heard a man scream like Chaz did when our lights illuminated the tunnel behind us. A giant arachnodog, standing only a few feet away, held Alex's headless body in one of its clawed limbs. Alex's legs still twitched as the demon munched on his severed head, shards of skull fragments and brains exploding from its jaws, Alex's blood raining down over us.

Gunfire erupted as Chaz emptied his rifle into the beast, the marine hollering in both terror and rage.

But the monster was a hybrid demon, and its hide was made of the same tough skin that hellhounds possessed. Most of the bullets ricocheted right off as the beast lunged for us, nipping Chaz on the shoulder with one of those clawed, hairy legs. Those hairs might've been spikes; it was hard to tell in the poor lighting.

Knowing bullets were mostly useless, I fired off an arrow bolt aimed at its head, but the ugly shit was fast and ducked in time. Kelsey took advantage of the beast's brief distraction and sliced her swords through the air, hacking two, then three legs off the demon. Black blood splattered our faces as the creature hissed and belted an ear-piercing screech.

I aimed again, and this time, didn't miss as the arrow found purchase between the many eyes on its disgusting face. Its skull exploded and relief swam through my veins as its body keeled over. "That's for Alex, you piece of shit."

"Clint," Kelsey said, pulling my attention away. When I faced her, blood drained to my feet. Hunched on the floor next to her, Chaz clung to his injured arm. "Fuck, man. You okay?"

He moved his hand away from the gash. The demon had sliced through meat and bone, the wound already festering. "We need to get you to Kate," I said.

He grunted, breath hissing through clenched teeth. "Nah,

kid. There's no time. You need to get your asses to that church."

"I'm not leaving you."

"The mission, Clint. Remember what I told you." His dark gaze zeroed into mine, and I knew what he meant. No attachments. But that wasn't how I was wired. Growls and groans echoed from the dark. The dead were rising—that's what those bodies had been, the infected who'd been dumped down here. We had no choice but to keep moving toward Saint Mary's.

"Get up, Chaz." I reached under his shoulder and helped haul him to his feet.

His breaths grew shallow. "I'll only slow you down, kid."

Kelsey nudged my elbow. I didn't want to meet her gaze. I knew what would be etched in those eyes, what that furrow between her brows would say.

Though it wrenched my gut to accept it, Chaz was right. He'd only slow us down. Unholstering my gun, I handed it to him, along with an extra clip—my only clip—hands shaking. "Here, you get back to Kate. She can heal you with her blood."

Chaz's lips quivered, either from pain or fear. Maybe both.

"Dude. Don't you fucking let me find you turned into a demonic zombie. You find Kate or get to the clinic."

His lips upturned into a strained smile, sweat coating the top of his upper lip. "If I turn into one of 'em shits, you better put an arrow right between my eyes, kid." He gripped my arm. "Promise me."

I gripped him back. "You ain't turning."

He pulled me closer, his voice grim. "Promise me."

I bit the inside of my cheek, struggling to form the words. Saying them would feel like I'd accepted there was no hope for him, that he was already dead. But I knew he needed to hear me say it; that, despite his motto of having no attachments, in the end, he wanted it to be a friend who put him to rest. So, I said the words, even if they burned my tongue.

"Go, before you lose more time. I'll handle these fuckers." He took the flashlight off his rifle and put it between his lips, using his uninjured arm to aim the handgun I'd given him at the incoming horde. "Go," he shouted again as he began to pellet the zombies one bullet at a time—all head shots—bodies dropping like fallen trees.

I sent a silent prayer to Mikha'el, hoping the archangel would hear me and maybe send someone down to help Chaz from the other end.

"Let's go," I said to Kelsey. "Time to haul ass."

Shots rang behind us, and I knew Chaz would soon run out of ammunition. I tried not to dwell on those thoughts. If there was one way to honor my friend, it was to do as he'd said, and that was to stick to the mission. Kelsey ran ahead, slicing through newly risen zombies like they were nothing but meat sacks, blood spraying everywhere.

Provided we didn't run into any more giant spider dogs, we could handle the occasional undead. We turned right, then left, and encountered a blockade of fallen debris. "Fuck," Kelsey groaned. Seemed the ceiling had completely collapsed, closing off the way through.

"Don't tell me this is the only way to the church."

"There's another tunnel, but the floor collapsed and now it's flooded."

"How deep are we talking?"

"Waist high, at least."

"Shit. That's gonna slow us down."

"We have no other alternative."

She led us down a few more turns until we finally came to the entrance of the flooded tunnel passage. The water was so dark and still, it looked like a magic mirror hiding a monstrous nightmare below its shimmering surface. The sound of slow dripping water echoed off the walls. When I pointed the flashlight through, I couldn't even see to the other end. "How far does this go?"

"Couldn't tell ya. We never used it because it was flooded."

"We're fucked."

"Royally." Kelsey didn't even stop to think about it as she took a cautious step toward the water.

I put a palm on her shoulder. "Hold on. We don't even know what might be in that water."

She twisted to look at me, face covered in dried demon blood, mouth curved into a mocking grin. "Scared?"

"Fear is a survival skill."

"And it's a death sentence if you let it paralyze you."

"Since you're so brave, lead the way, Guardian."

Her eyes narrowed. "So gallant of you."

"Not to sound gruesome, but you saw what happened to Alex. Taking the rear is not exactly the safe option here."

She angled her head, pausing for a breath as she thought back to the Texan, to *her* friend. I regretted the words immediately. "Kels, I'm sorry. I..." The humor she seemed to always wear as a security blanket fell from her, revealing the truth we all kept hidden. The truth that would otherwise unravel us much too soon if we allowed it to surface.

The brief but poignant pain in her eyes tugged at something deep inside me, evaporating the words that sat on my tongue. Our gazes locked, and we both realized at that moment how fickle our lives truly were. Four of us had gone into that tunnel. Two of us remained, and we hadn't even reached the church.

Choosing silence, she twisted back toward the tunnel, but this time, her shoulders seemed a tad more deflated.

Dark and oily fear slithered through my heart as I watched Kelsey waddle into the tunnel, swords held above the water as she slowly moved into the deeper parts. I knew then exactly what Chaz had warned me about, but his warning had come too late. My blood had already begun to thrum with something sweet and warm since I'd met her days before, a feeling too foreign yet beckoning.

One I'd been too scared to entertain, but one I was now scared shitless would end before it ever grew into something… more.

Following her, I hissed as I took my first step into the dark icy water and immediately began to second guess our decision. The air was thick and stale, filled with a faint, metallic scent. The light from our flashlights barely penetrated the darkness ahead, the water rippling with each cautious step we took.

Wet coldness seeped through my clothes and deep into my bones. The slick, moldy walls of the tunnel seemed to close in around us, the silence oppressive, broken only by the sound of our breaths and the faint echo of that one single water drop. My boots hit the uneven bottom, and I nearly fell over as I slipped on a broken slab of concrete. I kept pace at an arm's length behind Kelsey, the water reaching my navel while I kept my crossbow at shoulder level. "So, how'd you end up in Barcelona, anyway?" I asked, needing to focus on something else.

"When Hell broke loose, and the world was in a panic, headquarters knew we needed to fortify all our strongholds. I'd been a newly minted Guardian, and they assigned me to the Saint Mary's scion to support La Sagrada Familia."

"How did you become a Guardian?"

"It's a duty passed down through generations—that's how most of us get indoctrinated into the order. My entire family, dating back centuries, were holy warriors."

"That's incredible. I… didn't even know any of this shit was real, let alone that Guardians, who had been fighting the forces of evil since the beginning of time, existed. It's enough to make anyone go mental."

She scoffed. "I think we're all mental at this point."

"Where's your family now?"

"I… lost contact with them once the grid went down." She halted for a moment, her back stiffening as if saying those words out loud had carried a load heavier than she'd anticipated.

"I'm so sorry, Kels. We all carry the loss of someone in our hearts."

Shrugging as if she could so easily flip a switch to her emotions, she said, "But now that the stones have been recovered, perhaps we can finally end this war once Mikha'el decides to close the fucking gates."

"Hold up. Do you have an issue with the archangel?"

She looked over her shoulder. "All I'm saying is that Mikha'el better have those stones protected. We've lost too many people to this war to lose them again."

"Of course they're protected. Why wouldn't they be?"

"He's just really focused on Kate and finding that baby… and after what happened with Gavri'el… I don't know. He seems… different."

This time, I was the one who stopped wading through the murky water, a dark nail of unease trailing up my spine. "That *baby* is Kate's son, Kels."

Taking note of the firmness in my tone, she took a calming breath, eyeing me cautiously, perhaps realizing she'd trudged on a touchy subject for me. She knew how I felt about Kate and Jax. "I understand that's her son, but Mikha'el has the power to close the gates with those four stones. He could end this war now, yet he's choosing to keep them open, and for what? To rescue one baby when there's a million other babies on this planet who are suffering. They need saving, too, you know. They matter, too."

"I'm not saying that they don't matter, but closing the gates is not the end game, Kels. Samael must be destroyed—killed for good or the risk of him coming back will always be there. They can't do that until they know Luke and Jax are safe. Luke may be just one baby, but he's Kate and Jax's son." I raised my empyrean steel-plated arm. "And Gavri'el made me swear an oath to protect him—to protect them all. She saved me for that purpose, and I'm not giving up on that mission."

"I'm not asking you to."

"Then what *are* you asking?"

"Nothing. I just… He better have a plan, that's all."

"He does. And the stones are well warded inside the sacristy. No one is getting in there."

Her eyes glinted under the pale light of my flashlight and she half-smirked. "Let's hope you're right, then." She was about to turn back toward the tunnel exit when her back muscles flexed under her black shirt. Scanning the surface of the water, she asked, "Feel that?"

"What?

"Something just touched my leg."

I chuckled. "And here I thought you were the brave one."

"Shh. I think something's in the water."

There was a slight disturbance on the surface of the water, and my heart raced as I shone my flashlight on the ripples, only to find nothing there. "Probably just debris—"

Kelsey got pulled under before I had a chance to reach her, arms and swords flailing in panic as she disappeared.

"Kels!" Without thinking, I strapped my crossbow behind my back and plunged into the dark water, diving for her. My hands reached out, but instead of grabbing hold of Kelsey, my fingers gripped around cold, slimy, rotting meat. I pulled it back, the devoured and I breaking the surface at the same time. Its grotesque, deformed face was inches from mine, jaws snapping to rip a chunk out of my head.

I grabbed onto its neck with my empyrean-steel arm, fingers digging into the soft, decomposing flesh. I was about to decapitate it, but my foot got caught between two large rocks and I fell backward into the water, taking the creature with me. I clamped my mouth shut as I plunged into the chilling wet darkness while still trying to hold the monster from sinking its nasty teeth into me.

Then it suddenly went limp.

A hand reached down and pulled me up, my head breaking the surface, lungs gasping for air. "You okay, pretty boy?" Kelsey asked with a toothy grin as she pulled her sword from the devoured's head, its body floating between us.

Wiping water from my eyes, I stood and stared at her cocky smile. "I rescued you first."

"I had that totally under control."

"Sure, you did, Goldilocks."

She sheathed her swords and readjusted her headband, the attached flashlight blinking back to life. "Let's go. I think we're at the end. The church's basement entrance should be around the corner."

Pulling ourselves out of the flooded tunnel and stumbling onto dry ground, we groaned in relief to be out of the freezing water and whatever else might've been lurking under the black surface. Kelsey was first on her feet, though her muscles seemed stiff. I jumped to my feet as well, and instinctively rubbed her arms when I noticed her lips, and practically her entire body, quivering uncontrollably. "Hyperthermia is going to settle in if we don't get dry soon."

She nodded. "Th—this-s-s way," she stuttered, though the fierce determination in her eyes told me this girl wouldn't let hyperthermia do her in when we were so close to the finish line.

We set off down another winding tunnel until we came to an open circle, a set of metal double doors embedded into the rock, four other tunnel entrances surrounding us like the spokes on a wheel. When she tried to yank the doors open, I wasn't too surprised to find them locked.

She kicked the door. "Fuck."

"What do we do now?" I asked, scanning the darkened

tunnels surrounding us. I couldn't see down those halls, but I knew we weren't alone.

"This is it. This is the only way into the church."

"Can't we exit out into the street and access the church from the outside?"

"Not without losing more time. We could wind up blocks away, or worse, in the middle of a horde."

An all too familiar and bile-inducing clicking sound echoed from the tunnel to our left. We needed to get through those doors. I banged on the metal with my fist, once, twice, three times. "Anybody there? We're from *La Sagrada Familia. We need help.*"

The clicking drew closer. Lips still quivering, Kelsey whirled toward the sound, swords drawn. The tunnel circle began to fill with the other distinct sound I'd grown too accustomed to—the groans and high-pitched squawks made by the devoured.

I drew my crossbow in the direction of the sound while continuing to pound my fist against the metal doors. "Help us!"

The Sin Ojos demon who'd been lurking in the shadows, and who'd likely been hunting us since we entered the tunnels, lunged out of the darkness, its needle-sharp teeth glinting under the light of Kelsey's flashlight. The air hung thick with the stench of sulfur, the echoes of our panicked breaths bouncing off the damp stone walls.

We'd cornered ourselves, and now there was no way out of this mess but to fight our way through. The demon's haunting screeches reverberated through the tunnel, sending chills down my spine as the horde of zombies lurched closer.

Kelsey and I stood back-to-back. I raised my crossbow, the loaded bolts ready to be unleashed on the undead approaching us, their gnarled hands reaching out, their mouths full of rotted teeth, hungry for our flesh.

As the Sin Ojos drew closer, its claws scraping against the

tunnel walls, Kelsey pushed off me, her swords poised for an attack as she confronted the beast head on. "Though I walk through the valley of the shadow of death, I fear no evil, for thou art with me, O Lord."

The demon hissed at her words, but Kelsey didn't relent as the creature screeched its displeasure. She swung her blades as the vile beast launched itself at her, claws ready to rip her to shreds. I aimed my crossbow, but hesitated. Kelsey was an anointed Guardian, and the last thing she needed right now was my help, especially when I had my own demons to slay.

One at a time, I shot my crossbow at the decaying bodies spilling out from one of the tunnel entrances, bolts finding their marks, heads exploding. My heart raced as the undead fell around me, but they kept coming, their numbers seemingly endless. The double doors to the sub-basement of Saint Mary's church still lay closed behind us, our only hope of escape turning to dust.

"In thy name, O Lord, I wield these swords as instruments of thy righteous wrath," Kelsey shouted breathless, leaping around the tunnel circle like a deadly ballerina, striking the Sin Ojos with blunt force. Her shadow danced on the ceiling as she delivered blow after blow, hacking the demon to pieces. "To smite the darkness and banish the shadows." Her voice was raw, drained, black blood spraying everywhere until there was nothing left of the demon but a pile of severed limbs and guts.

Ragged breaths huffing from her chest, Kelsey limped toward me as I shot my last bolted arrow. Her eyes were wide, almost lost in some type of panicked fury. She raised her swords, but I put a hand on her shoulder. "You okay?"

As if startled, she jerked her head to me, eyes still wild. "Rolled my ankle. I'll survive." She'd wanted to sound unbothered, but her words came out breathless, almost shaky.

I knew she was as tough as they came. It had only taken that one battle I'd first seen her in to know she could hold her own, and could probably fight better than any of us. A rolled ankle wouldn't stop her from kicking demon ass. But that's not what I'd truly asked her.

"Kels, you were just attacked by a demon."

"Yeah, and I killed it."

"You know it's okay to *not* be okay, right? To be scared."

She seemed to snap out of her angered daze for a fleeting moment, pausing for a second as her eyes roamed my face. She looked at me like something I'd said had tugged at some chord she hadn't even realized was there. Her expression softened, lips parting as if she was going to say something, but then a gear clicked in her mind, her jaw going rigid.

Whatever she'd meant to say at that moment turned to smoke, and instead, she nodded at the endless horde of devoured inching toward us, her expression freezing over like black ice, those beautiful, warmed-honey-colored eyes hardening to cold stone. "Worry about keeping yourself alive, Clint, and I'll worry about myself." Whirling away from me, she spun her swords, cutting down zombies like she was a scythe slicing through tall grass.

I'd not been prepared for the way her harsh words smashed into me. It was as if, for a brief second, she'd shown me the real part of her she kept hidden. The part she masked with wit and sarcasm because otherwise, it would consume her.

But there hadn't been any time to dwell on those thoughts, those emotions. There would be time to peel back her layers, provided we survived this tunnel. With my bolts used up, all I had left was my army knife and my empyrean arm. Pushing into the horde, I stabbed zombie after zombie in the head, using my arm to elbow and shove others aside. We were lucky these zombies seemed freshly dead and were slow as fuck; otherwise, we would've joined their ranks by now.

Still, the fuckers kept coming, the tunnel circle practically swarming. I'd even lost sight of Kelsey at one point. I tried shouting for her, but the droning of the devoured muffled all other sounds.

Right when it seemed we might meet our end, the double doors burst open, and a flood of light poured into the tunnel. The blazing brightness seemed to startle the zombies. The sudden quiet was pierced when I felt water rain over us, and the hissing began.

No, not hissing. *Burning.* The sound of burning flesh when demons were sprayed by…

Holy water.

"Padre!" The words poured from Kelsey's lips like an answered prayer, the sound emerging from somewhere within the pit of the undead.

Saint Mary's priest, along with other Guardians, rushed through the doors. That's when I noticed the priest was using an aspergillum to spray us with holy water as he chanted a prayer. The zombies retreated from the light and water, falling back into the shadows.

Arms grabbed me from behind and I thrashed, accidentally elbowing a Guardian in the face, thinking I'd been grabbed by a zombie. Another Guardian rushed in to help him. Kelsey was also being dragged through. As the heavy doors slammed shut behind us, I collapsed against a wall, my breath ragged. Kelsey stood beside me, her body still vibrating with an adrenaline surge.

Two men pointed the muzzle of their rifles at our heads. The one wearing a Superman T-shirt under his green bomber jacket said, "What the fuck were you two idiots doing in that tunnel?"

A broad smile slowly slashed across her face. Kelsey dropped her swords and smacked the man's rifle away, crashing her body into his and roping her arms around his neck as he wrapped his arms around her body.

Chapter Three

SAMAEL

The always-mocking heatless fire inside the monstrously sized, black-stone hearth of my bedchamber fed my silent rage as I stared at the flickering flames, the ache at the base of my wings spreading across my shoulder blades, the strain of their weight hanging off my back like boulders of lead. I'd been sitting there for hours—maybe days… who the damn-demons knew anymore.

Time was irrelevant here. It had no fucking meaning. And now… now I struggled to find any meaning at all—in anything.

Because everything I'd ever done, I'd done for *her*. For Gavri'el, Virtue of the Second Sphere, Emissary to the Lord God. Even the bleeding heart I'd laid at her feet.

All of it.

For her.

And still, it had not been enough.

I had not been enough.

So, I'd chosen to kill her. Chosen to end her life, knowing that angels possessed souls but didn't have an afterlife. It was

God's final insult to our kind. Upon death, we died. Simple as that. Our essence becoming nothing but cinders and dust.

I'd known it, yet I'd sanctioned Gavri'el's death. She'd known it, and out of spite, had chosen to gift her last breath to Mikha'el to slight me. To keep me from claiming retribution for the way she'd filleted my raw, beating heart.

But had I truly wanted Gavri'el dead because she'd loved another? Had I ordered her execution because she'd taken my best friend to bed? Because she'd offered him her soul-bond when I'd craved it more than life itself? The festering wounds of that betrayal cut deeper than anyone would ever know, but no, that's not why I'd ordered Beleth to kill her.

I knew it had all been in vain the instant she'd chosen to fight for the humans. The sacrifice I'd made, this misery… it had all been for naught. And in the end, she'd chosen to punctuate her final farewell by becoming a fucking martyr for those insipid beings at the hands of God's mightiest warrior.

But she'd not screwed only me. She'd given poor, dear, intolerable Mikha'el the ultimate shaft—he'd been a victim of her venomous lies as well. If she'd loved him with the true power of their supposed soul-bond, she would've never asked him to take on that burden. The golden, perfect son with his virtuous heart could never bear the guilt. It should've pleased me greatly that at least his anguish would likely consume him more than my own would.

But she'd played a wicked game, robbing me of that final blow.

Unable to contain the wrath scorching me from within, I shot to my feet, knocking back the wooden chair I'd been sitting on. I picked it up and flung it into the fireplace, a roar erupting from my chest as the chair splintered into a million shards of burning wood. "God damn you, Gavri'el!"

Tearing myself away from the hearth, I marched to the large open window and fixed my gaze on the drab, colorless landscape of punishing frost and rock that stretched for infinity. Such a contrast to the beautiful sandy shores of Elysium's Vermillean Sea, its blue-green waters crashing on the coast of Halcion Summit. Cursed demons. I couldn't even remember the last time I'd felt the warm rays of Luminora or tasted the salty ocean mist on a cool, windy morning while riding my steed.

A suffocating weight settled on my chest. I hadn't thought about my home in so long.

I'd sunk so deep into my revenge, consumed by nothing but hatred and anger, that I'd cared little about my previous life—because all I'd cared about had been the new life I'd planned to create.

But Gavri'el's death…

It had unearthed so many buried memories. Had reminded me of everything I'd taken for granted. Of everything I'd willingly left behind because I believed one day everything I'd done—for her, for us, for our kind—would *mean* something.

And that something had turned to vapor. I now stared up at Abaddon's leaden sky, its bruised grayish hue an echo of the mourning that coated my insides like the tar clinging to the dead trees of the Wastes.

I fisted my hands, choler fermenting in my gut. This imperishable woe could not be my end.

Looking over my shoulders, I cursed the sickness eating at my detestable frail wings.

If only I could fly myself out of this forsaken realm. I gritted my teeth as I attempted to stretch each wing, the brittle bones cracking as if I was some decrepit, hollowed-out ancient husk. My back muscles spasmed, the throbs making my entire body tremble.

There was no use. Without the Creation Stones and a viable host, I would never be able to heal myself. I'd never be able to fly or rift myself out of this fucking hell.

My lifeless wings fell at my heels with a loud *thump*.

Defeated. I felt so damn defeated, I wanted to shred myself in half. I'd waged this fucking war in her name. I'd defied my Father, my Creator, my home, to give her a kingdom. To make her a queen. And in the end, it had not been enough. The realms I'd secretly visited against my Father's wishes, and the gifts I'd thieved…

None of that had meant anything.

The Creation Stones—I'd taken them to grant her the child God had denied us. I'd spat on His most treasured children, willing to destroy their glorious Earth, all to show her that we deserved the same gifts He'd granted them. The suffering that had been bestowed upon me, upon my court, my friends. I'd brought it down upon us because I'd wanted to give her everything that should've been ours from the beginning of time. Because I'd wanted to give her the eternal happiness she deserved.

And how did she show me her gratitude? By denying me her loyalty. By refusing to offer me the bond—the bond I'd fought so hard to earn. And now, I couldn't even claim her death. I wasn't even worthy of that. I was nothing but a spurned lover, a scrap of rubbish to be tossed aside.

I looked around my bedchamber. The cold, black stone walls. The bed dressed in stale white linens that offered nothing but restless sleep. I would've taken a bed made of nails if it meant I could at least find an ounce of peace, that I could sleep this sorrow away.

This… this dreadful castle had been my home for thousands of lifetimes, and for what? I'd given everything up for an angel who'd so easily given *me* up.

I'd pretended—lied to myself, more like—that I'd not shed a single tear for that blasted angel. That I'd been wholly unperturbed. But the crack that rumbled through my body when I felt her die—because despite not being her soul-bonded, I'd felt it the moment her heart had stopped beating —that crack had been loud enough to make Abaddon's dead sky thunder, to make the ice crusting this cursed kingdom shatter and splinter all the way to its bottomless depths.

My lips quivered as I continued to stare at the unending reminder of my solitude. The burning behind my eyes grew unbearable, but I refused to let another single drop of sorrow roll down my cheek. I pounded a fist against my heart, wishing I could pummel it to a pulp so I could stop feeling the crushing agony of her absence. Even if I hadn't felt the warmth of her skin for thousands of years, knowing she still lived had been a balm against the persistent ache in my core.

Foolish imbecile, that's what I'd been. Allowing myself to believe that somehow, her death could fix me, that it could free me of this torment. I should've known better. Hope didn't exist in Hell, it couldn't. That was the cruel beauty of its irony. This was my kingdom, and even *I* had fallen victim to its vile deception.

Gavri'el's death hadn't brought me peace; it had submerged me in a boiling vat of immeasurable torture. If that was even conceivable, given the countless millennia I'd spent trapped in this wretched place.

Now, more than ever, the humans would truly witness the horror of the heinous devil their world had conjured from their darkest, most depraved nightmares. With Gavri'el gone, there was nothing left for me to do than to willfully surrender myself completely to the black, oily nothingness that had swallowed up my soul.

This was who my father had always wanted me to be—had needed me to become. He'd tasked me with testing his humans, with showing them the fragility of their existence.

So be it.

I would not only bring those mortals to their knees, but I would find my father and yank His cowardly ass out of His damned hiding hole and make Him watch as I cut down His warrior priests, starting with His newly anointed saint.

Shutting my eyes tightly, I sank within myself, searching for the quiet, for the space at the center of my damaged soul. I'd stopped feeling His presence long ago, but I knew that no matter where He'd gone, He could always hear me. Hear my clamors, though He'd chosen to ignore them all.

Hear me, Oh Father. You wanted me to drown in my regrets, to despise what I am, to loathe the odious monster I've become. Bravo. Victory is yours. But no matter the guilt that rots me from the inside, I will never fall at Your feet and beg You to wash me of my sins. But know this: wherever You are, I'm coming for You. You and Your damn crown.

A knock sounded at my door. "Come in."

Chemoth, my Horseman of Pestilence, pushed through the entrance, his body now fully healed from the wounds Mikha'el had carved into his flesh, though without his Creation Stone or a host, he'd reverted to his demonic form. He didn't bother using glamor to disguise his charcoal-colored hide, his hooved feet, fanged mouth, or horned face. Shoulders squared, he tucked his wings tight against his back, choosing to keep them in view instead of spiriting them away.

Despite the black-as-tar diseased feathers that stemmed from each plumaged shaft, he wore the wings with pride. Because even sickly, our wings defined who and what we were —Fallen, but angels, nonetheless. We were still the universe's most divine creations, and we would refuse to relinquish our birthright, no matter how many more epochs we were forced to endure our banishment from Heaven. "Khama'el has arrived, my lord."

It was about time the noxious worm showed up. "Well, let's not keep our honored guest waiting." Donning my pre-Fall skin, I let Chemoth lead the way.

Chapter Four

SAMAEL

Khama'el hadn't arrived alone. He'd been accompanied into my great hall by a small legion of sicarii, all fitted in luminous silver-colored Empyrean armor, their sapphire and gold-trimmed white hooded cloaks draping over their shoulders. Crossbows and swords strapped across their backs, the holy assassins glinted across my throne room like a wave of deadly starlight, their famed platinum-tipped wings spirited away. The metallic clatter of their thudding boots echoed off the stone floors as they marched in perfect synchrony.

Slouched over my throne, I listlessly stared at Khama'el, a Power of the Second Sphere, overseer of God's elite covert forces, and Prime Judge of the Holy Council. He ambled toward the dais, chest puffed as the sea of armored angels fell into formation behind him. Though I'd decided to welcome him in the skin he was most familiar seeing me in, I'd made sure to un-spirit the crown made of crooked bones that my father had so graciously fused to my fucking skull.

"Samael." He and his warriors took a knee before me, lowering their heads in respect. I was the Fallen One, but I was still my father's first angelic creation, and subjugation had been bred as second nature into every angel of the lower spheres.

"Stand, Khama'el."

Nodding, he straightened, the sicarii following suit. One of the oldest angels in my father's court, Khama'el had also been one of the Lord God's most trusted advisors, and now, he'd come to pledge his fragile fealty to me. I hated that I needed his damn assistance and fought sneering at the slimy courtier. If he could so easily betray my father, I held little reservations that he wouldn't do the same to me.

Loyalty was never absolute.

I'd lived long enough to know that greed was merely a dormant seed that lived inside all of us. It was only a matter of watering the soil with the right dose of temptation to get its nasty roots to germinate.

Khama'el's long, white hair was tied into a tight knot at the nape, his high cheekbones sharp, eyes glimmering like pools of liquid silver. The snake had the gall to meet my eyes, as if he didn't stand before the King of Sins, as if he could hide the slimy scales slithering beneath his angelic skin.

Clad in court regalia, he adjusted the collar of his tunic. Proudly dressed in the sapphire and gold of Elysium's standard, he raised his chin as if his mere presence here wasn't treason against God's kingdom.

Ever the grimy politician; he played both sides.

He raised a hand to the hilt of the sword strapped to his hip, the platinum-tipped plumage of his wings shimmering with the metallic sheen of newly preened feathers. The strong scent of the especially perfumed oils used was a deliberate show of his elite status amongst my kind.

Such a pompous display of his privilege was infuriating. My gut twisted at his need to provoke my jealousy. Perhaps he'd forgotten he was about to conspire with Satan.

His shoulders straightened, and he fluffed his wings before

spiriting them away, as if finally noticing his blunder. "I came as soon as I received word, my lord," he said boastfully, though every syllable that spilled from his lips dripped with disingenuous concern for the matter at hand.

"Your sense of urgency is lacking," I replied, unimpressed by his feeble attempt at competency. "My emissary delivered that message days ago. Do you have any idea how long one Elysium day is in Abaddon?"

He shifted uncomfortably on his feet, color draining from his face. Of course, he knew—*everyone* knew time in Abaddon was warped. Moving thousands of times faster than any other timeline in the universe, yet at the same time, feeling excruciatingly and impossibly slow, almost inert. The bastard had taken his fucking time to respond to my demand of his presence, showing up at my doorstep preened like a pampered courtier, as if every minute spent in this cursed realm didn't feel like one revolution on The Breaking Wheel.

Inclining his head, he remained silent, jaw tightening as his silver eyes cut across me with repugnance. Finally, a touch of honesty. We didn't need to pretend we were anything but enemies about to strike an alliance out of sheer necessity.

My eyes flicked to his host. "Did you expect an unfriendly reception?" I asked, my voice unnaturally still.

Khama'el swallowed thickly. "Truthfully, I did not know what to expect. It's been long since we last stood face to face."

"You might have deigned to visit this prison occasionally, Khama'el. Taken a gander at the hell you've sentenced an innumerable amount of our brethren to. Perhaps then you might've had better consideration of my time."

He glanced at Chemoth, who stood to my left, the Horseman's hands clasped behind his back. Then to Beleth, whose smoke-like body seemed to ripple beside me on my right. My Horseman of Death bristled at Khama'el's disdainful gaze. Beleth took one step forward, but I halted his advance with one slight raise of my finger, my hand barely moving.

Khama'el's hand tightened around the hilt of his sword and a collective silence overtook my throne room. Every demon guard lining the perimeter gently placed a hand on the hilts of their swords. Though the sicarii remained unmovable, not bothering to reach for their weapons, I knew their bodies were more than primed for an attack, should I give the order to my guards.

"Did you summon me here to toss your grievances at my feet?" Khama'el asked, shattering the awkward silence.

Sitting up straighter, I leaned forward on my throne. I'd spirited my wings away, but I wore my royal cloak, one made from the black fur and hide of my hellhounds. It draped off my shoulders as a heavy reminder that, despite being a prisoner here, this was *my* home, and here, *I* was king.

Making sure my eyes reflected nothing but the dark truth of the alliance we were about to forge, I said through tight lips, "I summoned you here so you might have a glimpse of what awaits, should you fail."

He rolled his shoulders, as if stunned by my words. "I meant you no offense, my lord. Though, if you permit me to be honest, I don't take kindly to threats."

"I have no need for threats. Banishment to Abaddon is an inevitability of your actions, Khama'el. Treason has a cost, and the laws of our people are clear about punishment for such acts of betrayal. You stand before the Throne of the Fallen One, about to strike a deal with the Devil—the seraphim you spat on before signing off on my sentence. Being here is enough to cast you out of Heaven. Rest assured, if we don't prevail, you will not stand trial, Khama'el. You and every traitorous angel standing behind you will simply Fall to Abaddon."

"God has abandoned us all, Samael. Failure is not an option. Victory is our *only* chance at survival. The other realms have taken notice; they know Elysium is vulnerable right now, that we are without a king. Many already plot to overtake the throne of God. It is my job—my duty—to ensure our kingdom continues to be ruled by angelkind. Despite your transgressions, you *are* Heaven's rightful heir. If power and control are not restored soon, our kingdom will fall. Angels will no longer be the ruling race across the cosmos."

"While I believe you have Elysium's future at your forefront, if there is anything I've learned while sitting on this throne is that no one does anything without an ounce of self-interest." My gaze narrowed. "Not even the most righteous."

Furrowing his brows, his lips thinned as he gritted, "I've served my kingdom since the dawn of time. Have stood by God's side, even when my convictions did not align with His."

"A most faithful servant," Beleth snarled.

Khama'el took a step forward, making Beleth and Chemoth stir, forcing them to draw tighter around me. "Am I not due a recompense?" Khama'el demanded, ignoring my Horsemen. "Aren't us all, after eons of servitude?"

"Which brings us to the reason you've been summoned," I said. "Beleth has informed me of your price."

Softening his tone, he splayed out his palms. "The universe is vast, my *prince*, rife with infant realms in need of stewardship. Mine is but a meager request."

My wavering patience with this slippery worm made the jagged bones of my crown feel like they were sinking deeper into my skull. His hunger for power practically oozed off his pores, which meant his loyalty was even more fickle than I'd thought. Alas, as much as the thought of having some inept king rule even the youngest of realms made my skin blister, I needed the slithering snake if I was to have a substantive opportunity at recovering the stones. "I have considered your demands and have decided to accept your terms."

He stared at me in silence for several breaths, shadows of doubt glazing over his eyes.

"Something the matter, Khama'el? Is that not why you came? To pledge your fealty to me. To offer me assistance in recovering the stones in exchange for stewardship to your own realm once I escape Hell and take my father's throne?"

He breathed deeply. "Then it is true. You have an angelic hybrid in your custody?"

"I do."

"The fledging would be the first Nephilim born in thousands of years."

"A miracle some might say," Chemoth offered with pride.

"An abomination more like," Khama'el replied harshly, as if merely speaking of the child's existence was blasphemous. "Our Lord God forbade such unions—angels procreating with humans."

"My father forbade a great deal of things, Khama'el," I replied with similar venom. "It's the reason I'm here." My eyes roamed the dank vastness of my great hall.

"Nephilim are dangerous," Khama'el warned, his gaze glinting like blades. "Their powers are almost as strong as an angel's, if not greater. It's why they were eradicated ages ago."

I took note of the warriors lined up like rows of stone pillars. "Yes, the sicarii left quite the river of blood in the wake of that mass assassination."

"The Lord God sanctioned that order."

"Of course He did. My noble father would never allow anyone to have such immense power. Stars forbid any of His children exhibited any signs of true free will."

"If Nephilim had been allowed to walk the earth unchecked, they would've decimated it."

"Or they may have made it better," I retorted.

Khama'el kept his eyes trained on me. "You intend to make the child your vessel," he said matter-of-factly, his voice staid, fear simmering underneath his rigid demeanor. Taking the body of a Nephilim would make me more powerful than I'd ever been. I'd be almost god-like. He was right to fear me.

"How else did you suspect I planned to heal myself from the sickness of this place? To have my full powers restored, I need a new body, and an angelic hybrid is the only one able to contain my essence."

Khama'el remained silent, his silver gaze churning. He was second guessing his decision to come here, to align himself with me.

"Did you think betraying a kingdom would come with zero risks?" I leaned back on my throne and took a deep, untroubled breath. "Tell me, would you rather our people be ruled by a different race—an *inferior* race—Khama'el? The Lord God has abandoned us all; were those not your words? He's left you little choice but to hand over the throne to the shadowed prince. But have you considered if having me as your king would truly be such a terrible ordeal? I am not my father's son, Khama'el. My plans are for a new world order, one where all angels will have full autonomy. Where all of us will be free."

He stared at me, awed, or maybe confused, I couldn't be certain. He seemed at a loss for words, as if what I'd said had been such a novel idea. "Freedom?" he asked cautiously.

A frosted smile crusted over my lips. "It's why you came, Khama'el. Is it not? To take a slice of the universe as your own? Don't deny yourself the opportunity to choose how you *live* your eternal life."

He looked around my throne room, contemplating, assessing. Noting the way Chemoth and Beleth's muscled bodies tightened, how my guards widened their stances, gripping their swords. When he met my unwavering gaze again, he finally realized I hadn't invited him here to accept his bargain, but to give him an ultimatum. "I don't believe I'm being given much of a choice," he said.

"Oh, there is always a choice with me, Khama'el. It's simply about choosing wisely."

"What is it you require of me, Samael?"

"Glad you asked. Come, let us take a walk."

Khama'el seemed apprehensive about leaving the assumed safety of my great hall, especially when I told him I wanted to speak to him privately. Couldn't say I blamed him for not wanting to be alone with me. My father had ordered my capture, Mikha'el had done his bidding, but when it came to issuing out my formal sentencing, as Prime Judge of the Holy Council, Khama'el had signed the decree that had locked the invisible shackles that bound me to this realm.

I'd promised him I'd rip out his beating heart the next time I saw his face.

If he'd been cleverer, though, he would've known his current qualms were misplaced. My time was too valuable to focus on an infinitesimal quarrel with a pampered politician and oily courtier when my freedom and the fate of *my* court were at stake. His true *recompense* would come in due time. Right now, I needed him docile and cooperative.

His warrior angels had looked less than pleased when I informed them their presence was not needed, and that not even a sole escort would be allowed to accompany us. The Power may have trusted his assassins, but many of them had trained under Mikha'el, and it was my understanding some of his former lieutenants had joined the archangel on Earth. I couldn't risk letting a potential spy through.

Beleth and Chemoth hadn't been any happier when I instructed them to stay behind. They were intimately familiar with Elysium's court affairs and didn't trust a word that spilled from Khama'el's lips. I almost took offense to that. If there was something I was terribly skillful at, it was sniffing out greed, and Khama'el reeked of it. He was so eager to be the king of anything, he would stoop to whatever level I placed before him. He wouldn't be foolish enough to try anything against me while visiting Abaddon.

With our wings spirited away, Khama'el and I walked in silence, our shoulders almost touching as we ambled down Dolorem Castle's narrow, winding corridors. The black stone walls were slick with frost, icicles menacingly hanging from the arched ceilings, some dripping water that instantly froze upon hitting the ground, creating jagged, uneven patches of ice.

One could easily slip if not paying attention.

Our breaths were puffs of vapor against our faces. The air was impossibly frigid, but after so many lifetimes, I no longer trembled from the biting cold that made a home inside my bones. Khama'el, on the other hand, was not faring so well. His lips had leeched of their rose color and were now a bruised slash across his face, the clacking of his teeth quite audible. Unfortunately for him, he might still feel the effects of this unforgiving world long after he returned to his.

His gaze lifted to the flickering torches embedded in the walls. Their flames struggled against the pervasive cold as they cast eerie, shifting shadows down the passageways. "Fire has no warmth here…" he said, marveling, if not terrified.

I placed a hand on his shoulder as I urged him forward. "The cold is a living thing here, a relentless force that strips away all pretense and leaves nothing but the raw essence of despair."

He shivered as we passed a row of iron doors, the moans of condemned souls echoing through the cracks. "It's nothing how I pictured it would be."

"Imagine that…" I said with a smirk. "I'm supposed to be the Prince of Lies, but who's the one who's been truly lying all along, letting the humans believe Hell is all fire and brimstone?"

He spun to face me, shrugging my hand off his shoulder. "Enough of the politicking. Why did you bring me here, Samael?"

"Patience, Khama'el," I said, continuing to urge him onward until we were met by a large spiral staircase that led up to the battlements.

After we ascended about one hundred steps, I threw open the large wooden doors at the top of the staircase and a frosted gust blasted across our faces. The courtier had not been prepared for the brutality of Abaddon's howling, ice-cold wind. Whipping his neatly tied hair undone, the furious gale likely felt like thousands of tiny razors slashing across his skin. He used his wings to shield himself as we approached the edge of the battlements.

Above, the sky was a swirling maelstrom of dark clouds, an ever-oppressive ceiling of gloom. Below, the expanse of Abaddon stretched out in a desolate panorama, the landscape a mix of craggy ice formations and treacherous icy plains, devoid of any signs of life, save for the wind's constant, mournful wail.

The ground, covered in a thick layer of rock, frost, and snow, rumbled as my demon army marched toward the keep. The frozen Stygian River cut across the terrain behind them —a natural barrier between my castle and Nolafyr, Abaddon's cursed, charred forest and the gateway to the Wastes.

From our vantage point, we could gaze upon the full scale of the gathered masses of my army. Thousands of dark, twisted figures stood in formation, their outlines stark against the white expanse. Clad in black armor that seemed to absorb the feeble light, their breath rose like the smoke from countless smoldering fires, merging with the icy fog that clung to the ground.

A silence fell, the only sound the faint clinking of armor and the occasional crack of ice shifting underfoot. My generals stood at the forefront, their batlike wings folded, and their eyes fixed on me with unwavering attention. Behind them, the ranks of lesser demons and fallen angels waited, their expressions a mix of anticipation and simmering rage.

My heavy cloak sat wide on my shoulders, enhancing my size, making Khama'el look smaller than he was. "My army grows weary," I said to the angel as he stared into the distance. "They're hungry for violence, but now that all four stones are in Mikha'el's possession, the gates have weakened. Their instability makes it difficult to traverse across realms, especially to Earth."

He leaned in closer to the edge of the wall, making sure to stay clear of the spiked rocks on the ledge. "The gates are unstable, but that doesn't mean your demons can't cross over."

"Some can, yes. But to extinguish the Guardians, I need my full army."

Wind still whipping hard against his face, he said, "If Mikha'el has all four stones, why hasn't he closed the gates permanently?"

"Well, my dear Khama'el, thank the stars for that; otherwise, we wouldn't be having this conversation."

"It doesn't make sense. He would've closed those gates long ago, without the slightest hesitation. What's holding him back?"

"That female Guardian he's taken under his wing has him by the balls. I still have her child and the traitor who planted the seed in her. She'd never let Mikha'el close the gates until she was certain of their safety."

"Astaroth's vessel is still alive?"

"Depends on what you deem *alive*," I said, nodding toward Nolafyr.

"You've imprisoned him in the Wastes?"

"Killing him would hardly yield a lucrative outcome."

"You plan to bargain with his life?"

I planned a great deal of things, but I wasn't an imbecile, willing to reveal all my cards.

"You honestly think the female will trade the stones for his life?" he asked again.

"I think every player has a part in this game." I gestured to my army. "I may not be able to march them through the gates, but unlike those of us bound to this realm, you have no need for the gates. My human host moves against Mikha'el and what remains of the Guardians stationed at their eastern headquarters. They bring with them a horde of the undead. I need you and your cadre to join their efforts; plus assemble a team of your highest skilled assassins to extract the stones. I already have spies working to uncover their exact location."

"Mikha'el will not be taken down easily, especially if he's guarding those stones."

"Mikha'el murdered Gavri'el," I gritted. "You're Prime Judge of the High Council. Dole out his due punishment. Banish him to Abaddon, and I will handle the rest. Once he's cast down, your sicarii should make an easy meal out of what remains of his lieutenants."

"And what of the Guardians? Of the woman saint?"

"Stripped of their empyrean weapons, the Guardians will be a mere nuisance to cut down. And Kate… well, once I have the stones, there won't be anything she can do to stop me from taking my vessel."

"Where is the child, Samael?"

"In a safe location."

"In Abaddon?"

"You know time travels differently here. For a successful rebirth, where none of its essence remains, it needs to remain an infant. It's the only way my soul can extinguish his once I take over its body."

"On Earth, then?"

My silence was answer enough.

"What makes you think Mikha'el will accept this sentencing?"

"His guilt is likely already killing him. He'll go willingly. If not, use the Golden Shackles."

"They've not been used since—"

"Since he captured *me*. It's almost poetic, don't you think?"

Khama'el stared into the distance, his gaze fixed on the black trees of Nolafyr.

"Don't tell me you're growing too weary for this task, Khama'el."

Lowering his chin, he sucked in a deep breath. "Never thought it would come to this. Mikha'el… he's…"

"A traitor and a murderer."

He searched my eyes for the validity of my words. But I wasn't a liar; I simply revealed the ugly, despicable truth no one ever wanted to see. I extended a hand to him. "Are we to strike this bargain or not?"

The boisterous chants of my army intensified, and the clatter of their armor boomed like a loud crescendo as they beat their breastplates with their shields. Khama'el took in the sea of my shadowed soldiers, each demon birthed from my own soul. Each fallen angel, a brother in arms.

His shoulders sagged as if the weight of the entire universe had been draped over him. With hesitation brimming in his silver eyes, he accepted my extended hand. "You have my fealty, Samael. And that of my sicarii."

And as I gripped his hand tightly, I swore I felt a slight tremor rumble through his bones.

Chapter Five

KATE

Something trembled deep within me when I watched Clint disappear down the spiral staircase. Hank whined beside me, and it was as if he could sense the dark dread coating my bones. I couldn't shake the feeling that I'd sent the kid on a suicide mission, but I also couldn't let my emotions run amuck in my chest. I needed to stay focused if I was to have any chance of rescuing my son and Jax, of defeating that fucking bastard angel who had waged a personal war against me.

A sound like thunder vibrated through the church as the entire shield wall doming around the cathedral flickered from luminous gold to blood red, a sign the wards had weakened further. "Those assholes are going to break through," I said, rushing to the view port. Panic surged through my blood like a raging river as I took in the enormity of the horde pushing against the shield.

"Not if we can help it. But if we're going to join Remi and Cass, we need to do it now." With his wings spirited away, Mikha'el led us down the narrow staircase.

My knees and thighs ached, my throat burning from the dry

heaves that pushed from my lungs as we ran down the steep, darkened staircase. I grew dizzy as we kept spiraling and spiraling, almost without end, until we finally hit the ground floor. Mikha'el seemed unphased; meanwhile, I had to lean against the stone wall to catch my breath, a hand to the side of my abdomen. The archangel stared at me with impatience. Hank stood at his heel, ears perked as if shocked I'd stopped for a break.

Traitor.

I huffed a strand of hair away from my face and shot the angel an impatient look of my own. "What? That was like, three million stairs we just climbed down. Unlike you, I'm still mortal."

Mikha'el cocked his head, urgency deepening the creases on his brow. "With superhuman strength and angelic abilities. Get moving, mortal."

With a labored breath, I pushed off the wall. "Right. No rest for the weary when you're a woman tasked with saving the world and shit."

"And shit," he repeated with a smirk. "A poor comparison for what we're about to face."

"Was that your first curse word ever? Man, how you've stooped." I followed behind him as we rushed toward the central hub located in the eastern wing.

The archangel looked over his shoulder, his pace unaffected. "I curse, just not in your tongue."

"You can curse in Heaven?"

"We get creative."

"That's a *no*, then. Listen, unless you use fuck, shit, asshole, cunt—"

"Kate."

"Case and point."

Choosing silence, he jacked up his strides, forcing me to jog behind him. Emrandael, Mikha'el's legendary sword, was secured across his back, its gilded metal glinting with its own luminesce, its light casting a soft glow in the church's darkened corridors.

By the time we arrived at the hub, Guardians had already begun taking their posts to defend the church. I found Antonia Morales, the newly appointed leader of the Guardians, briefing a small team of young Guardians who were preparing to join the first wave of defense—those who were likely the unlucky ones to be sent to fight side by side with me and the angels.

A string of resentment tugged at my heart. If Antonia had been an anointed priest, she would've been able to bless our water, and I wouldn't have had to send Clint into those tunnels. Those damn arbitrary laws placed upon us by a God who'd gone MIA had once again found a way to fuck us. There was no logical reason for a female human to be denied the privilege of being ordained. None.

"Kate," Morales said, rushing toward me. "The shield is already cracking. The Unholy have begun to break through on the south end. I have a team of about ten Guardians keeping them at bay, but the crack is only going to keep widening."

"Mikha'el and I are going to join Remi and Cass and offer up our power to fortify the wall. We need to give Clint enough time to get to St. Mary's and back. Hopefully, with enough blessed water to blast most of the demons and zombies back to Hell."

"Lord hear you."

I wanted to scoff, but I kept my opinion to myself. If we got out of this alive, it wouldn't be because of God.

"What are our numbers?" I asked.

"We're a hundred strong."

"That's it?"

"We lost many Guardians during the fight against the Horseman of Death. I will send half with you; unfortunately, I can't spare any more. The rest of us need to remain inside to protect the civilians."

"Barricade the doors with anything you can find. We will hold them off as long as possible."

She placed a hand on my shoulder. "May the Lord be with you, Kate."

I didn't mean to shrug off her hand as abruptly as I did, but we were running out of time, and I had none to spare for pointless faith. "God abandoned me long ago. Prayers are lost on me, Antonia."

A soft, almost sad smile glossed over her lips. "You think you're the only one who has lost a loved one? This world is nothing but darkness, Kate, but if we let it consume us, then we are no different than they are. Faith strengthens us. It gives us something to fight for."

"I fight for those I love."

"Then let that be your beacon to salvation."

Salvation?

How could I worry about my soul when my life was measured by each passing hour that I survived this hell? All I had was the here and now—that was my beacon.

I gazed at the assembled team. Most were Spaniard, but we'd discovered that Guardians had been dispatched to *La Sagrada Familia* and nearby scions from across the world before the gates opened. The Guardians had been preparing for this long before anyone realized all this biblical bullshit was truly real.

Mikha'el stood beside me and was about to address the gathered congregation, but I put a palm on his forearm. "No. Let me." Right now, we were in this mess because of me. If Samael escaped his prison, it was because I'd failed to adequately protect my son. If these Guardians were going into battle to fight alongside of me, then they needed to know what was in my heart.

"Antonia, will you translate for me?"

Stepping forward, she nodded for me to begin.

I swallowed deeply as I stood before the assembled body of Guardians, their faces a mixture of hope and exhaustion. The weight of the impending battle pressed down on us all, but I knew we couldn't afford to falter. My heart pounded in my chest, not just with fear, but with anger—anger at the unfairness of it all, at the divine powers that seemed to toy with our lives. But it was now time to take back what was ours, on our terms.

"Guardians," I began, my voice echoing in the cavernous hall, "I stand before you, not as one of you, but as a mother with a broken heart. I'm not here to preach about faith in God because, frankly, my faith in Him has been shattered. I can't put my trust in a higher power that lets innocent lives be torn apart by evil. But I do believe in you and in what you represent for humanity, in what you fight to preserve—love. Because it is the one thing that separates us from the monsters knocking at our door. The one thing they can't possess."

I paused, meeting the eyes of each Guardian, letting my words sink in. "We've all lost something in this war: family, friends, our homes. This war took my husband and daughter. And for a long time, I thought it had taken my soul as well. But I was able to find love again. I was able to find a new purpose, a new reason to keep fighting. Now, Samael seeks to take more—not just from me, but from all of you. He wants to use my child as a vessel, to take Luke's body as his own and escape his eternal prison. He plans to turn us into his slaves. But I'll be damned if I let that happen."

The crowd murmured, the air crackling with the heat of their fervor. "But this fight isn't just about saving Luke or avenging our loved ones; this is about reclaiming our world. Earth belongs to humanity. It's *our* home, and we have to fight for it with every ounce of strength we have left. The demons think they can take it from us, that they can snuff out our light, but they're wrong. *We* are the light, and we will raise our weapons until the last one of us remains standing."

My voice cracked, fueled by the raw emotion surging through me. "You are humanity's Guardians, chosen not just by fate or God, but by your own will to protect this world. You fight for those who can't fight for themselves. For every child who deserves to grow up in a world free from this darkness."

I stepped forward, my pulse pounding like a troop of galloping horses. "I know you lean on your faith, and though I don't share that faith, I respect it. And I ask you to channel that faith into this battle. Not for me, not for my son or Jax, but for us all. For every human life that hangs in the balance.

"Let's show these demons what it means to be human. Let's show them our strength, our resilience, our unwavering will to survive and protect what is ours. We go into battle not just as warriors, but as the collective soul of our kind. Together, we will drive them back. We will reclaim our world. And we will make them regret ever thinking they could take it from us."

Antonia raised her rifle, pointing the muzzle to the ceiling. *"Bendito sea el Señor, mi roca, quien adiestra mis manos para la batalla, mis dedos para la Guerra."* She repeated it a couple of times, the Guardians all raising their weapons and chanting the phrase over and over again.

"What do they say?" I asked Mikha'el.

"Blessed be the Lord, my rock, who trains my hands for war and my fingers for battle."

Antonia approached me again. "The Guardians fight with you, but they also fight *for* you. They believe your son is a beacon for our salvation, Kate. What role he will play is not known to us, but blind faith is the foundation of our beliefs. We trust in you, but we also trust in Mikha'el and Gavri'el, who gave her life to protect your child. You may not have faith in God, Kate, but I'm certain, without a single ounce of doubt, that He has faith in you, sister."

I offered her a smile of gratitude. She meant well, and I wish I could've shared her sentiment, but I didn't know if I'd ever be able to forgive Him for all the pain.

But now was not the time to question my faith; it was time to face our nightmares.

Hank panted beside me, a toothy smile spreading wide. I knelt and cupped his furry face. "You're such a good boy, Hank." He always found a way to ground me, even in the middle of all this shit. His big brown eyes widened, tongue drooping to the side. I couldn't imagine my life without my buddy, and yet, here I was, about to send him into battle again. Tightening the straps on his tactical vest and securing his protective goggles, I patted him on the neck. "Time to get to work."

The instant we exited through the wooden double doors of the church and into the bone-chilled night, the deafening sound of devoured moaning and growling assaulted my ears. Mikha'el flared his wings, a show of his power and dominance. We'd grown so accustomed to each other it was easy to forget he was a myth turned flesh. But seeing him like this, in his black armor, brass-colored wings spread, and Emrandael gripped tightly in his hand, he looked more glorious than his fabled legend.

Remiel and Cassael had dropped to their knees. Their black-plumaged wings were still spread wide while they raised their glowing hands up toward the sky, pillars of light pulsing from their palms and shooting to the dome's flickering ceiling. As we neared, Remiel said, "Not… sure… how much longer we can sustain this." The angel's voice shook, his forehead gleaming with the sheen of fresh sweat.

Cassael didn't look any better. The female angel's black hair was damp against her face, her skin pale as moonlight. Mikha'el took his position next to Remiel, and I stood next to Cassael. "I don't really know what I'm doing," I said to Mikha'el.

"To activate your power, look within your heart, your soul. Find the light and imagine it shining through you."

I cocked an eyebrow at him. "That simple, huh?"

"You've used the power before. You just need to channel it." With that, he shot his gaze to the heavens, his arms spread as he aimed his hands at the dome. A pillar of light that seemed brighter than the sun burst from his palms, his power joining with the power from the other two angels. Their shoulders sagged in relief as the dome's golden glow brightened.

Closing my eyes, I reached deep within myself, seeking the spark Mikha'el spoke of. When I'd used my power before, it had been on pure instinct, a reaction to being attacked. Now, I had no idea how to activate it, and the urgency of the situation only gnawed at my concentration. The chaos around me threatened to pull me out of my focus, but I couldn't let it. Luke's face flashed before my eyes, followed by Jax's—a stark reminder of what was at stake. My pulse thrummed in my ears, each beat a countdown to either our victory or our annihilation.

And if I didn't tap into my power soon, the wall would fall.

In the depths of my heart, I found the flicker of light I was searching for. It was faint, almost shy, but it responded to my call. It grew as I concentrated, transforming from a mere glimmer to a fierce blaze. I felt it spread through my body, igniting my veins with a warmth that was both comforting and frighteningly powerful.

With a deep breath, I opened my eyes and raised my hands toward the dome. The light within me surged forward, pouring from my palms in a stream of pure energy. It collided with the powers of the angels, merging seamlessly. The effect was immediate—the dome recharged, its golden hue intensifying, the blood-red flicker banished for now.

The ground beneath us shook as the devoured continued to pound against the barrier, their guttural cries of frustration echoing through the night. "It's holding!" Cassael shouted, her voice strained.

Mikha'el nodded, sweat trickling down his temple—which meant even his power was waning. "Let's just hope the kid makes it back soon."

My arms trembled from the effort of maintaining the light. "He'll make it. He has to."

As if in response to our combined efforts, a chorus of howls erupted from the horde, their rage making the hairs on the back of my neck rise like tiny needles. They knew their window of opportunity was closing, and it only made them more desperate. I could feel the strain of their attack against the shield, each impact like a sledgehammer against my skull.

"Mikha'el," I said through gritted teeth, "what's the plan if they break through?"

Not taking his eyes off the dome, he said, "Remiel, Cassael, I need you both to lead the Guardians to cover our flanks. We'll form a defensive line and push them back as much as we can. Our priority is to buy Clint enough time, so each blow needs to count."

Cass tried to stand, but she collapsed back to her knees, then fell backward, her power blinking out.

"Cass." Remiel rushed to catch his twin in his arms. Without their power feeding the dome, Mikha'el and I felt the added push against our own power, and it forced me to my knees. Mikha'el held on, the warrior angel the epitome of strength.

Still, despite the strain, we held our positions, the tension vibrating in the air as we braced for the inevitable breach. We all knew it was only a matter of time before it gave way, but I was ready to face whatever came through those walls.

I glanced at Hank, who was standing alert, ready for my command. My heart swelled with both pride and fear for my loyal companion. I gave him a reassuring wink. "I've got you."

His tail wagged slowly, a sign he understood he was about to be put to work.

Out of nowhere, the dome began to flash with red rings, loud bangs coinciding with each flash, as if the dome were being pelleted from the outside with projectiles.

"Empyrean arrows!" Remiel shouted as he hauled his sister back to her feet.

"Blasted stars," Mikha'el hollered. "Sicarii have now joined their ranks."

After a few short breaths, the twins seemed to regain some of their strength, though Remiel looked at his commander with shadows of doubt in his glowing blue eyes. "I'm depleted. I don't believe I can rift."

"Me, too," Cassael added, wincing as she stretched her beautiful onyx wings… the source of an angel's power.

Remiel drew his double-bladed staff, a silver and gold shimmering instrument of pure death that looked like it could cut a Butcher in half. "Brute force it is."

Cassael drew her war hammer, its head forged from a radiant, silvery metal that glowed faintly with a golden hue. Intricate runes were engraved on the broad, flat striking surface—the side meant for crushing blows. Its opposite end was pointed, chisel-like, perfect for piercing armor. Glowering at the continued onslaught of arrows that were close to penetrating the shield, she said, "I've always known Khama'el and his holy assassins weren't to be trusted. He didn't waste a breath before siding with Samael."

Mikha'el grunted as more blasts hit the shield. "We are going to burn out if we keep trying to fortify the wall. We'll be useless once the horde breaks through."

Cracks started to appear as even more arrows smashed against the domed ceiling. "What are you suggesting?" I asked, cold hard dread threatening to crumble my resolve as I felt the blows vibrate through my bones.

His golden eyes met mine, and I didn't have to hear his

words echo in my mind to know what he planned to do. To reserve what little power we had left, we wouldn't be able to wait for Clint any longer. We would need to allow the shield to crack and fight the horde head on and pray we could outlast the attack until the kid showed up—hopefully, and with reinforcements.

Still, there was no way of knowing how many sicarii had joined the Devil's Army. And while we had Heaven's mightiest warrior and two of his best lieutenants, I knew we would be gravely outnumbered.

"Are you ready to give them hell?" Mikha'el asked.

"Ever since they took my family."

With that, Mikha'el counted to three, and we both cut our power source to the shield.

The first fracture was accompanied by an ear-splitting crack, like ice shattering in the dead of winter. The golden glow faltered, replaced by jagged lines of blood-red that spider-webbed across the dome's surface.

"Brace yourselves!" Mikha'el roared, his wings snapping out to their full span. The Guardians around us tightened their formations, weapons at the ready.

With a deafening explosion, the dome shattered, shards of light cascading down like deadly rain. The Devil's Army surged forward. From above, winged warriors dove down, their golden crossbows aimed for the Guardians. One bolt flew past my cheek, nicking my skin before plunging into the poor fellow's chest who'd been standing behind me. He didn't even have a chance to fire his weapon before he was gurgling to his death on the ground.

Ahead, a seething mass of demons and zombies scrambled over each other, their eyes gleaming with black hatred. They poured through the breach, a tide of darkness against the dim light emanating from the cathedral's illuminated interior.

"Hold the line!" I screamed, drawing my sword and plunging into the fray.

The first demon I encountered lunged at me, its claws extending. I ducked under its swipe and drove my blade into its chest, black blood spurting out in a vile torrent. I twisted the sword and yanked it free, and the demon collapsed into a twitching heap. Another one was on me in an instant, its teeth gnashing, but Hank leapt at it, his jaws clamping down on its throat. With a vicious shake, he tore its windpipe out, and it fell, gurgling and thrashing.

Around us, the battle was a whirlwind of violence and gore. Guardians fought with desperate ferocity, their weapons slicing through flesh and bone as they battled their mortal counterparts.

Mikha'el was a blur of golden light and steel as he flew high above the cathedral to fight off the sicarii, who were sniping down the Guardians, his sword cutting down anything that came within reach.

Covered in black blood, the twins fought side by side as they dodged the barrage of empyrean bolts being fired off by the sicarii, their powers searing through the ranks of the dead and the monstrosities that were the arachnodogs. Remiel hacked off the limbs of the demonic spider dogs while Cassael smashed in their heads with her hammer.

A hairy spider leg landed at my feet, and for a brief second, I gawked at the grotesque limb. But there was no time to process what my eyes were seeing, no time to be afraid. A zombie staggered toward me, its mouth opening in a silent scream. I swung my blade, decapitating it with one clean stroke. The headless body continued to stumble forward for a moment before it crumpled to the ground. I kicked it aside, already focusing on the next threat.

A demon with glowing red eyes and serrated teeth reached for me, its claws aiming for my throat. I parried its attack, but its hulking strength was overpowering, and I was driven back a step. Before it could strike again, Mikha'el's sword flashed between us, cleaving the demon in two.

He nodded at me with a half-smile, and I nodded back. "I still have more kills than you."

"Doubtful," he said before springing back into the air, resuming to hacking demons to bits.

As I continued to take in the never-ending swarm of devoured, I realized I'd lost track of Hank. A sick feeling curdled in my stomach as I scanned the plaza, unable to find him. "Hank," I hollered, but my words were nearly drowned out by the cacophony of screams and growls.

The onslaught was relentless. Blood and ichor coated the floor, turning the once sacred ground into a slick, treacherous battlefield. My muscles burned, my breath coming in ragged gasps, but I fought on, each swing of my sword driven by my need to find Hank.

I whistled and whistled, hoping he'd be able to at least pick up on the high-pitched sound. "Hank!"

A loud bark broke through the overwhelming din and a wave of relief slammed into me when I tracked the sound to a far corner of the plaza. Hank was perched on top of a beat-up car, barking at one of the spider dogs as it approached, trying to corner him. The beast lunged with its clawed front legs, but Hank stood his ground, growling at the demonic spawn, and dodging getting speared by the clawed legs.

"Hank!" I ran as fast as I could, leaping over bodies, almost slipping on the slick ground, but then a second spider dog appeared, and my heart nearly stopped. There was no way he could fight off two of those beasts.

A bloodied hand grabbed my ankle, and I went tumbling. Scrambling to my feet, I kicked off the devoured that was trying to gnaw at my foot. The beasts were too close now, denting the metal as they slowly climbed onto the hood of the car. "Hank!" My thighs burned as I tried to run as fast as I could, but I knew there was no way I could get to him in time.

Right as the spider demons were about to leap onto Hank, Remiel landed on the ground next to the car, the force creating a crater. Faster than I could blink, he spun like a dancer, using his double-bladed staff to hack off limb after limb before impaling the first beast and decapitating the second.

Covered in black and golden blood, he caught my gaze, and I didn't even manage to mouth *thank you* when an Empyrean bolt shot through one of his spread black wings. The pained bellow that erupted from his lungs sent a shock-wave through the plaza that almost knocked me to my knees. The bolt hadn't been a regular arrow, but one with anchors and rope. Then a second bolt was shot, spearing his second wing.

A guttural wail burst from me. I knew in that instant what the sicarii who'd fired those arrows meant to do.

In a moment's breath, Remiel was yanked backward into the air. The holy assassin swung the ropes, propelling Remiel into the side of the cathedral, a rain of shattered stone falling to the ground and pommeling everything in its path. The warrior angel's agonizing screams could be heard throughout the entire battlefield as his wings began to rip with each swing of those ropes and each collapse against the church's façade. The nativity wall was left in utter ruin, but it was Remiel's falling limp body that tore my heart from my chest.

The sicarii had ripped out both of Remiel's wings right from their base. His body landed with a thunderous crescendo at the foot of the ruined Nativity façade, and a piercing scream almost blew out my eardrums when Cassael caught sight of her dead twin. "Remi, no! Remi!"

Her voice was so choked with grief, her pain permeated through me. Tears bubbled in my eyes as I watched her run to her twin. Dropping to her knees, she turned his body over and cradled his head in her lap, her own tears pouring over him as she wailed. She barely had time to caress his cheek before his body turned to pixie dust in her hands. Time seemed to stand still as Cassael trembled, rage and agony transforming her face from one of beautiful grace to one of sheer brutality and hatred. Staring at her hands as if unable to accept, unable to make sense of the fact her brother no longer existed, she shook her head furiously, then shouted into the heavens.

Once she spotted the sicarii who had killed her brother, Cassael sprung to her feet and reached for Remiel's discarded staff, aiming it at the assassin and silently claiming his death before she shot into the air after him.

Hank found his way back to me and nuzzled my hand. I patted his neck, grateful he was okay, but the guilt that wrapped itself around my heart like a boa reminded me that Hank's life had been paid in blood—angel blood. Remiel had died protecting Hank. To many, Hank was just a dog, but to me, Hank was family, and the fact that Remiel had stopped everything to come to Hank's rescue… I would never forget the sacrifice he'd made. Or the eternal pain his sister would suffer.

But right now, there was no time to mourn. All around me the battle raged on, and even after all the carnage, the devoured and demons kept sprouting from the shadows like an endless swarm of killer ants. Hank and I worked in tandem as we made our way back to the main entrance. The Guardians Morales had given us had been cut down to about half their numbers. At this rate, we would not outlast this attack.

Where the heck is Clint?

The clash of metal against metal drew my attention to the sky. The sicarii who had killed Remiel hovered above us, his platinum-tipped wings gleaming. His face was a mask of cruel satisfaction, his eyes glinting with dark triumph. He already felt they'd won this battle.

Cassael's roar seemed to spring out of thin air as she rifted right into the sicarii's flight path. She launched herself at him, her wings propelling her with incredible speed. The two angels clashed in a blur of steel and feathers, their weapons striking with such force that the very air seemed to shudder.

I'd seen angels fight before. Seen how Mikha'el had defeated Beleth, but watching Cassael's ferocity was wholly different. This wasn't an angel seeking to protect, but one looking to exact revenge.

The sicarii was a formidable opponent, his movements precise and deadly. But Cassael fought with the strength of her grief and the power of her love for her fallen brother. Her war hammer crashed into the assassin's defenses, driving him back. She twirled Remiel's staff with practiced ease, the blades flashing as they sought out weaknesses in her enemy's armor.

The fight took higher into the skies, the two angels darting and weaving through the air. Blood and feathers rained down as they struck and parried, their wings beating furiously. The sicarii managed to land a glancing blow on Cassael's shoulder, drawing a cry of pain from her lips, but she pressed on.

With a rage-filled wail, Cassael slammed her war hammer into the assassin's side, the force of the blow sending him crashing to the ground at lightning speed. She followed, landing on his back with a bone-crushing impact. The sicarii struggled, but Cassael was relentless. She threw her weapons aside and used her bare hands, grabbing hold of the assassin's wings.

"You took my brother from me," she hissed, her voice trembling. "Now I will take your life as well, even if it damns me."

With a primal scream, Cassael tore at the sicarii's wings. The assassin howled in agony as his feathers were ripped away, his flesh tearing under her relentless assault. Golden blood sprayed in all directions, staining Cassael's hands and face. The sicarii's struggles grew weaker, his agonizing pleas fading to whimpers.

Finally, with a sickening rip, Cassael tore the wings completely off his back. The assassin's body convulsed until it went limp, and then he was nothing but dust. Cassael stood over the discarded mangled wings, her chest heaving, hands slick with death.

The entire plaza seemed to have stopped to witness the battle, but now that the show was over, devoured and demon alike stalked forward, meaning to box her in. She'd been able to rift earlier when she ambushed the sicarii, but given her heavy breathing, slouched shoulders, and caved-in chest, it was clear she'd used too much of her power in killing that sicarii—or she was so emotionally destroyed that her spirit was drained.

Hank and I ran toward the angel to help her fight off the horde. Cassael met my gaze as we joined her, and the sorrow etched in her luminescent blue eyes almost made me weep. All this death and bloodshed… and for what? She'd chosen to fight on humanity's side, only to lose her brother in the process. I wouldn't blame her if she decided to abandon us now.

"I'm so sorry," I mouthed to her.

Cassael shrugged as she bent down to grab her war hammer. She strapped her brother's staff across her back and said, "What's done is done, mortal." Gripping her weapon tightly, she sneered at the horde. "Now, let's make Remi's death count for something."

From behind, the remaining Guardians who had been protecting the barricaded door stepped forward, weapons drawn, ready to fight to the end if they had to. Mikha'el swooped in out of nowhere, his armor torn, his body slick with demon and angel blood as he landed in front of us. Emrandael gleamed in his hand as he took up a fighting stance, his wings spread wide as if trying to shield us.

I walked around until I stood beside him. "We do this together."

The entire outside of the cathedral was surrounded by the undead, alongside Samael's demon and human army. Above, several sicarii hovered, their arrows pointed down at us. The rumbling, loud thumps of footsteps echoed through the plaza, and I swore if Jax had been here, he would've made some stupid ass *Jurassic Park* joke about T-Rex, because that's exactly what is sounded like as a Butcher parted the sea of devoured, its sharp cleaver nearly the size of a full-grown man.

The monstrosity was about fifteen feet tall, maybe taller, and built like a bulldozer.

We were incomprehensibly outnumbered, and for the first time since I could remember, I felt true primal fear. Fear that we might lose, that Samael might actually win.

That I might never see my son or Jax again.

I gripped my sword and dug my heels in. If I was to die today, I would take as many of these fucking bastards with me.

Mikha'el spun his sword once with a flick of his wrist. "I don't know that I can promise you victory, Kate, but rest assured, I will fight with every ounce of my soul, even if that means all that remains is dust. I will not give up. Not now, not ever."

Cassael stood beside Mikha'el on the other side. "And neither will I. We fight until the end."

"Until the end," I repeated.

The Guardians joined us at the line, the fierce determination in their eyes the strength I didn't know I needed. Hank growled as a devoured made the first move to attack, and I sent a prayer to the God I had no faith in, pleading for Clint's life and that he was on his way with that damn holy water, or we might not live through this fucking night.

Chapter Six

CLINT

I wasn't sure how I was supposed to feel when I saw Kelsey wrap her arms around that man, but a surge of male possessive anxiety sank into my stomach, making me sick. Christ. I wanted to hurl. I'd never felt anything like it, and it sucked, big time. So, when the guy pulled back and tucked a loose strand of her hair behind her ear, then kissed her forehead, and said, "Glad to see you survived, little sister," I not only felt like a complete jackass, but also shamelessly relieved.

"I thought I'd never see you again," Kels said, wrapping her arms around her brother once again.

He sighed as if life had just rushed back into his lungs. "I thought I'd lost you in the attack."

"It's a long story, but the Guardians at *La Sagrada Familia* took me and a few other survivors in. Just glad I was able to make my way back to you."

I cleared my throat. While I was happy about her reunion, we'd come here on a mission. As if she'd forgotten I was there, she snapped around, eyes wide. Swallowing deeply, she said,

"Clint, this is my brother, Kyle. Kyle, this is Clint. He's with the Eastern Headquarters."

With dark hair falling to his shoulders and a prominent brow that made it somewhat intimidating to look him straight in his deep brown eyes, he leaned in and shook my hand. "Pleasure to meet you, Clint." Looking between me and Kels, he added, "While I'm excited to see you, I need to ask: why the hell were you two idiots in the tunnels? It's a fucking death trap. We happened to be down here by accident; otherwise, you would've joined the walking dead in there."

The guy was about five, maybe ten, years older than me. These days everyone looked haggard and older than their years, but I didn't appreciate his tone or being talked down to. Living in the end-times meant we all did stupid shit to survive, anything to get us to the next day. Strapping my crossbow over my back, I took a step forward and didn't miss the puzzled look in his eyes when he examined my empyrean arm.

I squared my shoulders and didn't bother to offer an explanation for my nifty weapon. "*La Sagrada Familia* is under attack by the biggest horde of the undead I have ever seen. Not to mention that Samael's demon army is threatening to break through the shield. We risked our necks in those tunnels to come for your priest and, hopefully, some holy water. We lost two of our own in there just to get here. Trust me, we wouldn't have come if we'd had another choice."

His brows dipped. "Back up. What do you mean *shield?*" he asked, ignoring everything else I'd said.

Kels cut in, eyeing her brother as if silently telling him to be patient, "A protective force field powered by Mikha'el and his lieutenants."

"Mikha'el? As in the archangel?"

We both nodded.

"The rumors are true, then?"

"What rumors?" I asked.

"That angels are assisting the Guardians."

The way he said *Guardians,* as if he wasn't one of them, made a spidery claw rake down my spine.

Lowering her voice, as if to keep the rest of the men gathered in the room from hearing, she said, "He's recovered all four stones."

They locked eyes, and their continued wordless exchanges were unnerving. I didn't know what was going on between Kelsey and her brother, but I couldn't waste any more time trying to figure it out. Finding the priest amongst the armed men of the Saint Mary's scion, I decided to go straight to the source. "Do you speak English, Padre?"

"I do."

"If we don't get holy water to *La Sagrada Familia* before that shield falls, many people will die, not to mention that the Devil's Army is searching for the Creation Stones, and we all know what will happen if Samael gets a hold of them."

"But even if they get the stones, Samael needs a vessel to escape," the priest said, clearly behind on current events.

"News flash, Padre, he *has* a vessel," I said more poignantly, trying to drive home the urgency of the situation. "Now all he needs are the stones, and we have all four at *La Sagrada Familia*. And if we don't get our asses moving, Samael is going to make the last two years of this apocalypse look like a day at Disney World."

Blinking fast, the priest looked at me like he'd forgotten how to speak. I snapped my fingers in front of his face, and he finally shook out of his stupefied gaze. "We... we knew the Horsemen were going to seek to impregnate a woman as soon as the gates opened, but after two years without signs of Samael having escaped..."

"He hasn't yet," I told him, grabbing him by the shoulders. "But he will if he gets a hold of those stones. Can you help us or not, because we ain't got much time left."

The priest's eyes widened, and he made the sign of the cross. "*Dios nos ayude.* Come with me."

Kyle and Kelsey exchanged another glance, then followed as the priest led us through a series of winding corridors deep into the heart of the Saint Mary's scion, the three other Guardians tailing behind us. I could hear Kelsey and Kyle whisper behind us, but I couldn't make out a thing they said. I tried not to let it bother me; after all, he was her brother, and they'd just reunited.

But I didn't understand why she hadn't mentioned him before. Why she didn't tell me that's why she'd volunteered to come on this mission. Plus, something was off about her, about them both. Ever since we'd arrived, she'd been different with me, cold even. As if we hadn't just spent the most terrifying forty minutes of our lives trapped together in that tunnel.

As if she hadn't felt the pull between us.

And maybe she hadn't. Maybe she didn't feel the same way about me, but that didn't mean she had to treat me like a stranger.

I grew impatient as we continued to walk down corridor after corridor. Unlike *La Sagrada Familia*, this church didn't seem to have solar power. All we had were flashlights and the occasional fire sconces, making everything look unnecessarily eerie. The walls were lined with icons of saints and angels, their serene faces offering a stark contrast to our grim reality. The church gave me a strange vibe, and I almost couldn't wait to get the heck out and back to my crew.

"In here," the priest finally said, pushing open a heavy wooden door. Inside was a vast room lit by multiple lanterns, its shelves lined with gleaming silver and glass containers filled with what I could only imagine was holy water. There were also racks of water guns and an assortment of projectiles designed to deliver the sacred liquid.

"Impressive," I said, running my hand over a row of water guns. They looked like something out of a sci-fi movie, all sleek lines and water reservoirs. These weren't the Supersoakers I'd grown up playing with. "You've been busy. The New York arm had to learn on the fly how to make holy water-infused bullets."

"Our department for the development of holy weapons was here in the heart of Barcelona. We had been preparing for decades. The signs were there, for those who knew what to look for," the priest said solemnly. "Unfortunately, we couldn't get these weapons to all of our operations across the globe, not even to *La Sagrada Familia*, before the gates opened. Our weapons facility was attacked, and almost everything was destroyed. What you see here is everything we were able to recover months later from storage units that survived the blasts. As you can see, it's barely enough for our Guardians here."

Kyle stepped forward, his strong jaw tight as he eyed me. "How many of us do you think you'll need to make it back?"

"As many as you can spare. The entire cathedral is surrounded. It's just a matter of deciding how we're gonna get there. The tunnels are clearly clogged with undead and demons. We can brave them, or we can try our luck on the streets. Either way, we need to act fast. We had about an hour from the time we left to make it back before the shield fell." I looked down at my watch. "We're down to fifteen minutes."

The priest clasped his hands. "Our Guardians know the streets well. It's a safer passage than the tunnels." Gesturing to their weaponry, he added, "Take what you can carry, but use it sparingly, as I won't be able to join you. We have civilians here to look after. I hope you understand."

"No need to apologize, Padre. This is more than we could've hoped for."

As we armed ourselves, a group of Guardians—six men and women who looked like a special ops team—joined us. Kyle pulled Kelsey aside, and I continued to stuff water bombs into my pockets but kept my ears peeled to their conversation.

"I want you to stay behind," he whispered.

"You need me. Otherwise, you won't know where you're going."

"I think I can figure my way through a church."

"This is my fight, too, Ky."

"Kels, I've already lost too much. I can't lose you, too. Not again."

I peered down at my watch. Ten minutes to go. Gently approaching them, I said, "Hate to interrupt, but we need to get going."

They shared a heated stare before Kels said to him, "I'm your best fighter. You need me."

"I can't argue with that," I said, sheepishly smiling at her, though I wasn't entirely certain I knew the details of everything they were discussing.

Kyle's eyes darkened as he looked at me. "Easy to say when it's not your little sister you're sending out into a demonic zombie-infested battle."

Straightening, I closed the gap between us, this time not cowering my gaze from his. "I lost my sister to this damn war, so I think I understand perfectly well what the risks are. At least you still have your sister. If there is anything I've learned since Hell broke loose, it's that nowhere is safe. The faster we accept that, the easier we can protect those we love. Kels can hold her own better than any other Guardian I've seen fight. If she wants to go, then let her."

"Nobody *lets* me *do* anything." Seething, she stormed off to fill up with ammo.

Once she was out of earshot, he drew closer, those dark eyes as sharp as blades. "Best mind your own business, Clint. This has nothing to do with you."

"Is… is that some kind of threat I hear in your tone?"

"If anything happens to her…"

"I'd worry about your own skin. If there is anyone that I

know who can handle themselves out there, it's Kels. Nobody I'd rather watch my back."

"And who watches hers?"

I patted him on the shoulder with my bionic arm. "I guess that would be you, big brother."

Not having any more time to entertain his temper tantrum, I made sure we were all loaded up with as much holy water ammunition as we could carry before setting out.

I'd never visited Spain prior to the gates opening—never truly traveled anywhere outside the United States—so I had no idea what Barcelona looked like before it was overrun by zombies and demons, but I could still feel the dark sadness of the ruined city. Could almost hear the ghostly, woeful echoes of its once vibrant life now snuffed away. Smoke billowed from collapsed buildings and the air was so thick with the stench of decay, we had to wrap the bottom of our faces with scarves.

Even after two years of this shit, there were still days I struggled to accept this new world. A world now covered in perpetual shadows and coated in eternal sepia. Looking around at all the blown-up apartment buildings, the burnt cars, the random, abandoned army tanks, and all the raided homes, the immensity of everything we'd lost snuck up on me like a tsunami.

It wasn't like this was anything new. The streets of New York were a carbon copy of the streets of Barcelona, but here, in this city, on this side of the world, the concept of centuries upon centuries of history, all gone in a moment's breath, just took on a different meaning. The loss here hit harder, like a heaviness that was almost too much to bear.

I usually stayed focused on the task at hand, unaffected by my surroundings—it was easy to do when you were following orders. First from my sister, then Father Ortega, then Jax and Kate. But when you were the one leading people to their potential death, everything landed differently.

I was hyperaware as I kept a careful watch on Kelsey. She was quick on her feet, sticking to the shadows as we avoided the small roving bands of undead that prowled in the same direction—probably following a summons to *La Sagrada Familia*.

"Stay close," I whispered to Kelsey as we darted across an open plaza, our footsteps echoing eerily in the empty space. The Guardians led the way, while Kelsey and I took the flanks, and Kyle took up the rear. Everyone's eyes scanned for any sign of movement.

From the hand gestures one of the Guardians shot my way, it seemed we were close to our destination. I checked my watch and tried not to panic when I saw our window had expired, and we were now on borrowed time. To my relief, we didn't encounter any demons, but that only meant Samael's entire army had converged at the cathedral.

The evidence of that was confirmed as we neared our destination and the horrific, all-too-familiar hum of an army of moaning zombies beat against my ears. With my crossbow secured on my back, I double checked that the reservoir on my slick, silver-coated SanctiBlaster, as I'd dubbed it, was locked and ready to blast those motherfuckers back to Hell.

Kelsey gripped one of her swords in one hand, and in the other, some type of machete-looking blade that seemed to have a reservoir of holy water in the pommel. The weapon was constructed so every time she sliced the blade, it would be coated in holy water. I truly wondered why we hadn't thought of that back in the States.

Kyle had chosen a firearm that resembled a shotgun. The bullets were large globes made of some silicone material filled with holy water that would explode on impact, obliterating its target. Chaz would've loved that one.

An uncomfortable heat spread from my heart as I thought back to my friend. The asshole better have made it back to the clinic or I...

I didn't even want to contemplate a different outcome.

Knocking the thoughts from my head, I crouched lower as we rounded a corner, and my gut twisted when I finally saw the historic landmark. One entire façade had been completely obliterated and lay in utter ruin.

The shield was down, and the entire front plaza was clogged with zombies and demonic creatures climbing over a bloody mountain of mangled corpses, trying to get to the front door of the church. Kate and the angels were nowhere in sight, but I prayed they were holding the line.

Fuck. Had we been too late?

Above, winged warriors aimed with their crossbows, shooting bolts like snipers. Fuck. Sicarii.

Panic snaked around my throat like a tentacle wanting to cut off my breath. No. Not again. I wouldn't let fear paralyze me from doing what I needed to do. Steadying my shaking fingers, I gulped down my dread and nodded to the rest of the team. "Time to bring down the rain."

My gaze snagged on Kelsey, and her eyes softened above her partially covered face. A weight settled right between my breast plate. There was something close to sadness dulling those beautiful eyes of hers, like a glint of regret. For what, though? It was as if she was apologizing for something that hadn't happened.

I wanted to run to her, and maybe, just maybe, risk pulling down her scarf and stealing the kiss I'd been craving since I'd met her, because angels knew if we'd ever get the chance after tonight.

Kyle and the other six Guardians wasted no time running into the mayhem, blasting zombies and melting the skin off every demon doused with holy water. But Kels and I simply stared at each other for another two breaths that felt like two lifetimes. It was as if she'd sensed that same pressure against her chest, as if she too was struggling with understanding what the hell was happening between us.

But I'd hesitated too long, too damn long to run to her and taste her lips before they would be coated in demon blood. She slowly batted her eyes, an acceptance of some sort, then she ran into the horde, slicing her blades through the air, incinerating demons with each blow.

"Kels!" I ran after her, but she was swallowed up by the chaos, and I soon lost track of her bouncing ponytail. An anchor sank deep into the pit of my stomach, angst chasing it down my esophagus as if I'd taken a gulp of acid. I knew in that instant that whatever it was she'd wanted to tell me, it was something I would likely never know.

Chapter Seven

KATE

Mikha'el charged at the Butcher at full flight, his wings beating so fast and harsh, the wind at their wake whipped furiously against my face. The air crackled with his power as he closed the distance, sword raised high and shimmering with its internal light. I held my breath as the loud clang of metal against metal echoed over the loud drone of the snarling devoured. Mikha'el slashed his sword against the Butcher's cleaver, but the beast was barely affected by the archangel's blows.

Towering and grotesque, the demon roared, its ginormous maw displaying row after row of needle-pointed teeth. With a single, brutal punch, the Butcher struck Mikha'el in the gut, sending him hurtling backward, right into the church's Passion façade. The impact reached my ears in a sickening crunch of stone and bone; the boom sending a shockwave barreling through the horde and making the ground vibrate like a freight train.

Mikha'el slumped to the ground, wings sprawled and sword slipping from his grasp. A strained scream erupted from my lungs. "Mikha'el!" Heart in my throat, I dashed forward, but a screeching arachnodog coming from out of nowhere landed right in front of me. The monstrous creature lunged, pincers glistening with venom. Hank barked furiously at my side, but the creature was undeterred.

On instinct, I summoned a small shield of golden light around us. The divine energy pulsed weakly, the effort draining what little angelic power I had left. Each time the demon's massive limbs struck against the shield, it flickered and dimmed, and I knew I wouldn't be able to hold out much longer.

Just as my strength faltered and the shield began to collapse, a young female Guardian appeared in a blur of motion. She leapt between us and the arachnodog, her short sword gleaming like liquid metal. Each strike she landed made the beast's hide sizzle and smoke. Her movements were fluid and precise, her blonde, curly ponytail whipping through the air as she fought. The creature recoiled, shrieking in pain, and before I could thank her, she vanished back into the chaos, swallowed by the wave of devoured.

There was something oddly familiar about her, but there was no time to think about that now. Reorienting myself, I caught the glint of Cassael's war hammer as she landed blow after hard blow on the Butcher, giving Mikha'el time to recover. Though weakened, the archangel managed to push himself back to his feet, his eyes aflame with a fury that seemed to burn right through him.

Fuck. I'd never seen Mikha'el so consumed by rage—not like this, not even when fighting Beleth. And though the dread that had coated my limbs when I'd seen him fall thinned a little, my insides still quivered. He was more than vengeance turned flesh. When he wiped golden blood from his brow, then spun his sword over his wrist and stretched his mighty wings like each feather was a razor-sharp blade, he looked like a ruthless god.

His eyes flared with a savage, unyielding golden light, his presence radiating such raw, unrestrained power that it seemed to ignite the very air around him. Cassael dove from the sky, landing on her feet right beside her commander in a thundering crash. The female warrior angel looked just as deadly, if not more brutal. The Butcher took two steps back, its inhuman face scrunched in disgust, maybe disbelief.

This fight was not over.

Mikha'el's voice boomed across the battlefield as he charged once more, Cassael at his heels as she leaped above him. This time it was Remiel's staff that glinted in her grasp, one of its sharp blades aiming right for the Butcher's head.

The demon had no time to register what had happened as Mikha'el rifted out of view in one blink, then rifted back behind the beast just as quickly, skewering the demon straight through its spine. Coated in black blood, Emrandael protruded from the Butcher's chest. The demon's painful roar was cut short as Cassael sliced Remiel's weapon across its neck, sending the Butcher's head flying across the courtyard before turning to ash, along with its body.

I'd been so distracted by the battle, I failed to notice when a devoured charged at me. Hank's jaw snapped closed over its hand as it tried to dig its claws into my arm. I spun around and split the vile creature in half. Taking a moment to assess, my world whirled in and out of focus, everything seeming to move in slow motion. It didn't matter how many of these shits we killed, because where one fell, three more appeared. This was a never-ending battle. A few yards in front of me, two more Guardians lost their lives, their bodies thumping to the ground like felled trees.

My limbs ached and the exhaustion that smashed into me felt like I'd been clobbered by Cassael's hammer. I gasped for breath as I summoned the strength to keep fighting, as I reached within my soul, searching for a spark of my angelic power.

I desperately needed a boost. I couldn't die here. Luke needed me, Jax needed me.

Suddenly, a burst of water showered over us, like that time on the Brooklyn Bridge when Jax had launched a water cannon of holy water over the pack of hellhounds who'd surrounded me. The sound of sizzling flesh choked the air, joined by the sounds of demons and zombies howling as the water fell over their bodies like acid rain.

Clint. The fucking kid had done it.

I shouted his name into the chaos as Hank and I hacked through the horde. "Clint!"

"Kate!"

My chest ballooned with relief when a jet-stream of holy water sliced through the wall of the undead. The words got lodged in my throat when I saw the kid sporting what I could only describe as a futuristic machine gun straight out of a *Terminator* movie. And the fact I kept thinking of movies, even in the middle of all this death, made me realize that despite the fact Samael had separated me from Jax, the man I loved was still with me.

It was going to take more than the forces of Hell to keep me from the ones I loved.

Clint unleashed another torrent of holy water on an advancing demon. The creature writhed and screamed, its flesh bubbling and disintegrating before becoming dust. I flung my arms around Clint, letting every muscle absorb the fact that he was alive, and he'd been able to find help. Taking a step back, I ruffled his hair. "Your timing is impeccable."

We ran behind a broken-down van and took a moment to catch our breaths. Hank jumped up on his hind legs and licked the kid's face as if it was covered in ice cream. "Happy to see you, too," Clint said, though his voice sounded heavy.

"Where's everyone?" I asked.

The kid simply stared.

"Clint, the team you gathered. Chaz?"

Lowering his chin, he said, "We were attacked in the tunnels. Chaz… he…" He couldn't finish his sentence.

Placing a hand on his shoulder, I said, "Don't you dare blame yourself."

He swallowed the grief embedded in his throat. "Kelsey and I, we were the only ones who made it to the church. Turns out her brother is also a Guardian, and he helped us once we arrived." He handed me a water pistol he pulled from inside his jacket, also made of the same shiny metal as his weapon, and a couple of what I figured were water grenades. "Their priest offered us these weapons, but we need to use the water sparingly. We only brought what we could carry. The priest stayed back to protect the civilians at Saint Mary's."

"Did any Guardians come back with you?"

"Kelsey and her brother and six others, but I lost track of them in the mayhem."

I rubbed a tired hand over my face. Even equipped with holy water, eight Guardians would barely make a dent in this battle. I peeked over the hood of the van and couldn't help the wave of panic that crashed into my chest. I wanted to convince myself that we could win—that we could actually make it out of this alive—but watching Guardians crumple to their feet, and Mikha'el and Cassael get swarmed by sicarii…

I sank back behind the van, trying to keep it together. At this rate, we wouldn't be able to last the night. Closing my eyes, I searched my consciousness for my connection to Mikha'el.

Hey, are you there?

A little busy at the moment, he grunted.

Even with you and Cassael fighting off the sicarii, we are not going to outlast this attack unless we get reinforcements. And I mean the angelic kind. This water is only holding them back temporarily, and we only have a limited supply.

I'm… working on it.

What exactly does that mean?

Help is on the way. We just need to hang in there, Kate.
For how long?
As long as it takes.

With that, he cut off our connection. I hated that he had the power to decide when our conversations were over. I knew he was a trained holy warrior, and that I should trust him, but right now, despite my best efforts to remain positive, watching Guardians fall left and right was slowly chipping away at my resolve.

I sagged into the side of the van, feeling defenseless. Paralyzed.

Clint put a hand on my shoulder, snapping me out of my daze. The deafening sounds of the war raging around us rushed back into my ears. Hands trembling, I took in the utter savagery engulfing our world. Mother above, there was so much death.

"Come on, Kate," Clint said. "There's only one way out of this."

Meeting his gaze, I uttered, my voice tired, "Fighting."

He nodded.

With that, I found the strength to push to my feet, and Clint, Hank, and I pulled away from the safety of the van, holy water weapons drawn, and we ran into the fray, hollering until our voices melded with that of the enemy's.

The next thirty minutes felt like a thousand revolutions around the sun as we hacked our way back to the front doors of the church.

I shot streams of holy water at the devoured, watching their flesh sizzle and melt. Clint mowed down scores of demons, each burst of water a mini explosion of guts and ash. Hank was a mesh of fur and teeth, savaging anything that got too close.

Despite our best efforts, the horde kept coming. My arms ached from swinging my sword, and every breath felt like I was inhaling fire. Clint and I fought back-to-back; our movements synchronized out of sheer necessity. A particularly large demon lunged at me, and I barely had time to bring up my weapon. The creature's claws raked across my shoulder, and I screamed in pain.

Clint used his empyrean arm to beat the demon in the face until all that remained was a bloody pulp. "You okay?" he shouted, not taking his eyes off the advancing horde.

"Yeah," I gasped, clutching my bleeding arm. "Keep fighting!"

The battle seemed hopeless. More Guardians fell around us, their bodies crumpling to the ground like rag dolls. My heart pounded in my chest, fear threatening to overwhelm me.

Suddenly, Clint spotted the girl with the ponytail—the one who had helped me—and he called after her when he noticed she'd been cornered by two hellhounds. "Kels!" he shouted again, and the girl lifted her gaze to him, black and red blood streaking across her face. She was cradling one arm, her hand barely gripping the short sword she'd used when she'd aided me. Then she took a couple of steps away from the dogs, and that's when I noticed she was also limping.

Shit. If she'd been scratched or bitten…

Her gaze dimmed as she shook her head at Clint's approach, as if telling him not to come closer. But I'd seen that look in his eyes, the one that told me this girl was more than a Guardian; she was someone he cared about, and that quiet panic in his gaze said he wasn't about to listen to her. He checked his water reservoir and flung the gun aside when he realized it was empty. I was out, too, but I had one grenade left and handed it to him.

Using large chunks of fallen debris as cover, Clint crouched, inching as close as possible to achieve the biggest payoff.

Make it count, kid. Make it count.

The hellhounds snarled, fangs dripping with black venom. Hackles raised, they poised for the attack. Taking a few more steps back, the girl finally hit the stone wall of the church behind her. The beasts pawed at the ground, their claws digging into the concrete.

Something was off. Why weren't they pouncing on her?

The girl locked eyes with Clint again, fear flooding her gaze. The kid was ten feet away now, well within throwing distance. The air became too thick to breathe as I watched him try to move in closer, trying to find a better angle, but all he was doing was making himself the target.

Throw the damn thing, Clint.

He finally made it to about two yards when the beasts inclined their heads, nostrils sniffing the air. Fuck, they'd caught his scent. Clint noticed and immediately pitched the grenade through the air. The beasts spun right as the grenade clocked the bigger demon dog right on its forehead. The explosion of holy water had the hellhound bellowing in pained anger, but there was a reason the motherfuckers were so hard to kill—their hides were as thick as plated armor.

Though the acid-like liquid melted through its hide, it wasn't enough to kill it, only to piss it off. Now that the beast had turned around, its silvery mane was on full display. An alpha. Nausea rippled through me. One of those beasts had nearly killed Jax. "Run!" I screamed, but I knew there was no outrunning those monsters.

Clint immediately registered the same threat, but he didn't let fear freeze his muscles. Spotting a discarded Empyrean bolt on the ground, he snatched it up and quickly nocked it into his crossbow. As the first hellhound leapt, Clint fired the bolt directly into its open maw, the projectile piercing through the back of its throat and into its brain. The beast crumpled mid-leap, collapsing into a heap of lifeless muscle and fur.

But the alpha was upon him before he could take his next breath. Clint's bionic arm shot up in a defensive motion. The hellhound's jaws clamped down on the arm, but the holy metal repelled its bite, burning the inside of its mouth, causing the creature to recoil with a snarl of frustration.

Without much thought, I slid my sword across the pavement in Clint's direction, and the kid didn't hesitate in grabbing the blade just as the beast leapt at him again. This time Clint plunged the Empyrean steel into the hellhound's chest without much resistance, twisting it to maximize the damage. The beast howled, but Clint didn't stop. He pulled the blade out and slashed at its throat, the blade cutting through the thick hide like butter.

The hellhound staggered back, its lifeblood spilling onto the ground, but Clint didn't give it a chance to recover. He swung his bionic arm in a wide arc, smashing the alpha's head with the force of an anvil. The beast fell, its body twitching before it lay still.

Heaving, Clint took a second to catch his breath before running to the girl, quickly assessing her for injuries. "Kels, are you badly hurt?"

She blinked slowly, dazed or maybe she had lost a considerable amount of blood. Shrugging, she said, "I'll be fine. Just—"

"Rolled an ankle?" he finished for her. "Not buying it this time. If you're bitten or scratched, we need to get you to the clinic." Fighting her protests, he slid an arm under her uninjured shoulder, then shot me a glance.

"Go," I told him. "There are Guardians holding the line toward the back entrance; it's your fastest route to the infirmary."

But before they could take a step, a loud *boom* blasted across the courtyard, snatching our attention to the sky, where a luminous orb seemed to float toward us.

No, not an orb. A luminous angel with platinum wings hovered above, flanked by a squadron of about one hundred sicarii. With a voice like a thousand trumpets, he spoke as if he wanted the entire world to hear. "Mikha'el Bar Elah,

Archangel of the Third Sphere, former commander of God's Heavenly Army, by holy decree of the High Council, you're hereby ordered to surrender yourself."

The Devil's Army went completely still, as if caught in a trance by the angel's words.

With blood caked over his torn armor, Mikha'el stepped out from the shadows, Emrandael slick from a fresh kill. He spread his wings wide in an act of defiance, peering up at the hovering angel. "Under whose authority do you command me to surrender, Khama'el? Our Lord God no longer sits on the throne."

"This world was condemned by His Grace long before He left His seat. You disobeyed His orders and came to the mortals' aid. By the laws that govern our kingdom, you have been declared an enemy of the realm. Furthermore, you are being confined for the murder of Gavri'el Barat Shemaya, Virtue of the Second Sphere, and Emissary to the Lord God. Murder of a higher sphere angel is a crime punishable by eternal banishment to Abaddon."

I watched in horror as Mikha'el lowered his head. No. No, Mikha'el couldn't surrender. Then he dropped Emrandael, the sword clanging to the floor. "I will surrender, but you must give me your word that you will leave Kate and the Guardians unharmed."

"You have my word," the Power uttered, a slimy smile curving his lips.

Oh God, no. I ran toward Mikha'el, not caring that several assassins had their crossbows aimed at my head from above. "What are you doing? Why are you surrendering?"

Mikha'el didn't' answer; he simply looked at me with his golden eyes as if pleading with me not to make this more difficult. Cassael stepped toward Mikha'el, Remiel's staff in one hand, her war hammer in the other as she aimed it at the Power. "Khama'el, you deceitful, vile wretch!"

"Watch your tongue, lieutenant."

"I'm not afraid of vermin like you. You're willing to sell your soul for what? The crown of an infant realm?"

The angel's eyes widened. He'd clearly underestimated Cassael's abilities as Mikha'el's Shadow Keeper.

"I know about the deal you planned to make with Samael," she went on. "How could you betray our kind by aligning yourself with the same serpent you sent to Hell?"

"*That* serpent is the rightful heir to the Kingdom of Heaven, and I serve the crown. And on the authority of our new king, all those who conspired with Mikha'el will, too, be cast down."

No. No. No. I pinned Mikha'el with a fiery glare that would've burned right through his skull. *You can't let them take you and Cassael. This is wrong. Please…*

Kate, the laws of my people are clear. Gavri'el died by my hand.

But you didn't murder her. It wasn't your fault. She made you do it.

It doesn't matter. I took her life.

And Cassael? She's here because of her loyalty to you. You're going to let them take her when she was just following orders?

She knew the risks, Kate. We all did.

What about us? What about this war? What about the promise you made to me? You're sworn to protect me.

"You've never truly needed me, Kate," he voiced out loud in a whisper only I could hear, caressing my cheek with such tenderness my heart cracked straight down the middle. "And I'm not abandoning you." He bent down and picked up Emrandael, handing it to me, the metal cool to the touch and so heavy, I nearly dropped it. Taking blood from a gash in his arm, he traced the sign of the cross over my forehead. "With my blood, I anoint thee, Katherine Elizabeth Jones, Daughter of Eve, Defender of Mankind. For those who wait on the Lord shall renew their strength. They shall mount up with wings like eagles. They shall run and not be weary, and they shall walk and not faint."

"What are you doing?" I asked, my voice shaking, hands

trembling as a river of golden light snaked through my palms and up my arms, the spectacle hidden under my jacket.

I'm giving you my power, my lowly mortal, he said into my mind, his lips quirking with a playful, yet sad, smile. *And I'm entrusting you with my sword. Treat her well. She can be temperamental.*

Stop this right now, I said, smacking a palm against his armored chest. *Stop being such a righteous asshole all the time.*

My time has ended, Kate. Please, don't fight this inevitability. Can't you see I'm trying to protect you? To give you a fighting chance to save Luke and Jax and put an end to this war. If I don't surrender, that squadron will finish us off. All of us.

Fuck that.

Turning to the sky, I shouted up to the Power, "Mikha'el is innocent! Gavri'el made him do it because of what Samael planned to do to her! You know this to be true. Mikha'el would've never murdered her, and the fact you can condemn him without even having the balls to come down here and face him yourself is a sign of your own cowardliness. You are no better than Samael."

"You think the words of a mortal woman are enough to change the judgment of the heavens?" Khama'el sneered, his voice dripping with contempt toward me. "Your defiance is both amusing and pathetic, Kate. But it will not save him."

Heartbeat pounding in my ears, I tried to summon every ounce of courage I had left. "You underestimate the strength of humanity, Khama'el. It's not just the power of the words, it's the truth behind them. Mikha'el is innocent, and you know it."

Khama'el's eyes narrowed, a flicker of irritation crossing his face. "Innocent? He has defied the celestial laws, interfered with divine plans. His crimes are unforgivable."

I tightened my grip on Emrandael, feeling the weight of its power, of the power wielded by Mikha'el. "He did it to save me, to save all of us. You can't see beyond your rigid laws, but we humans fight for love, for family. We bend the rules when we need to because life is more precious than some arbitrary law created to control us, and that's what makes us strong. Stronger than you. That's what truly terrifies your kind. Why you fear humans. Why you seek to destroy us."

Khama'el whipped his wings, descending until he stood mere feet from me, his luminesce and majestic presence a stark contrast to the darkness brewing in the depths of his silver eyes. He took a closer step, each movement of his muscles slow and imposing, his wings tucked but rustling. "You speak of strength, yet you are nothing but a fragile mortal. You rely on the power of others to protect you. Look at you now, trembling and desperate. Your will to live, though admirable, will not save your people."

I met his gaze, refusing to back down. "I might be fragile, but I have something you'll never understand. I have the hope of a whole civilization that refuses to be squashed out of existence, and I have the courage to stand up to cowards like you. You can shackle Mikha'el and Cassael, but you can't break our spirit."

A dark smile curled Khama'el's lips. "Spirit? Let's see how long that lasts." He raised a hand, and shackles of gleaming light materialized around Mikha'el and Cassael's wrists, binding their powers.

"Remember your word, Khama'el," Mikha'el warned, his lips taut.

Mikha'el's eyes met mine, a silent plea and a promise in their depths. *I believe in you, Kate. You will not be defeated. And no matter what happens, I will always be with you. Take my oath and embed it into your heart.* His words were barely audible over the crackling energy of the chains around his wrists.

Tears stung my eyes, but I forced them back. "I *will* find a way to free you."

Khama'el chuckled, a cruel, mocking sound. "Such touching resolve. Let's see if it saves you when the real battle begins."

With a flick of his wrist, a rift opened behind him, a swirling vortex of dark energy. "Take them," he commanded the four assassins standing guard, and Mikha'el and Cassael were pulled into the void, their forms disappearing into the darkness before either could offer another word.

"Wait!" I shouted, but it was too late. They were gone, leaving me standing there, alone with Khama'el.

He looked down the slope of his nose, his eyes cold and unfeeling. "I'm sorry for your people, Kate. Truly, I am. Our Lord God, He… He had great intentions. Your race had the potential to become great, but you squandered it. And now… now the time of the humans has come to an end."

As he turned to leave, I felt a surge of panic snake around my heart. He wasn't planning on keeping his word… All around us, the sicarii took positions around the perimeter of the cathedral. This wasn't going to be an execution; they were planning an extermination.

Taking flight, Khama'el rifted out of our world in a blink, and in that moment, I knew if I didn't act fast, we would all be dead in a matter of minutes. Without time to even think, I gripped Emrandael and focused all my energy, imbuing the sword with all my love and courage, and drawing from it the power needed to ignite the angelic magic Mikha'el had poured into my veins.

Heat, unlike anything I had ever felt, flared within me. I was a raging volcano about to spew a torrent of flaming lava. I screamed so loud I thought I'd bust my vocal cords. Holy stars, Mikha'el's power was a galaxy… and it had turned me into a fucking supernova.

Body trembling, I let out a slow trickling breath, trying to control the vortex of star energy swirling inside me.

"Kate!" Clint's faint voice reached my ears, but I put my palm out, warning him to stay back. I had no idea what would happen once I unleashed the power Mikha'el had gifted me. Hank barked furiously, and I knew I only had seconds to act.

Reading my desperation, Clint took Hank by his harness and yanked him back, though my canine fought him with every muscle in his body.

"I'm gonna be okay…" I whispered to him, but I struggled to believe my own words, could barely hear my own voice from the thundering rumble in my ears.

A guttural scream ripped from my throat as I let the vortex consume me. Suddenly, everything went incredibly still and silent, then with a sonic boom, a blast of blinding light exploded from my body and into the darkness, expanding into a dome of energy that covered the entire cathedral. Every devoured and demon in its path exploded into ash.

Rivers of flames circulated through my body as I tapped into the angelic power seated at my core. My body trembled, and I fell to a knee as red rings began to appear across the dome. The sicarii were firing against the shield with their bolts and magic.

Fuck. I felt the strain deep in my marrow. I didn't know how long I could hold out. Once the shield fell, those assassins would pick us off one by one. Clint ran to my side with Hank at his heel. "Kate, are you okay?"

"For now. Every bolt they shoot at the dome eats at my energy."

"What can we do?"

"Once the shield cracks, there's no fighting ourselves out of this one. That's at least a squadron of one hundred sicarii, if not more. We're sitting ducks."

Another Guardian approached. "There's gotta be something we can do," the woman said.

"You need to get back inside the church. Barricade it. Find the civilians and get to safety. Clint, you know the way through the tunnels. Maybe you can get them to Saint Mary's. I will hold the dome for as long as I can."

Clint eyed my body, noticing the layer of sweat on my

forehead dripping down the side of my face. All my limbs shook as I fed light into the dome.

"You're going to burn out."

"Don't worry about me, kid. Take Hank with you. Make sure those fucking stones are secure and get the fuck out of that church."

"You're out of your mind if you think I'm leaving you."

"Clint," I gritted, fire blazing across my shoulders and singeing my skin as Mikha'el's power kept pouring from me. "It's an order. Please. You're my last hope." I fell to another knee. "If Samael gets the stones…"

"Shit. Shit. Shit." The kid climbed back to his feet. "I don't like this. Fuck. Alright. Everyone, we need to get back inside the church and get everyone out through the tunnels. Once the shield falls, those sicarii are going to hunt us down. Without holy weapons, we don't stand a chance of survival."

Without question, the Guardians gathered all the wounded and headed back to the front entrance. Clint and Kelsey hung back as Hank ran to me. Whining, he licked my face and nuzzled my neck, sniffing profoundly, as if wanting to absorb my scent into him.

I dropped to all fours, the weight on my back from each blow the sicarii were inflicting on the dome beating into me like a sledgehammer. Hank refused to leave my side. "Buddy, you have to go…" I huffed out with each breath.

He simply laid down at my feet, and this time, I couldn't hold back the tears. "I'm gonna be okay, I promise," I whimpered. "But you won't be if you stay. You need to go with Clint."

He let out a grumbling whine, his stubborn heart refusing to abandon me.

"Damn it, Hank. Please! Go!" When he still didn't budge, I screamed at him, and my heart shattered into a million pieces as he quirked his ears at me and lowered his gaze. "I'm so sorry…"

Noticing the strain on my body, Clint rushed in and took Hank by the vest and dragged him away. I couldn't bear to look at them as they ran for the doors.

Stars. The searing burns were spreading across my body like wildfire. I screamed until my voice echoed off the stone walls of the church.

I needed to hold on.

I needed to hold on.

The first crack rumbled through the ground, and I slowly craned my neck to look up at the top of the dome where the assassins were focusing their attack. About twenty more crossbow bolts hit the dome, and another crack thundered through the shield. Shit. It was too soon. There was no way the Guardians would have enough time to get to safety.

I could feel my strength waning, the shield cracking even further under the relentless assault. My vision blurred, but I knew if I didn't push myself harder to maintain the shield, everyone would die. I needed something, anything, to keep me going.

When all is lost, faith is the last thing to die… Mikha'el's voice echoed in my mind, and I wasn't sure if I'd imagined it, or he'd managed to reach me across realms somehow. It was almost as if I could feel what he was asking of me. Like his words were a warm, comforting blanket on a cold wintry day.

But I shook my head, rejecting what he was asking of me. *Not that. I can't. I won't.* My stubborn ass wouldn't let me. Mikha'el wanted me to pray… he wanted me to lean my faith on God. But I was the last person He'd listen to. And He was the God I resented with every fiber of my existence. How could I now seek His help? Why would I, when I'd made it this far without it…

But have you?

Damn it, Mikha'el. Even when he wasn't around, his will still pound against the well-barricaded walls of my heart.

But what other option did I have, really? We'd done all we

could, fought with everyone and everything we had. I was now near burn out, and only a miracle could save us. And as much as I hated the idea of praying to a God who had already let me down so many other times, I needed to put my damn pride aside. This was bigger than me, and I wouldn't be doing this for my own personal preservation. I was doing it for all those people in that church. And for everyone who would suffer at the hands of Samael if I let him win this war.

This was our Hail Mary, and I wouldn't be able to live with myself, in this world or the next, knowing I hadn't tried everything, including prayer.

"God, if you're there, if you're listening…" I choked out through gritted teeth. "I know I've questioned you, doubted you, even hated you, but right now, I need your strength. Not for me, but for them. Help me protect them. Please."

I closed my eyes, desperately searching for any source of power to draw from. Then, a verse from my childhood came rushing back to me, a prayer I hadn't uttered in years. A prayer my grandmother had taught me, and one I'd chosen to forget.

Heaving, I began chanting the words that had been shoved into the deepest recesses of my soul for so long. "Lord, You are my foundation, my fortress, and my deliverer. You are my rock in whom I take refuge, my shield, and the horn of my salvation, my stronghold. I call to You, my Lord, who is worthy of praise, and the only one who can save me from my enemies."

I paused, my throat dry and burning. The next words poured from me as if my spirit was speaking of its own volition, as if each word carried the weight of every soul that had ever lived. "Please, Lord, grant me Your mercy, Your strength, Your blessings. That I may draw upon Your well of power and grace and offer protection to those who follow You and even those who don't. For we are all members of Your flock, and I beseech You, do not forsake them."

I repeated it like a mantra, forcing myself to believe in its power, to believe that somehow, someway, it would be enough.

Above, the shield flickered, the light dimming and brightening as I fought to maintain it. The cracks widened, each one a clobbering blow as the sicarii attacked, the tremors reverberating through my bones. My muscles screamed in agony and my skin blistered from the heat of the power still surging from within me.

"Please, God," I whispered, tears streaming down my face. "Give me the strength to save them."

Suddenly, a coolness spread through me, comforting and soothing. As if gentle hands had been placed upon my back, lifting my burden and lessening the pain. The reprieve was a balm against my scorched skin.

The shield's light steadied, and the fractures slowed, though they didn't stop.

"Thank you," I breathed, feeling a sliver of hope amidst the pain. I knew it wouldn't last forever, but it gave me just enough to hold on a little longer.

Another crack spider-webbed through the dome, but I gritted my teeth and poured everything I had left into maintaining the barrier.

Images of Jax and Luke filled my mind, my love for them blooming like a flower inside my heart. Roger and Isabella… their memory a flicker of light among all this darkness. Clint, Chaz, the girls back home. My boy Hank… I needed to hold on for them. For all these people.

Peering up at the top of the dome, I watched as the shield began to fracture into pieces, the shards of golden light falling around me like rain.

Just a few more breaths… give me a few more breaths.

I gritted my teeth, letting the last vestiges of Mikha'el's power burn through me. My body blazed with white-hot energy, nearly blinding me, but then… something snagged my attention. Something far and faint…

My vision blinked in and out of focus, sound muffling in my ears as I felt myself fading. Was that a winged horse I saw flying above the dome? But how? And who? Not just one, but several of them, holding armed riders. Was I hallucinating? I tried to rise to my feet, to push myself just a bit more… but as the last surge of star energy burst from me, I collapsed to the ground with bouldering force, my world plummeting into a depthless, black sea until all I saw and felt was absolute nothingness.

Chapter Eight

JAX

I walked down the dark, narrow hallway of the Devil's Army headquarters, my footsteps echoing off the tiled floors as I ambled my drunk ass toward my mother's office. I could already picture the scowl on her face. I'd missed her mass from earlier in the day, which also meant I'd missed rehearsing the Summoning ritual.

It wasn't like we hadn't practiced it a million times already.

We were mere days from D-Day, when the gates of Hell would fling wide open, and I would take my last breath as a mortal man, sacrificing myself to bring forth one of the Horsemen. I deserved to at least enjoy myself a little before meeting my end on this earth.

I mean, did we really need to keep going over something I'd been practically preparing for my whole damn life?

Stand on the southwest corner of the pentacle, accept the amulet with the Fire Creation Stone, recite the Horseman's prayer, and drink the warm blood of the poor asshole whose neck my mother would slice open. The fucking ritual had been seared into the back of my skull. But my mother was a methodical woman, and this wasn't just about remembering a stupid ritual; it was about the control she had over us—over me.

Finally reaching the door at the end of the hallway, I gently pushed it open and was immediately hit with the strong scent of Dragon's Blood incense, my mother's favorite to burn. The air was so thick with it, the smell had permanently attached itself not only to the dark paneled walls, but to the furniture and carpet, and even to her hair. I smelled it on her every time she made me kiss the hematite ring on her finger, like she was doing now by extending her hand out to me, her gaze not lifting a fraction from her lap.

Dressed in her funeral-black, ankle-length skirt and knit cardigan, she sat in her usual paisley wingback chair, her face illuminated by the glow of the gas fireplace. She didn't bother to look up at me as she waited for me to kiss her ring.

"Mother," I said as I took her delicate slim fingers, kissed the ring, then sat opposite her on the matching love seat.

She resumed to busying herself with her crocheting, her fingers moving a million miles a minute as she manipulated the needles, probably making some new scarf. God, how she loved making those ugly scarves nobody wore. A long string of black yarn snaked down to a rolled-up ball inside a wicker basket full of other balls of yarn.

My mother, the high priestess of the Devil's Army, looked as cold and distant as ever. There was such disdain in her aura, she even made crocheting look like the prelude to a nightmare, as if she could snap and stab me in the eye with one of her needles at any point. She probably would. "You reek," she said, her eyes still glued to her moving fingers as she forcefully looped and looped.

Oh, she was more than pissed. She was nuclear.

I sniffed my pits, but I knew she meant my breath. Pitchers

of beer would do that. "I'm not *that* rancid. I showered two days ago," I said with a mocking grin.

Her scoff was barely audible, and I hated that the wordless response grated on me more than the insults she was accustomed to hurtling at me.

"Tell me, Mother, why have you summoned me?"

Her eyes finally snapped up at me in an almost inhuman way, as if her body was made of stone and only her eyes could move. A sharp blade of unease cut down my spine, and I sat up straighter, needing to shake off the feeling.

But the color of her eyes… something was off about that, too, though I couldn't put my finger on it. The shade of blue seemed wrong. Maybe it was my own eyes playing tricks on me. It was dim in here; the gas fireplace and the lone desk lamp in the corner provided poor illumination.

Wait, has that lamp always been there?

"Jax," she crooned in that raspy, commanding voice of hers, drawing my attention away from the desk lamp. I stared at her, nausea curdling in my gut. Maybe I'd gulped down one too many beers. I was so inebriated, I couldn't even remember how I'd gotten here. I should've eaten something. I'd skipped breakfast and had gone straight to the bar, drinking well past lunch. What time was it now? Four in the afternoon?

But was it?

Why is it so dark outside?

"Jax," she said again, and this time, her mouth curled a little, as if trying to mask her dead soul with a smile. "I know I've been hard on you, but you know why that is, right?"

Because you are a heartless, evil woman who probably should've never been a mother.

"Enlighten me," I said, my mind swimming. I'd definitely drank too much. I tried to focus on the wall to help ground myself, to keep my head from spinning, but as I kept focusing, strange symbols flashed on the walls, as if some type of red, luminescent writing was layered under the dark paint.

What the hell?

"I don't think you understand your importance. How critical your life is to our cause. You were created for more, Jax. You were created to change the world."

"I've heard this speech before, Mother."

"Yes, but I need you to understand that everything I've ever done, I've done for you. Because I… love you, son."

I quirked my head at those words, blinking at her in shock. "Love? Mother, do you even know what that word means? The only person you've ever cared about in your entire life has been yourself." More red writing on the walls flashed, flickering like a dying light going in and out of focus. What the fuck was going on?

"What is this? Why am I really here?" I asked, pushing up to my feet, my skin prickling as if the temperature in the room had suddenly dropped twenty degrees.

I looked around her office and more things seemed to be out of place. The gas fireplace was replaced by a wood-burning stove. The curtains… there hadn't been curtains before. Memories from my childhood began to rush into my mind. I spun. This room… this wasn't her office at headquarters. There hadn't been carpet at her office. The walls hadn't been black. That seat she was on, the yarn… none of it belonged here.

This whole entire room was wrong. It was… I stared the woman down. "Who the fuck are you, and why am I here?"

"What do you mean, darling? Where is it you think you are?"

That right there, the tone of her voice. Warm. Pleasant. Calling me *darling*? There had never been anything motherly about my mother. And in that split second, my body began to thrum with understanding. Sweat beaded down my neck and every muscle in my body tightened into a coil. "What do you want?" I asked the demon before me.

It ignored my question, maintaining its ruse. "Jax, where are you?"

"You brought us here. You tell me."

"No, Jax," it said, gently placing the yarn and needles neatly beside her before pushing up to her feet. "You conjured this."

I took a step back, watching as that writing continued to flicker. Those symbols… I'd seen them before. What the fuck did they mean?

"Jax," the demon crooned, its voice now distorted. "Where did you bring us?"

My old baseball glove was in the corner next to a bat… a bloodied bat. Dread surged up my throat. I looked around, the room morphing even more. I would've never come back here of my own volition. Not to this place. Not to my …

"You wanted to find something, remember? Something that was lost."

"There's nothing but evil here…" I trailed as I continued to stare at all the memories of my past, of everything that reminded me of the awful things I'd done. Of the terrible things she made me do.

It stalked closer, those inhuman eyes now swirling like a blackhole. "A secret. Where did she keep it?"

The walls. The answer was on the walls. But what?

My body trembled. I needed to get out of here. Looking around in a panic, the symbols slowly started to make sense. Runes… they were magical runes. I remembered now. My gaze narrowed over the poorly executed rendition of my mother. "I'm under the spell of The Dreamer's Descent. But why?"

"The location, Jax," it hissed. "Tell us where we are, and all will be forgiven."

I let out a slow, trickling breath as I took in every detail of the monster's demeanor and that familiar, bone-crushing stare. The creature before me was no ordinary demon. Fuck.

"Vigilantiam voco, ut ex tenebris in lucem trahar. Ut a diaboli manibus liberer et ex hoc regno eruar," the words spilled from my lips in a rapid chant, the words that had brought me back from this nightmare realm countless times while my mother had been grooming me into accepting my fate.

But when the walls of my childhood home fell away, I was left naked inside a small, barren cabin. A weak breath leaked from my lips. I knew this fucking place, and it was enough to coat me in a permafrost of fear. A fire crackled inside a brick hearth. My body shivered, craving the warmth of the flames. But there was no heat in this place, only the taunt of it.

Was this another trick of my imagination? Another attempt to give me false hope? Because if I was, in fact, in the Wastes, then it meant the heart beat I'd felt inside my chest hadn't been a lie.

"Sit, Jax," said a deep, melodious male voice, a voice that had haunted me as a little boy. Clearly, it still did. "We need to talk."

A wooden dining table and two chairs materialized in front of the fireplace. Dressed in his usual impeccable black suit, the figure occupied one of the chairs, one leg crossed over a knee, as if patiently waiting for me to join him. Then I noticed the steaming bowl of soup on the table and my stomach grumbled so loud, it echoed in the small space.

Wretched demon. Samael never showed up empty-handed; an offering always accompanied these visits—for those fools too dumb to realize his gifts were never meant to satisfy your yearnings but intensify them.

"Come on," he sang. "I know you're hungry."

"My mind might be a shattered mess, but I remember enough about this place to know that's not a hot meal." Body shivering, I didn't bother covering my nakedness, and simply stared at the brutally stunning fallen angel. His platinum blonde hair was slicked back and those twilight eyes devoid of anything but the sheer wickedness that existed inside him shone like the stars in the galaxy.

"It's been a while since you and I had a chat. Come, sit."

"I'll stand."

A guttural chuckle rumbled within him. "You and that woman of yours truly delight in vexing me. Now. Sit."

My muscles responded to his command of their own accord, and I sat in the chair, my body still quaking uncontrollably. "You could at least conjure some clothes for me."

"Clothes in this realm won't stop you from feeling that chill in your bones."

My teeth clattered. "I'd still rather not do this with my dick hanging out."

Samael blinked and instantly, I was dressed in a pair of faded jeans and an I Love NY T-shirt. "Better?"

The clothes did nothing for the cold as he had said, but at least I felt less exposed, though I knew if he wanted to lay my spirit bare, he could do it with another blink of those otherworldly eyes. "How about a cigarette?" I asked with a twitching grin.

"Don't press your luck, Jackson. My patience has limits." The shadows in the room seemed to vibrate with warning, tendrils of icy darkness snaking around the room, as if something else was in the room with us. I swallowed thickly. There was always something lurking in the shadows of this realm, something ancient and rotting with evil.

"What do you want from me?" I asked, meeting his gaze.

The way he tapped his fingers on the table unsettled every fiber in my body. "By now, you've likely puzzled out why that little incantation didn't pull you back into your realm."

I'd traveled to the Wastes enough times in my youth to know that the souls of the damned weren't trapped here. This was the in-between place, where the consciousness traveled to commune with the devil. "I'm not dead."

"No, you are not."

My eyes welled with relief, but I held back my tears. "But my mind is imprisoned."

"Somnolent stasis."

A shudder ran the length of my back, confirming what I already feared. A coma. How long had I actually been trapped in this hellish place, in these nightmares? When I'd been in that hole, time had felt meaningless, an endless loop of agony and confusion. But now that I knew I was still alive… How much time had I truly lost? Days? Weeks?

What if I'd lost years? My gut twisted, nausea making me dizzy. Deep, suffocating dread wrapped around my throat. But why choose to keep me alive after everything I'd done to keep him locked in *his* prison?

And that's when it hit me. "I know how your realm works. To sustain itself, it feeds off the souls of the damned. Keeping me alive serves you no purpose, unless you need something from me. Which means *you're* still imprisoned." He cocked his head, narrowing his gaze, and a flicker of satisfaction burned in my heart. If he was still trapped in Abaddon, that meant the war still raged on. He had Luke, but he probably didn't have the Creation Stones.

"It's not quite so simple. You see, my father, in His infinite wisdom, decided life would be more exciting if He created all these insufferable rules that make sense only to Him. Unfortunately, there is no way around them. In order for me to be reborn in your son's body, I not only need the four Creation Stones and a perfect vessel, but I need a particular spell. One only your mother possessed."

"The rebirthing spell was kept secret, even from me. What makes you think I know it?"

"I believe you know where she kept her grimoire."

"Everything was destroyed when we won the battle in New York. The spell you need died with her. Her soul is probably somewhere in Abaddon; ask her for it, but it will do you no good without the stones."

"Alas, her soul was so dark and unpure, Abaddon greedily devoured her sins with each turn of the Breaking Wheel faster than some of the most wicked souls your kind has ever encountered. Seems she was a bit too delicious to savor. And sadly, by the time I tried torturing the information out of her, she had been reduced to nothing but a whimpering dolt, unable to remember why she was even in Hell.

"Can you believe it? Your mother finally got to meet her Over Lord, and she couldn't even remember she'd pledged her soul to me. You should've seen it, though, how she begged for mercy with each revolution, her bones breaking one by one, until her body was torn apart, limb by limb, over and over and over for countless millennia. I would've loved the opportunity to personally oversee the torture of her pathetic soul for another ten thousand years—no other priestess had ever failed as miserably as she did—but duty calls. I have a throne to steal."

He seemed genuinely disappointed, and as much as I hated my mother for everything she'd ever done, picturing her soul in perpetual torture brought me no pleasure.

"And you assume too much, Jackson," he went on. "I already have the Creation Stones." His stark smile sent ragged claws scratching all over my body.

Lie. It was a filthy lie. It had to be. "Mikha'el would've never—"

"Do not speak his name here, human. That traitor has already been dealt with."

I didn't think it could possibly get colder in this place, but the frigid panic that reverberated through me made my bones rattle like they were about to splinter into a million frozen shards. What could he possibly mean by *Mikha'el had been dealt with?* He was Kate's sworn protector. Without him, Kate was too vulnerable.

"Your mother was entrusted with the most potent magic of my kind. And every priestess before her passed down the original grimoire, along with its duplicate. The original was always kept safe and secret until it was time to pass it down to the next priestess."

I trembled, but it wasn't from the intolerable cold of this place. "I never even knew there were two. I have no idea where she kept it, and even if I did, what makes you think I'd tell you?"

"Jackson, how many times do you think you and I have sat here at this table, having this exact conversation?"

The question almost had me teetering off my chair. I was stuck in a dream loop? Oh God. For how long?

"Days may have passed since your capture, but here, in my world, your mind has been imprisoned for over a thousand years. We've been at this for a millennium. I've been pulling your fucking mind apart, thread by thread, searching for clues to the location of that goddamn book."

I almost couldn't breathe. A thousand years? I shook with sheer terror. The dark hole… that's where he sent me after each dream loop to recoup from the mental strain. Into a void inside my subconscious, where each day, I lost even more of myself.

"Do you think I would be sitting here in front of you, year after fucking year, if I didn't know that the location of where you mother hid that book lived inside your pitiful head?"

The idea that I'd been stuck in the Wastes for so long made me spiral. There was a reason trips to this realm were kept short. They usually lasted minutes, if that. If a mind stayed too long down here, the ramifications would be unfathomable. Waking up from a thousand-year dive into the Wastes would be like sticking your brain inside a blender. My hands trembled so violently, I had to clasp them together. Even if I ever managed to escape this realm, I would likely never fully wake up, my mind would be lost like a soul in purgatory.

Tunneling my gaze into his, I gritted, "It's been a thousand years and you're no closer to discovering its location.

Don't you think you've wasted enough time?" I'd wanted to mock him, but my voice cracked too much, revealing the horror raking at me from the inside. Would we go on for another thousand years if he didn't get what he needed? The idea was enough to make my bowels churn.

He pushed up to his feet, his form towering over me, and those shadows that had been slithering on the walls converged onto him, forming his grotesque wings. I jumped to my feet and tried to walk backward away from him, but he rushed forward and pinned me to the wall, a strong hand wrapped around my neck.

"Impudent fool," he gritted over my face, his breath a blistering gale against my skin. "What's a thousand years to an immortal? I've been imprisoned here longer than your kind could possibly comprehend. We're only getting started. I will break apart your consciousness until your mind is nothing but a husk. I already know much more than you think. That baseball glove, the bat… Oh, Jackson. Do you not remember the conversations we used to have when you were a little boy? The things your mother made you do? I know all your secrets."

The coldness of his breath spread over my body, seeping deeper into my bones, until it burned, until it felt like my body was on a pyre. "It's only a matter of time before I crack you open like a shell. And once I do, there will be nothing left of your miserable mind. Your mother always told you that you were meant for more, but I wager you never imagined you would be solely responsible for the death of millions and millions of your kind. That you would be the true antichrist your people foretold."

"I never wanted to be a part of your army. I tried to stop the gates from opening. Tried to atone for all my mistakes——"

"Save your excuses, Jackson. You can no more escape your fate than I can. Didn't your mother teach you that? Your bloodline was bred for one purpose alone——sacrifice. You see, the spell can only be activated by the blood of a Constantine.

Your mother was prepared to offer her life in exchange for my rebirth, but now that you've killed her, your blood will be the key that unlocks my shackles once and for all, so I may take your son as my vessel and finally claim my father's throne."

He peered deep into my pleading eyes, and I felt that stare probe all the recesses of my mind. Samael saw every fear, every regret, every weakness. He saw all my despair.

He leaned in closer and smiled so brightly, he could've lit up the entire world if his heart hadn't been crafted of the darkest and coldest stone. "You'll never see your child grow, Jackson. Never know the meaning of being a father. He will be stolen from you, just like my daughter was taken from me. And Kate? Oh, I have special plans for her. When all my demons are done defiling her body, I will peal the flesh off her bones with my bare hands before I feed her entrails to my hounds." With his serpentine tongue, he licked the tears that streamed down my face. "How delightful, the taste of your sadness. Lamentably, she won't have the opportunity to witness your death, but I will still bask in the knowledge that, once again, I will take everything she loves from her."

"Is this the part where you offer me a bargain?" I croaked, his fingers still tightly wrapping around my throat.

"Seems to me you're looking to offer *me* one."

"My life is already forfeit. Even if I were to escape, I might as well be turned into the walking dead—my brain will be so fried I doubt I'll even know my name. I also have no desire to spend another thousand years in this place, fighting to preserve a worthless existence. If my blood is required for your rebirth, then I'm a dead man already. And as much as you claim that a thousand years is inconsequential to you, we both know you don't want to spend another intolerable second stuck in Hell. So do us both a favor and cut the bullshit. The last thing you want is to spend lifetimes stuck in a dream loop with me, waiting for breadcrumbs to piece together your little puzzle."

"What is it you propose, Jackson?" it hissed.

"I will tell you where I believe the original grimoire might be, and you will swear not to touch a single hair on Kate's head."

The beast snarled in my face. "Once I take my father's throne, I will burn your planet to the ground. Her death is an inevitability."

My gaze hardened. I was not backing down from my offer. If there was even one glimmer of hope that I could give Kate a fighting chance to make it out of this, I was prepared to give this asshole anything he asked of me, including my soul. "Swear that you won't touch a single hair on her head, Samael. And remember that, even once you regain your freedom, you will still be bound by the rules of the bargain."

"You bargain for a less painful death for her. How noble of you."

"It's called love—something you'll never understand. Now take the deal before I change my mind and decide to prolong this dream loop for tens of thousands of years. I've had practice with dreams and know how to manipulate them. Heck, we could be stuck in here until I die, and then there won't be a Constantine to offer their blood up for your rebirth."

He let go of my throat and took a few steps back, eyeing me like a lion assessing its prey.

"It's a wise choice and you know it. Kate means nothing to you, but she means everything to me." I stuck my hand out. "Take the damn deal, you fucking demon."

Then, with an ice-crusted smile, he took my hand and accepted my bargain.

Seemed I couldn't stop damning my soul, no matter how hard I tried. Perhaps my mother had been right all along. Perhaps I was destined to bring destruction, destined to be the antichrist, as Samael so poetically put it. It appeared that, regardless of the countless times I attempted to make up for the sins of my past, I would never be able to escape my true fate.

Closing my eyes, I reached for the only thing I had left. *God, if you can hear me, please give Kate and Luke all my love and all my strength. I might not deserve your mercy, but Kate and Luke… they deserve the world.*

Chapter Nine

CLINT

Tightly gripping Hank's harness, I dragged him away from Kate. Barking and growling, he practically dug his claws into the cobblestones, trying to run back to her. I found Kelsey leaning against a wall and reached for her hand, dragging her as well, her limp slowing us down, but I wasn't about to leave her behind. By the time we joined the surviving Guardians at the barricaded doors, the loud cracking sound of the dome breaking reverberated through the church and ground.

We all turned to Kate, knowing it was her power that was buying us these precious moments, but also knowing that while she was trying to save us, she was killing herself in the process. Bellowing in agony, she was on all fours as a pillar of brilliant light pulsed from her back, feeding the dome, repairing it inch by inch to keep the sicarii from breaching the shield and executing us all.

The light was burning her body and watching her cry out in pain tore my heart in two. Hot tears welled in my eyes as I saw her skin blister, as I watched her entire body tremble, struggling to hold herself up. She was burning up just like Mikha'el had warned.

There was no way she could hold on for much longer.

The doors to the church swung open, and the Guardians rushed in. I lost my grip on Kelsey as everyone pushed and shoved. There was so much chaos, I was unable to find her amongst the throng of Guardians trying to find a safe place to hole up. Hank continued to pull toward Kate, and I had to give up looking for Kelsey. Kneeling, I snapped my fingers until his attention flicked to my eyes. He sat down and huffed. "I know, buddy. Trust me, I know. But I promised Kate I'd keep you safe. I can't let you go out there." He let out a grumbling whimper, but at least he'd settled down. I needed to give him a job to keep him focused. "Hank," I said, pointing to my eyes, then to some of the wounded Guardians scattered by the entrance. "Guard them."

His head cocked, and I knew he'd understood the command. I was finally able to let go of his harness, and like a good boy, he set to work. Needing to see what was happening outside, I climbed onto one of the scaffolding platforms and peered out into the courtyard through a broken stained-glass window.

From my vantage point, I had a clear view of the insanity unfolding outside. The dome shimmered with cracks spider-webbing across its surface. Kate's light, so intense it hurt to look directly at it, was the only thing keeping the shield from shattering entirely.

Another thunderous crack shook the foundation, and I peered up at the dome again. My breath stilled. Through the fractures, I caught a glimpse of what I could only describe as a legion of winged horses carrying female riders. The shield continued to fall away, revealing the battle raging in the sky. The riders looked like female Viking warriors, with their long-braided hair and glinting armor, as they jetted through the air on their flying horses, golden war paint on their faces, war cries piercing the air as they sliced their swords and scythes, cutting through the sicarii ranks as if the assassins were nothing but gnats.

Bodies thumped to the ground and bounced off the church roof as angels fell from the sky. The sight was gruesome, but a wave of relief crashed through me. Had these warrior women been the reinforcements Mikha'el had told Kate about?

One rider, her blonde hair flowing behind her, drove her spear right through the heart of an assassin as he'd tried to aim a bolt at Kate. Another swung her sword in a deadly arc, felling two angels with a single strike.

Kate now lay unmoving on the ground, her body severely burned, the brilliant light that had burst from her now completely snuffed out. I couldn't leave her body out there, not while that aerial battle raged on, and the assassins were still trying to aim at her. Heart jack hammering against my chest, I descended the scaffolding, leaping off as I neared the ground. Hank barked at me, but I barked a command right back. "Stay here, Hank," I ordered, and the shepherd obeyed.

I pushed through the tumult of Guardians blocking the exit, ignoring their shouts and protests for me to stay inside. There was no way I was leaving Kate's body out there—I didn't care if she was alive or dead. The courtyard was a bloody battlefield, and I would not let those demons or fallen angels have at her or take her body as a trophy.

Angels continued to fall from the sky and even one of the flying horses dropped like a boulder, splattering guts and blood everywhere. The sight of its broken body and that of its rider was something I'd never be able to erase from my mind. A bolt flew past my head as I zigzagged my way through the courtyard, but one almost found purchase, nicking my non-bionic shoulder as it zipped by, forcing a grunt from my lungs, but I kept running, blood dripping down my arm.

Kate was still not moving, and I felt my stomach bottom out.

Please, God. Don't let her be dead.

With my mind so focused on getting to Kate, I failed to notice as a wounded sicarii, who had been pushing back onto his feet, lunged at me with his dagger. Before I could react, a warrior on a winged horse swooped down, her sword slicing through the air and decapitating the assassin in one swift motion. She nodded at me, a silent acknowledgment, before flying back to the battle in the sky.

Frayed platinum-tipped white feathers gently fell all around us, coating everything in silvery white, like some type of serene winter storm, except we were covered in the wing feathers of fallen angels instead of snow.

Finally reaching Kate, I fell to my knees, heart in my throat. Blistered and burned, her skin looked worse than I imagined. I checked for a pulse, relief flooding me when I found one, albeit weak. I needed to get her to the infirmary and hope that the med unit could use the same concoction they'd made with Kate's blood to somehow heal her.

I tried lifting her into my arms, but her dead weight was more than I could manage with my injured shoulder. I tried heaving her up into my arms again, but the gash was clearly worse than I'd thought. I was startled when someone appeared from behind me. I turned, ready to fight, but was met with the gentle eyes of a behemoth of a man—one of the Guardians had decided to brave the battle to lend me a hand. "I'll help you," the man said in accented English, lifting Kate with ease. He carried her back toward the church; our steps hurried but careful as we tried to avoid any more falling sicarii and the bolts that kept flying in our direction.

We burst through the doors and rushed to the infirmary at the back of the church, Kate laying limp in his arms. Hank was at our heels in an instant; I knew this time there would be no one who would be able to pull him from Kate's side.

Reckoning

"Get out of the way!" I shouted as we hurried through the corridors. The small clinic was in utter chaos when we arrived, filled with injured Guardians. Medics tended to the wounded, the air reeked with the scent of antiseptic and the sounds of pain. We laid Kate flat on her stomach on one of the makeshift beds, and one of the nurses immediately began working on her, gently peeling the burnt clothing from her skin.

I stood back, my chest heaving, watching helplessly. "Is she going to make it?" I asked in half a panic, my legs unable to stay still as I paced back and forth.

More medics rushed to her bedside, and the horrified look in their eyes told me they felt exactly how I did. It would be a miracle if Kate managed to survive her injuries, but I didn't want to say it. I refused to even allow myself to think it. Kate needed to survive. I couldn't lose another sister.

So, I stepped close to the gurney and whispered in her ear, "You're going to make it out of this, Kate. You have to." I gripped her hand and gently squeezed her fingers. "Jax and Luke need you, Kate. And Hank… he's here, too. You know he's not going to leave your side, so I'll tell you the same thing you told me: don't you go breaking his heart, Kate."

And I need you, too. I couldn't bring myself to utter the words out loud, but I knew she felt them. As I wiped my eyes, someone tapped me on the shoulder. When I turned, they pointed to the door. Antonia stood at the entryway, her face pale as a ghost. "Clint," she said, her voice grim. "You need to come with me."

I didn't want to leave Kate's bedside, but the glacial look in Antonia's eyes made my skin ice over. Something was terribly wrong.

We stood outside the sacristy—rather, what used to be the west sacristy. The entire room was a mountain of ruined wood, glass, and marble. The large armoire that used to house the church's holy relics and ceremonial artifacts was nothing but splintered wood. It had been destroyed to gain access to the secret opening to the underground floor where the most treasured holy items used to be stored, and where Mikha'el had hidden the Creation Stones.

I dropped to my knees, chest heaving, both from exertion and despair. "The stones…"

"We checked; everything is gone. It wasn't just the Devil's Army; angels did this."

I struggled to take in the destruction, to accept the implications of what this meant. If the stones had been taken, then it was all over. We'd lost. It was only a matter of time before Samael would be reborn in Luke's body. I trembled, trying to contain my anger and the utter helplessness bulldozing through my body. "How did this happen? It was heavily warded. The stones were completely undetectable unless you knew their exact location."

"The wards must have fallen when Mikha'el was taken. With the wards down, any angel would've been able to detect the power of the stones."

I shook my head. "Even with the wards down, someone needed to have known where the stones were located. Mikha'el purposefully stored them inside gold chalices to prevent angels from detecting the power of the stones—the gold should've been able to mask the power emanating from them. Someone leaked the information to the Devil's Army that the stones were in the sacristy…"

"I'm so sorry, Clint," Antonia went on. "With the battle raging outside, we didn't realize we'd been infiltrated. We had Guardians stationed here, but we found their dead bodies under all the rubble."

Reckoning

I stared down at my bloodied and dirt-covered hands, at the empyrean steel woven through my flesh. A piercing cut slashed across my heart, and I gasped as I held back the tsunami of emotions threatening to burst through my chest. I'd failed them; I'd failed my family all over again. I'd sworn an oath to Gavri'el, been given a second chance, and for what? Samael had still won and everyone I cared about was gone.

Antonia placed a hand on my shoulder. "We were able to apprehend a member of the Devil's Army as he tried to make a run for it. We may still have time to find out where they've taken the stones."

I jumped to my feet and faced the Guardian.

"Hope is the last thing to die, Clint. And *we* are not dead yet."

"Take me to him."

THEY'D PUT the individual inside a storage room in the crypt. When the door was opened by one of the Guardians and I spotted the man sitting on a metal chair, a black hood covering his face, my blood drained. The shirt he wore… it was covered in black blood, but I knew I'd seen that Superman T-shirt before. "Take the hood off," I said, voice shaking.

I held my breath, hoping I was wrong, praying it was just a coincidence, but the instant the captive's brown eyes met mine, the world fell away beneath my feet. His face had been beaten up, one of his eyes almost bloodshot, but there was no mistaking who he was. "Kyle." The word was a mere whisper on my lips, as if the realization of what this all meant had knocked the air from my lungs.

With her rifle strapped across her back, Antonia shot me a surprised look. "You know this man?"

Swallowing thickly, I said, "You're certain he's a member of the Devil's Army?"

"We caught him climbing out of the secret passage. When we tried to approach him, he fired at us and killed one of our men," said the Guardian who'd taken Kyle's hood off. "I'd say we're pretty sure."

Kyle said nothing as I approached him; he just branded me with the same heated stare he'd given me back when I met him. "You're a member of the Devil's Army?"

He sucked on a tooth, then spit red-tinged saliva at my feet.

"How did you know where the stones were hidden?"

With a twitch of his busted top lip, he smirked, his bloodied teeth gleaming.

Fuck. Fuck. Fuck. I should've known. I should've fucking known…

I ran out of the room and bee-lined it for the crypt stairs, Antonia running behind me. "Clint! What's going on?"

"Kelsey!" I screamed her name as I ran through the destroyed cathedral and through the corridors. "Has anyone seen Kelsey?" I stopped random Guardians as Antonia trailed behind me trying to figure out why I was so frantic.

Finally, someone stepped forward. "I think I saw her limping toward the plaza. Said she'd lost her swords during the battle. She didn't look well, though."

Antonia grabbed me by the shoulders and spun me around. "Clint, what the hell is going on?"

"That's Kelsey's brother you captured."

"Kelsey… the Guardian from Saint Mary's we rescued? Didn't she go with you into the tunnels to fetch the holy water?"

"Yes. But it seems she's also the mole who led the Devil's

Army straight to the sacristy. And I'm the fucking asshole who gave her the location of the stones."

"What do you mean, you gave her the location of the stones?"

Ignoring her question, I ran to the large wooden doors leading to the plaza.

"I'll come with you," she said.

"No. I need to do this on my own."

I stepped out into the blood-stained night and stared up at the dark sky. The battle had ended, but the winged riders continued circling the perimeter around the cathedral, probably patrolling in case the sicarii returned. I wanted to thank them for their aid, hopefully learn more about who they were and why they'd come, but first, I needed to find the golden-haired traitor.

Spotting a discarded empyrean arrow on the ground, I reached for it and nocked it into my crossbow.

"Clint," Antonia called after me. "What do you plan to do when you find her?"

My fingers flexed around the stock of my Empyrean weapon. "Shoot a bolt through her fucking head."

Chapter Ten

CLINT

Kate's initial blast of celestial light had obliterated every demon, zombie, and Devil's Army member in what seemed to be a three-block radius, if not more. The plaza was so eerily quiet my footsteps echoed off the stone buildings, a stark contrast to the screams that had reigned moments ago. Blood and feathers coated the cobblestones and the acrid smell of burnt flesh still hung in the air.

I pushed through the carnage, heart pounding, eyes scanning for any sign of Kelsey. Anger roiled within me. I'd done this; I'd allowed myself to be blinded by this girl. Had it been lust? The hope of something more? It didn't matter, did it? I had literally handed Samael the Creation Stones on a golden platter. If Kate survived, how could I face her? How could I tell her that I gave away the location of the stones because of my stupidity?

She'd never forgive me. It wasn't just about losing the hope of rescuing Luke and Jax; it was about damning the entire world. I wouldn't be able to live with myself. I had to find

Kelsey. I had to find a way to get her or her brother to talk. One of them had to know where the stones were taken.

A few yards in front of me, I caught movement in the shadows, followed by the distinct sound of someone's ragged breaths. Drawing closer, I finally found her slumped against a shattered pillar, her usually vibrant hair matted with blood and grime. Her face was pale, almost translucent, and her eyes, once sharp and full of fire, were now dull and unfocused. She looked up at me, and for a moment, I saw the girl I had thought I knew. But then I remembered the devastation in the sacristy, the loss of the Creation Stones, and my resolve hardened.

Fingers slightly trembling, I aimed the crossbow at her head. I knew what I needed to do. She was a member of the Devil's Army, and she'd betrayed us—she'd given Samael the stones. But I couldn't bring myself to pull the trigger. A slow, quaky breath leaked from my lips. "Why did you do it, Kels?"

She blinked slowly, her breath wheezing. "You wouldn't understand."

I stalked closer, my crossbow still aimed right between her eyes. "It was all a lie, then? Everything you told me, this *thing* between us, it was just to get me to open myself up to you, to give up the location of the stones?"

She wheezed harder as she struggled to stay upright. "This isn't about us, Clint."

"You're right. It's about the fact that you're one of *them*," I gritted. "That you used us—used *me*—to give Samael the stones. Shit. How could I have been so stupid? So wrong about you, Kels?"

Tears welled in her eyes, and she coughed, a spray of blood flecking her lips. "It wasn't… personal." She fell to the ground, and a string tugged at my core.

"It sure as hell feels personal to me." But despite the fact she'd betrayed my trust, I couldn't just shut off my feelings. Mere hours ago, I thought I was falling in love with this girl.

My instincts were to protect her, to take her in my arms and rush her to safety. But then I noticed the dark veins crawling up her neck, and my world collapsed all over again.

God damn it. She was infected.

"I'm sorry, Clint," she whispered, her eyes closing. "I never wanted this. I had no choice."

"Don't you dare die on me," I growled as I knelt beside her, trying to shake her awake. "You don't get to get away with this that easy. Where are the stones, Kelsey? Where did the sicarii take them?"

She mumbled something incoherent, her breath more shallow and uneven. My hand tightened around my crossbow. She was going to turn soon. Fuck. Killing her was the right thing to do—it was what she deserved—but if we lost her, we'd lose our chance at finding the stones. And I was not about to fail again.

"Let's go, Goldilocks. You're not dying today." At least not until she gave me the information I needed. I wanted to believe that was the only reason I was doing this. That it wasn't because I couldn't bring myself to put a bolt through her head. That the reason my heart felt like it was going to gallop out of my chest wasn't because I wasn't ready to accept that she wasn't who I thought. Propping my bionic arm under her shoulder, I hauled her to her feet and dragged her across the plaza and back to *La Sagrada Familia*.

The doors swung open as we neared, and two Guardians rushed out to help. "Take her down to the crypt. She's infected, so make sure she's tied up."

Antonia met me at the entrance. "Did you get anything out of her?"

"Nothing useful." My voice sounded hollow. "But she's infected and doesn't have much time left, so we need to act fast," I said as I headed toward the infirmary.

"Wait, where are you going? I thought we needed to interrogate her now?"

"To get a vial of the antidote."

"You plan to heal that bitch?"

The insult made me flinch, and I had to hold myself back from looking like I wanted to defend a Devil's Army member. "She won't make it through an interrogation unless she's healed. Once she turns, it's game over. I don't think her brother will talk, no matter how much you beat him up or torture him. But I know he loves his sister."

"You're going to use her to get him to talk…" She almost seemed elated, and it made my skin tingle with unease. If it came down to torturing Kelsey, could I go through with it? Fuck. I prayed it didn't have to get to that.

"I'll meet you down in the crypt."

As I neared the infirmary, I was flummoxed by the commotion outside the door. "What's going on?" I asked the crowd assembled.

"It's a miracle," someone said.

"A sign from God…" said another.

"What are you all talking about?"

"Clint!" Jasper called to me from down the corridor. "I've been looking for you." The Guardian who approached was one of Antonia's men. "You need to see this."

"See what?" I said impatiently.

"Come. Everyone, move out of the way." He opened the door to the infirmary as the crowd cleared, and I was almost blinded by the bright golden light that exploded from within. My breath caught in my throat as I stepped into the infirmary. The golden light was so intense that it forced me to shield my eyes. But as they adjusted, the source of that light became unmistakable.

Kate.

She was sitting on the edge of the bed, her skin glowing with an ethereal radiance. The burns that had marred more than fifty percent of her body were gone, replaced by a pristine, unblemished complexion. But that wasn't what left me rooted to the spot, as if the floor had turned to quicksand beneath my feet.

It was the wings.

Two massive, feathered wings unfurled from her back, glowing with the same golden light that filled the room. They were pure, almost iridescent white, each feather shimmering with a soft luminescence that seemed to pulse with life. Kate looked like herself, but there was something undeniably different about her now. She looked… otherworldly.

The room was dead silent, save for the faint rustle of her wings as they shifted. Hank sat at her heels, staring up at her like she was the only thing that existed in his world. The medics and Guardians in the room stood around her, their faces a mixture of awe and reverence. Kate seemed as bewildered as the rest of us. She glanced at her wings, her brow furrowing in confusion. "Clint… what's happening to me?" Her voice trembled as she searched my eyes for an answer.

I had none.

Unsure if what I was seeing was even real, I took a hesitant step forward. A heaviness settled over my chest, and I could hardly contain the river of tears that wanted to rush down my face. Kate was alive. She'd made it. And now she was…

I didn't know what she was. "Kate, I—" My words faltered as I tried to process everything. "The antidote… it worked. You're healed, but…" My gaze drifted to her wings, then back to her eyes. "It must have been the power Mikha'el gave you."

She tried to walk, but the wings threw her off balance, and she stumbled awkwardly, her hands flailing to catch herself. I rushed forward, catching her just before she fell. She was warm to the touch, almost too warm, and the golden light seemed to seep into my skin where our hands met.

"This… this doesn't make sense," she whispered, wide-eyed.

"I don't know what to say," I said, trying to keep my voice steady. "But you're alive, Kate. That's what matters. You're alive, and you're—" I glanced at the wings again, still unsure how to finish the sentence. "Different."

A ghost of a smile tugged at her lips, though it didn't reach her eyes. "Different… yeah, that's one way to put it." She flexed the wings experimentally, wincing as they responded with a jerk, clearly Kate was unsure how to control them. "I don't even know how to use these."

I managed a weak laugh. "There will be time to figure that out, I guess. Right now, though, we have another issue." The weight of what I had to tell her pressed down on me, almost suffocating the oxygen from my lungs. I took a deep breath, my throat tightening. "Kate… there's something I need to tell you. About Kelsey… and the Creation Stones."

Her gaze snapped to mine, and the lighthearted confusion in her eyes was replaced by a sharpness that cut straight to my soul. "What happened? Where are the stones?"

I rubbed the stubble on my jaw, scratched at my scalp. I didn't know how to tell her other than to just…

"Spit it out, Clint. What the hell happened to the stones?"

"It was my fault, Kate. I-I trusted her. I let her get too close. She… she used me to find out where we were keeping them. And I just…"

She took me by the shoulders. "You just, what?"

"I inadvertently told Kelsey where Mikha'el had hid them not realizing she was a member of the Devil's Army."

Kate just stared at me, her eyes darkening like an impending storm.

I couldn't stand the weight of her gaze and dropped my chin. "I'm so sorry. I failed you. I failed everyone."

The silence stretched on, and it became unbearable. I expected her to lash out, to blame me—hell, I deserved it. But instead, she placed her hand on my cheek, gently pulling my gaze back to hers. Her touch was warm, almost soothing.

"You didn't fail, Clint," she said softly. "You couldn't have known." Her voice was steady, filled with an understanding that I didn't think I deserved. "And we're going to get those stones back."

I had nothing left to say, and even if I tried to speak, I was too choked up to utter a single word. Without thinking, I reached for her and took her into my arms, and an overwhelming rush of relief washed over my entire body when she wrapped her arms around me. Wetness coated my eyelashes, but I didn't try to hide the tears. She had no idea how much she meant to me, no clue at all.

"Where's Kelsey now?" she asked, pulling from me and wiping the tears from my cheek.

"She's down in the crypt with her brother, her accomplice. She's infected, though. I came here looking for the anecdote. If she turns, we may lose our only chance of finding out where the stones were taken."

She was already trying to retract her wings, her brow furrowed in concentration. Slowly, the wings seemed to shimmer and fade, folding into her back until they were completely gone. Satisfied they were properly spirited away, she nodded to the medic that was nearby and asked for a vial of the blood-made serum. Taking the small syringe into her hands, she narrowed her gaze, fixing her eyes to mine. "Let's go make those assholes squeal."

Chapter Eleven

SAMAEL

Mikha'el's arrival to Abaddon had made the entire realm shudder. Even though weakened and stripped of his holy weapons, it seemed the rock and ice itself feared him, sending shockwaves through every corner of this wretched, frozen wasteland. I would be lying to myself if I said his presence here hadn't sent a ripple of apprehension down the jagged peaks of my spine. I'd not seen my best friend in countless millennia. Had plotted this moment innumerable times inside my head, wondering if it would ever come to pass.

Well, it finally had, and despite the turbulence riding my veins and the tension coiled around my muscles, I was more than ready to face him.

The large stone doors of my great hall scraped open, the sound of rock grating against rock heralding the archangel's arrival. My fingers dug into the armrests of my throne chair as I beheld the creature who had pushed me through the gates of my prison and locked me inside without ever looking back. Ragged breaths sawed in and out from my chest, but I tried to breathe through my nose, tried to calm the rage boiling me from the inside.

Hands held firmly behind his back by the Golden Shackles, Mikha'el was dragged into my throne room by Beleth and Chemoth, their fingers gripping his arms with enough force to bruise an immortal, though Mikha'el did not show any sign of pain. His eyes were partially obscured by his long black hair, but I could still feel the heat of his golden gaze unflinching as he was brought before me.

The throne room was silent, save for the footsteps against the black stone floor. My court watched with bated breath, their eyes darting between Mikha'el and me, waiting to see what I would do. Even in chains, even after all he had lost, Mikha'el was still a presence, a force to be reckoned with. And it infuriated me beyond measure.

As he was forced to his knees, I stood from my throne, the echo of my movement filling the chamber, reminding everyone, especially him, that although I was the Fallen One, down here, I held all the power. My sickly wings unfurled behind me, casting long shadows across the floor. I had no intentions of glamouring myself for him. He'd only bask in my shame.

No. Today, I would wear every scar, every single grotesque imperfection. I wanted him to see what our Father had done to me. What *he'd* helped orchestrate.

"Mikha'el," I said, my voice low and dripping with venom. "It's been too long, brother."

There was no fear in his eyes, no anger, only quiet defiance. "Samael," he replied, his voice steady as he eyed the craggy bones protruding from my skull. A small, taunting smile tugged at his lips. "A crown fit for the Prince of Hell. Tell me, brother, have you grown fond of your blighted kingdom yet?"

A surge of anger raced up my neck. Even here, in the heart of Abaddon, surrounded by my demons, he dared to mock me. "This *blighted* kingdom," I gritted, stepping closer, "is now your home, Mikha'el. Do pay it some respect."

He said nothing, but his silence spoke volumes. It was the same silence I remembered from the day he cast me down, from the moment he turned his back on me to claim everything I had ever wanted: my Father's approval, but above all, Gavri'el's love and loyalty.

The memory of her name still sent a fresh wave of bitterness coursing through me. She had always looked at Mikha'el with such adoration, such devotion, that thoughts of our days at court twisted like a rusted knife in my chest.

She had been mine, would've been my queen, if not for him. And when she had chosen the humans over me, when she had begged Mikha'el to take her life rather than allow me to claim her death, it had shattered something in me that could never be repaired.

I stepped closer, looming over him, my shadow engulfing his golden glow. "Do you know what it's like," I said through clenched teeth, "to have everything you desire ripped away? To be cast down into darkness by your own brother?"

His eyes flickered, just for a moment, but it was enough. I saw it—the faintest hint of guilt, of regret—and it only fueled my rage.

"You imprisoned me in the land of the forsaken," I continued, my voice rising, "left me to rot while you ate at my Father's table. While you made a whore of the angel I loved."

He lunged forward, teeth gnashing, but Beleth and Chemoth held him back. His neck muscles strained as he kept pulling on his shackles, unable to break free. "How dare you sully her name, you infernal beast," he spat.

"I speak only the truth," I barked back. "She was betrothed to me, or did she not tell you?"

The way he seethed, those golden eyes of his finally aflame with the ire I knew he was capable of, told me she hadn't. I grinned. Cracking his shell had been easier than I thought. "You took Gavrie'el as your mate, yet she'd promised herself to me long before I Fell. I still bear the scars of her nails as she scraped them against my back when I made her mine—their sting so fresh, it's almost as if she carved herself onto my skin just last night."

Mikha'el's jaw tightened, the muscles in his arms flexing against the chains that bound him. "She was never yours, brother. That was your first mistake. The second was believing she could ever love a monster like you."

His words hit me like a blow to the chin, fanning the fury that had kindled for millennia. "Mikha'el, Mikha'el. Always so fucking righteous. Always so sure of your own goodness, your own purity. But where did all that bullshit get you? Look around you, Archangel of the Third Sphere. You lost. Your soul-bonded is dead. Our Father has abandoned *you*, His golden warrior. Who He always favored over His first son. You've been stripped of your titles, your armies, your weapons. Your little human pet is nothing but a charred corpse, her pitiful lover my slave, her son my vessel, and now that I've taken back the Creation Stones, even her world will be mine to claim."

The utter terror in his gaze made the skin around his eyes crinkle. He'd clearly not known about the final battle at the Guardians' Eastern headquarters.

"Khama'el gave me his word that he would leave Kate and the Guardians unharmed if I surrendered."

"You better than anyone should've known that courtier could never be trusted. That was *your* mistake, brother," I mocked.

"All of you will answer for what you have done…" he gritted, those muscles of his straining so hard to break free of the chains, I flinched and took a step back, half-believing he actually could break free. But the shackles held true. Stalking closer, I gripped him by the hair and bore my gaze into his. "I think I've answered for my crimes long enough.

It's now your turn to answer for yours. Welcome to Hell, brother."

With a single nod to Beleth and Chemoth, they yanked Mikha'el to his feet. His wings, still majestic despite the filth and blood that stained them, flared in defiance, but he could not fight the Golden Shackles. The chains were too strong, the magic too potent.

"Strip him," I ordered, my voice like steel.

The room seemed to hold its breath as Beleth and Chemoth tore off his armor and undergarments, leaving him naked before me, before all of Abaddon. Even now, there was no shame in his eyes, no plea for mercy. He stood tall, his back straight, his wings still unfurled, as if daring me to do my worst. As if being sentenced to this eternal damnation was an *honor.*

One of my demons handed me my final welcoming gift, an iron collar crafted specifically for angels. "Do you know why they called this the Seraph's Death?"

Mikha'el kept his eyes trained on me, lips tight, but I knew horror had begun to course through his veins. "Iron is known for its ability to absorb heat energy—it devours it, makes it null. And what is celestial power but the most intense star energy in the entire universe." His nostrils flared, preparing himself for the searing touch of the metal as I clasped it around his neck. The instant I latched it closed, his golden glow was snuffed out and he sagged, dropping to his knees. "String him up," I demanded.

My demons moved quickly, dragging a heavy wooden beam into the center of the throne room. I watched as they laid him down and stretched his arms, the archangel so drained of his power, he was unable to fight back. Beleth and Chemoth brimmed with exuberance at the chance to exact their revenge. Each of them took turns nailing Mikha'el's arms to the wood, the sickening sound of metal driving into flesh echoing through the chamber. Mikha'el gritted his teeth, his face twisting in pain, and though his eyes watered, he did not cry out, though his pained grunts echoed through the chamber.

The next part, I would do myself.

Taking the hammer Beleth had used, I stepped into a puddle of Mikha'el's golden blood. Ragged breaths sputtered from his trembling lips. I leaned down and stared into his half-closed, pained eyes. "I want you to know that I will delight in every thunderous cry that will explode from your lungs. This entire realm will know you have been broken… by *me*."

They flipped him over, and I took my time with each wing, stretching them across the back of the beam and caressing the beautiful feathers before driving the first of the nails right through the bones. This time the archangel couldn't hold back his cries, and he bellowed in pure agony with each strike of the hammer.

One by one, I swung downward with the full force of my strength, feeling the resistance of reinforced marrow and sinew as I secured each wing to the beam. Mikha'el's body trembled uncontrollably from the sheer pain, and a grin split across my lips as I relished every groan, whimper, and scream that erupted from him.

On and on I went, Mikha'el hollering in sweet misery as I hammered nail after nail across the entire length of each wing, first pinning the upper wing bones, followed by the forearm bones, all the way down to the wing fingers. By the time I was done, his glorious, brass-colored wings were nothing but a bloodied mess of torn feathers and mangled tissue.

I'd made sure I slammed down so hard with each nail, even the tar-crusted trees in Nolafyr would've trembled from the sound of Mikha'el's wings breaking—the sound akin to branches cracking.

When I was done, I stepped back, surveying my handi-work with pride until my Horsemen flipped him over and the beam was lifted by chains anchored to each end, Mikha'el's head hanging to his chest—the exertion and torment had knocked him unconscious. They suspended his crucified body above the dais, naked and bloodied, putting him on full display, his spirit broken, arms and wings brutalized, nailed in place for all to see that even the mighty can fall.

Golden blood dripped from his extensive wounds, staining the stone beneath him. "There," I boomed, addressing my court, my voice reverberating through the great hall. "Let all who enter bear witness that my brother, Mikha'el Bar Elah, Archangel of the Third Sphere and former commander of God's Heavenly Host, has finally been brought to heel."

Chapter Twelve

KATE

Wings.

I had *wings*. Even thinking it felt surreal, like some fever dream that wouldn't release its grip on my reality. The words alone were impossible to reconcile, even though I could feel the wings like they were a new set of limbs—every feather and twitch of muscle a new sensation that was both familiar and uncomfortably strange. I had control over them, yet they could move with a life of their own as well, a foreign presence now stitched into the very fabric of my being.

The first time I instinctively made them disappear, it wasn't relief I felt, but a gnawing awareness that, although you couldn't see them, they were still there, hidden just beneath the surface, their weight ever-present on my back.

It was as if my body had been invaded by something alien, something that didn't belong. My shoulder blades ached with a new kind of pressure, and my spine tingled as if my nerves were raw with regeneration. Bones I'd never given a second thought to were now the only thing I could focus on.

I couldn't shake the feeling that my entire skeleton had

been restructured. My chest was broader, my sternum more pronounced. Every muscle across my breastbone seemed stronger, my bones denser, heavier somehow, yet paradoxically lighter—to make them strong enough to carry my weight into the sky while allowing me to soar through it, I supposed.

To fly…

I puffed a long breath as we walked through the church's corridors toward the crypt, trying to calm the anxiety that raked through me at the mere thought of flying. I was terrified and awed. How could I ever trust these wings, these strange extensions of myself, to lift me off the ground? To actually let me *fly*? The idea scared the living hell out of me, a fear that was both visceral and bone-deep.

But just like everything else in my life recently, things were moving at lightning speed, and I didn't even have the chance to properly process the fact that I'd grown wings like an angel.

Mikha'el had been taken prisoner, the Creation Stones were gone, and if I didn't figure out a way to get them back soon, I'd probably never see my son or Jax again. My emotions were twisted into a jumbled web of unease that was impossible to unravel, but there was at least one thing that kept my feet moving: the thought of losing my family forever.

It was enough to make me jam all thoughts about having wings into the deepest recesses of my mind, allowing me to focus on one thing alone: getting my family back. And at this point, I was willing to do anything to make sure they were returned to me safely.

Anything.

Hank trotted at my heel while Clint trailed a few steps behind me. I had the subtle inclination that the kid was ashamed of what happened with Kelsey, which was why he didn't even want to look me straight in the eyes. He felt wholly responsible, but I couldn't put the blame on him. The Devil's Army had infiltrated us. They would've figured it out sooner or later.

Not to mention that, if it hadn't been for those riders on winged horses Clint had told me about—who I'd yet to thank for coming to our aide—we would've had our asses handed to us. We were lucky to even be alive.

But gratitude for being alive was not enough to drive away my rage. My entire body vibrated with the need to make someone pay for all the Guardians we had lost today. And I was more than ready to start with the two assholes in that crypt.

As we descended the stairs, I tugged and pulled on the fresh shirt I'd been given before leaving the infirmary, the material feeling too snug. Now I knew why Mikha'el preferred to keep his wings out rather than spirited away. Hiding them from view made them ethereal, but even though they seemed to lose their physical properties, they were no less real, which meant I still felt them, except it was as if they'd been tucked under my too-tight shirt and the feathers pricked my skin and made me itchy.

It was driving me mad not to be able to simply spread them wide and let them breathe, which only added to my already rattled mood. However, until I felt completely in control of my new appendages, I didn't want to risk potentially hurting someone if I swung them too forcefully. I'd seen angels use their wings as weapons, and they could be deadly.

We finally made it down to the crypt, and I couldn't help the surge of blood that flared in my veins at the memory of the last time I'd been down here. All the mangled bodies had been removed after the battle against Beleth, including Amada's, but the stench of stale blood and death still clung to the walls. Not to mention the last time I'd been down here was also the last time I'd held Luke.

Taking a few cleansing breaths, I collected myself. Breaking down and becoming an emotional wreck was not going to help me get my son back. There was no room for that version of myself, not for what I needed to do. I let the cold dampness of the crypt seep into my bones, chilling every part of my body, numbing even my heart.

Jax had said once that to win this war, we would need to fight monsters with monsters.

So be it.

Two Guardians flanked the entrance to Kelsey's brother's holding cell, their expressions grim as they watched me approach. Antonia stepped forward and ordered them to let us in.

I felt Clint's unease radiate behind me as I stepped inside. I'd already told him what I'd planned to do, and although he hadn't tried to talk me out of it, I saw the apprehension in his eyes. I gave him the opportunity to sit this out, but he chose to come, and I didn't have the time to fight him on it.

Kyle was bound to a chair in the center of the room. His bruised-up face and bloodshot eyes hid his emotions, but the sweat that dripped down his brow gave him away. I sat on the metal chair opposite him and crossed a leg. "Do you know who I am?"

He narrowed the one eye that wasn't completely swollen shut. "If I had to guess, you're the cunt who fucked everything up."

Here we go.

I nodded to the two Guardians by the entrance and a minute later, they dragged Kelsey's body in, her feet barely moving, a hood over her head. I stood from the chair and allowed them to plop her ass on it to face her brother. Kyle sat up straighter, as if he'd just been caught completely off guard. He couldn't see who was under the hood, but from the way his breathing hitched, it seemed he was starting to get the idea of where this interrogation was headed.

Standing behind Kelsey, I waited a few breaths, giving Kyle time to work himself up before I pulled her hood off. "To be more precise, I'm the cunt who's going to give you a chance to either save your sister or let her die."

Kelsey's hands were secured behind the chair, but she was so weak she could hardly keep herself upright as she looked at her brother, her glassy eyes at half-mast. Drenched in sweat, her hair was plastered to her pale, balmy face, the black tracks of the infection running through her veins spider-webbed across her skin.

He leaned forward, as if he couldn't trust what his eyes were seeing. "Kels…?"

Kelsey could only expunge a breathy moan as she tried to speak her brother's name.

The man yanked on his restraints as he snapped his one eye at me. "What the fuck have you done to her?"

Using my dagger, I sliced open her already frayed pant leg, exposing the large bite mark on the side of her calf. I had to cover my nose from the putrid smell that wafted from the festering wound, the tissue decaying and oozing with pus. "She was bitten during the attack. Quite frankly, I have no idea how she's made it this long without turning. Most humans with such a severe injury succumb to the infection fairly quick."

His face sagged as he took in the totality of Kelsey's condition. "Hey, Kels… listen. You're going to be alright. Okay?"

"No, she won't," Clint added from the shadows. He'd been standing behind Kyle, leaning against the back wall, arms crossed. "Her body is rotting from the inside. You're doing her no favors by lying to her. She doesn't have long."

"Fuck you, asshole." Lifting his gaze to me, he said, "So what's your plan? To let me watch her die in front of me. Is that it, you sick bitch?"

I sighed, already losing patience with this man. "We know you led the sicarii to the sacristy. I need to know where they took the Creation Stones."

"What makes you think I'd tell you, even if I knew?"

"I believe you do know. You just need a little motivation."

I gestured for Clint, and he handed me the syringe with the angel blood serum.

"What the fuck is that?"

"Your motivation. Let me make this quick and easy for you. Inside this syringe is the cure to your sister's condition."

"Bullshit. You can't cure this infection. It's hellborn."

"It's a serum made from my blood. Don't ask me how; I'm not a doctor and I'm not a priest. But I am the cunt who was anointed by two angels and who bore the first Nephilim born in God knows how long. The Nephilim your master wants to use as a vessel." This time I couldn't hold back the intense itching on my back, and I let my wings spring free. I breathed with relief as I stretched the bones, letting the feathers flutter. All Kyle could do was stare in utter awe as my white-as-snow wings expanded the entire length of the room and the golden sigils on my arms flared to life.

"But you don't have to take my word for it." I nodded to Antonia, and her men dragged in another infected Devil's Army member. "They found this one trying to make a run for it through one of the underground tunnels. Clint says he's one of yours."

The man writhed as two Guardians tackled him to the ground, and one put a knee to his back. I knelt beside him. The guy grunted in anger. "Feisty, this one. Trick is to time it right. According to Father Ortega, it must be done before the infection crosses the blood-brain barrier, or some shit like that. Otherwise, the serum will simply incinerate the individual from the inside." I peered down at the Devil's Army member. "I've seen it… it's not pretty. You don't want that, do you?"

His mouth frothed as his veins blackened, roping around his neck. "Now or never." I went to give him the injection in his neck, but he continued to thrash.

"Hurry, Kate. We're losing our window," Clint said, but I had the feeling he was referring to Kelsey.

With one quick plunge, I jabbed him in the neck and

pushed down on the syringe, delivering a dose of the golden serum. "Don't let him go yet," I said to the Guardians holding him down. The guy continued to seethe as the black tracks began to fade. His breathing slowed, the bloodshot eyes began to clear, and in a matter of seconds, any signs of the infection were gone.

I gestured for the Guardians to let him get to his feet. The man pushed up slowly, blinking in surprise, as if he didn't know where he was or how he'd gotten here. He looked down at his hands and at the now-healed bite mark on his forearm, what had just happened finally registering. Raising his gaze to mine, he asked, "How?"

Shrugging, I unholstered my pistol and pointed it right between his eyes. "I don't really give a fuck how it works, just that it does." Then I pulled the trigger and blew the man's head off, splattering blood and skull fragments everywhere. Then I pressed the barrel to Kelsey's temple. "So, what will it be? The location of the stones or your sister's brains all over your face?"

Chapter Thirteen

CLINT

Fuck.

Everyone in the room collectively flinched when Kate pulled the trigger and splattered the dude's brains all over the room, his body hitting the ground with a loud *thump*. She'd told me she'd planned to use the guy to show good faith on the serum, not that she was going to off him right in front of everyone after healing him.

I also hadn't expected my heart to jump as it did when she pressed her gun to Kelsey's head.

"I don't have time to waste, Kyle," Kate said, gritting her teeth. "And neither does your sister. Either you tell me what I need to know, or I kill her first, then shoot you between the eyes after."

"They have my family," he said, breath shaky. "If they find out I told you anything, they'll kill my wife and daughter."

She didn't have to say it for me to know the thought that had crossed her mind at those words. Everyone had something to lose in this battle, and Samael had Jax and Luke. She understood Kyle's predicament, but when everyone was in the same boat, it was hard to show sympathy.

Kate pulled back the hammer on her pistol, the cocking sound echoing in the room. "Guess that means you've made your choice."

"Wait, wait," Kyle sputtered. "Wait."

"D… don't…" Kelsey managed to whisper. "It's… okay."

Tears trickled down the side of his busted-up face. Kelsey barely resembled herself any longer, and I could feel my pulse echoing in my ears. The black veins were weaving over her face. She had less than a minute, if that, before it would be too late for the serum to work.

My gaze lifted to Kate's and something in me went completely still at the darkness brewing in her eyes. It sent icicles raking over my skin. She was going to do it. She would let Kelsey turn, then blow her brains out before her brother.

"Kyle," I breathed. "Don't let your sister die like this."

He shot me a poignant stare. "If you gave a single shit about her, you wouldn't have let this cunt use her like this." After a pained breath, he said, "Utica State Hospital. Now give her the fucking antidote."

Pulling the second syringe from my pocket, I ran to her and plunged the needle into her neck, half expecting her body to explode into cinders. She gasped for breath as the serum raced through her veins. "Unshackle her," I told the Guardians. Once she was free, I took her into my arms and laid her on the floor. The glassiness in her eyes became clear and the black tracks retreated, leaving only unmarred skin.

Her chest rose and fell in even heaves, and I was finally able to breathe freely myself. But damn if I didn't hate the fact that I cared if this girl lived or died. She was a fucking member of the Devil's Army. She'd betrayed us…

But then again, at one point, so had Jax. Wasn't it possible for there to be some good in her heart as well? As I peered down at her face, her eyes gently fluttered opened. "Clint?" she choked, her lips tugging at the corners in a feeble smile. Something deep in my chest squeezed, and I felt my throat tighten. Fucking hell. How could she still have this effect on me after everything she'd done?

Chaz's words echoed in my brain. *No attachments.*

Big guy had been right. This emotional shit wasn't for me, not in this new fucking world. Not when it would be so easy to lose myself, to lose my focus. I had other responsibilities, other people I couldn't let down. I fought the tingling in my fingers that begged me to reach for her cheek. I wanted so badly to touch her skin, to feel her warmth, to have further confirmation she was okay, but I couldn't show any sign that I was glad she was not dead or turned.

I tore my gaze from her without offering her a smile back. "Take her to the infirmary," I said to the Guardians who had brought her in, and as I slipped away, I felt her fingers grip my shirt as if she didn't want to let me go. I pried them free. "Make sure she's not left unsupervised."

After they took her away, Kate retracted her wings, then sat on the metal chair and leaned forward. "I need to know everything."

"I've already told you where they took the stones."

"Yes, but why Utica State Hospital? Is that one of the Devil's Army's hideouts?"

I stood behind Kate, arms crossed, as I eyed him down. "Wasn't that an asylum in upstate New York? I did a haunted tour there on Halloween one year when I was a kid."

Kyle flicked his gaze to me, that bloodshot eye twitching as he tried opening it. "Those tours were bullshit, run by fake ghost hunters looking to make a buck off idiots who would pay for a thrill boner." He paused, as if insinuating I was such an idiot.

Maybe I had been.

"You probably visited Old Main, the restored main building they let the public see," he went on. "But the true horrors of that place live in the abandoned wings and sub-levels they kept off limits."

Kate sighed in agitation. "Everyone knows that back then, people with mental illness were treated poorly; some of the practices implemented to treat them were barbaric. It's why those asylums closed. I fail to see what any of that has to do with Samael's rebirth. For all I know, you could be trying to send me on a wild goose chase."

He cocked his head, as if shocked Kate didn't understand. "The majority of the patients in that building weren't just treated poorly; they were tortured, abused with such brutality all semblance of humanity was wiped from them, as if they were less than animals. The impact of their suffering, their torment, their pain and sadness... all of it is embedded in the walls, in the stone and dirt, and in every single speck of dust that exists in that place, in the very fabric of the air around it, like a living, breathing organism."

My eyes widened. "That's why people used to say the hospital was haunted. The bad vibes that place gave off were not a hoax, then."

Kyle shook his head. "It's more than bad vibes; the hospital is literally a direct gateway to Hell. *That which is above is like that which is below, and that which is below is like to that which is above.*"

Kate's gaze drifted, as if lost in thought, as if remembering something from her past. "My grandmother used to always say... As above, so below."

"Thy kingdom come, Thy will be done, on Earth as it is in Heaven," Antonia added. "It's part of our creed."

"Except," Kyle said, "the phrase is not of Christian origin. It's much, much older. At its most basic, it simply means that what happens in a higher realm or plane of existence also happens in a lower realm. Abaddon or Hell, whatever you want to call it, is where the souls of sinners go to be tortured. The two planes, Earth and Samael's kingdom, are strongly linked by the intense spectral energy concentrated at that hospital. It's why the Devil's Army chose it for the rebirth."

"Well, if I'd known I'd been literally standing on a gateway to Hell, I might've shit myself."

Kate shot me a glance that told me if I didn't keep my mouth shut, she would shut it for me. Permanently. "How to I break into the hospital?" she asked.

"How the fuck do I know that you won't kill me or Kelsey after I tell you?"

"You don't. But what is certain, is the fact that if I don't have use for you, I have no reason to keep either of you alive."

"You're sure you're the anointed one?"

"Being the anointed one doesn't mean I'm not willing to do whatever is necessary to get my family back."

"You have our word," I interjected, regretting it the moment the words came out of my mouth. Kate glanced over her shoulder at me again, but didn't say anything. I was grateful she didn't hand me my ass in front of Kyle.

"You'll forgive me if I don't just take your word for it. I need assurances."

"What kind of assurances?" Kate asked.

"The hospital is heavily warded with ancient runes, spells woven in angel tongue. If you want a chance at stopping Samael from using the stones and taking your son as his vessel, you'll not only need me to break into the sanctum, but you'll need someone familiar with the rebirthing ritual and how to stop it."

"And how do I know you're not lying just to keep yourself alive?"

"I don't care what happens to me; all I care about is my family. I was born into this cult, but my wife wasn't. When I met her, she made me realize I didn't want to spend the rest of my life in servitude. I didn't want to be a puppet for the Devil. And when my daughter was born, I knew there was no way I was going to raise her up in the cult. I'd seen what the cult did to little girls. I'd been forced to witness the horrors Kelsey was subjected to."

My body shifted uncomfortably at those words.

"If I could prevent my daughter from being indoctrinated, then I would. But when I decided to leave… Let's just say, my presbyter didn't take it so well. The Devil's Army took my family and threatened to kill them unless Kelsey and I agreed to infiltrate the Guardian's Eastern headquarters in preparation for the Summoning. I haven't seen my family since before the gates opened… I don't even know if they're alive."

"What exactly are you asking of me in exchange for your help in stopping Samael?"

"When I heard about the location of the stones, I knew that was my ticket back home. I traded the information to one of Samael's spies in exchange for a rift. I was supposed to be transported back to Utica with the sicarii. From there, I was going to try to find my family. That is, until you all fucked everything up."

"So, you'll break us into the hospital and show us how to stop the ritual all for a ride to the States?"

He nodded.

"I don't know about this, Kate," Antonia chimed in. "Despite what he says, he's still a member of the Devil's Army. The asshole could be walking you right into a trap."

Kate wiped a hand down her face. "Perhaps. But I'm running out of options here." She leaned in closer to Kyle. "How much time do we have before the rebirthing ritual?"

"When's the next full moon?" he replied.

"What does the moon have to do with the ritual?" I asked.

He sat up straighter and adjusted his shoulders, the handcuffs jangling. "Despite being linked at that site, opening the portal between Earth and Abaddon is no easy feat, even with the Creation Stones. However, during a full moon, the veil between the physical and spiritual worlds is thinner, making the portal less unstable and easier to traverse."

Kate stood, placing her hands on her hips and surveying the group. "Okay, well, who the hell here knows how to read the phases of the moon?"

Everyone looked at each other, all of us equally confused. When no one said anything, Kate rushed out of the room. Hank and I followed behind her. She'd walked to a far corner of the crypt where a statue of Mikha'el stood high on a pedestal. The statue did not resemble the archangel at all, but this iconic depiction of the angel standing atop the slayed serpent hit me square in the sternum. As it had Kate, too, it seemed. She wiped at her face angrily with her fingers, clearly dabbing away tears she didn't want me to see.

"Kate," I whispered gently. "You okay?"

"No. I'm not," she said dryly, her back still to me as she looked upon the statue. "Mikha'el and Cassael are gone; the stones were taken by the sicarii. Now Samael has everything he needs to win this war, and I might never see my son and Jax ever again…" She choked up and had to take a few quick breaths before turning around.

Eyes rimmed red and wet with tears, she said, "My only hope of getting my family back is to rift back to the States and hope that the information that guy gave us is not bullshit. Except, how the fuck are we even supposed to rift to New York? We have no angels."

The desperation in her eyes drilled deep into me, and I couldn't help the sinking feeling in my gut. She was right. How the hell *were* we supposed to rift? She searched my gaze, anxious for a reply, hoping I had some answer, some crazy out-of-the-box solution, but I had nothing. Then… I blinked, my eyes widening as I took note of the sigils that glowed on her skin, an idea flaming to life like a spark off a flint. "What about *you*?"

"Me?"

"Kate, you have angelic power flowing through your veins. You have *wings,* for Christ's sake. You're practically an—"

"Clint, I'm not an angel."

"Well, you're the closest thing to one, and right now we gotta take what we've got."

She unspirited her wings, but she seemed to struggle a little to unfurl them. "I don't even know how to properly use these things, so how the heck am I supposed to figure out how to rift? Not to mention that there's no way I can go up against the cult on my own, plus devoured, plus demons, *plus* a legion of sicarii." Hands on her hips, she paced, smacking me with a wing as she passed.

I pretended the powerful new appendage hadn't almost knocked me down.

"I can't do this alone. When Mikha'el rifted me and Jax here, he was so depleted of his power, he nearly lost his life to one of those Butchers. Explain to me how *I'm* supposed to do it, because there is no way I'm leaving you and Hank behind. Not a fucking chance," she said, pausing to anchor her glowing eyes to mine.

Shit. Glowing eyes. Mikha'el's power was definitely flowing through her, which meant she was probably stronger and more capable than she gave herself credit for.

"I don't have the answers, Kate. I wish I did. But we've been walking in the dark since those gates opened, and all I do know is that we've made it this far—against terrible odds. I gotta believe it hasn't been out of sheer luck.

"Look, I've never been a person of faith. Sure, I grew up Catholic and went through the motions of celebrating the big Christian holidays with family, but I never went to church. I didn't pray to God or believe that angels were watching over us. And even after everything I've witnessed, after finding out that God and all this bullshit is real, I still don't know how to make sense of it.

"I mean, I've been searching within myself, trying to find a connection, needing to find hope, but how does a person pray to a god they've never known?"

Kate stared, those gorgeous luminescent wings lighting up the crypt, making the air in my lungs evaporate with utter awe. "They can't," I said, answering my own question, my chest tightening. "But guess what? I may not know God, but I know *you*. I've seen what you're capable of. I've seen you fight with such love in your heart, you practically glow like the sun. So, if there is anything I need to believe in, it's the fact that someone or something up there picked you for a reason. And that's enough for me."

"I'm just a woman looking to save her family, Clint."

"That's all you need to be." Reaching for her, I took her into my arms and this time, it was me who squeezed her like I never wanted to let go. "We're going to figure this out. Hope is the last thing to die... isn't that what these Guardians keep yapping about?"

She chuckled, and we pulled free. Ruffling my hair, she said, "You've grown up, kid."

I smiled, but despite the warmth in my heart, I knew our biggest battle still loomed. Nevertheless, the promise of war didn't eclipse what I knew to be true. "We're gonna get Jax and Luke back, Kate." They weren't empty words, and I wasn't trying to just make her feel better. Somewhere deep in my soul, I knew we were going to get out of this.

She parted her lips to say something, but before she could reply, her attention was snatched by someone approaching.

"Kate," Antonia piped up from behind me. "There's someone who wishes to speak to you."

"Who?"

"She says her name is Loriana Evengale, Queen of Aetheria, realm of the Elementals."

Kate took a step forward, her eyes scrunched. "Come

again?" For a second, she seemed to have forgotten about the help we'd gotten against the sicarii.

"She's the leader of the riders who arrived on the winged horses. The female warriors who saved us from the sicarii. She says she arrived here at Mikha'el's behest and is requesting an audience with you."

Chapter Fourteen

KATE

After seeing angels, demons, and zombies in the flesh, nothing should've shocked me. Boy, was I wrong. My recollection of the female warriors was so brief and faint, it was like a flame that flickered and died in one breath. When I saw them flying over the church, their bodies had been mere silhouettes against a pale moon. Now, my entire body shuddered as I stepped out into the predawn and noticed the two-dozen or so armored riders atop their steeds, the courtyard, a field of carnage around them.

Demons and angels turned to cinders when killed, humans and zombies did not. And it seemed, neither did these alien riders and their beasts. Dead winged horses and their accompanying riders lay strewn on the ground, bodies broken in ways no one should ever have to witness. Needing to keep my stomach from turning inside out, I kept my eyes trained on the row of riders perched atop their steeds. The beasts were larger and more muscular than any horse on Earth—if any still existed.

As I neared closer, I realized how enormous their wings

truly were. Even tucked and loosely drooped to accommodate the rider sitting behind their shoulder blades, you could tell their wingspans would be wider than anything I'd ever seen on an angel. Equally marvelous was the fact that the beasts' bodies weren't covered in horsehair, but small, sleek feathers that looked dense and soft as velvet, kind of like that of a penguin. Their tails were also feathered, as were their manes.

A soft breeze brushed through the courtyard, the wind gently ruffling the short feathers on the body of the black steed before me, revealing hints of iridescent blues and greens that played across the black surface, reminiscent of the ocean's depths as they shimmered.

Being in the presence of these creatures felt like stepping foot into a fantasy novel, though the allure was quickly overcast by the gruesome backdrop of the now ruined church.

Taking a deep breath, I steadied the nervous energy vibrating in my blood. I had no idea who these warriors were. Antonia had said their queen mentioned being summoned here for aid at Mikha'el's request, but I had no idea where their loyalty or friendliness would lie once they learned that the archangel had been taken prisoner by Khama'el.

From the leather diadem encrusted with one emerald stone in the center between the eyes, I figured the rider on the black steed was the queen. She dismounted with the grace of a dancer; the green cloak anchored to her shoulder guards billowed behind her, and the bladed staff gripped in her hand glinted like sunlight. I took note of the peculiar, scaly leather that made up not only her shoulder guards, but the gauntlets that protected her hands, which were adorned with sharp, talon-like extensions. The reddish leather wrapped around her shins and a pair of boots that looked like they could crush stone.

Towering at about seven to eight feet tall, she dwarfed me just as much as Mikha'el and the angels did, and I had to wonder if humans were the smallest of God's creations across the cosmos.

The rest of her armor was an assortment of quilted fabric and metal that made her look both regal and lethal all at the same time. Her bronzed skin, though streaked with angel and demon blood, gleamed under the first light of dawn. Her caramel-colored hair, tightly plaited, was coiled in a pattern of intricate braids that framed her face, each held together by golden rings and woven with thin strands of metal.

Her eyes were sharp and calculating, the color of molten amber, and they seemed to pierce right through me as she approached. Every step she took was measured and purposeful, the metal of her armor whispering softly with her movement. When she finally stood before me, I had to crane my neck to meet her gaze, her towering height making me feel small and insignificant. Yet there was a calmness in her demeanor, an assurance that came from knowing her own power.

The leather of her armor, which I now saw up close, was indeed like no material I had ever seen. It was thick and textured, with a pattern that resembled the scales of some ancient, powerful creature. It had a sheen to it, almost like the hide of a dragon—if such a creature existed. Though, if I was being honest, the existence of dragons couldn't be that far-fetched if the female warriors and their flying horses were any indication of the types of beings that existed beyond Earth's solar system.

Another rider, who had dismounted her steed alongside the queen, stepped forward as well. Dark skinned and long black hair also intricately plaited, she was similarly dressed, though less dramatic. The rider bowed her head slightly as the queen whispered something to her. She nodded, then met my gaze, her violet eyes shimmering.

Speaking in a tongue I couldn't understand, the queen's voice followed, strong and melodic. The rider, acting as her translator, relayed her message: "Queen Loriana Evengale of Aetheria," she said for her queen, the rider's accent thick but her words understandable.

"I am Kate Jones of Earth," I replied, feeling almost sheepish saying those words, as if I was someone significant, like a president or a ruler of a nation. I was merely a former cop from New York trying to find her way back home. "Thank you for coming to our aid. We are very grateful."

The female translated once more, "We lost many great riders today."

I swallowed thickly. I had no idea how many riders they'd lost, but from the forlorn faces on the queen and the rest of her cavalry, I could tell it was a considerable amount. "My condolences for your people. We are indebted to you." The phrase tasted sour on my tongue. *Condolences…* I hated that word; it was cold and meaningless. We'd lost many Guardians as well, friends. Nothing anyone could say would heal the wounds caused by their deaths.

And I knew I could say nothing that would heal *their* wounds, either.

Not to mention that there was nothing our kind could possibly offer her people that would ever repay this debt. The apocalypse had rendered our advanced weaponry and technology useless—not that even if it wasn't, we could offer them anything of value. These warriors could literally traverse the cosmos on flying horses. And they'd defeated Heaven's elite squadron of assassins and prevented a massacre all without our aid.

To them, we were probably nothing but a speck of dust on a faraway rock.

The queen's gaze softened slightly as the rider translated my words, her expression one of reverence mixed with a hint of sadness. She glanced around the courtyard, taking in the devastation that surrounded us, her eyes lingering on the fallen warriors and their steeds—on our fallen Guardians as well. She turned to her rider and spoke.

"Her Majesty appreciates your words, but our people owed Mikha'el a great debt for the assistance he provided our realm in a time of dire need. Once, when we were on the brink of destruction, and our people faced annihilation at the hands of a powerful enemy, it was Mikha'el who came to our aid. His bravery and strength turned the tide of the war, saving our kingdom from ruin. We answered Mikha'el's call for aid because we could not refuse the one who saved our people. Our debt is paid. *You* owe *us* nothing, Earth child."

Mikha'el had cashed in an invaluable favor with the queen of another world to save our asses. *Of course he would.* Joy and sadness wrapped around my heart. "Please tell your queen we are forever grateful for your great sacrifice."

The queen listened, then stepped forward, her eyes catching on the hilt of Mikha'el's sword. I'd strapped it across my back before coming to meet them using a harness one of the Guardians lent me. I'd hoped that seeing Mikha'el's legendary weapon on someone like me might help my diplomatic efforts if the need should arise.

Her eyes narrowed with scrutiny, and her hand tightened around the grip of her staff. For a moment, I wondered if perhaps wearing the blade had elicited the opposite effect. She decided not to use her translator, and instead, asked the question herself, her accent very thick, but her darkened tone was unmistakable. "Where is Mikha'el?"

The queen meant to intimidate me, and I'd be lying if I said she hadn't. I could've unspirited my wings, maybe let the sigils flash over my skin, but I didn't want to do anything they could interpret as a threat. I kept my bravado in check, and solemnly said, "He was taken prisoner by Khama'el and brought to Abaddon on charges of murder. He's accused of killing Gavri'el."

Her rider assisted in translating my words, and all the

riders around us shifted on their beasts as they heard the words spoken by their translator. They murmured amongst one another, and the queen quickly returned to her steed.

"Wait, where are you going?" I said, rushing toward them, my heart in my throat. I didn't understand why what I said had seemed to spook them or why they were anxious to leave, but my heart sank to my stomach when I saw the queen's face harden before she mounted her beast.

When Mikha'el was taken, I felt the world crumble beneath my feet. It wasn't the same emptiness I'd felt at losing Jax or Luke, but it had still caused this hollowness in my gut that drove absolute fear into my bones. I'd felt utterly alone, like I had no other plan, no options left. It was the same fear I'd felt when Kyle mentioned the stones were taken back to the States.

How the hell was I supposed to get across the Atlantic before the next full moon? Clint's suggestion that I try to rift using the power Mikha'el had imbued me with seemed logical, but I knew it was a pipe dream. I hadn't had the chance to try, but I didn't need to. There was no way I could master it before the next full moon, starting with the fact that I wouldn't even know how to even begin practicing.

It wasn't until I'd come to the courtyard and seen the winged horses that a tiny flower of hope began to bloom. Those riders had come here from another realm. What if they could transport us back home somehow using their beasts or their method of traversing realms?

Panic surged within me like a volcano about to explode when I saw that hope wilt like the petals of a dying rose.

The queen looked down from her beast as someone handed her a helmet.

"Please," I begged. "Don't leave yet. I… *We* still need your help."

She looked at her translator, who said, "If Mikha'el has been taken prisoner to Abaddon, then our realm is in danger.

We will be seen as traitors to God's kingdom, and Khama'el will send Heaven's legions to Aetheria. Our people will be caught defenseless. Our queen must return to gather and lead our armies against Khama'el."

"Tell her I understand her need to want to protect her people, but Khama'el is not who you need to fear. Samael is the true enemy. If everything Mikha'el has said about Samael is true, then I refuse to believe the rest of the universe doesn't know what Samael is capable of. That *you* don't know why he was sent to Abaddon. Just look at what he's done to my planet; the utter destruction he's unleashed upon humanity."

The queen had her interpreter translate again. "Why should we risk more of our riders for your people, Earth child?"

"You think he's not capable of doing the exact same thing to yours? That he'll spare you knowing that you helped *us*? You might be able to fight back against Khama'el now, but what happens when Samael takes the throne? When he inherits God's power? This is why Mikha'el asked for your aid. He didn't call in his debt to save some group of humans holed up in a church; he called you because we need your help to defeat Samael. If we defeat him, all those who stood beside him fall, too."

"And if he wins, despite our efforts to help you?" the translator asked for her queen.

"Losing cannot be an option—for any of us. I don't know what the rest of the universe knows about my kind, about our home, about why God created us only to abandon us, but we are just as worthy as any of you are to exist. We've been kept in the shadows, blind and ignorant to the worlds that exist beyond our solar system, but that wasn't our doing. The veil has come off now, though, and despite still playing catch up, humanity is stronger than you think.

"We may not have magical gifts or abilities, our technology is now obsolete, and our numbers are depleted, but what makes us weaker in your eyes is what makes us stronger. Because, despite being left to rot on this planet by God, despite Samael's best efforts to eradicate our kind from existence, we're still here. Fighting. And rest assured, we will continue to fight to our dying breaths to protect our world, our families, and the people we love. And that right there, that is what we bring to the fucking table—our heart and our courage and our drive to live."

The queen looked at her riders, as if trying to read their reaction to my words, as if looking for the answer she already knew. Even if she didn't think my planet was worth much, that resigned look in her eyes told me she didn't want to be under Samael's rule.

"Look, for reasons I still don't fully understand, Samael has chosen to make Earth his battleground, has chosen our people to be his sacrificial lamb, but I'm certain he will not stop with us. Because if Samael takes God's throne, this is what he will do to anyone who opposes him, and you know it. That fear I see in your eyes—in the eyes of all your riders here —that's because you know he would come after your realm, too. It's not just Earth that faces annihilation, but anyone who refuses to bend the knee to him. So, tell me, Queen Loriana Evengale of Aetheria, are you willing to bend the knee to Samael?

"Because if you've fought alongside Mikha'el like you say you have, then you know he would've never asked for your help if he didn't think our people were worth saving and if the fate of your world was also not at stake. Again, I implore you, please help us stop Samael before it's too late… for everyone."

Chapter Fifteen

CLINT

Queen Loriana Evengale had requested to meet exclusively with Kate and no one else, so we were all forced to watch from inside the church as Kate practically begged the queen to help us get back to New York. There hadn't been much time to plan a diplomatic discussion before Kate had to walk out into the courtyard to play ambassador for our planet. It was surreal. I'd been out there earlier when I'd run out to retrieve Kate's body, but it wasn't until I stood atop the scaffolding, watching through a broken stained-glass window that I was finally able to fully appreciate the magnitude of who these warriors were and the fact we were breathing because of them.

Angels and demons were one thing—I'd grown accustomed to the fact that the supernatural world was real—but it wasn't until the winged riders showed up that I realized these weren't supernatural beings, and neither were the angels and demons for that matter. They were… Shit. Even saying the word felt weird.

Aliens.

I always thought if we ever got visited by aliens or if they ever made themselves known, we'd be seeing big spaceships descend from the sky and that the beings who stepped off those ships would look like gray humanoid creatures. Seemed we'd gotten it all wrong. These riders looked like they walked off the pages of one of Tolkien's books. I'd read his books years ago and never thought I'd be living my own personal dark fantasy one day.

But the most remarkable thing about this whole situation wasn't even the alien female warriors or their flying horses, but the way Kate handled herself. She'd been a nervous wreck as we made our way from the crypt all the way back out to the courtyard. All color had drained from her face and her hands had turned to ice. I rubbed them together and tried to calm the tremors that ravaged her body.

In the end, she'd swallowed down her nerves and strutted her ass out there with Mikha'el's sword strapped to her back, head held high, and pretty much represented us—all of humanity—like she was our leader, even if deep down, I knew she doubted her worth. My chest swelled with so much pride. I wish Jax could've been here to witness this, to see Kate be the leader we all knew she was, despite the fact she was always downplaying how much she meant to us.

Kate was out here fighting to get Jax and Luke back, but she was also fighting to give us all another chance at survival.

For a moment, the entire church took a collective breath when we saw the queen climb back onto her horse. Kate had conjectured on our walk to meet the queen that perhaps she wouldn't have to figure out how to rift if she could somehow convince the riders to use whatever methods they'd used to reach us from their realm to transport us back to New York. I'd let Antonia and some of the guardians in on Kate's plan, so when the riders looked like they were about to leave, everyone's stomachs must have bottomed out at the same time.

Short of getting on her knees, Kate implored the queen to

help us defeat Samael, and we all finally released the air from our lungs when the queen dismounted her beast. They spoke quietly for about ten minutes, and unfortunately, I was not able to make out much of what they were saying before Kate ran back to the church. I jumped off the scaffolding and rushed to the door, Hank at my heels. "What did she say?"

Antonia and the dozen or so Guardians in the room surrounded her as well.

"She's worried that Khama'el is going to launch an attack against her realm after he learns of her aid, but she understands that this war is not just about protecting humanity. If Samael takes God's throne, every realm ever created will be at his mercy."

"Does that mean she's going to help us?" Antonia asked.

"She can't leave her realm unprotected. As their queen, she must return to Aetheria, but she's agreed to give us two of her best riders, including Ta'herah, their translator. If, for some reason once we get back to the States, we're unable to recover the stones and stop the ritual, she's agreed to pledge her armies to us to fight against Samael. She's also agreed to speak to the leaders of something called the Astral Concord."

"The what?" I asked.

"It's a secret coalition comprised of about a hundred realms that wish to establish their independence from God and Heaven's rule."

"Holy shit."

"Yeah, it's kinda blowing my mind, too, but right now we don't have time to worry about that. She said she can transport us, but the mechanical orb they used to traverse realms is powered by the elemental magic of their home world, and right now it's depleted. We have thirty minutes to gather our gear and put together a team—no more than ten people. The orb lost a lot of power in getting them here, and they need what remains of it to get back. Transporting us to New York is already putting them at risk of the orb being too depleted, but she's willing to take the risk if it means we can stop the rebirth."

I ran a hand through my hair. "Fuck. Okay, tell me what you need me to do."

"To open a wormhole or portal to our destination, she needs coordinates. I have no idea how we're going to translate our coordinates to something the orb can calculate, but I'm hoping that by showing the queen a map, she'll be able to navigate us there. Please tell me you brought your maps with you when Remi rifted you here."

"I don't go anywhere without my maps."

"Perfect. I need you to go to the infirmary, get Kelsey, and pack several syringes of the serum. I don't want to lose anyone to the infection."

My spine froze. "Wait… we're bringing Kelsey?"

"If I'm bringing Kyle, I'm gonna need an insurance policy to keep him cooperative once we get back to the States. For all I know, he could ditch us once we get there. I know the girl means something to you—"

"Past tense, Kate. You don't have to worry about me doing my job."

Her gaze paused over my face for a moment, as if assessing if what I said rang true. I didn't divert my eyes. I wanted her to see that whatever feelings had begun to bloom inside my heart had been yanked out by the root. "Kate, I'm good."

She cupped my cheek and smiled. Then she turned to Antonia, but the Guardian was already on task. "I'm coming with you, Kate. No discussion. I'll gather a small team, grab Kyle, and meet you back here in fifteen."

Kate simply nodded.

I was about to run to the infirmary when an idea came to mind. "Sun's about to come up. I can probably make it to

Saint Mary's in fifteen minutes now that the streets are cleared of devoured and the demons are stuck in the shadows until nightfall."

"Why go to the church?"

"Holy water. We're all out."

"No. We can't risk it. There could be more Devil's Army members imbedded in the scion. We don't need anyone getting suspicious and potentially hurting you or following you back. Can't take the chance of someone alerting Samael of our plan. Stick to the original task. Find Kelsey, get the serum, grab your gear, and make sure you have your maps. And get back here ASAP."

Kate plopped down on a pew, and I noticed she was holding her hands together, trying to keep them from shaking. I knelt beside her, placing my hands over hers. "Hey, what's going on?"

She released a long breath, and it was like she let go of the dam she'd been trying to hold back for too long. "I'm trying to be strong, but this is a lot to deal with. Between losing my family, Mikha'el being taken, understanding these strange powers in my blood, and now somehow being the spokesperson for Earth… I don't know how I'm even standing. It's like I'm on autopilot, looking out through my own eyes like they're windows, and I'm inside just watching everything unfold."

She lifted her gaze to mine and her brown eyes were close to cresting with tears. "I… I killed a man in cold blood, Clint. That's not me. I crossed a line, and it's not something I can take back." She looked back down at her shaking hands. "I'm afraid I don't know what I'm doing anymore, or if I'm even doing the right thing."

"What you did wasn't right or wrong. You did what you had to do to get the job done. We need to get the stones back. No one said it would be easy… or that we wouldn't have to get our hands dirty."

"I don't know, kid. I'm out of my league here. What if Kyle is lying? What if I'm just leading us all to some gruesome death? It's not just about Jax and Luke anymore—"

"I think we've always known that. This is bigger than you or me, or any of us."

"Yeah, but now there's a whole new group of people from another realm depending on me… on us, to not fuck things up."

"Listen, we are going to get through this."

She sat up straighter and looked ahead at the half-destroyed church. "We have less than forty-two hours to find that Asylum, break in, and stop the ritual. You think we can do that by tomorrow night?"

I pushed to my feet. "Tomorrow night?"

"I told the queen what Kyle said about the veil between Earth and Hell being thinnest during the full moon and what that meant for the rebirth. She showed me a bronze hand-held mechanical device they use to navigate the stars. It projected a small hologram of our solar system, kind of like an orrery. It was able to track the position and movement of our moon. According to its calculations, the next full moon is set to rise over New York tomorrow night. Based on my own math, and the time difference between here and back home, that's approximately around seven-thirty P.M Eastern."

"Shit."

She pushed up to her feet and looked me straight in the eyes. "Still feeling confident we can do this?"

"Losing is not an option. Isn't that what you said to the queen?"

"You heard all that, huh? That was just me grasping at straws."

"Not all of it was bullshit."

She smiled, and it was the first one I'd seen in a long time that seemed genuine. "Go. That queen is not one to wait around if we're not ready to leave on time."

BEFORE HEADING to the infirmary for Kelsey and the serum, I stopped to collect my crossbow and picked up a few discarded bolts that had been left behind on the courtyard. I also found my backpack and triple checked that I had all my maps.

I wasn't about to lie to myself about why I was checking my maps when I knew I had them.

I'd told Kate I was good, and that she had nothing to worry about in terms of how I felt about Kelsey. *Had* felt. Yet, there I was. Stalling.

Fuck. I didn't have the luxury of time to figure my shit out, so I just resigned myself to the fact that I was going to be playing babysitter to a traitorous she-devil and made my way to the infirmary. As soon as I pushed through the door, I caught sight of her lying flat on a gurney, handcuffed to the metal frame, sleeping, it seemed.

She looked so relaxed and peaceful, as if the whole world wasn't about to burn to hell all because of her.

I shook my head and was about to walk to her when a male voice piped up from behind me. "Clint?"

My heart dropped like a lead ball. Spinning around, I nearly broke into tears when I saw Chaz sitting up on a gurney while someone checked his vitals. Rushing toward him, I didn't care that I pushed the poor male nurse away as I threw my arms around the big guy. "Dude, you're alive! You're fucking alive!"

He chuckled and patted my back, and I pulled away, still stunned that I was actually looking at my friend and he wasn't a zombie. "You made it out of the tunnel."

"Barely. If it wasn't for Mikha'el showing up at the last minute, there wouldn't have been much of me left to even turn into one of them shits."

I remembered the prayer I'd sent to the archangel before leaving Chaz in the tunnel, asking him for assistance. Something tugged deep in my chest. We'd been so focused on the stones and finding Jax and Luke that we hadn't even stopped to think about rescuing Mikha'el. He'd done so much for us, sacrificed *so* much. There was no way we were going to let him rot in Hell. But first, we needed to stop the rebirth. "We have lots to catch up on, big guy."

"Yeah, I heard I missed the big fight against the sicarii, and that Mikha'el got taken captive. And apparently, we got visited by some hot Amazonian-looking women on flying horses? Don't you let me snooze on the next fight, kid. I'm ready to kick some demon ass."

"You won't have to wait long for your next fight. Those Amazonian women are giving us a lift back home so we can crash the Devil's Army rebirthing party. But we gotta haul ass or they'll leave us behind."

"Did you say home?"

"Get dressed. I'll explain on the way. I need to grab Kelsey first."

A nurse was checking her IV as I neared the gurney. "Wake her up, please."

"She's still recovering. She was far gone when the serum was administered."

"I get that, but we don't have time to wait for her to be fully recuperated." Before the nurse could protest, I leaned over the gurney, keeping my voice low and cold. "Kelsey."

She stirred, her eyes fluttering open. For a split second, I caught a glimpse of that soft vulnerability she'd always tried to hide, but then it was gone, replaced by the wariness that had become her armor.

I waited as she blinked herself into consciousness, the reality of her situation crashing back in. Her wrist tugged at the handcuffs as she shifted, a reminder that she wasn't a free woman anymore.

"You're being taken back to the States," I told her, my tone flat. "Your brother told us where he thinks the sicarii took the stones. You're coming as insurance; in case your brother decides to pull anything. And if you so much as think about betraying us again, I won't hesitate to put a bolt through your head. Got it?"

Her eyes softened, and for a moment, she looked genuinely remorseful. "Clint, I didn't have a choice."

I kept my face stony, though her words stirred something inside me. "Everyone always has a choice. You just made the wrong one."

She sat up a little, wincing as the nurse took out the IV in her arm. "You don't understand. I had to do what they asked, or they would have killed my brother's wife and daughter. I was raised in that cult; it's all I've ever known. The Devil's Army… they don't let you walk away."

I couldn't meet her gaze—didn't want to, for fear of being tangled back in her web. But her words yanked on my heartstrings, especially when they reminded me of what Kyle had said about the horrors Kelsey was subjected to as a kid growing up in the cult. Despite the sadness I felt for what she'd gone through, she was no longer that little girl. "Doesn't change what happened between us. You used me, and the damage you've caused… I can't forgive that."

Her eyes welled up, her voice a whisper now. "I never wanted to hurt you."

Something inside me twisted, threatening to make me say things I no longer believed in. I pushed them back down my throat. "Doesn't matter now. And I'm not here to talk about us. We need to get going or we're going to miss our ride."

She reached out with her uncuffed hand, her fingers brushing mine, a desperate plea in her touch. "Clint, please…"

I pulled my hand back, my resolve hardening. "Don't," I warned. "The only reason you're coming is as collateral.

Though, if it were up to me, I'd leave you behind. So don't get any ideas."

Her face crumpled, but she didn't say anything else. She knew, deep down, that whatever friendship we'd built, she'd crushed it beneath the weight of her betrayal.

Just then, Chaz appeared behind me, still looking rough, but alive. "We good to go?"

I gave a sharp nod. "Yeah. Let's move."

The female Guardian who had been supervising Kelsey uncuffed her and Chaz helped her off the gurney, her steps shaky but determined. Before leaving, the Guardian accompanied Kelsey to the restroom, and I used the time to grab a small medical bag and stuffed it with serum-filled syringes and briefed Chaz on everything that happened, including what went down with Kelsey and her brother. The big guy didn't have much to say about Kelsey; he just gave me a deflated look, like he knew his advice had come too late. "I'm okay," I told him. "I'm over it. Right now, what matters is getting the stones and stopping the rebirth."

"Alright. But I'm here for you if you need to talk, kid."

I offered him a short smile.

Once Kelsey got back, I barely even looked her way and simply led us out of the infirmary and into the morning light shining through the windows of the cathedral. I let the sun caress my face, let it warm my skin, and pretended, even if just for one sweet, tranquil moment, that going home was going to feel like when you took too long of a vacation and you couldn't wait to sleep in your own bed. I let my mind transport me to the years before the gates opened. To my days coming home after school, climbing the stoop of my family's Boston brownstone, heading up to my room, and plopping on my bed while I mindlessly scrolled through my phone, waiting for my mom to finish making dinner, smelling the mouth-watering aroma of her homemade garlic bread.

Yeah, it was time to get back home. Even if home was no longer what I remembered… far from it.

Chapter Sixteen

JAX

The sun hung high, a brilliant ball of fire in the sky, warming everything it touched. I tossed the baseball to Luke, his tiny fingers clumsily gripping the glove as he caught it with a wide grin. He was five now, taller than I'd imagined he'd be at this age, his dark hair messy from running around the yard. Every time I looked at him, my chest swelled with pride. He was the best parts of Kate and me combined—a perfect little piece of our love made real.

"Nice catch, buddy!" I called, my heart lifting as his face lit up with joy. His laughter rang through the air, pure and sweet, a sound I could've listened to forever.

The breeze was gentle, carrying the scent of fresh grass and blooming wildflowers. Kate lounged on a sunbed nearby, legs stretched out, her skin radiant under the golden light. She had a book propped open on her lap, one hand holding a glass of iced tea, the condensation running down the sides. Her long, brown hair cascaded over her shoulders, and every now and then, she'd push it behind her ear with a graceful, absent-minded flick. Hank sat at her feet, ever the protector, his dark eyes tracking every movement in the yard, never fully relaxing. But here, in this slice of blissful happiness, even Hank seemed at ease.

I threw the ball back to Luke, marveling at the peace of it all. It was the kind of day that made you forget the world outside your own little bubble, the kind that made you believe everything was just as it should be. The Devil hadn't been released from his prison. Demons hadn't poured through the gates to ravage Earth. It was as though Hell had never touched us.

Kate laughed softly at something in her book, and for a moment, I let myself sink into the sound, into the beauty of it all.

But then… the light shifted.

It was subtle at first, as though a shadow had passed over the sun. I blinked and looked up. The sky, which had been a brilliant blue moments before, was darkening—slowly at first, then speeding up with an unnatural quickness that prickled at the edges of my mind.

Luke threw the ball back to me, but my hands fumbled. I caught it, barely, my eyes fixed on the horizon.

"Daddy, I'm ready."

"Hold on, buddy." The clouds were rolling in, thick and black, swirling like a storm was coming. But there'd been no sign of one, no warning. The breeze shifted, turning colder, more urgent.

I turned to Kate. She hadn't noticed yet, still lounging, still peaceful. Hank, though, had lifted his head, his ears perked, a low growl building in his throat.

That's when I saw him.

A figure, walking slowly down our driveway. His black suit seemed to soak up the fading light, his slicked-back platinum hair gleaming like it had been cut from solid starlight. My stomach twisted into knots, cold dread creeping down my spine as I recognized him.

Samael.

He walked with that same unnerving grace—calm, deliberate, unstoppable—like a predator with all the time in the world. The world around him seemed to darken further with every step he took. Hank's growl deepened, and I knew. I *knew* something was wrong.

"Kate," I said, my voice tight as I tossed the baseball to the ground. "Take Luke inside."

She looked up, her brow furrowing. "What's wrong?"

"Now, Kate," I snapped, urgency lacing my words.

She didn't argue, didn't ask another question. She stood, scooping Luke into her arms, and hurried toward the house, Hank trailing after them, his gaze never leaving Samael.

I turned back to face the Devil, my pulse racing. "What do you want?"

He smiled, that same cold, infuriating smile that never reached his eyes. "Looks like you've been enjoying my little gift." He glanced around the yard, his eyes narrowing on the backdoor of the house where Kate stood inside with Luke, looking out. Samael's slimy grin grew wider, and my protective instincts flared like a melting core reactor.

My hands clenched into fists at my sides, every muscle in my body screaming for me to grab a weapon, to fight, to protect my family. But I knew better. I knew who I was dealing with.

Samael's gaze flicked back to me, and something in their twilight depths made my insides churn. He looked at me with a bit of puzzlement, but then he laughed. "Oh. You think this is *real*. The pitfalls of spending too much time in the Wastes, Jax. You should know this."

My heart slammed in my chest, but I kept my body steady.

He took a step closer, his black shoes sinking into the soft grass, but it didn't slow him down. "I've let you play *house* long enough. It's time to go."

I swallowed hard, the taste of fear bitter on my tongue. "I'm not going anywhere with you."

He tilted his head, brows dipping. "Have you forgotten our bargain? You'd tell me where to find your mother's grimoire, and I'd leave your precious Kate alone." His eyes gleamed, cold and merciless. "And I've upheld my end. Kate is unharmed. But the grimoire, Jax…" His voice dropped to a chilling whisper. "It's out there, and now that I have all four Creation Stones, you're going to help me find it."

I shook my head, stepping back, the world warping around me. "I don't know where it is."

Samael sighed, a sound that was almost pitying. "You know what the problem with this damn dream realm is? People forget—they forget who they are, where they came from, why they are here, *what* they did."

The ground seemed to shift beneath my feet, the once peaceful yard now dark and menacing, shadows creeping closer with every second. An onyx sky loomed above, the sun swallowed whole, and the wind whipped through the trees like a howling beast.

"I won't let you hurt them," I growled, my voice, thick with desperation, was barely recognizable.

Samael's smile never faltered.

I felt an impossible cold settle into my bones, freezing me from the inside out. My heart pounded in my ears, the perfect world I'd been living in crumbling away with every breath as the truth hiding behind his ice-crusted smile began to surface.

This wasn't real.

Kate, Luke, our house… None of it was real.

But the terror was.

Samael took another step, and my pulse thundered. "Wake up, Son of Adam."

Suddenly, my world blinked out of existence. The next thing I knew, my lungs were bursting with violent breaths, as if I had been drowning and was finally able to break the water's surface to take in oxygen. Feeling disoriented, I tried to sit up, but I realized I was shackled to a bed with nodes and wires hooked up to my bare chest. Somewhere in the room, machines beeped and whirred. "What is happening? Where am I?" I choked, my throat feeling like it was lodged with rusted nails.

My eyes darted around the dimly lit room. I didn't recognize anything or anyone. The four people standing by my bedside were dressed in lab coats, their faces covered with surgical masks. "Let the High Priest know he's awake. We'll need to ready him for the procedure."

My mind felt like it was tangled in a spiderweb. I couldn't see straight, couldn't think clearly. "Procedure?" I asked but was ignored.

Then one of the people in the lab coats finally leaned down, her voice soft. "Don't worry, Jax. The procedure won't hurt much. You're familiar with this. Once the demon is inside you, you won't remember much about yourself."

Demon? I thrashed, trying to break free of my restraints. "Let me go. Where's Kate? Where's my son?" I asked, panicked. Had Samael taken them?

A man suddenly walked into the room dressed in red ceremonial robes. My heart raced, beating so hard I thought it might burst through my ribcage. I recognized those robes...

The Devil's Army.

The man stood by the side of my bed, hands clasped, his short white hair neatly combed. "Welcome back to the world of the living, Jackson. You've been under the Dreamer's Descent for quite a while and are a bit confused. Let me bring you up to speed. You were taken from *La Sagrada Familia*, along with your son. He's fine. We've been taking good care of him here. Lovely baby. He's going to make a fine vessel for Samael. Unfortunately, you were under for longer than we expected, languishing in the Wastes. We didn't think it would take this long for Samael to crack open the code to your childhood memories. I know the cost of such a deep descent, but we appreciate your sacrifice. Soon none of this will matter, anyway."

Baby? Dreamer's Descent? The Wastes? Childhood memories? What the fuck was he talking about? Luke was five years old, and I hadn't been in the Wastes; I'd been at home with my family when Samael showed up out of nowhere. "Who the hell are you? Where am I? I demand to see my wife and son."

"Jax, I know this is rough for you right now because you've been trapped in the Wastes, but listen to me, you're awake now."

A slow breath trickled from my lips as distant memories flooded my mind. The black hole. The cold stone. The solitude. My head spun, and I felt so dizzy I wanted to vomit.

"Jax, do you know what year it is?"

"It's… it's…" I fumbled through my words as my head continued to spin. My brain hurt as I tried to recall the year, as I tried to orient myself. "I can't remember. Kate and I… we recently bought a house. Luke is going to be starting kindergarten. It's…" I looked at the man in the robes and a new surge of panic churned in my chest. "I don't know what year it is."

"Do you know where you are?"

"I'm…" But I couldn't remember that, either. I thrashed, yanking on my restraints. "What is this? Why can't I remember anything? Where's Kate? Where's my son?"

"His blood pressure is too high; we need to sedate him," someone in the room said.

"No, please. I need to see Kate."

The same woman with the soft voice approached. "It's going to be okay. This is going to make you feel better."

She showed me a syringe and my body went cold. "What is that? No. No."

But she plunged the syringe into my IV line much too

quickly. I strained against the restraints bound around my wrists and ankles as a warmth spread through my veins. With every passing second, my muscles grew too weak, my nerves becoming almost numb.

"How much did you give him?" the man in the robes asked. "We need him awake for the procedure."

"It's just a mild sedative. He'll be drowsy, but awake."

"Jax, Jax," the robed man said. "Can you hear me?"

I narrowed my eyes, trying to focus. "Yes," I hissed slowly.

"You've been under the Dreamer's Descent for about three days. Do you understand?"

My entire body shivered, my chest heaving as I absorbed his words, as I painfully began to understand what he was saying. The Dreamers Descent… it was a form of induced sleep, a trancelike state that allowed the consciousness to travel to the Wastes.

"Do you remember anything?"

I blinked several times, my mind struggling to piece together the fractured images of my memories. My breathing slowed as the warmth from the sedative sank deeper. "But what about the last five years? Kate and I… Luke. We had a life. That wasn't…"

"I'm sorry to say, whatever you experienced while you were under, none of that was—"

"Real." A hollowness dug inside my chest, and I felt the need to vomit again. I wretched until bile rose up my esophagus and someone wiped the sick off my lips.

"Samael can be very cruel when he wants to be." The man almost sounded sincere.

I stared up at the ceiling, barely able to move. I focused on the hanging yellow bulb. At the paint chipping from water damage. At the exposed pipes. I had no idea where this was, but I finally knew *when* this was. The air stunk with the scent of staleness and decay. No more fresh grass, no more wildflowers. The room reeked of an all too familiar smell—the smell of the world after the gates opened.

I closed my eyes and swallowed, my saliva feeling like thick molasses down my throat. Three days in the Wastes meant I'd spent lifetimes down there. Centuries. I recalled the hunger, the sadness, the despair. Yet, it wasn't the memory of my time spent suffering in the hole that made me tremble. It was the loss of the last five years that sliced my chest up like I'd been put through a meat grinder.

Tears rolled down the side of my face.

That bastard angel had given me the five best years of my life, only to steal them away in one single breath. The blow felt like someone had taken a chisel to my heart.

It was a miracle I could remember anything at all. My brain should've been mush. Thankfully, it wasn't, probably because of all the practice I had in visiting the Wastes growing up, but that didn't mean I wasn't feeling the effects of the time warp. As much as it killed me to know that the life I'd shared with Kate had been nothing but a ruthless game that Samael had played to torture me with when I woke up, there was something that gave me a bit of hope.

If I'd only spent three days in the Wastes, and if they still needed me for something, then Samael must've still been trapped in Hell. The man had mentioned that Luke would make a perfect vessel. All of that meant that there was still time.

Everything wasn't lost yet.

"What are you planning to do to me?" I asked the priest.

"You must forgive me for the shackles and makeshift ceremonial room. We couldn't take any chances. You're not exactly a willing subject anymore." He leaned down closer, his dark brown eyes meeting mine, almost softening. "I knew your mother, Jax. She wanted so much for you. It's a pity how things ended. But thankfully, there are contingency plans for these sorts of things. When your mother died…

rather, when you killed her, another leader had to take her place."

"You're the new High Priest."

He smiled. "Someone had to step in and finish the job. Or did you think that by killing your mother, we'd stop trying to liberate our king?"

"Your nurse over there mentioned something about a demon being put inside me. Am I to become a vessel for Beleth or Chemoth now?"

"That would be too risky."

"Samael needs four horsemen for the rebirth."

"Yes. Suitable replacements have been secured."

"Who?"

"Nothing for you to worry about. Samael has chosen well. But enough chitchat. The full moon is almost upon us, and we need to secure the grimoire. So, let us begin."

"Grimoire?"

"Yes, we need to know where Judith hid the original grimoire. We need it for the rebirthing ritual. It's why you were put under. The fact that you woke up means Samael unlocked your repressed childhood memories. In those memories lie the clues to where your mother hid it."

"And if I refuse to tell you anything?

"Oh, I don't need *you* to tell me anything, Jackson. You've done enough damage; I don't need you trying to sabotage any more of our plans. Now that your memories are unlocked, Barbatos can do the dirty work for us."

My eyes grew wide, my heartbeat rising. "Barbatos? You're putting that spineless, driveling, low-ranking swine inside me?"

"Given your track record, we couldn't exactly give you access to a demon with great power. Barbatos is low-ranking, but he's still a duke of Hell, and an obedient servant. You'll be useful, but not a liability. Not that this should matter much. Once we acquire the book, the only other use we have for you is your blood to complete the ritual."

Rage built inside me as I remembered what Samael revealed while in the Wastes. The Constantine bloodline had been chosen for the final sacrifice. With my mother dead, I was the last Constantine alive besides Luke.

The High Priest must have seen the anger in my eyes, the desperation, but also the resolve. "Don't even think about fighting the compulsion. Barbatos might be a grunt compared to Hell's other demons, but he's still stronger than a human. The more you fight it, the more damage he will do."

He was right. To get to my memories, the demon would need to shred through my mind. He would destroy neurological pathways that could essentially erase portions of my past, memories I would never be able to get back. Even if I found a way to fight the possession, or to rip him from my body, there was a good chance I might not even remember who I was once I was free of him. But it was a risk I was willing to take if it would give Kate just a little extra time.

"Go ahead, priest. Do your worst."

He smiled, and this time any softness I'd seen in his eyes turned to jagged ice. "Let me remind you that you've made a bargain with the Devil. You agreed to give us the location of the grimoire in exchange for Kate's safety. Fight the compulsion and you'll be gambling with her life."

The sedative was beginning to wear off, and I could feel life returning to my muscles. I yanked on my restraints and gritted my teeth at the High Priest. "When this is all over, I'm coming for you."

Something like horror flashed deep in his eyes. Perhaps a part of him believed my words.

He leaned in, lips terse. "I know why you're doing this, Jax. You think that by fighting this, you're going to be giving Kate a chance to stop us. But I'll let you in on a little secret. Kate's in Barcelona; you're back in the States. And before you start twisting your head into knots, trying to figure out how she can possibly make it back here in time to stop the rebirth… Mikha'el has been taken to Abaddon, and his lieutenants have also been incapacitated. Kate's not coming. It's over. We won."

I didn't even have a chance to process everything he'd just said before someone was holding my head, another was forcing my mouth open with some device, and warm blood was being poured down my throat. I gagged, my survival instincts making me thrash.

Fuck, this was it. Breathing sharply through my nose, I braced myself for what was to come next and prayed with every cell in my body that whatever memories the demon would destroy to get to the location of the grimoire, that somehow, any memories of Kate, of the love we had, of the child we made together would remain untouched. That somehow, I could find my way back to her.

I closed my eyes as I heard the priest chant the ancient words spoken by the angels and made sure the last image, the last thought I had before I was once again thrown to the mercy of a demon, was that of Kate.

I love you, angel. Please know that no matter what happens to me today, that love will never die.

PART II

Chapter Seventeen

KATE

It didn't dawn on me until I'd been sitting on that pew by myself waiting for Clint and the others to assemble that if we left so early in the morning, the six-hour difference between Barcelona and New York meant we'd be arriving around one in the morning, Eastern Standard Time. It would still be dark out, which also meant we'd have to deal with the creatures prowling the streets in search of a snack. At least if we arrived during daylight hours, we'd have one less thing to worry about. We could cover considerable ground without having to fight off demons or the devoured.

It wasn't easy convincing Queen Loriana to at least let us wait until noon before leaving, but eventually, she relented. We'd lose five hours, but after the battle we'd just fought, the extra time to rest and eat was much appreciated. Plus, it gave us the opportunity to iron out some details before arriving in the States, guns blazing and without a plan.

A heaviness settled over the church when the clock bell chimed twelve times, announcing our departure. Many gathered to bid us farewell as we exited the large, wooden double doors. I had to put a hand up to shield my eyes from the noon sun as it cast a bright glow over the plaza-now-turned-graveyard. Taking a solemn breath, I took in the devastation. In the daylight, the carnage was harder to stomach, and I hated the fact we were abandoning the remaining Guardians to the arduous and soul-crippling task of piling the dead into a burning pyre. My team and I had to cover our faces with scarves as we walked out to the center of the plaza, past the burning corpses, shielding our noses from the soft breeze that carried the stench of death and decay.

To my right, Antonia walked with a determined stride, rifle strapped over her chest. Behind her trailed Talia, a silver-haired woman with fierce eyes, and Mara, a lean and tall dark-skinned woman holding twin daggers that caught the noon light. Behind them, a set of red-headed brothers from London, Jasper and Tristan, dragged a shackled Kyle.

To my left, Clint held Hank by his lead, and Chaz escorted Kelsey. It wasn't hard to miss the way Kelsey kept glancing at Clint, something like hope and sorrow flashing in her eyes. Clint was the perfect picture of composure and didn't show an ounce of awareness that Kelsey was even part of our company. He was either truly over whatever feelings he'd developed for the girl in such a short time, or he was delivering an Oscar-worthy performance.

Chaz met my eyes, and we shared a smile. He had no idea how relieved I'd been to see that he'd made it. I broke down when he told me how Mikha'el had showed up and rescued him from the horde in the tunnels. With the battle raging outside the church, Mikha'el could've easily ignored the prayer—and it would've been understandable if he couldn't abandon the courtyard—but Chaz wasn't just any body. Chaz was a friend, he was family, and the archangel dropped everything to save him.

Picturing Mikha'el being tortured in Hell by Samael after everything he'd done to help us made my blood burn nuclear.

I hadn't said anything to anyone, but once we stopped the ritual and I found Jax, I planned to go after Mikha'el. I didn't care how, but I would find a way to break into Abaddon to rescue him.

It was the least I could do after how much he'd done for us. I owed it to him, but it went beyond gratitude. He had been more than my sworn protector, more than the legendary commander of God's holy army. He'd been my friend, and I would not let him perish in Hell.

I tried to not let myself be too distracted by my rage and instead focused on the mission at hand.

Surrounded by her small calvary, Queen Loriana was waiting for us, an impatient look in her eyes. I knew waiting five hours had been more than she had originally agreed to, and the cost of her sacrifice sat heavy on my heart. Her people were vulnerable, and she'd delayed rushing to their aide to help *us*. It was a debt I knew we'd never be able to fully repay, but that didn't mean I wouldn't try.

The queen, flanked by two of her warriors, Ta'herah and who'd she'd earlier introduced as Khai'runē, strode toward us. The breeze had blown strands of the queen's hair loose from her braids and the ringlets billowed softly over her face. Her eyes, wise and piercing, held mine, and I felt the weight of worlds in that gaze. In her hands, cradled like a fragile heart, was the Eldohn-rhā, the orb-like mechanical device that would create the wormhole between Barcelona and Utica.

It gleamed under the sunlight, its metallic surface shifting, mutating. Gears clicked softly, rearranging themselves with each subtle movement, as though the orb was alive, thinking, calculating. Intricate markings pulsed faintly, reflecting the hidden energies contained within. It was both an object of great beauty but also of terrible power. I felt that power as we neared the object, and the humming energy that pulsed from it almost made me drop to my knees and worship it.

As mesmerizing as it was, it wasn't hard to tell that in the hands of someone nefarious, the device could be abused.

"The Eldohn-rhā," the queen said through Ta'herah. "Its power is weakened more than we thought."

I stepped forward. "Can it still get us there?"

The queen's gaze chilled.

"It will," Ta'herah answered, taking the orb from her queen's hands, "but it requires more than it has left to function properly. The journey between realms demands balance—the four elements to guide it, to feed it." She glanced at the riders behind her, their faces a mask of calm, though I could sense the tension simmering beneath. "We will provide what it needs."

Antonia shifted on her feet, her face awash with concern. "How?"

Ta'herah held the orb higher so we could all see the subtle glow coming from its core. "All Aetherians hold a drop of elemental magic in their blood," the translator said. "Some more than others—considerably more—especially those chosen to serve in the queen's guard. The Eldohn-rhā feeds off the elemental magic of our realm, but as we are far from home, those of us blessed by the elements will feed it the fuel it needs to open the gateway."

Chaz, standing off to the side, shook his head slightly, his deep voice rumbling. "Won't that drain you?"

"Yes, but it is necessary. The portal must be precise, or you'll be lost between realms."

I couldn't stop the question from spilling out. "And what happens if *you're* depleted?"

Her shimmering eyes met mine, unwavering. "You need not worry, Earth child. We shall recover, eventually. Rest assured, the Eldohn-rhā will guide you to Utica. From there, the task is yours to complete."

The thought of leaving the queen and her riders weakened unsettled me, but we had no choice. Samael's ritual would not wait for us to find another way.

"How does it work?" Clint asked, his eyes on the orb, brow furrowed with the weight of whatever calculations were racing through his mind.

Ta'herah shifted her grip on the Eldohn-rhā, holding it up higher to the sun. "I was able to use your maps to calculate an approximate location marker of our destination and have pre-entered coordinates in our navigational language. I can't guarantee it will drop us off directly at the asylum, but we will be close. All it now requires is elemental magic to align the coordinates and breach the veil between realms. We need Earth to stabilize the journey, Fire to ignite the opening, Water to smooth the transition, and Wind to guide our path." As she spoke, the orb began to shift, its gears clicking and whirring faster, the markings glowing brighter with each word.

Ta'herah lifted her hand, palm open, and the orb responded—rising from her grasp, floating in the air between us. It hovered for a moment, then began to change, shifting and expanding as thin metal arms extended outward from its center, like the hands of a clock. Each spoke reached out toward the four Aetherians among them who seemed to possess the required elemental magic.

The queen extended her arm first. "Tírěn," she said softly, her voice laced with reverence. A faint green glow surrounded her hand as she pressed her palm against the orb. The metal responded, the engravings shifting, pulsing as the energy flowed into it. The ground beneath our feet trembled ever so slightly, and I wondered if she'd offered the element of Earth.

Khai'runē stepped forward next and pressed her hand on the orb. "Éthren." Flames flickered around her hand, casting a fiery glow across her bronze skin. The device whirred, the gears moving faster, absorbing the raw heat and power.

Ta'herah followed, her voice calm as she placed her hand on the metallic surface. Felndír," she said, her voice barely a whisper, but it carried the strength of a storm. The air around us stirred as she touched the orb, and a rush of wind swirled around the courtyard, lifting the hairs on the back of my neck.

The last rider, a younger warrior named Fellára, stepped up. "Lūiné." A soft, cool mist formed around her fingertips, and the orb shuddered as the liquid energy was drawn into its core. The markings glowed a faint blue, soft and fluid, as though waves were rippling across its surface. *Water.*

The Eldohn-rhā spun faster now, a soft hum emanating from its center as the magic of Aetheria fueled its transformation. The gears aligned, the orb's intricate structure glowing brighter, until a thin beam of light shot from its core, cutting through the air and opening a swirling vortex before us.

The wormhole.

It wasn't like anything I had ever seen before. It wasn't just a portal; it was alive, shimmering with layers of light and energy, each color representing the element that powered it. The air rippled with the force of it, a mixture of calm and fury, as though the elements were held together by sheer will.

In order for Ta'herah to have a chance to return back to her home realm, the orb would need to remain in her possession, which meant the queen and the rest of her riders needed to enter the wormhole first. Ta'herah had already programmed the orb to take them back to Aetheria. The queen waited until all her riders had passed through the portal, then she turned to me.

"Thank you. For everything," I said to her, my hand tightly gripped around Mikha'el's sword.

Her gaze softened slightly. "Your path is not finished, Earth child," she said, her accent thick. "Thank me when we meet again." With a final farewell to the two riders she was leaving behind, she stepped through the portal and was gone.

"Once *we* step through," Ta'herah said, her voice almost drowned out by the hum of the portal, "we must move quickly. The Eldohn-rhā will hold the connection as long as it can, but it will weaken with every second we delay."

With that, she stepped back, and I turned to my team. Clint was already at the front, his crossbow slung over his shoulder, ready as ever. Hank sat obediently at his heel, unphased he was about to enter a churning hole. I loved seeing them together. If something ever happened to me, I would have peace knowing Hank had the kid to look after him.

Chaz stood next to them, his massive frame a comforting presence as he held on to Kelsey by the shoulders. Antonia and her Guardians were lost in silent prayer, while Kyle simply looked on in terror as if he knew only nightmares awaited us. I could only hope it wasn't a trap.

I took a deep breath and stepped toward the portal. The wind from the vortex pulled at me, tugging at my clothes, but I didn't hesitate. With one last look at the church, I stepped into the light, my team following close behind.

The world around me stretched, twisted, and folded in on itself as we passed through the wormhole, the elements swirling around us, guiding our path. The sensation was both exhilarating and terrifying—like being pulled apart and put back together at the same time.

And then, just as quickly as it began, it was over.

Chapter Eighteen

KATE

We tumbled out onto the cold, hard ground of upstate New York—at least, I hoped it was New York. The air felt different—thicker, more frigid. Looking around, I spotted a mangled *No Parking,* American-looking street sign, so it seemed we were at least back in the States. Luckily, using the wormhole appeared to be easier on a human body than rifting was. I remembered puking my brains out on the streets of Barcelona when Mikha'el first rifted us—granted, I'd also been in labor at the time, but Jax had keeled over on the side of the road and vomited his innards, too.

While I felt slightly disoriented now, for the most part, I felt fine.

I took a couple of steadying breaths as I checked we had all made it across safely.

Clint was already checking his maps while Hank sniffed the air, ears perked as he scanned the surrounding area for potential threats. Chaz had sat Kelsey on the curb next to Kyle while he shared some words with Ta'herah. The Aetherian looked to be at least two feet taller than him and had muscles that could rival his, but the marine had clearly caught her eye, and Chaz didn't seem to mind the attention.

Antonia drew closer as she checked her watch. "Something's off," she said, looking up at the darkening sky. "It was noon when we left Barcelona. It should be six in the morning here, but it feels like dusk is approaching."

"Ta'herah, Khai'runē," I called the riders over. "Did we somehow time jump? This feels like it's later in the day from when we were supposed to arrive."

Ta'herah dug into a satchel and pulled out another mechanical-looking device that resembled a compass."

"What's that?" I asked.

"We call it narhkhā," she said, staring up at the slate-gray sky. "It can help us find a path to your desired location, as well as give us an approximate alignment of your solar system's celestial bodies to help us determine a time."

When I just stared at her in quiet puzzlement, she lowered her gaze and added, "Inside the portal, time and space exist in a different state, flowing in a non-linear fashion. To create a portal, the Eldohn-rhā not only needs to sync spatial coordinates but temporal ones as well. Manipulation of time during our journey shifted our arrival time."

"Did you know this would happen? That our arrival time would be affected?"

She tapped on the device she held in her hand. "Yes, but the shift in time shouldn't have been this severe. The depletion of elemental power likely complicated the process, especially after my queen and fellow warriors passed through to Aetheria." She tapped on the device a few more times, her brows dipping as she stared at the spinning needles.

I tried to look at what she was seeing, but I couldn't decipher what any of the symbols meant. "How much did it shift?"

"I can't be certain, the narkhhā is still calculating. Usually, it doesn't take this long."

I ran a hand over my brow, trying to smooth out the tension I knew was building. "That doesn't sound good. We need to know exactly how much time we lost."

She tapped on the device again, causing the needles to spin. She sighed and something in me went completely still as her demeanor changed, her face going pale.

"What is it?" I pressed.

She looked up at the sky, as if trying to pierce through the gloom. "These clouds are too dense, making it hard to mark your sun's path, but according to the narhkhā, the sun should be setting soon."

"Feels like late afternoon to me. It's probably five P.M, maybe six," Antonia said, placing her hands on her hips, shoulders slouching as she took in a deflated breath.

"Maravilloso," Talia said, spinning away from us in frustration. "We lost eleven hours."

Ta'herah's expression sagged, knowing full well we'd not prepared for this. "Lamentably, we lost more than that. I'd say a lot more than a full Earth rotation."

My jaw tightened, and I felt my blood drain to my feet, the air feeling too thick to breathe. "You can't be serious."

By now the rest of the group had begun to suspect something was wrong, and they all drew in closer to the conversation.

"What's going on?" Clint asked.

I blew out a rankled breath, trying not to lose my composure. "We lost more than twenty-four hours in that portal. We're now mere hours, if that, from the full moon."

"What?" Chaz blurted, "We were in that tunnel less than thirty seconds. You're telling me that we traveled into the future?"

Antonia grunted. "Apparently so. Seems they forgot to tell us that little gadget of theirs is not just a portal maker, but a time traveling machine."

"We did not travel into the future," Ta'herah said tersely,

correcting the Guardian. "Not exactly. It's true that the Eldhon-rhā warps time and space to create openings between realms, but normally the time differences are insignificant."

"So, what happened here?" Antonia asked.

"I don't have a clear answer for you, Guardian. Our people seldom have need of the Eldhon-rhā since we don't travel between realms often. The power it requires would drain our world if used consistently. We use our beasts or ships to travel within our own borders. But to come to Earth when Mikha'el called, we had no choice but to use our sacred artifact. Still, we lost only fractions of time when we crossed into your realm. For this to have happened, I can only surmise that its depletion of magic is what may have caused this severe time lapse."

"So, we didn't travel through time, then?" Chaz asked, and I noted slight disappointed in his voice. I understood why —time traveling seemed cool, but right now, it would be our worst enemy.

Ta'herah's eyes softened over the marine. "What may have felt like a mere breath inside the portal was, in actuality, more than a full Earth rotation out here. In simpler terms, we didn't necessarily leap through time, we were stuck in the portal longer than anticipated, but you didn't feel the passage of time due to the great forces at work that made this trip even possible." Her last words were aimed at Antonia.

Everyone now stared at one another, our heads spinning, trying to make sense of the time warp. The tension in the group practically crackled as we all realized what this meant for the mission. I hated that we'd gone from having almost forty-two hours to find the asylum and figure out a way to break in, to having two, maybe three hours to execute our makeshift plan.

We had zero time for error, which meant we had zero time to bicker about how the artifact fucked us over. We'd made it to the States, and now we just needed to focus on finding that damn building.

One of the red-headed brothers stepped in closer, eyeing the Aetherian rider. "How do we know we're even in New York?"

Ta'herah's eyes narrowed over the Englishman. "I charted our path using the navigational parchments your people provided. If your *map* was accurate, we should be near your destination."

I shot a glance at Clint, who gave me a reassuring wink as he laid his map over the hood of a broken-down Toyota Corolla and flicked his flashlight on. "Luckily, I have really good spatial memory and actually recall the area from the time I did the haunted tour," he said, pointing to a spot on the map, then gesturing to the large domed building several hundred yards behind us. "That right there, is Utica University's Sports Dome. Well, *was.* Now it's just another relic from the past. Either way, we're in the heart of Utica."

"Kid's right," Kyle chimed in from his sitting spot on the curb, his voice startling me. I'd half-forgotten he was with us and hadn't realized he'd been listening in on our conversation. "We're about a thirty-to-forty-minute walk to Old Main from here."

"Yeah, but with nightfall approaching, that may as well be a trip to Mordor," Clint said.

"Mordor?" Ta'herah asked, but Clint ignored her, and I had no time to explain *Lord of the Rings* to an alien.

"So much for the daylight advantage," Chaz said. "Now the streets will likely be clogged with demons and the devoured." As if hearing his words, a howl went off in the distance, followed by the distinct whooping chorus of a pack of nightcrawlers waiting in the shadows like racehorses at the gates.

"Seems the shaitan have already caught our scent, and they're hungry for blood," Tristan added.

"Aye," his brother Jasper agreed. "They will hunt us down as soon as this place is covered in complete darkness. We need to get our asses out of the open and into a more residential area if we want to throw them off our scent."

Ta'herah tapped on the narhkhā again and the needles spun.

"We won't need that," Clint said, eyeing the device in her hand. The Aetherian tilted her head, but Clint tapped his temple and offered her a crooked smile. "*I'm* the compass."

The rider simply cocked a brow.

"Alright, everyone," I said. "Listen up. According to Ta'herah's fancy thingamajig, the sun will be setting shortly, and we have about two and a half hours before the full moon reaches its peak. With these clouds clogging the sky, we won't be able to keep track of it. So, if you have a watch, synch it. We can't afford to lose track of the moon's trajectory or it's game over—for our entire species. Understand?"

Everyone nodded and another chorus of whooping calls erupted in the distance, louder now. Hank's ears perked up, and from the direction his snout was pointed, it seemed the nightcrawlers were south of our destination.

I unsheathed Zadkiel's sword and kept Mikha'el's strapped to my back. "I'm gonna keep this short and sweet. We've all faced off with the beasts hiding in the shadows, so I don't need to tell you how important it is to keep ahead of those hellhounds. We'll need to haul ass, but we can't be careless. I don't doubt there are devoured lurking the streets, and heavens knows what other hell-born creatures Samael has unleashed here.

"Keep your eyes peeled and weapons ready. Kill anything that moves. I don't care what or who it is. There might be Devil's Army members patrolling the area, and we can't take any chances. Any civilians who've survived this long would know to keep off the streets after dark. If they are stupid enough to be out… Well, I guess they didn't learn about Darwin's theory on natural selection."

Hank's sudden posture change and alertness made the angel blood in my veins tingle with alarm. The way he scanned the area meant things were already out here, watching us, hunting us, and it wasn't the hellhounds. We'd be minced meat if the beasts had already caught up to us.

Time to wrap things up and get our asses moving.

"Clint, here," I said, nodding toward the kid, "he's a human GPS, and the one who's gonna get us to Old Main. Wherever he goes, we go. We clear?"

"Copy," Chaz and the Guardians said in unison. Ta'herah and Khai'runē pounded a fist to their chests. Good enough.

"Wait," Kyle said as Chaz reached for Kelsey and Jasper yanked the Devil's Army member to his feet. "What about me and Kelsey?"

Clint squared his shoulders and took a few steps too close to Kyle. "What about *you* and Kelsey?" Sometimes I forgot the kid was not really a kid. The two men stood chest to chest now, Clint eying Kyle with an intensity I thought would burn right through Kelsey's brother.

"You're leaving us defenseless if you keep us shackled."

Clint practically snarled. "You're out of your fucking mind if you think we're taking those off."

"We're skilled fighters," Kelsey said softly, her frame dwarfed by Chaz's muscles. "Let us help."

Clint didn't chance a look her way, he just kept his gaze trained on her brother. "Now you want weapons, too? The two of you can't be trusted."

"Don't be stupid," Kyle spat, raising his shackles and shaking them in Clint's face. "We'll be liabilities this way. At least give us a chance to defend ourselves."

"He's not wrong," Antonia said, resting her arms on the rifle across her chest. If we get ambushed, they'll get picked off first. It's your call, Kate, but make it quick. We don't have time to waste."

I didn't need long to consider. "They stay shackled. Liability or not, I'm not taking any chances with the two people who handed the Creation Stones to the devil himself."

The siblings both sighed in disappointment and agitation.

"If a time arises where I need to reconsider, I will. But for now, you'll remain bound."

Strapping Hank's leash to my waist, I said to Clint, "Lead the way."

Chapter Nineteen

KATE

It wasn't long before any traces of light were snuffed, and we were covered in darkness. We moved quickly as the distant howls of the hellhounds being released from their shadowy prisons pushed us to move faster through the remnants of Utica University's sports field. The ground was soft, riddled with mud and broken pieces of metal and concrete. Overgrown weeds reached our knees, slowing our pace. Clint scanned every building, every turn, before finally deciding on the best route.

Clint's words stuck in my head: *Might as well be a trip to Mordor.* That's exactly what it felt like. Nightfall had closed in, and with it, the cold bite of death lurking in the streets. The shadows around us stretched like the fingers of some unseen hand, ready to pull us into the void if we strayed too far from our path.

My back tensed as we left the open field and we slinked down a residential street, that ever-present itch down my spine constantly reminding me that, despite being able to hide my wings, I couldn't ignore the fact that I was no longer myself.

I was something *other*; something I couldn't quite under-stand. Keeping the wings spirited away took a mental toll, and now I understood why Mikha'el only spirited them away when he absolutely had to. I knew if I released them, I'd have relief, but until I learned how to properly use my wings, they would be more of a nuisance than anything else.

Hank looked up a me, eyeing me through his goggles. He knew there was something different about me, though he still couldn't place it. I rubbed behind his ears. "Nothing for you to worry about, buddy. Stay focused on the path ahead."

Chaz loomed behind us, his broad shoulders casting a long shadow over Kelsey. She kept her head lowered, her breath easy, knowing her life depended on how quiet she remained. Her eyes darted to mine every so often, pleading for release for her and her brother, but I had no time to consider it. The second we unshackled them, we risked betrayal.

As we stepped onto another street lined with crumbling homes and overgrown vegetation, Clint raised his hand. "Hold up." He crouched low and pointed to the shifting shadows ahead. Something was clearly waiting to ambush us.

Hank growled low and his hackles rose, bracing himself for whatever would come. Clint pointed to a nearby alley. "We cut through there and avoid the main street."

I turned to Ta'herah, who still held her navigational device, her eyes tracking the spinning needles. When she looked back up, she nodded, as if the narhkrā had confirmed Clint's assessment. "Lead the way."

The alley was tight, forcing us to squeeze together. The scent of rot grew stronger the deeper we ventured, and it wasn't long before I saw the source. Human bodies lay strewn across the ground, their limbs twisted at unnatural angles. Some looked to have been there for days, others for much longer. Flies buzzed around the corpses in thick clouds, filling the air with a sickening stench.

Chaz whispered from the rear, "Keep your eyes sharp.

They're never truly dead." The Marine had recent first-hand experience with dormant zombies in the tunnels below the streets of Barcelona. They'd encountered something similar when traipsing down there—piles of corpses that later reanimated.

As if on cue, one of the bodies twitched. I barely had time to react before a withered hand shot up from the heap of flesh at my feet, clawing at the air.

Kelsey stumbled back into Kyle as she tried to steer clear of another twitching limb. Clint moved quickly, his crossbow already aimed. He fired, the bolt slicing through the air and embedding itself into the skull of the thing that had begun crawling toward her. The body dropped to the ground with a sickening *thud*.

I speared the devoured who tried to grab my ankle through the head before it even had a chance to crawl.

"Keep moving," Clint said. "We're almost through this section."

But the alley wasn't going to let us through that easily. The dead were rising from every corner, every heap of decay. First one, then another, until the narrow passage was crawling with zombies, their black, sunken eyes glaring at us, their mouths gaping in grotesque, skin-crawling moans.

"Talia, cover our rear!" Antonia ordered. The Guardian was already moving, drawing her sword and slicing through the nearest corpse. The headless body slumped to the ground, but more took its place.

"We're outnumbered," Antonia gritted, her voice strained as she held off another group of the undead.

"We have to keep moving," I yelled, cutting down a zombie as it lunged at me. "We can't stay here."

The group surged forward, hacking and slashing through the seemingly endless swarm of bodies. Clint fired his crossbow over and over, each bolt piercing skull after skull, but the devoured just kept coming.

Suddenly, a scream shot through the alley, and we all turned in the direction of the sound. Talia had been grabbed from behind by a large zombie, its gnarled fingers digging into her shoulder. She cried out in pain, swinging her sword in a desperate attempt to free herself. The blade connected with the creature's arm, severing it at the elbow, but it didn't let go.

Antonia rushed toward her. "Talia!"

The Guardian locked gazes with her leader, her eyes wide with fear, and I saw the moment she made her decision. With a fierce, determined cry, she allowed herself to be dragged backward into the horde. "Get to the hospital," she managed to scream as the zombies swarmed her.

She'd given herself to the horde to buy us time to escape. Antonia screamed and I had to hold her back from going after her friend. "We can't help her."

She thrashed as I held her by the arms, but I was much stronger—stronger than I realized. "I can't let her die like this," Antonia whimpered.

"It's too late, there's nothing we can do. We gotta go, we gotta go!" With one final pull, I managed to drag her away as the horde converged onto Talia's body, burying her beneath a pile of rotting zombies, the devoured temporarily forgetting about us as they feasted. The Guardian's agonized bellows as she was ripped apart hammered into my skull, a sound birthed of nightmares I'd never be able to forget.

We burst out onto a side street, gasping for breath, but we couldn't stop. Not yet. Old Main loomed in the distance; its silhouette framed by a sliver of glowing light that poked through a puff of dark gray clouds. The full moon was partially visible now, and it looked like our calculations had been off. She was much closer to reaching her peak than we thought. The sight filled me with hope and dread. We were close to the asylum, but I couldn't be certain we'd make it in time to stop the ritual.

As if things couldn't get worse, the loud chirping and

squeaking noise of flying bats *boomed* out of nowhere. The sound of flapping wings as the creatures swooped down enveloped us, claws and teeth tearing as they made contact. We ducked for cover, and when I finally managed to glance upward to see what was attacking us, I realized they weren't bats. The creatures had leathery wings with sharp, bat-like membranes, but their bodies were humanoid—pale gray and abnormally elongated. Their faces were skeletal, with gaping jaws lined with serrated teeth.

They attacked from the sky like torpedoes with heat sensors, screeching so loud that the sound pierced my eardrums like needles. Everyone tried to shield their ears while slashing at them with their weapons, but they were fast, diving and clawing at us with razor-sharp talons. Hank barked viciously, snapping at the creatures whenever one got too close, but even he was starting to struggle.

"Move! We have to move!" I yelled over the deafening chaos. Clint fired his crossbow, the bolt impaling one of the flying demons mid-flight, sending it spiraling to the ground with the sickening *splat* of cracking bone and mangled flesh.

Kelsey tripped backward as she tried dodging a clawed talon that slashed across her face. Chaz hauled her up over his shoulder to keep them moving, blasting the winged beasts from the sky with his one-handed, short-barreled shotgun. Kyle was struggling to keep up, and I realized then that there was no way we were going to make it, not with those two slowing us down. "Unshackle them," I yelled over the whooshing sound of flapping wings. "Do it!"

I didn't know how Chaz heard me above the screeches and screams and the blasts from his shotgun, but he lowered Kelsey to the ground and quickly unlocked her cuffs. Jasper did the same for Kyle.

When they were free, I pointed to what looked like an old, dilapidated diner on the side of the road. The broken windows and a sagging roof had me second guessing myself if they'd be safe in there, but we had nowhere else to run. "There. We need to get off the streets. Everyone get inside. I'll cover you. Clint, take Hank."

"I'm not leaving you out here."

"Clint, I've got this. Go. Get everyone inside that diner! That's an order."

"What are you planning to do?"

I stared up at the enormous black mass moving across the sky. "Incinerate them."

The clouds cleared as if by some mysterious force, unveiling the full moon now nearly at its peak. Fuck. We were truly running out of time. I turned toward the diner and spotted the group huddling inside, Clint standing by the doorway holding on to Hank as my shepherd barked and barked, warning me of the danger looming above.

I know, buddy…

Eyeing Clint, I made sure the kid understood. *Don't try to be a hero.*

Planting my feet, I faced the incoming wall of flying demons, the creatures sailing like a single organism across the sky. My nose twitched from the putrid sulfuric stench that hit me like a heat wave as the bat-like demons flapped their massive wings, their leathery hides blotting out the moonlight as they drew closer. Their screeches tore through the night, sharp and jagged as broken glass, the sound making my entire body cringe.

My heart thudded, slow and steady, each beat sharpening my focus, narrowing the world to the demons in front of me. I twisted Emrandael over my wrist like it weighed nothing, the sword humming beneath my touch, the ancient power thrumming through my veins. It felt like an extension of my arm now, a part of me.

The demons were close now, close enough that I could see their serrated fangs glinting, their claws reaching with talons sharp enough to rip through bone. A shudder ran the length of my spine, and I knew, *knew* Samael must have sensed our arrival and this was our welcoming committee.

Bring it on, you fucking asshole.

I spread my wings and the air around me ignited as light unfurled from my back—blinding, pure, searing through the darkness like a dawn that came too soon. The wall of flying beasts tried to slow their approach, their mouths agape in terror, but they faltered mid-flight, eyes wide and wild, their bodies recoiling from the angelic power they were too wretched to endure.

It was *my* turn to bring *their* nightmares to life.

On instinct, I launched myself forward, my wings responding as if I'd done this countless times, their force shooting me into the sky, even though I had no clue how to fly. Baptism by fire, I guessed. Reminded me of how I learned to swim—by being thrown into the deep end of the pool and told to swim or drown.

Higher and higher I rose until I was met head on by one of the demons. Emrandael arced in my hand, its edge slicing the creature straight in half. Black blood sprayed across the night, the demon's body crumbling into ash before hitting the ground.

Another one dove from above, talons outstretched, aiming for my face. I twisted midair, spinning my wings around me like a shield. Its claws ripped across my feathers, and I screamed at the biting sting that raced through the shafts and down my spine. Son of a bitch. My wings snapped open again, flinging the creature back. It tumbled, spiraling through the air, and before it could recover, I was on it, Emrandael plunging through its chest in a flash of silver light. It bellowed a high, keening wail before dissolving into dust.

I landed in a crouch a few yards in front of the diner, wings wrapped tight around me as more demons circled over-head, their shrieking rage making the air vibrate.

The angelic sigils flaring along my arms glowed white-hot

beneath my skin, the power building like a thunderstorm, lightning ready to strike. I slowly raised to my feet, spreading my wings wide. I could feel every shaft, every feather as I stretched each wing to its full span.

Heavens, it felt magnificent. Currents of power ran along each bone down to the tips. No wonder angels were so arrogant, so sure of their might. Their entire essence, their power, surged from their wings, and now that power, *Mikha'el's power,* surged through mine. I glanced down at my palms as my fingertips crackled with forks of electrified light—*starlight,* the raw energy of the universe.

The same energy that had erupted from me and pulverized the demons back at *La Sagrada Familia.*

My eyes flicked to the sky where the flying shits still hovered, waiting to strike. Idiots. With a guttural scream, I lifted Emrandael skyward, letting the empyrean sword act as a conduit, amplifying my power. A torrent of bright light blasted into the swarm like a beam of white fire. The screams of the demonic creatures shattered the air, the light searing through their wings and their flesh as the blinding brightness spread in all directions, turning the hell-born nightmares to nothing but smoldering cinders in an instant. Ash rained down around me, covering everything in a blanket of disintegrated remains before being carried away on the wind, leaving nothing but death and darkness in their wake.

I lowered my hands, my wings folding back slowly, the sigils on my arms fading as my power receded. I felt light-headed, limb-heavy. Emrandael, still glowing faintly in my hand, felt lighter though, almost peaceful, satiated, it seemed, on the blood and ash of the fallen demons.

Closing my eyes, I let myself take a couple of steadying breaths that were cut short when Clint's hollering voice suddenly sliced through the unnatural silence, sending a jolt of alarm up my spine.

Chapter Twenty

CLINT

"Kate," I called out, the fierce pounding in my heart loud enough, I swore what remained of the world could hear it. "Get inside, now." The glow of those angelic sigils was fading on her skin, the light in her wings dimming as she stumbled inside. She looked… drained, like the power had bled her dry. She leaned against the doorframe, swaying slightly.

Her head snapped up, and for a second, she looked at me with glassy eyes, like she didn't know where she was. But then her gaze sharpened, and she pushed herself off the door jamb, staggering toward me. I caught her by the arm before she could fall, steadying her, expecting to find her partly charred as I scanned her over, but she seemed unscathed by the star power that had exploded from her moments prior.

Maybe it had been Mikha'el's sword that had protected her. They way she'd used it seemed to have channeled the energy, allowing it to flow through the empyrean weapon rather than her. Either way, using it had still weakened her, but at least she wasn't burnt to a crisp.

"You're weak," I said, trying to keep the edge out of my voice. "You need to sit down."

She took another step forward, but the movement was slow, lethargic. "I'm okay. We need to get moving. The moon is nearly at its peak. We might even be too late."

My stomach twisted. Clearly, she hadn't seen what was out there, the dark shapes creeping toward us, low to the ground, their glowing red eyes cutting through the blackness. Ushering her completely inside, I shut the diner door closed—well, what remained of it as it half-hung off its hinges. She spirited her wings away and leaned against what used to be the hostess station. Old menus and a check-in computer were buried under mounds of dust and debris now covering the surface of the small podium. "What is it?" she asked, noting the pained expression on my face.

"Nightcrawlers. The hellhounds have caught up to us."

"How many?"

"A full pack led by an alpha," Antonia said, pushing to her feet from the red-vinyl chair she'd been sitting on, the cuts and scrapes across her forehead and cheeks leaking blood.

Chaz peeked through the mangled blinds. "Huge motherfucker, too"

Tristan wheezed on the floor, his breaths running ragged. "Why haven't they attacked?"

All we had were our flashlights to cut through the darkness, but I could see the Guardian was covered in blood, a hand over his abdomen, his brother Jasper sitting beside him, his hand pressed over whatever wound they were trying to staunch.

"They likely saw Kate's lightshow and aren't eager to be turned to ash." I nodded toward his injury. "How bad is it?"

"Bad enough, mate," he said through tight lips.

Jasper met my gaze, and his red-rimmed eyes told me what we all already knew.

"What about the serum?" Mara asked as she stepped into the beam of my flashlight. "Can't it heal him?"

I quickly unstrapped my backpack, and my heart sank to my gut. The outside had been ripped apart like someone had taken razors and shredded the leather. Those fucking flying shits had torn it up with their talons. When I reached inside, I flinched as I cut my fingers on a broken vial.

"What is it?" Tristan asked.

Swallowing thickly, I could barely look the Englishman in the eyes. "The vials… they're all broken."

Kate pushed herself off the podium. "What do you mean? Are you sure?" She took the bag from me and looked inside. "Fuck!"

"Now what?" Mara asked. "That was supposed to be our fail-safe, in case any of us became infected."

Tristan's ragged breathing filled the air, the blood from his wound pooling in slow, steady drips on the floor. His skin was turning pale, too pale, and the gashes on his chest and arms looked deep enough to see bone. Those beasts had done a number on him.

Ta'herah was suddenly in front of Kate, eyes narrowed. "What are you?" Her voice was sharp, cutting through the thick tension in the room. She didn't bother glancing at the wounded Guardian. "Those wings… the power. Are you an angel?"

Kate recoiled slightly but met Ta'herah's gaze with surprising steadiness. "I don't know what I am."

Ta'herah's expression darkened, her sword twitching in her hand. "That's not an answer. You hold angelic power; you carry Mikha'el's sword. You could have rifted. My people needed me, yet I came on this quest because you said you needed *our* help."

"Hey!" I snapped, stepping between them. "We don't have time for this. There's a pack of nightcrawlers coming for us.

Let's focus on surviving first, then we can figure out what she is."

Kate's gaze dropped to the floor. "It's okay, Clint. Ta'herah deserves the truth." She lifted her eyes to the Aetherian rider. "I've been anointed by two angels, including Mikha'el… He anointed me before he was taken by Khama'el. I think… I think he gave me his power, some of it, at least. But before now, I didn't even know how to use my wings, let alone rift."

"Hellhounds are moving in," Chaz piped in from the windows. "Looks like they're willing to take their chances with Miss Fireworks over here. They're splitting up, some are taking the flanks. They're gonna try to surround us."

Hank was perched on a busted-up booth table, looking out through another window, a low growl rumbling in his throat.

I looked between Ta'herah and Kate, the Aetherian's eyes blazing. "Look, we can talk about Kate's power later. Right now, we need to figure out a plan out of this diner without becoming nightcrawler dinner."

"We're not gonna make it if we stay here much longer, that's for sure," Kyle said suddenly, pushing himself up from where he'd been crouched next to Kelsey. His eyes were wide, but his voice still. "I can put up a protection shield… wards. Give you a chance to sneak out while I hold them back."

"But the wards, they'll…" Kelsey started, her voice tight with panic.

"I know. If I leave, they'll fall," Kyle said. He looked around at all of us, his face grim. "Which is why I need to stay."

"No," Kelsey said firmly, her face scrunching in pain as she stood and limped toward her brother. She'd clearly rolled that ankle again.

"Vēl Hanír." Khai-runē's voice was cold as steel, almost resigned. She didn't look up from sharpening her dagger, but the weight of her words settled over the room like a death sentence, though none of us knew what she'd said, so we all turned to Ta'herah.

"She said *she'll* stay," the Aetherian uttered.

"She understands English?" Antonia asked.

"Some. But most of those amongst my kind who understand other tongues prefer to speak only in ours."

Kyle placed his hands on his waist. "Doesn't matter who stays, you still need me to keep the wards up while the rest of you sneak out through the back."

Kate's eyes flashed in the darkness, as if her irises were made of flames. It only lasted a split second, but there was no way anyone missed it. She stepped up close to Kyle, her chest almost touching his. "This whole trip hinges on you getting us inside the asylum and to the ritual pit. *You* can't stay. And I'm not sacrificing anyone else, either." Her gaze flicked to Khai'runē.

"Tristan and I will stay behind, Kate," Jasper said, pushing to his feet.

"I said no."

"It's not your choice, nor is it ours." He pointed to his brother's wound. Tristan was barely breathing now. "He doesn't have long, and neither do I." He lifted his sleeve and showed us the bite mark."

"*Que maldicion*, Jasper," Antonia said, rushing to the brothers. "Why didn't you say something?"

"I just did…" He fixed his blood-shot gaze on Kate, the effects of the infection already manifesting. "Have Kyle still put up the wards. Once they fall, I'll hold the nightcrawlers back as long as I can to buy you more time to get to the asylum."

"A pack of hellhounds will shred you to ribbons faster than you can blink, Guardian or not," Antonia said. "Your sacrifice will buy us a minute, if that."

"It's better than nothing," Tristan said breathlessly from

the floor. "Besides, we're both already dead. Let us go how we want, Antonia."

His leader simply stared; arms crossed. It was clear she was trying to mask the pain of leaving them behind with anger.

I turned to Kyle. "How long do you think we have before the wards fall?"

"If we're running, a minute or two."

"How long will it take us to get to the asylum?" Kate asked.

Ta'herah pulled out the narhkhā and tapped it a few times, her eyes fixed on the shifting glyphs and needles. "We're only a quarter of a solar phase from the structure."

Chaz looked at the Aetherian rider like she had three heads. "Thanks, Xena darling, but can we get that in human measurements?"

"Who the hell is Xena?" Kelsey asked.

From the expressions on all our faces, the majority of the group had the same thought—even Ta'herah seemed confused—but there was no time to explain who the demi goddess was.

Kyle said, reeling us all back, "I think we're about a half mile from Old Main."

"That's a five-minute sprint," Antonia said.

I eyed Kelsey's foot. "Provided we can all make that run."

She caught my gaze and narrowed her eyes. "I'll be fine. It's just a—"

"Rolled ankle, I know. You won't be able to sprint, Kels—" Something inside me tugged when I called her Kels instead of Kelsey. I hadn't meant for it to come out the way it did, as if I gave a shit about her foot or the fact she wouldn't be able to run. The way her eyebrows quirked upward, as if she, too, had caught the slip, made me regret the way I'd said her name even more.

"Why can't you just put a shield around us while we're running?" Mara asked.

Kyle ran a hand through his blood-caked hair. "It doesn't work like that. The wards must be anchored to something, usually the ground. I can't ground them if we're running."

"Kate," Chaz called from the windows. "Why not just use that power Mikha'el gave you and blast these motherfuckers to smithereens?"

Her expression sagged as she glared down at her hands, her arms. The angelic symbols weren't glowing, but they were there, right underneath her skin. I swore I almost heard their power chime like distant ethereal bells. Maybe I could sense that power because of my arm.

"I wish it were that simple," Kate said. "Unfortunately, I haven't mastered its usage, otherwise, I would have done it by now. The amount of power I used to take down the flying beasts nearly drained me completely of my energy, let alone the star energy that seems to dwell inside me, dormant until I need it."

"If she were to use it again," I said, noting how much it hurt her to admit even an ounce of weakness, "she'd risk burn out. The fact she even survived raising the shields at *La Sagrada Familia* is a sheer miracle."

Kate looked at the Marine. "I need time to recover. And whatever energy I'm able to tap into, I need to save it for when I face Samael."

Chaz sucked in a deep breath and parted the blinds with his fingers once again. "Well, whatever the plan, we need to execute it ASAP. Those shits are getting braver by the second. They're practically a stone's throw away."

Kate tightened her ponytail and blew out a cleansing breath. "Kyle, put the wards up, now. We can't risk those beasts getting any closer."

"On it." The Devil's Army member rushed to the front door and got down on his knees. "I need a blade."

Kate hesitated and Kyle looked over his shoulder. "I need it to draw blood. Look, you don't have to give me the weapon, but someone needs to slice my palm open. The sigils need to be written in human blood."

Kate nodded to Mara and the Guardian obliged. We all watched as she took an army knife to his hand and gave Kyle a shallow cut over his palm. He hissed but didn't waste time dipping his fingers into the beads of blood and writing sigils on the smashed tiles on the floor and on the busted-up door.

"Anshu min bayta hana mashḥayna d'eshā w'aytyin d'ʿi-ran. Natrin ʿayna w'qayna ʿalhoun w'naʿṭun rūḥanaya d'nuhra, malka d'nuhra. La nqarrvon l'baita hana w'naḥshon b'nuhra." His head hung back as he continued to chant the words, his eyes seeming to roll to the back of his head.

Ta'herah's brows rose as she stared at the Devil's Army member. "He speaks the language of the angels…"

Antonia drew close to the Aetherian. "You can understand what he's saying? Is he truly casting a protection spell?"

Ta'herah looked at all of us. "He does not deceive you."

"Good to know. Need to save my bullets." Kate holstered the gun I hadn't realized she'd drawn—I hadn't even known she'd been carrying.

Kelsey limped forward. "You were just going to *shoot* him?"

Kate eyed Kelsey's foot, ignoring her question. "You need to do something about that ankle."

"I'm fine."

"You're not. And the sooner you stop being a fucking brat about it, the sooner we can get going. I'm not missing that ritual because of you. If you can't keep up, you'll be night-crawler chum, and I don't need your brother bailing on our deal because you chose to be an idiot. Clint, help her wrap up that ankle."

I knew that tone of voice. It was the one my mother and sister would use on me whenever they meant business, the kind of tone you didn't fuck with. Kate didn't even look at me as she passed me to go look through the blinds herself. I shivered when her shoulder shoved mine briskly and she didn't even flinch.

Swallowing thickly, I turned my gaze to Kelsey, already dreading having to even talk to her, but knowing I had no choice. Kate was right; Kelsey could seriously derail this entire mission if she wasn't able to keep up.

She slumped into a booth and wiped at the blood smeared across her cheek. Her sleeve was ripped and stained with blood. She winced as she touched her side, which meant she was more beat up then she was letting on. Thankfully, even if she'd been bitten or scratched by a demon, the fact that she'd received the antidote meant she was now immune to the virus. However, the wound would remain, pain and all. "Let me see."

"I'm fine, Clint," she snapped, pushing my hand away, but her breath hitched when she moved.

"Yeah? Well, you're not a very good liar." I knelt beside her, reaching for the wound before she could protest again. She flinched, but didn't stop me as I lifted her shirt. The skin around her abdomen was torn, blood seeping through. Her breath came out in shaky gasps as I pressed around the wound.

Her eyes flicked to mine—sharp and guarded. "Don't start acting like you care all of a sudden."

"I've always cared, Kels," I said, quieter than I meant to. "You know that."

For a moment, her guard cracked, and something softer flickered in her eyes. But just as quick, she looked away, jaw clenched. "Just hurry up."

I had some first-aid supplies in my bag that survived the flying freaks and was able to clean the clawed scratch and cover it with a bandage, all while ignoring the ache in my chest that had nothing to do with the fight outside. She was still the same Kelsey—tough as nails, walls up so high that even now, after everything we'd been through, I could barely reach her.

The others were scattered across the diner, battered and bruised. Ta'herah paced near the window, her sword in hand, every muscle in her body tense, like she was expecting the next attack at any second. Khai-runē sat in a corner, so still and quiet, it sent chills down my spine. The determination in her eyes told me she planned to stay and fight the hellhounds despite what Kate had ordered. At the end of the day, the Aetherian riders didn't answer to us.

Antonia sat on the floor next to Tristan and Jasper, holding hands as they chanted a prayer.

Even on the brink of death. Even with all this darkness and evil lurking right outside our door, the Guardians remained true to their faith. The brothers looked at peace, gladly accepting their fate, knowing they were dying for something they believed it, dying to protect others.

It was times like these I wished I had that same devotion.

My thoughts were abruptly interrupted by a piercing howl that erupted right outside the diner. Too close.

"Weapons check, everyone," Kate said. "Get ready to high tail it as soon as Kyle gives the word."

"Warding was never my brother's strongest suit," Kelsey said, drawing my attention back to her. She nodded toward Kyle. "It's draining him to keep them up, especially if the shaitan are pushing against them, which they likely are."

"More of a reason to hurry up." Propping her foot up on my knee, I slowly slid her pant leg up, conscious of the fact that I was touching her bare skin—skin I'd only dreamt of caressing, but never imagined it would be like this. A tingling awareness ran over my fingers as I took off her combat boot and slipped her sock off. Then my eyes widened, and I couldn't help the rough breath I inhaled when I took in the extent of the damage.

"Is it bad?" she asked.

It was more than bad. Her entire ankle was black and blue and swollen. She'd not only sprained it, but she'd probably torn something, too. "Fuck."

She reached for my arm. "Clint, what is it?"

Forget being able to run. No matter how I wrapped her ankle, there was no way she was going to be able to walk, not without limping or without assistance. I reached for the ace bandage in my bag and began wrapping.

"Clint, answer me. How bad is it?"

I flipped my eyes to hers and contemplated lying, but what use was it? "You likely tore something. You won't be able to run."

"I'll walk fast."

"Kelsey, you won't be able to put any pressure on it. Do you understand what I'm saying? You can't even walk, not without assistance. Which would put everyone in jeopardy. We need a new plan."

She shook her head. "Kyle won't help Kate if you leave me behind."

I wasn't sure if she was threatening me or simply stating a fact. "I'm not leaving you behind, Kels. But we can't go with them. We'll only slow them down."

"We?"

"You won't survive two minutes out there on your own. You and I will need to take a different path. We'll meet up with them at the asylum."

"Clint," Kate called. "Are you ready?"

I finished tying the ace bandage and putting her boot on loosely then stood and faced Kate. Her shoulders fell. She knew something was wrong before I even said anything. Chaz, Kyle, and the rest of the crew, except for Jasper and Tristan, stood behind her, waiting.

"Kelsey and I can't come with you."

Kyle pushed past the Aetherian riders and Kate until he

stood face to face with me. "What the fuck are you talking about?"

"Your sister can't walk."

"If she stays, *I* stay."

Kelsey tried to stand but she fell forward into my arms. I steadied her as she stood and placed a hand on her brother's arm. "Kyle, please. I'm dead meat if I try to outrun those beasts. You know that."

"I'm not leaving you alone to face those demons."

"You're not. Clint is staying with me. We're going to find a different path. We'll meet you at the asylum."

"Clint?" Kate said.

"There are some backroads I can take. With the night-crawlers focused on chasing after you, Kelsey and I will be able to sneak out. We'll meet you at the asylum."

"Kid, nightcrawlers aren't the only thing out there. With Kelsey unable to walk right, you're going to be easy pickings."

"We'll be fine."

"Don't you fucking try to bullshit me."

"What do you want me to say? Our odds suck, but what other option do we have? We can't leave her behind, and we can't just throw her out there and expect her to make it on her own." I clenched my teeth, my jaw muscles twitching in frustration.

"I'll go with them," Chaz said.

"No," I told him. "Kate needs you more than we do. She needs all the muscle she can get."

"Then I'll go with you," Mara said. "I don't have Chaz's muscles, but I can hold my own with pistols. You'll need someone to have your back, Clint. Don't be stupid by trying to be a hero."

"I agree with Mara," Antonia said. "It's too risky to send you both out alone."

I nodded in agreement and grabbed my bag. "It's settled,

then. Mara, Kelsey, and I will head out first. Kyle, give us a five-minute head start before you drop the shield."

Kyle took Kelsey into his arms and whispered something only she could hear before he gave us the okay to head out, eyeing me with a stare as sharp as daggers. "You better keep her safe, asshole."

I shot him some daggers of my own. "Just remember, we're in this fucking mess because of you."

Chapter Twenty-One

KATE

As Clint, Kelsey, and Mara got ready to head out, I called Hank over and adjusted his vest and goggles. "Clint, I want you to take Hank with you."

The kid took me to the side and lowered his voice. "With Kelsey injured, we're compromised. You'll be putting Hank in unnecessary danger by sending him with us."

"Nowhere is safe, Clint. And it's *because* you're compromised that I want him with you. He can help alert you to dangers you wouldn't see or hear until it's too late, and he'll be able to track me down when you get to the asylum."

He cocked his head, and I saw the thoughts crossing his mind. He knew I was right and puffed a resigned breath. "Fine."

I cupped a hand behind his neck and brought him close, our foreheads touching. "You're the little brother I never had. I'm not prepared to lose any more family, you hear?"

"I won't let you down, Kate."

Grabbing his cheeks, I anchored my gaze to his, bringing

my voice to a whisper only he could hear. "It's not about letting me down; it's about staying alive. Stay. The. Fuck. Alive. You and Hank. Kelsey is important, but not more important than you and my boy." If they encountered trouble, and it came down to saving Kelsey or himself or Hank, he needed to be okay with preserving himself and my shepherd first.

He nodded, and the dimmed look in his eyes told me he understood the sacrifice I was asking him to make. "I love you," I told him, and he pulled me in for a hug. Hank stuck his nose between us and looked up, and I rubbed behind his ears. "I love you, too, buddy. You keep Clint safe, okay?"

The canine panted, tongue drooping to the side. No matter the task, he was always ready to work.

Those hyena-sounding yelps erupted outside the diner, so deep and boisterous it drove a chill through my marrow. They wanted us to know they were getting tired of waiting. Soon, they were going to try to break through the shields.

Jax had warned me once that wards and shields acted as strong deterrents, but they were not impenetrable, albeit demons would likely not survive or be severely injured trying to traverse through them. But nightcrawlers were like battering rams, and their instincts were simply to kill. They would risk their own hide to catch their prey.

More howls broke through the night, and everyone in the room shifted uncomfortably, our muscles filling with adrenaline as we readied ourselves for the sprint of our lives, especially since what waited outside was not a scouting pack, but a fully-fledged army of nightcrawler soldier-hellhounds led by an alpha that looked bigger and meaner than any I had ever seen. I'd spied him through the blinds before, and his sheer size was enough to make my bowels run liquid.

Its thick silver mane glimmered under the light of the moon, and each muscle on its body rippled with every movement. Two-inch claws scraped against the concrete as he'd pawed the street right outside the shield barrier, its face contorted in a gruesome snarl.

Clint strapped his backpack and crossbow over his back and he and Mara helped Kelsey up. She wrapped an arm around each of their shoulders and they carried her out through the back door, Hank trotting beside them as they disappeared into the darkened streets, their figures swallowed by the shifting shadows.

Five minutes later, I gave everyone the nod. "Time to move," I said calmly, though my heart pounded against my ribs.

Jasper and Khai'runē took their positions by the windows while Tristan remained on the floor; his body too weak to even speak. We bid them farewell, and sadly had no time for longer goodbyes. Antonia, Ta'herah, Chaz, Kyle, and I went out the back door and into the same darkness that had swallowed up Clint and his crew. We ran, our footsteps quick yet silent against the cracked pavement. We pushed into the heavy night, our breaths fogging the air. Overhead, clouds churned like a living creature, swirling around the rising moon now hovering right over the asylum looming in the distance.

We barely made it the two minutes Kyle said we'd have when the wards shattered with an ear-splitting wail and the world suddenly came alive with terror. I chanced a look over my shoulder and my heart squeezed. A wave of shadows slammed into the diner, the grotesque beasts emerging from the blackness, swarming the broken-down establishment, barreling through brick and glass like the diner had been constructed of cardboard. Their sickening growls filled the air, scraping against the night.

But what truly made icicles crystalize in my blood were the hollering screams that burst from the diner seconds later. Jasper, Tristan, and Khai'runē were under attack. I knew the brothers were doomed, though they'd claimed it was an honor to die in this battle, to sacrifice themselves to buy us these precious seconds. My heart ached for them, but there was nothing we could have done to save them, not with the wounds they'd sustained. I held an ounce of hope, though, that at least the Aetherian rider would survive the attack. She was a skilled warrior and hadn't been injured like the brothers.

Trying my darndest to block their screams, I focused on my run, on every burning muscle and every painful inhale. This five-minute sprint was beginning to feel like an hour from the exertion, but there was no time to stop to catch our breaths. Ta'herah had incredible stamina, and her long legs made her strides much longer than ours, pushing her yards ahead of us. Kyle ran right behind her, Chaz at his heels. I was a few feet behind them, and unfortunately, Antonia had fallen behind. My heart plummeted as we neared the asylum and the chain-linked fence surrounding the whole facility came into view—a fence we hadn't accounted for. "It's probably warded," Kyle yelled over his shoulder as he continued to run. "I'm going to need to disarm it. I don't know if I can before the hellhounds reach us."

Not what I needed to hear now, but with no other alternative, we were committed at this point. "We keep going!" I yelled. "We will hold off the dogs while you work." Pressing forward, we ran through overgrown grass and jumped over a dense thicket of bushes, all of us sounding like our chests were going to pop.

We made it another two minutes before another roar shot into the sky.

The alpha. And he was summoning his pack.

Fuck.

They approached from all corners. Fuckers had deceived us. The pack back at the diner had been a fraction of their numbers, and the alpha had clearly anticipated we'd try to escape. The beasts moved faster than I could have imagined, their muscled backs rippling like waves, skin gleaming like polished obsidian. I heard the unmistakable sound of claws against earth, which meant they were closer than I thought.

Much closer.

A sharp cry escaped Antonia's lips as she tripped and went down, her leg caught in a jagged root, the bone twisting at an unnatural angle. I didn't hesitate and ran back for her. My wings tore free, feathers glinting under the pale moonlight, and I swept her into my arms. The wind rushed past us as I took to the air, my wings beating strong and steady, lifting us high above the grasping claws of a trio of nightcrawlers that had nearly caught up to us.

"Don't stop running!" I called down to Kyle and the others, my back muscles straining, the extra weight making it harder for me to keep us airborne. I heaved from the exertion, but I kept Antonia tight to my chest.

I would not fail us. We would not fall.

Chaz fired his shotgun over and over, injuring night-crawlers, but barely making a dent in their tough-as-granite hide. He needed something stronger, something that could slice through demon flesh. "Chaz!" When the Marine looked up, I gripped Antonia with one arm and unsheathed Zadkiel's sword with my free hand, then flung it down to him. He leapt up and snatched it from the air, and I held my breath for a second, praying the angelic power wouldn't burn him. Mercifully, it did not. I had to think it was due to the serum he was given to heal his wounds back at *La Sagrada Familia*.

The Marine wasted no time slicing into demon dog after demon dog. "Now this is what I'm talking about!" he hollered as he stabbed one right through the chest, black blood spurting all over him before the monster turned to dust.

Ta'herah's retractable two-headed spear was about ten feet long, and the rider exhibited skill with the weapon I hadn't even seen displayed by a warrior angel, and I'd fought alongside Mikha'el and his lieutenants. She was a blur of flesh and steel as she twirled and jumped, landing blows that obliterated the beasts like they were blood balloons exploding upon contact.

Kyle made it to the fence and dropped to his knees. I landed right behind him and placed Antonia on the ground, then stared up at the pulsing red glow coming from the fence. It was indeed warded. Antonia grunted a whimper as she tried to stand but fell back down. Kyle was already at work, his fingers weaving through the air, muttering incantations under his breath as he worked to dismantle the shield. But the nightcrawlers' growls grew louder, more vicious as they were closing in.

I unsheathed Emrandael from my back and stretched my wings as wide as they would go. "Kyle, holler when the shield falls." Mikha'el's sword felt like fire and ice in my hand, the sensation welcoming as I faced the oncoming pack led by the alpha. "Let's play, motherfucker."

The nightcrawlers lunged at us in throngs, their blackened forms moving with terrifying speed. I spun through them, my wings slicing around me like blades, cutting down the first one that got too close. Blood—thick and black as tar —splattered across the ground, but more beasts spilled from the darkness.

God. These shits wouldn't stop coming.

Ta'herah was a continued blur of motion, her spear flashing as she cut through another beast, then driving the spear deep into the chest of another, the creature shrieking in pain.

Still, more flooded in like a broken dam.

My muscles burned, every slash of my blade feeling heavier than the last as exhaustion began to creep in. But there was no room for weakness, not here, not now.

"Kate, the wards are almost down!" Kyle shouted, his voice strained. He was pale, sweat beading on his forehead as he worked, the red glow on the fence flickering like dying embers.

I turned just in time to see one of the nightcrawlers leap for him, claws outstretched.

"No!" I surged forward, wings propelling me faster than my legs could carry me. My blade found the beast's neck, severing its head in one clean strike. But another was already on me, its claws tearing through the flesh of my shoulder. Pain flared, hot and sharp, but I gritted my teeth and spun, driving my blade through its chest.

"Kyle, now would be a good time!" I gasped, blood dripping down my arm.

With a final surge of power, the wards crumbled. The fence shimmered for a moment before the magic dissolved, leaving nothing but cold metal behind.

"Go!" I shouted as Kyle climbed the fence, followed by Chaz and Ta'herah. Antonia hadn't moved from where I'd left her, but I noticed a downed beast by her side. Damn.

Her face was covered in black blood and her eyes strained to focus as she stared up at me. "Leave me. I'm no use to you now."

"The hell I'm leaving you here to be torn apart by these monsters." Wings fluttering wide, I raised Emrandael to the heavens and the sword erupted into a white flame that illuminated the entire open grass area, revealing the wall of beasts. The alpha stood, front and center, snarling at me.

I was about to charge when a gunshot blasted through the night, startling me and the beasts all at once, as if someone had ordered them to stand down.

"Kate!" Chaz's voice boomed and I spun around, only for breath to be stolen from my lungs. Antonia laid keeled over, half the side of her head blown off. I was so stricken, I couldn't even scream. Behind the fence, armed men and women held Chaz, Ta'herah, and Kyle at gunpoint. One man held a rifle pointed at me, the nozzle still smoking.

"*You* killed her?"

"She was dead weight. Now, why don't you fly yourself over the fence, sweetheart, unless you want me to blow one of *their* heads off, too," he said, nodding toward my crew.

I could barely process what I was seeing. My chest heaved in rapid succession. This couldn't be happening. How had I come this far, this close, only to lose now?

"I ain't got all night," the man pressed, pointing his rifle at Kyle's head.

"Wait!" Kyle squealed. "I'm Devil's Army. I can prove it." He pointed to his chest, asking for permission to lift his shirt. The man holding the rifle nodded, and Kyle showed him the strange runes tattooed over his chest.

Fucking worm.

"You're not part of this sect," the leader said.

"I'm still a member."

"Who is far from home. And for a Devil's Army member, you're sure keeping some strange company." He gestured to all of us with his rifle.

"Strange maybe, but I'm sure the high priest would be pleased to know I'm the one who gifted him the Creation Stones, and the one who brought him the cunt who birthed Samael his hybrid vessel. A nice little treat for the king to savor once he is reborn."

The man raised a brow in my direction as the rest of his crew shared confused glances. "She has wings. How's that possible?"

"How's *any* of this shit possible?" Kyle challenged. It wasn't a real answer, but something in the leader's mind seemed to tick as he glanced at Chaz and Ta'herah.

To me, he said, "Let's go, angel-wings. Get yourself over the fence or I pop the Amazonian in the face." He pointed at Ta'herah and I had no doubt he'd follow through with this threat. I flew myself over and landed softly on the other side.

"Now hand over the sword."

I smiled gently and offered it to him. "Go on, take it."

His eyes narrowed, suspicion glinting in their depths. Yet, he still took a step forward. He'd clearly seen the light show, not to mention the sword was grandiose in size and shimmered like liquid gold. There was zero doubt the sword was crafted of empyrean steel, yet the Devil's Army soldier seemed willing to try his luck.

"That's Mikha'el's sword, asshole," Kyle warned him. "Touch it and it will incinerate you before you even register what happened."

"You traitorous fuck," Chaz gritted, earning a blow from the butt of a rifle. He turned to his assailant. "Touch me again and—"

"And, what?" Kyle said. "He'll just blow your head off, so shut your mouth before you get us all killed."

Chaz's nostrils flared and I knew it was taking the Marine every ounce of strength he possessed to keep his lips sealed.

The leader trained his eyes on me. "Spirit those wings away and drop the sword on the ground."

As much as it burned me to my core to do as he said, I had no choice. I couldn't risk him hurting Chaz or Ta'herah, though I couldn't care less if he blew Kyle's brains out.

The rest of our weapons were confiscated, and we didn't have to tell them to be careful with Zadkiel's sword. That too was clearly an empyrean weapon, and no one was stupid enough to test if it was true that only anointed Guardians could wield such a weapon. They bound our hands behind our backs, including Kyle's. Guess the leader wasn't taking any chances. Someone threw a heavy leather coat over Emrandael, wrapping it tightly before shoving it inside a duffle. Stepping closer to me, the leader grabbed my chin and pinned his gaze to mine. "If you are who he says you are, then you're just in time, angel-wings. The show is about to start, and you've secured yourself a front-row seat."

As they dragged us across the front lawn of the asylum,

Kyle's eyes met mine. I wanted to bare my teeth at him, but something in his gaze gave me pause. It was like he was trying to tell me something. And as if I could hear his thoughts clearly in my head, that look in his eyes jogged my memory.

Clint, Mara, Hank, and Kelsey were still out there.

And no one realized the shields were still down…

Chapter Twenty-Two

CLINT

The moon's pale light flickered through the cracks of shattered rooftops as I led the group through dark, narrow alleyways. Mara stayed back covering the rear while Hank scouted up ahead. Kelsey limped beside me, her injured ankle barely holding up. I'd offered to shoulder her weight, but she'd spotted a long wooden beam discarded in the alley and decided to use it as a makeshift crutch, refusing my help every time I reached out to steady her.

The tension between us gnawed at me, and I had to clench my jaw to keep from huffing in frustration. This wasn't about what had happened between us, at least not anymore. Despite the shit she'd done, I still fucking cared about her—hell, I cared way more than I wanted to admit—but keeping her ass alive now was less about my feelings and more about ensuring that Kyle kept his end of the bargain.

"Clint, I'm fine," Kelsey muttered, her voice tight. "You don't have to keep looking over your shoulder. I can keep up."

I glanced at her, seeing the way she was trying to hold herself up despite the pain. The guarded look in her eyes was the same as always, but there was a fragility there, too, something deeper than her defiant words. I kept my face schooled. "You don't *look* fine."

She shot me a sharp stare, then bit her lip, glancing away. "If you think I'm slowing you down, then just fucking leave me behind, Clint. Honestly, it's the kindest thing you can do for me. I can't stand seeing the disgust in your eyes anymore. I know the burden I'm causing you, the danger I'm putting you, Hank, and Mara in. It's literally tearing me up inside a lot more than the throbbing pain in my foot."

Lowering my crossbow, I closed the distance between us and stared her down the slope of my nose, fire burning in the depth of my eyes. "Does it also tear you up knowing that you're responsible for all this? For the death of those who had to stay behind at that diner—not to mention all the people who died back at *La Sagrada Familia* and the countless more who will die if we don't stop that rebirth?"

Her lips trembled as she held my gaze, her eyes filling with fat tears. "Go on. Blame me for everything if that's what makes you feel better. I'm not proud of what I did, but I know why I did it. And if I had to do it again, I would. And don't, for a second, think yourself more righteous than me, because if the tables were turned, I know you'd do the same for the people *you* loved."

My nostrils flared. "Don't fucking compare yourself to me, Kelsey. You and your people worship Satan. Our definition of love doesn't align, not even in the slightest."

She swallowed a thick sob as tears poured down her face, but she said nothing, clenching her teeth, trying to hold back the words that wanted to burst from her lips. But that wordless pain hidden behind those tear-soaked eyes boomed louder in my ears than anything she could have uttered, and I immediately felt like a piece of shit.

I knew Jax's story, knew the horrors he'd faced as a kid. And from what Kyle had said, Kelsey had been subjected to the same kind of abuse. Like any child indoctrinated into any religion, her choice was taken from her. I probably shouldn't have blamed her for everything. Even if, as an adult, she could have chosen to leave the cult, I could understand why it wouldn't have been easy. This wasn't all just her fault, I knew that. And maybe she was right—*more* than maybe, if I was being honest. There wasn't anything I wouldn't do for those I loved.

So, who the hell was I to judge her? I'd probably make the same terrible choices if faced with the need to save the people I cared about.

Including her.

That one act of betrayal wounded me in ways she'd probably never know. In ways *I* never knew I could be wounded. And that was from knowing her for only a few measly days. How deep could she cut me if I truly allowed myself to feel the things I knew were skimming over the surface of my heart?

Suddenly, the weight of my backpack seemed to pull on my shoulders and I took a moment to shift on my feet and take a deep breath. "Look, I know what you went through in that cult."

"You know nothing," she spat.

I softened my eyes over her. We weren't going to make it to the asylum in one piece if we kept jabbing at each other every chance we got. "I never wanted to be your enemy, Kels… I still don't. You think I like this version of us? We made a great team back in those tunnels. So, if we want to live through this, we need to work together again, and that means we need to be able to put our differences aside."

Her eyes clouded with doubt.

"I'm not saying it's going to be easy," I whispered, realizing we'd probably been speaking too loudly. "But we gotta start somewhere." I stared as her eyes rounded, her shoulders slacking a bit. Fuck. The strong warrior girl I'd met back at that church peeled away and all I saw now was her broken soul, and I ached so hard to take her into my arms.

I took a step closer, my heart thundering as her scent filled my lungs. The smell of grime and blood stung my nose, but there was also something else there, something that beckoned me closer, and before I could stop myself, I reached for a golden curl and tucked it behind her ear, my fingers lingering over her soft skin for two-seconds-too-long.

She shuddered at my touch, and in that instant, I knew I wouldn't be able to keep my promise to Kate.

"Glad you two are making up, but how about we keep the conversation to a minimum?" Mara whispered as she drew up nearer. "We have company."

"Are you sure?"

"Something's tracking us. Just look at Hank."

Hank's spine had grown rigid, his ears twitching as he scanned the darkness ahead. He suspected something was out there, but he wasn't alerting us to danger just yet. I raised my crossbow again, aiming at the shadows as I followed Hank. "Let's keep moving. Ears and eyes open."

We emptied out into a residential area and the dark streets felt suffocating, empty houses looming over us, their windows hollowed out. Mara's eyes darted to every corner, sharp and focused, which made me tense. She seemed to have a sixth sense and was certain there was some unseen danger hunting us.

Then the sounds started—far off, like distant thunder, but unmistakable. I froze, listening as the low growls and guttural roars of the nightcrawlers echoed through the night. The others heard it, too. Mara's posture stiffened, and Kelsey straightened, the pain lacing through her ankle visible on her face.

"They're at the diner," Kelsey whispered, her voice barely above a breath.

My heart clenched. If the hellhounds had attacked the

diner, that meant Kate was on the move. We had split up to give Kelsey a chance, knowing her injury would slow us down. But now… now the nightcrawlers were on *them.*

A scream pierced the air—far off, but close enough that it clawed at my chest. Hank growled, ears pressed flat as he looked back toward the diner, his instincts mirroring my own. But I couldn't go back; I couldn't leave Kelsey out here defenseless. "There's nothing we can do to help them. Best option is to stick to the plan. We stay to the shadows, quiet as a mouse," I said.

Kelsey glanced at me, something flickering in her expression—fear, concern, maybe even understanding—but she didn't say anything. Instead, she kept pace with me, hobbling forward as fast as her injured leg would allow.

The howls of the nightcrawlers carried through the night, their terrifying cries mingling with more screams. Every shriek was a fresh knife cut to my gut. I wanted to rush back, wanted to tear those creatures apart, but we had to keep moving.

Mara sped up to me, her gun aimed up ahead. "I can't shake the feeling that we're being hunted."

More screams echoed in the distance. "Could be a hell-hound scout."

"Nah, this feels like a different kind of shaitan."

I raised a brow. "I'd forgotten that's what Guardians call the demons."

Kelsey stumbled, her breath catching in her throat, and without thinking, I grabbed her arm, steadying her. She tensed, her gaze locking with mine. "Not what *they* call them; it's what they are."

"And what's this one that's hunting us?"

Mara sniffed the air. "There's a slight sulfuric scent in the air. High order demon. But I don't think it's just one…"

Hank suddenly lifted his nose from the ground, letting out a low growl. There it was. His warning. The shadows twisted and churned around us, and every hair on the back of my neck stood tall, like tiny needles over my skin.

And then, like a nightmare unraveling in slow motion, they appeared.

Wraith-like figures emerged from the shadows, their ghostly forms flickering in the moonlight, gliding toward us with unnatural speed. They didn't growl, didn't roar like the nightcrawlers, just the eerie silence of death itself.

"Ruhadim!" Mara shouted, terror lacing through her voice as she began firing her gun. "Don't let them touch you!"

I aimed my crossbow at one of the floating demons and fired off a bolt. The creature shrieked as the bolt flew right through its dark, misty form, like its body was made of smoke.

What the hell… They are immaterial.

Despite her injury, Kelsey slashed at one of the wraiths with the wooden beam she'd been using as a crutch, her movements slower but still forceful. Again, the beast shrieked, but the beam seemed to go right through it. Kelsey hadn't been ready for there to be no resistance, and she stumbled, her ankle buckling beneath her, but I caught her in time and pulled her close.

"Watch yourself," I growled, the words harsher than I intended.

"I don't need saving," she hissed back, though her voice lacked bite.

I almost argued back, but another wraith raced toward us and Hank lunged. Remembering Mara's words, I grabbed his harness before he collided with the wraith. He snarled viciously at the demon, foaming at the mouth as he barked, but I held tight and managed to fire off a bolt right through its face. The thing vanished into thin air with a fading screech.

I stood back-to-back with Kelsey while holding on to a feral Hank. Two more wraiths approached, and I fired off two more bolts, and the demons vanished in puffs of smoke. "What the hell are these things?"

Kelsey heaved her wooden beam and swung it a wraith that wanted to test its luck. "They're death wraiths. Easy to kill, but if any part of their body touches you, your soul will be sucked right out of your body."

"Shit."

A human scream erupted, and Kelsey and I both turned toward Mara. The Guardian had been surrounded by three wraiths, and one had wrapped its smoke-like fingers around her throat, I could only watch in horror as Mara struggled to breathe, her face ashen.

"Shoot it!" Kelsey shouted, but the bolt left my crossbow too late. Mara's body slumped to the ground.

"Mara!" I shouted, but I knew she was already gone. "Fuck. Hank, stay." Leaving Kelsey's side, I checked my crossbow. Two bolts left. The demons shrieked as they watched me charge at them. If I missed, I'd end up an ashen husk just like Mara.

But I didn't miss; I shot one wraith right through the face, the other through its chest.

"Clint, watch out!"

I spun around just as another wraith I hadn't noticed reached for me from the darkness. I'd run out of bolts, and out of instinct, I reached for it with my empyrean arm. My fingers wrapped themselves around its windpipe… or whatever it was I was holding on to because it was like I was strangling air. A hissing sound billowed from where I held it, like the steal was burning it somehow. I held my breath, waiting for my soul to evaporate out of me, but instead, the demon turned into thin smoke before vanishing.

Rooted to the ground, I heaved several breaths, pressing a hand to my chest as if half expecting my soul to be sucked out of me. Satisfied I was still alive, I stared at my empyrean fingers, the metal still smoking and molten orange. I'd literally burned that demon to death. "Fucking hell. That was mental."

"Holy shit," Kelsey said, a somewhat horrified yet amused whimper escaping her lips. "We survived a shatra of ruhadim."

"A what?"

"A squadron of death wraiths. I'd never seen one in person, let alone a whole group of them. And to have survived an attack…"

I looked down at Mara's dead body. "Not all of us survived."

Kelsey's face sagged. "I'm… sorry."

But there was no time to mourn the dead. Not knowing if death by a wraith left a human infected with the virus, I shot Mara's corpse through the head once. The last thing a Guardian would want was to be reborn as a fucking zombie. I found a tarp discarded by a dumpster and used it to cover her body but made sure to confiscate her weapons first. Before heading back toward the asylum, I took Mara's pistol, and I handed it to Kelsey.

"What's this?" she asked, eyebrows quirked.

"What does it look like?"

"You're trusting me with a weapon?"

"I'm trusting you with my life. It's just us two now. I can't have you covering my back with a wooden beam."

She eyed me cautiously, as if assessing if this was a trick, a test. Then in a blink, she quickly cocked the gun and aimed it at my chest. "See, that's your problem, Clint. You're too quick to trust."

"You're not going to shoot me."

"What makes you so sure?"

"Because if you wanted to shoot me, you would've pulled the trigger already. Also, Mara emptied her clip before she died." I held up a new magazine, a smile tugging at the corner of my mouth.

"You knew I'd turn the gun on you."

"I know you're wounded and scared, and I also know

scared, wounded creatures lash out. But I told you already, Kels. I don't want to be your enemy."

She knew the gun was empty, but she still aimed at my chest, hand shaking. I stepped toward her until the barrel pressed against my heart. "It's too late to shoot me, Kels. You've already made my heart bleed."

A laughed escaped her lips. "You can't stop with the cringey lines, can you?"

I smiled back. "Not within my nature to do so."

Her mouth tugged downward, but she kept the gun pressed against my chest. "I can't change my past, Clint."

I put a hand over hers and gently took the gun from her. "No one can change their past." Discarding the empty clip, I reloaded the gun with a full magazine and handed it back to her.

Slowly taking the gun, she stared at it, then at me, with utter awe. "You're too good for this world, Clint."

I huffed a low laugh. "We all have our dirty secrets, Kels. No one is free from sin… not even me."

As we skulked through the darkened streets toward the asylum, I couldn't shake the image of Mara's dead body, of how that wraithlike creature had snuffed out her life with a mere touch. It wasn't the first time I'd watched someone die, but that didn't make it any easier. And all I could hope for was that there weren't any more ruhadim hiding in the shadows.

Kelsey limped beside me, trying to mask the pain in her foot, but the groans she bit back with every step weren't silent. She seemed annoyed with herself, mumbling a soft curse every time she tried to walk quicker but failed.

"There's no need to push yourself harder if it hurts too much, Kels."

She said nothing and simply pressed her lips into a tight line, her nostrils flaring as she fought through the jolts of pain. That was just who she was—a girl who only knew how to fight her way through things and who hated asking for help. I swallowed deeply and kept walking, unable to ignore the thickness of the air hanging around us, both from the weight of what lay ahead and from the tension that seemed to always hum whenever Kelsey and I were alone. It was a gentle pull, like some tether that held us together, reminding us that we both wanted something more from the other, but not able to say it.

Not being able to just seize it—whatever the fuck it was—that we needed to ease the electric current running over that tether.

Another scream pierced the air from behind us, making my lungs tighten. I clenched my jaw and forced my feet to keep moving. Hank stayed close, his sharp eyes constantly flicking to the dark corners around us, a low growl simmering in his chest.

Then we heard it again—the too close, telltale growls of the nightcrawlers. They must have caught up to Kate's group. Every scream sent a tremor through me, but I had to keep us moving. I slung Kelsey's arm over my shoulder, despite her gritted-teeth protest.

"She'll make it," Kelsey whispered, almost like she could hear the doubt scratching inside me.

I didn't answer, couldn't answer. The asylum was only about three-hundred yards ahead, a looming white building against the moonlit night, a chain-linked fence surrounding it like some kind of cage. But that wasn't what stopped me cold.

It was Kate.

A bright flash of light exploded, drawing my eyes to the sky, and there she was—wings out, a blur of motion and flame as she wielded Mikha'el's sword, tearing into a pack of hellhounds. Her body glowed like a beacon, fierce and beautiful, her movements deadly and graceful.

Kelsey stiffened against my body as I wrapped an arm around her waist, and I pulled us both behind a dumpster with Hank at my heel. I sat her down slowly and instructed Hank to sit beside her. "Stay down."

I peered over the dumpster and silently gasped at the sight. God, I wanted to rush into that light and fight beside Kate—like I should have been from the beginning. Hank sensed it, too, his body trembling beside me as he stuck his snout out and stared up at Kate, poised to lunge.

"Hank, no." I gripped his harness, holding him back as I saw movement at the base of the asylum.

Fucking hell. The Devil's Army.

They came out of the shadows like ghosts, surrounding Kate's group as they climbed over the fence. I cursed under my breath, tightening my grip on Hank. Kate landed with her back to the fence, focused on the wall of nightcrawlers before her, unaware of the danger behind her. Hank growled, locking his eyes on the snarling alpha. It took everything I had to keep him from barking, from running headlong into a fight we couldn't win.

Kelsey pressed her back against the dumpster and reached for my hand. "What's happening?"

I put a finger to my lips.

Kelsey peeked around the corner, and we watched as Kate, Chaz, Ta'herah, and Kyle were stripped of their weapons and taken prisoner, the Devil's Army members dragging them toward the asylum's large doors. The nightcrawlers slipped back into the night after a command from the man who appeared to be their leader, the hellhounds' haunting chorus fading into the darkness. Seemed they believed no one else was out here.

As soon as they were inside, we scanned our surroundings for any more threats. Thankfully, though surprisingly, we didn't spot any more Devil's Army members on the grounds. I would've thought the place would've had more security, but perhaps they figured that since they had Kate, no other idiots would try their luck against the demon dog pack.

After waiting a few more seconds to make sure there weren't any guards around, we abandoned the dumpster and hurried to the fence border. Taking[SC1]. hold of the chained metal with my empyrean arm, I ripped a section wide open. Kelsey let out a soft breath beside me, her eyes flicking between me and the opening in the fence. "Impressive," she muttered.

I smirked. "Stay close."

Kelsey gripped my forearm. "There might be no guards out here, but inside Old Main, the entrance will be clogged with members. I know another, less trafficked way inside."

"You've been here before?"

Her faced sagged, her crystalline eyes dimming. "This is where the children are *educated* in the faith."

My heart squeezed thinking about the horrors she'd likely experienced here. "Kels, if this is too much for you—"

She straightened, using the wooden beam she'd been hauling all the way here for support. "I have no doubt there's children in there now, probably even my niece. There's no chance in hell I'm staying behind."

Chapter Twenty-Three

KATE

The air inside the asylum felt *wrong*.

A heavy weight pressed down on my shoulders, on my chest, each breath tasting of damp decay and rot. The dim lights flickered in the corners of the hallways, casting long shadows that played over the walls like the specters of the souls who had once been tormented here. But it was more than just the memories of what had transpired in the past; it was what had seeped into the bones of the building—an ancient, tangible malice clinging to every surface like smoke after a fire.

Chaz walked beside me, his jaw tight, his gaze flicking to every corner, every half-open door. I could tell he felt it, too. Even Ta'herah, whose stoic grace never faltered, seemed uneasy, her steps slower, as if she were wading through the muck of the unseen atrocities committed in this place.

Kyle, though… his silence was unnerving. He seemed unbothered, his steps languid, unrushed, as if he were on a lackadaisical walk through the park. Of course he would be unperturbed; he probably felt at home here. Meanwhile, I felt like my body was being coated in tar.

The grim tour through the abandoned east wing of the building felt much longer than I cared it to be, adding to my already frayed nerves. I'd seen the moon dangling right over the asylum before they dragged us in, and I knew the ritual would be starting soon—if it wasn't already underway. But these assholes were taking their sweet ass time to bring us down to the pit…

At least, I hoped that's where they were taking us.

My heart pounded so loud I could hear the pulsing blood in my ears. Anguish flooded through me as I continued to scan our surroundings, trying to orient myself, making sure I'd remember my way back out. Though, the fact they hadn't blind-folded us or covered our heads wasn't a good sign—it meant they didn't expect any of us would make it out alive.

The walls were so old and crumbling in places, I thought the building might collapse at any point. But it wasn't just time that had ravaged this place, it was something else, something worse. Graffiti that was scrawled in desperate, jagged letters was barely visible under layers of grime. Each word a warning, a plea for help. Faint outlines of claw marks raked through paint and plaster, and I swore I could hear the echoes of distant wails, as if the cries of those who had suffered here were trying to force themselves into the present.

I shuddered, wishing I could erase the sounds from my mind.

"This place is… fucked up," Chaz muttered under his breath, mirroring my thoughts.

The Devil's Army members surrounding us walked with cold, methodical precision, dragging us farther into the depths of this nightmarish labyrinth. They'd donned dark cloaks before marching us through the east wing, their faces shadowed under their hoods, but I could feel their gazes on me, could feel their disgust as they stared at the sigils on my arms, as if the angelic words inscribed over my skin were an abhorrent insult to their dark faith.

The corridor twisted ahead, leading us to an old stairwell. The wooden steps groaned underfoot, each creak sending ants crawling over my body. As we descended, the air grew thicker, colder. Ta'herah's eyes narrowed, her lip curling in distaste. "There are… remnants of angry, seething energies here. Spirits, maybe. Some are human, but others are dark, forgotten abominations."

She didn't need to elaborate. The weight of the ancient evil that breathed here clung to the walls, saturating the space with an oppressive energy that seemed to close in with each step. After three flights of stairs, we came to another floor. The hallways here were lined with heavy iron doors, some still intact, others hanging off their rusted hinges.

Through the slivers of darkness beyond those doors, I caught glimpses of what lay forgotten in those rooms: chains dangling from the ceilings, tattered straitjackets abandoned in corners, old gurneys, broken wheelchairs… But what truly made nails scrape down my back was the rusted, white metal crib with a worn, black vinyl mattress in the middle of a dark, empty, crumbling room, like a relic left over from some long-ended war. The thought of a baby once having laid in there made my gust twist. This was supposed to be a mental hospital for adults. Why was there a crib in there?

The stench of mildew and something far fouler reached my nose and I retched, bile rising in my throat. Chaz and Ta'herah gagged as well.

The members leading us deeper into the bowels of this cursed place snickered at our disgust.

I clenched my teeth. This place was beyond deprived, and if Kyle had been telling the truth, and this *was* where the rebirthing ritual was about to take place, the mere thought of my baby being down here made me want to rip out of my shackles and slaughter every deplorable human being that dwelled here.

But there was nothing I could do, at least not yet. I knew that if I tore my wings free and let my angelic power flare in my veins, I could potentially take out the guards escorting us, but not before they hurt Chaz and Ta'herah. I had to bide my time; I had to at least confirm that the show they'd promised us was in fact the rebirthing ritual.

Then, and only then, would I risk it all to save my son.

Chaz shot me a look, his eyes dark with understanding. I smiled inwardly. Glad the big guy and I were on the same page.

We reached another staircase and went down another two flights, my heart beating faster every time I thought about how deep underground we were, as if this place was literally descending into hell. The flickering lights above us dimmed further, and Kyle turned his head slightly, enough where I was able to read his lips as he mouthed the word *sub-basement.*

My insides recoiled. I couldn't fully read him. One minute it seemed he'd rejoined his brethren, and the next, he seemed recommitted to helping our cause.

With terrified eyes, I stared at the condition of what Kyle had just claimed was the sub-basement, the location of the pit, where the rebirthing was to take place. The floors were rougher, torn up, as if some demon had clawed itself out of the earth to make its home down here—a place now reeking of sulfur and death. That unseen, oppressive presence was more potent this deep, and I never wanted to bolt and run away from somewhere more than I did at that moment.

Ahead of us, the corridor opened into a wide chamber. The room was vast, the ceiling arched high above, but the center of the room was sunken in, like an amphitheater surrounded by rows upon rows of spectators. What little light there was seemed to come from strange, twisted iron sconces set into the walls, casting a sickly greenish glow that only made everything seem more monstrous.

The center of the chamber was dominated by an altar—a massive structure carved from black stone. Runes I couldn't decipher glowed a faint red light along the surface, pulsating with a rhythm that set my teeth on edge. Attached to the altar were iron manacles secured to the stone by chains.

This was it—the heart of the pit. Where the rebirthing was to take place.

The whole room seemed to quiet upon our entrance, the multitude of seated, cloaked individuals spinning around at the same time to stare at me and my companions. My wings twitched instinctively, as if sensing danger. They ached to unfurl, but I held them back.

Not yet. Not yet.

A hooded man stood at the center of the pit, looking up at us, the alter looming behind him. Next to him was another man, also hooded, but kneeling before the alter and with his back to us. The one who faced us lowered his hood, revealing an old, weathered face framed by thinning white hair that sat like a puff of cotton on his head. "Behold, my children," he announced. "Our guests of honor have arrived."

The man kneeling beside him rose to his feet, his movements slow and steady until he stood at his full height. When he turned around and lowered his hood, my world burned to cinders. Eyes the color of freshly-spilled blood stared back at me through an unfamiliar gaze, but the rest of him…

The rest of him was unmistakable.

The man standing at the bottom of the pit cloaked in Devil's Army ritual regalia and holding a baby—*our* baby—in his arms, was Jax.

Chapter Twenty-Four

CLINT

We managed to slip through a small window at the back of the building which emptied us into a long-forgotten, small storage room. The tight enclosure was dark, and the atmosphere hit me like a punch to the gut. It reeked of mold, a sickening combination of decades of neglect and rotting wood. I glanced at Kelsey, whose face was pale, her lips pressed together in a thin line. She mentioned kids used to hide in this place, but as she learned one night, hiding was useless.

At night, the corridors were patrolled by what she called an az'guhrath, some type of demonic beast in charge of making sure the kids didn't stray at night—so no one tried to escape or tried to break in.

Hank huffed as he sniffed at the crack at the bottom of the door. *Was such a creature patrolling the hallways now? Only one way to find out.*

I gently pulled the rickety door open, a soft creak echoing down what Kelsey claimed was the children's dormitory hall. It stretched out in front of us, narrow and lined with rusting metal doors. The fluorescent lights above flickered weakly, casting just enough light to make the shadows twist and move like they had a mind of their own. I tried keeping the creaking to a minimum, but the damn door was too loud, far too loud in the otherwise silent corridor.

We didn't even have a chance to exit the storage room before we heard it.

A low, guttural growl reverberated from the far end of the hallway, followed by a slow, heavy dragging sound—like claws scraping across the floor. "Get behind me," I muttered to Kelsey, already raising my crossbow. Thankfully, before leaving Mara's body behind, I'd recouped some of the bolts I'd used on the wraiths.

Hank lowered his head, a growl rumbling in his throat. His hackles were raised, and every muscle in his body was tense, ready for whatever was coming.

The creature skulked down the hall on four legs, its scaley skin reminding me of the banshees we encountered back when we were on the hunt for the sanctuary.

Damn. That seemed ages ago.

The demon's body was hunched, bones sticking out at odd angles, with limbs far too long for its twisted frame. Its face was skeletal, hollow eyes glowing bright red. Black ooze dripped from its mouth, and its claws were as long as daggers, scratching the ground as it lumbered toward us.

The demon let out a screech, its voice a twisted mix of human and animal, a sound that made my insides cringe. The monster was going to hit us head on, so I charged, slamming an empyrean fist into its chest, the force reverberating up my arm like a freight train. The demon shrieked, but its claws lashed out, catching my side and sending me flying against the wall, a sharp pain shooting through my body as I landed on the ground with a crunching *thud*, plaster debris falling around me.

Whirling around, the creature was about to pounce but

Hank darted forward, snarling, his jaws clamping onto one of the beast's limbs, and with a savage shake of his head, he tore it clean off.

Holy shit.

Black blood sprayed everywhere as the demon staggered. I took the opportunity to aim and shoot my crossbow, the bolt embedding itself right between its eyes. The demon let out a final shriek before collapsing into a heap of twitching limbs and dissolving into ash.

Kelsey hobbled over. "Clint, are you alright?"

I wiped the black goo from my arm and flinched as I stood and the gash on my side pulled open, sending fresh jolts of pain spiderwebbing across my entire upper torso. "I'm alive, so I guess that means I'm okay."

She wrapped her arms around my neck and hugged me tightly. "You idiot! You scared the living shit out of me."

For a moment, I allowed myself the reprieve and returned her embrace, even if it hurt to lift my arms. I simply relished the feel of her body pressed against mine. God, she felt amazing. "Just a scratch."

"That was a fucking high order demon. It could've shredded you to pieces."

Grunting from the pain, I pulled away. "It didn't. Thanks to Hank."

"Yeah, another idiot," she said, rubbing behind Hank's ears as he stuck his snout between us. "Let's just hope all that commotion didn't alert any guards."

"Then we better get moving. Hank, let's find Kate."

As Hank put his snout to the ground and began sniffing, Kelsey's attention was snatched by one of the closed metal doors we passed. Inching closer, she pressed her face against the small, grimy glass view port and her breath hitched, hands shaking as she tried to see through. "Oh God," she whispered, her voice barely audible.

I peeked inside and couldn't help the sharp inhale. Rows

of beds lined the wall, children laying on top. Some seemed asleep while others were tied down to their beds, their tiny forms writhing in what looked like nightmares. A few were motionless, too still. I couldn't tell if they were alive. "The fuck is this?"

She backed away from the door, her hand covering her mouth as she sank to the floor, chest rising and falling so fast, she looked like she was hyperventilating. Her body shook like she was about to break apart.

"Kelsey—"

"This place—" she cut herself off, a sob breaking free. "I was locked up here. Just like them. I saw... I saw things. Horrible things. They-they *did* horrible things to me, Clint." She lifted her gaze to mine and my heart shattered. The absolute terror embedded in her gaze dropped me to my knees.

Tears welled in her eyes, her breath hitching harder as if the memories were suffocating her. "My niece. She could be in one of these rooms."

"We'll find her."

She grabbed my arm. "I... was her age, Clint, when one of them took me... I was seven, when he..." She couldn't finish the sentence, but she didn't have to. I could only imagine the atrocities committed against her.

I took her into my arms and held her tight. "I'm so sorry, Kels. I'm sorry you had to grow up in this hell. That these people hurt you. That I wasn't there to protect you."

"I... can't let them do that to her."

Pulling her back a little, I wiped the tears from her eyes. "We'll get her out, Kelsey. I swear it. We're gonna get all these kids out."

"You promise you'll help me?"

I took her chin in my fingers and leaned in so close our breaths became one. "I promise you, I will tear this place apart until every single child in here is safe."

Her body shook, and before I realized what was happening, she pressed her lips to mine. It wasn't planned; I hadn't meant to lean in that close. But I also wasn't able to fight against her kiss—not when she melted into my arms, her fingers clutching my shirt as if I were her lifeline.

When her mouth parted, her tongue reaching out to brush mine, a moan rumbled through me. Fuck me. This wasn't it. This wasn't how I had envisioned kissing her. Not after knowing who she was, what she'd done. Not when we were covered in demon blood. Definitely not while we were in a fucking broken down, haunted asylum where children were being held captive and were likely being tortured. When we were supposed to be helping Kate escape while also stopping Satan from being reborn.

Shit.

But when I tasted her wet, salty lips, my mind went wild. Every fiber in my body shot to attention and I hated that I needed to pull away from her, away from this delicious heat spreading from my chest, reaching like tentacles to all my extremities… all the way down to my…

Fuck. I had to stop this. Had to pull away from the male need hankering to be sated. Maybe it was all the adrenalin running through our veins that made it hard to end the kiss, but we both knew this was not the time, nor place, to explore this—us—further.

"Kels…"

"Don't," she said, breathless. "I know what you're going to say."

I took her chin into my fingers again and forced her to look at me. "You know shit. Have you any idea how long I'd been dying to kiss you? But if we're going to do this, if I'm to kiss you right, it isn't going to be on this cursed floor. In this fucking place."

"We don't know if we'll even have tomorrow."

"Oh, Goldilocks, I never enter a game I don't think I can win. Now, get your ass up. We're going to go stop this fucking ritual, save my friends, then we're coming back here and rescuing every one of these children, including your niece."

"I don't think I can leave them, Clint. What if another of those demons shows up? Or a guard?"

I pulled her up to her feet. "I'm not leaving you here alone. And rescuing these kids won't matter if we can't stop the ritual. I promise, we'll come back. You have my word."

She nodded, her gaze lingering over the row of doors lining the walls. Sadness clung to her like a lead cloak, but she knew there was nothing we could do right now. There was no way we could safely walk out of this building with all these children without alerting the Devil's Army. Not to mention, where would we go from here? Into the night where hellhounds, zombies, and all other sorts of demons lurked?

If we were to have a chance at helping any of these kids then we needed to finish what we came here to do.

Kelsey's breath was ragged beside me, her face tight with pain as she limped along, favoring her injured ankle. Every step was an effort, and it tore at me to see her like this. Hank trotted ahead, nose to the ground as we made our way through the shadowed asylum halls. The walls felt like they were closing in on us, their peeling paint and water damage stains reminders of this building's long history. Every dark room we passed reeked of fear, of suffering long gone but not forgotten.

"I hate the way this place makes me feel," I said as we passed another room, a lone, abandoned metal bed frame sitting in the middle, a relic that anchored this place's despicable past to the present. "This asylum should've been demolished ages ago. Perhaps then the spirits still lingering here might've been able to find rest."

"That's the reason it *wasn't* demolished. These tortured souls are what allowed the Devil's Army to use it as the location for the pit. It's also what enabled the Devil's Army to acclimate kids to the horrors of hell. The thin veil made it easier for us to traverse into the Wastes."

"Acclimate? That's an interesting way to put it."

"You *don't* acclimate; you simply learn to survive. Most of us just shove the trauma into a closet. Some of us grow up and do the same shit to the new kids, while the rest of us try to find ways to get as far away from this place as possible."

"I'm sorry we forced you to come back."

"If I can save those kids from the shit I went through, it's worth it."

We moved forward in silence for another few minutes until Hank alerted us to a potential threat. Kelsey leaned against the wall as I peeked around the corner of an intersection. Five Devil's Army soldiers stood just ahead, seemingly unaware of our presence. Their black cloaks caught the dim light from the flickering bulbs above. Hank's fur bristled as he let out a soft growl next to me. "Easy, buddy."

With Kelsey hurt and barely able to move, we were at a severe disadvantage, even if we had a demon-killing German Shepherd on our side. All five of the guards were heavily armed with rifles. I checked my bolts—definitely not enough with barely a handful left. I flexed the fingers on my empyrean hand. Even with the strength the metal afforded me, there was no way I could take them all without putting Kelsey in danger. But what other choice did I have?

"You can't fight them all," Kelsey whispered, as if she could read my thoughts. Her face was white as a ghost, lips drawn tight.

"I don't see any other way," I muttered, looking down at Hank, his sharp ears twitching. He knew it, too.

Just as I was ready to commit to a reckless charge, a shadow tore through the soldiers like a lightning bolt. A whirlwind of motion shredded them apart, and before I could register what happened, bodies lay crumpled on the ground in twisted heaps. A figure emerged, tall and covered in blood, but unmistakable.

Khai-runē.

I blinked, not quite believing it. She had survived the nightcrawler attack. The Aetherian rider straightened, powerful and imposing, wiping blood off her blade as if she had done this a thousand times before. But when she spoke, it was in her Aetherian tongue, and I had no idea what the hell she was saying.

I shrugged, but she just motioned for us to follow.

Glancing at Kelsey, I said, "She seems to know where to go."

Kelsey nodded, though I could see the fatigue lining her face. She limped even harder now, each step slower than the last. Then I spotted it—an old wheelchair, rusted but seemingly functional—in the corner of the hall. I rushed toward it, the metal handles feeling unnaturally cold to the touch, but I had to shake the eerie sensation running over my fingers. We needed speed, and with her injury, there was no other option.

"Here," I said, bringing the chair to her. She didn't protest, plopping her ass on the black vinyl seat. She was too exhausted for pride now. "I'll push."

The chair squeaked and rattled as I maneuvered it down the narrow, ghostly corridors, every creak of its wheels echoing off the walls like whispers from the dead. Khai-runē led the way, her silent presence more commanding than any words.

Finally, we reached a staircase that descended deeper into the asylum, and Hank's ears perked up. His tail wagged furiously; nose pressed to the ground—he had picked up Kate's scent.

The Aetherian rider scouted up ahead before returning and giving us the universal nod that meant all was clear. I helped Kelsey off the chair and down the stairs, while Khai-runē carried the chair down. Hank trotted beside her.

We traversed through another maze of halls, letting Hank lead the way, his pace quickening as the scent he was chasing seemed to grow stronger. We increased our pace to keep up, but eventually the ground became too uneven. The tiles were broken, the exposed dirt underneath making it difficult to wheel the chair through. "You'll need to do the rest on foot," I said apologetically, as if it was my fault.

"It's fine," she replied, pushing herself up. "I remember this place. We're close to the pit."

After another few short minutes, we finally arrived at a set of double doors, massive and foreboding, with wards faintly shimmering in the dim light. I could feel the power thrumming through them. "Fuck," I muttered, stepping back. "How the hell are we supposed to get through?"

Kelsey's hand gripped my arm. "Let me try."

She shook, both from pain and, no doubt, from the memories this place was dredging up, but we were running out of time—if we weren't already too late. Limping forward toward the wards, her breath steadied as she reached under her shirt and opened the bandage covering her wound.

"Kels, what are you doing?"

She winced as she dipped her fingers inside the gash. "Blood," she croaked. "Every spell requires a price."

"Do you even know what you're doing?"

"I've seen my brother practice. I know the runes, the words." She looked over her shoulder, her gaze challenging. "Unless you have a better idea?"

My shoulders sagged. I didn't.

Raising her bloodied fingers, she began tracing symbols in the air. She tapped on the erected wards, but her fingers were zapped by the flickering shield. "Shit," she uttered, sucking on her fingertips. "That fucking hurt."

"What's the matter?"

"It's a little more complex than I thought. I need to concentrate. Figure out the correct order of the runes."

"You've got this," I whispered, though it felt more like a prayer. "Just take a breath."

Suddenly, Hank and Khai-runē whirled toward the hall where we'd come from.

"What is it?" I asked, though neither the rider nor the dog could answer me. But I didn't need them to tell me anything, I could already see what lurked in the shadows. "Fucking hell."

"Clint… what's going on?"

"You keep working on those wards, Goldilocks. Whatever you hear, don't stop. Your job is to get us through that shield."

"What's yours?"

"To make sure we survive to see what's on the other side."

Chapter Twenty-Five

KATE

"Bring them," the high priest ordered.

Our captors dragged and pushed us down the steps toward the center of the amphitheater. Lanterns flickered along the rows of seats, the flames casting baleful shadows over faces twisted in reverence, breaths bated in silent worship, gazes tracking every step we took, as if watching precious lambs being marched to slaughter. The pit loomed before me, as if it had always known I'd come. And at the heart of this gateway to hell, standing before the altar made of wet, black stone, stood the man I loved, holding our child.

"Jax..." The word slipped from my lips in a gentle summon, hoping that somehow the man I knew and loved was still somewhere inside that demon-possessed body. Heavens. It had been mere days since I'd last seen Jax, but it may as well have been years. He looked like he'd dropped thirty pounds; the robe he wore seemed to hang off bony shoulders. Ashen skin was streaked with grime, and his gaunt face and sunken eyes shattered my heart. He looked like he'd aged a decade or two.

He was a ghost of himself, and I couldn't even imagine what he might have gone through these last few days, what manner of torture he was subjected to be this broken. Whatever demon had taken over his body was leaching the life out of him. I wanted to roar, wanted to dig my hands into his chest and rip out the demon's essence with my bare hands.

I tried to take a step toward him, desperately needing to touch him—to feel his skin, to know he wasn't completely lost—but the individual holding my son stared at me with utter indifference, like I was not even standing before him. I nearly buckled to the ground. How many more times would I need to keep losing the people I loved to this hellish plague?

Then a soft cry leaked from the bundle cradled in his arms. Luke's tiny fingers poked out from the red blanket he was wrapped in. A sharp exhale burst from my lungs, my soul aching to reach for him, to hold him in my arms. It was physically excruciating to stand with my hands shackled behind my back and not be able to soothe my baby. "Please," I begged, trembling. "Let me hold him."

The man who wasn't my Jax simply continued to stare right through me, dank coldness glossing over the surface of his eyes like a lake made of ice.

This onslaught of heartbreak after heartbreak was too much for any person to bare. It needed to stop. I needed to end it, or I would not survive through this night.

"Katherine Elizabeth Jones," the high priest crooned, pulling me from my spiral, his voice a blade wrapped in velvet. His robes rustled as he stepped forward, dark eyes flickering with a sinister glow. "What an unexpected pleasure to see you here."

I flicked my gaze from my baby to meet his. "Where else would I be, you maggot? You have my family."

"*Your* family? How presumptuous of you. This child does not belong to you—you weren't even supposed to bear children. It is because of Samael that you can even call yourself a mother, Kathrine. Your lover's soul belonged to Samael long before the traitor ever met you. It was Jackson's demon seed that fathered this child. Luke belongs to us. You have no claim to him. None."

My nostrils flared, and I squared my shoulders, breath hitching. "I *grew* him in *my* body. I felt him *move* inside *my* womb. *I* birthed him, right out of my fucking vagina. So, pardon me if I don't give a shit about your paternal rules. Luke *is* my son, and neither you nor Samael can change that."

The priest grinned, anger dripping like acid from his lips. "You'll be fun to break."

I sneered. "What kind of person delights in torturing others? You hide behind your spells and twisted rituals, but deep down, you're just another scared, power-hungry coward."

"You do have quite the tongue on you, but your sedition ends here, woman. You've caused enough trouble as it is. It's time you learned the consequences for fucking with the Devil's Army."

"If you hurt my son or Jax, I *will* gut you."

His eyes softened over me, something like pity washing over them. "Women like you are a nuisance to the world. Look around you. You're defeated. Your friends will pay with their lives because of your pigheadedness. Because you thought yourself mightier than the Devil." He leaned in close, his breath reeking of days' old smoke. I cringed in disgust. He was taken aback and glowered. "Oh, I will enjoy watching Samael wring every gasping breath from your pitiful lungs."

My body tensed at his words, but I didn't let him bait me. He wanted me unhinged, but I would not give him the satisfaction, not yet at least.

Next to me, I could feel the heat of Ta'herah's rage. She too was holding back, but it wasn't hard to read the damage she envisioned she'd unleash on this priest. Chaz also trembled with fury; his jaw clenched so tight I thought his teeth might crack.

Kyle, though, breathed steadily, holding the high priest's gaze as the robed man approached him. "I hear *thanks* are in order, loyal servant. They tell me it was you who gave Khama'el the location of the stones."

Kyle looked around the amphitheater, scanning the entire enclosure. "I did. But where is the Power and his sicarii? I wanted to personally thank him for abandoning me at *La Sagrada Familia*. If he hadn't, I wouldn't have been able to bring you this gift." His gaze slithered in my direction.

"Despite aligning themselves with Samael, their essence is still too holy for this place."

I wanted to bare my teeth at the bastard, but another part of me realized what Kyle had done. He'd gotten the priest to confirm there were no angels present. Without the sicarii here, we stood a better chance, even if that chance was minuscule at best.

One of the guards dropped the leather-wrapped weapons on the ground with a loud *clank*.

"Be careful with those," Kyle warned. "Emrandael is in there. She can be temperamental, or so I hear."

The priest's eyebrows hiked, eyes flooding with greedy desire. "Mikha'el's legendary sword… A splendid gift, indeed."

"For our lord," Kyle added, eyes narrowed.

The priest laughed nervously. "Yes, yes. Of course."

Kyle pulled on his restraints. "Is there a reason you still see fit to bind me, high priest? It is my honor to serve you, to serve my king. Let me worship at the altar as a true believer. Or have I not proven my worth by not only bringing you the woman who bore the child, but empyrean weapons as well?"

The priest clasped his hands behind his back, his gaze darkening. "Oh, Samael will be greatly pleased. But do elaborate. How were you able to traverse the ocean so quickly?"

Kyle nodded toward Ta'herah. "Alien technology from another realm."

The priest eyed the Aetherian thoroughly, as if examining an oddity, rubbing his chin as his slimy gaze lingered over her muscles and stature. "While I believe you gave Khama'el the location of the stones, I find it hard to believe this alien warrior and the Marine," he said, toying with Chaz's dog tags, "plus *this* woman…" he paused as he stood before me, sneering as if I was a vile, filthy creature, "were brought here *by* you."

The priest smiled mirthlessly while he circled Kyle. "I know who you are, and I know why you gave Khama'el the information—a bargain to buy yourself a trip back home. But you missed your train, and now you think me so stupid that I would believe a grunt like yourself would be capable of capturing the anointed one and bringing her *and* her friends here as *your* captives?"

All Kyle could do was swallow thickly, his eyes darting around the room as if he was expecting someone… "I promised I would help her stop the ritual, but it was a lie. I planned to hand her over to you as soon as we were through the wards."

Two men emerged from the shadows, one holding a woman and another holding a young girl.

Kyle's face went pale, a sheen of sweat coating his forehead. "What are you doing?"

"I hope you understand why I can't just take your word. I can't risk this ritual going wrong. Now, tell me who else is here. Who accompanied you? Answer wisely, or your daughter's neck will be sliced first." As if to show he was serious, he nodded to the cloaked man holding the girl, who then yanked her head back, exposing her neck as he put a knife to her throat.

"Daddy!"

Kyle fought against his restraints, the veins in his neck

looking like they were ready to pop. "It's okay, baby. It's gonna be okay."

The woman, presumably his wife, whimpered as her head was also pulled back. "Kyle, please. Just tell him whatever he wants to know."

"You bastard," Kyle seethed at the priest. "Let them go. They're innocent. They have nothing to do with this."

The priest stalked closer. "Tell *me* what I need to know, or you will become a childless widow all in a moments breath."

Life leached from Kyle's face as he let his head hang to his chest. "There *were* others, but we lost them on our way here."

"How many?"

"Four," he lied. I understood Kyle knew the risk he was taking, knew the sacrifice this would cost him if the priest found out he lied. But the man was grasping for hope, hope that perhaps Clint, Kelsey, Mara, and Hank were still alive. That maybe there was a chance we could all still make it out of this.

"And you believe them to be dead?"

Kyle raised his gaze, his lips pulled back in a snarl. "Yes. We were attacked by a horde of undead, then by a pack of hellhounds at the diner in the center of town."

The priest sucked in a deep breath and adjusted his cloak. "And why should I believe *you*?"

"Because I'm a man with everything to lose. But just have your people check. They'll confirm I'm telling you the truth. You'll find the bodies."

The priest didn't look half convinced. "Kill the woman."

Kyle's spine went rigid, his eyes wild. "Wait, what? No! Oh God, no."

Terror gripped my spine as we all watched the man holding Kyle's wife drag her to the center of the ritual circle. The woman screamed, pleading for her life.

Sobs choked Kyle's voice as he begged the priest to stop. "Please don't do this, please! Kill *me*! Kill *me*!"

But it was too late. Her life was snuffed out with the slice of a blade across her throat, her body dropping to the floor with an unceremonious flop. She seemed to gasp for air as blood flooded out of her neck like a river breaking through a dam.

Face wet with tears, Kyle's eyes flared in horror as he watched his wife's life leak out of her. He shook, tremors raking his entire body, then he fell to his knees. "Oh, darling… I'm so sorry. I'm so sorry."

"For the record," the priest said, looking down at Kyle's miserable, whimpering body. "I do believe you were telling me the truth. *That* was for the trouble you caused this coterie by bringing this unfaithful lot here. The veil is the thinnest at full rise, and you've caused us precious minutes dealing with your transgressions."

"You didn't have to kill her," Kyle seethed.

"I didn't, but I *did*. And it would serve you well to know your place here, lest you want your daughter to meet the same fate." He turned to his guards. "Remove him and his dead wife from the circle, but seat him at the front with his daughter. Let them bear witness to the birth of our king."

Watching Kyle's defeated body be dragged away, his feet brushing against the blood soaking the ground, made my chest tighten with grief. I knew that pain, knew what it was like to watch someone you loved die before your eyes. I turned to Jax one more time, my voice cracking when I tried uttering his name. It was barely a sound above a whisper, but the beast finally blinked, acknowledging me.

A cruel smile curved on my lips, a grin that was all sharp teeth and venom. "I know he's inside you, and I know he can hear me. It won't be long before he rips through your consciousness and sends you back to hell."

"Or I rip through his," the beast uttered in a voice too calm to be human, a voice too similar to Jax's that it sent icy shockwaves rippling down my vertebrae. "He will die tonight. As will your son."

I lunged for the demon, but the chains holding me shackled were yanked back. "I will kill you before I let you hurt my baby!"

"Silence!" the high priest barked, his attention shifting to me. "You. Will. Do. Nothing. I've had enough of your insolence. Tie her to the stone. It's time we got this ritual underway."

I thrashed as two men grabbed me by the arms, but my strength faltered. I couldn't understand it. My angelic abilities were failing me. I couldn't stop them. Not as they dragged me to the altar, not as they lifted me onto the stone, nor as they strapped me to the cold, unforgiving slab. The chains tightened around my wrists, biting into my skin, snuffing out the power that coursed through me.

My wings… I couldn't feel them at my back anymore. The starlight power that burned in my veins didn't respond. "What did you do to me?"

"The wet-looking veins in the stone, sweetheart," one of the guards said with mirth as he secured the latch around my wrists. "It's raw iron."

"Raw iron?"

The high priest peered down at my spread-eagle body. "Iron is the antithesis to angelic power. It takes high quantities of the substance, or an expert smith to craft the perfect shackles, to nullify an angel's power, but you… You're not fully an angel; you're just an anointed one. Just being near it is enough to render you… well, render you defenseless. Another useless woman in the end."

"If I'm so useless, why not just kill me? Why strap me to this rock?"

"Well, maybe you do have one more role to play. See, all magic requires a sacrifice, and before Samael can take his vessel, he must first drink the blood of a still-beating heart—

Kyle's daughter was supposed to serve that purpose. Purity is power, and nothing's purer than a child. But then you decided to crash the party, and it got me thinking… What is grander than a child's purity, but the fierceness of a mother's love. Samael needs power, strength, and taking yours will be more than retribution for your sins; it will be poetic justice."

Panic clawed at my throat as I struggled against the restraints, my breath coming in shallow gasps. The only thought reverberating inside my skull was that of Luke. My baby. I'd finally found him. I'd crossed through time and space; I'd battled the undead and slaughtered demons. But in the end, I hadn't been able to protect him from these people, to rescue him from the Devil's clutches.

I'd failed my family when it had counted the most.

My eyes darted toward Jax, who stood unnaturally still beside the high priest. His eyes burned red, and it tore my soul to shreds. This was all up to him now. Jax needed to find a way to save his son—to save humanity. He needed to prevent this rebirth. He'd fought Astaroth's compulsion once, and he could fight again.

He had to.

He fucking had to.

Tears trickled from my eyes and spilled down the side of my face, but the wetness coating my cheeks wasn't self-pity. That wetness was utter rage—rage at not being able to rip myself off this stone slab and ram Emrandael straight through the high priest's gut.

All I could do now was hope that, somehow, through our bond, through our ability to simply know what the other was thinking with a mere gaze, I could reach Jax's soul and push him to fight. To fight with every ounce of himself, even if nothing remained in the end, because despite my love for him, despite my love for my son, despite wanting to share a life with them both, I was ready to lay my life down for them.

We had to stop Samael at any cost.

I clenched my teeth and bore my hardened eyes into his. He was still in there; he had to be. *You are not your mother's son. And you would also never treat your son like your father treated you. You would never sacrifice your family for this. So, wake up, Jax. Wake the fuck up. Wake. Up!*

With a lifeless expression, Jax drew nearer to the altar. "He's locked up in a dream loop. He can't hear your desperate pleas."

I trembled. "Release him."

That impossible coldness in his eyes cracked me in half. There were no traces of Jax in there. None.

Please… God.

The demon tilted his head. "He can't help you, either. This will all be over soon. Accept your fate, Kate. We all have."

"No. Jax, this isn't you. Don't do this. Wake up! Please, wake up!"

A hard *whack* burned across my face, sending a piercing shriek ringing through my ears. Hot tears welled up in my eyes, and I could barely discern the outline of the figure who stood beside me. It was like looking through a glass filled with water.

Blinking away the wetness, I finally made out the scrunched up, wrinkled face of the high priest. He shook his hand, cradling it like he'd injured himself slapping me across the face. "You will obey when I tell you to be silent, or I will make sure to shatter your jaw into grains of bone the next time you utter a single word."

Satisfied with himself, he faced his congregation. "My brothers and sisters," he began, his voice dark and somber, like a dirge carrying over the sea of robed figures. "Tonight, we stand on the edge of a new world. The time has come to finally complete the purification of our people." He slid his gaze to me, his face twisted in disgust. "*This* woman sought to stop us, but in her desire to sully our sacred rite, in her quest to prevent the rebirth of our king—the one and *only* true king —she has succeeded in offering herself as the lamb."

The crowd stirred in a low, guttural rumble, a sound that seemed to rise from the very earth beneath them. The priest outstretched his arms and spoke into the gathered mass again. "But first, let those who have been chosen come forth, for we must now call upon the Four Horsemen to prepare the way."

As the high priest's words echoed through the chamber, the worshippers began to beat their feet against the stone floor in unison, creating a deep, rhythmic thudding that reverberated through the pit. It was slow at first, almost like the pulse of a heart, but with every passing moment, it grew faster, more frantic, as though they were summoning some ancient evil from the depths of hell…

Because they were.

But how? Beleth and Chemoth were the only ones I remembered had survived and sent back to Abaddon.

Four young bare-chested men were dragged forward, each wearing the cold expressions of those who had given themselves willingly to the cause, ready to become vessels for Samael's lieutenants—yet again. The priest gestured to them as they took their places at each of the four points of the pentagram that had been drawn in front of the altar, and a different young man was made to kneel on the fifth point.

"To each of these chosen, we will gift the power of Creation," the priest continued, raising his arms as someone brought forth the first pendant—the Fire stone. My mouth went dry. This was it. They were going to use all four Creation Stones to fully open the Gates so Samael could pass through from Abaddon.

One by one, the high priest placed the Earth, Water, and Air Creation Stones around the necks of the remaining three men, each pendant glowing with its power. The priest's eyes gleamed in the dim light as the pounding of fists against chests began, the dull *thud* of flesh meeting flesh, a sound that grew louder and more chaotic, filling the air with a wild, fevered energy.

The noise rolled through the amphitheater like a storm, building in intensity as they chanted in what I believed to be the angel's ancient tongue, their voices merging into a single, terrifying roar. "Shlama l'Samael, Shlama l'malka didan." Over and over, they chanted until at last, the priest was given a long, ceremonial-looking knife.

He walked toward the man already prepared for his death, kneeling on the fifth point of the pentagram. Staring blankly at the ceiling of the chamber, he took one breath before the blade came down swiftly, slicing through his throat with a sickening sound that echoed through the amphitheater. Blood gushed, thick and dark, pooling into a silver bowl. My stomach churned, bile rising in my throat, but I couldn't look away.

The blood was passed to the four men, each one taking an oath to serve Samael before drinking from the bowl without hesitation. Their bodies stiffened, their eyes rolling back into their heads as the magic took hold. The pendants flared brighter, glowing like embers, and the high priest raised his arms in praise, chanting in the angel tongue—a language older than this world, older than time.

The ground trembled beneath me, and from the very air, a cold wind began to swirl, carrying with it the scent of rot and sulfur. The altar vibrated beneath my back, the stone cold against my skin as I watched, horrified, as a portal began to form behind the altar. The air rippled and tore open like a wound, revealing a darkness so deep it seemed to consume the very light around it.

From that swirling black hole, four shadowy figures emerged—twisted and grotesque, their forms barely recognizable as they slithered and clawed their way into the bodies of the four men.

Screams erupted as The Horsemen took their vessels; the

poor idiots who had willingly given themselves did not realize until it was too late that there would be nothing left of their essence once the transmutation was complete.

The chants and rhythmic beating continued as The Horsemen shed their demonic skin like molting snakes, leathery wings transforming into luminous angelic feathers. Tall and proud, the reborn angels stood like sentinels at each of their points. I recognized Beleth right away, his gaze snagging on mine. The angel grinned, a promise of pain and death etched across his face.

My heart thundered in my chest, but the chains held firm. Desperately, I pulled against them, but the stone was sapping every ounce of energy I tried to summon. Jax, still standing at the altar, stepped forward, holding Luke in his arms. His face was blank, his eyes glowing that vibrant red, and I could barely breathe as he handed the baby to one of the robed figures standing beside the priest.

"No…" My voice cracked, barely a whisper, but Jax didn't even flinch. Didn't even hear me.

I looked for Chaz and Ta'herah, but they'd been dragged away from the altar and I couldn't tell where they were. Panic threatened to consume me. I forced myself to inhale slowly, steadily, but it was too hard to calm myself, hard to even think when the congregation continued to chant, continued to beat their boots against the concrete floor.

The priest's voice grew louder, and he turned his attention to me, a wicked smile curling his lips. "Barbatos, it is time to call forth our king."

Jax was given a blade—the same blade that had just taken that poor man's life—its edge glinting in the dim light. He stepped toward me with slow, deliberate steps, the blade gleaming in his hand. My heart lurched, terror gripping me in a vice as he leaned over me. He used the knife to cut my tank top down enough to reveal the flesh over my heart.

Then he sliced his palm, blood welling up before he

pressed it to my forehead, my arms, and over my heart, tracing symbols over my skin with his blood, chanting in that same ancient language.

"*Al tēsūg nafshah, libbah b'oz yachrotz, lev ha-chayyim l'Samael. Nifrotz basar v'dam, kapot ha-mavet aleha, b'or ha-chashecha tit'arev. B'eyn moshia, lev nokesh yishta'aved, nishmatah tihyeh l'Samael.*"

Even though I had no clue what he was saying, each word felt like a shard of ice, cutting deep into my soul. His eyes were vacant, hollow, and I struggled to find a trace of the man I loved in that gaze.

"Jax," I whispered, my voice trembling. "Please… you don't have to do this. Wake up, Jax, I'm begging you."

But he didn't stop. He drew more symbols across my chest and arms, blood mixing with the cold sweat on my skin, and as his chant grew louder, the crowd joined in, their voices rising in a fevered pitch.

I screamed as the symbols began to burn. "What are you doing to me?"

Jax's eyes glowed brighter. "Your heart and soul now belong to Samael."

The portal behind me pulsed, a swirling vortex of black energy. The wind howled, and suddenly, the very air seemed to tear apart, as though reality itself was shuddering under the weight of the dark magic being wielded here.

Samael, Seraphim of the First Sphere, First Son to the Father and Heir to the Throne of God, stepped through the gates of hell and into the mortal realm of the living.

Chapter Twenty-Six

CLINT

They emerged from the shadows, their forms nothing but tendrils of smoke, their cloaks whispering over the ground as they glided toward us. Their hollow faces were barely visible through the tattered blackness in the poorly lit hall, but I saw enough to know what they were. Death wraiths. Three of them.

"Don't let them touch you!" I warned Khai-runē. "If they even graze you, they will rip out your soul before you have a chance to fight back."

Khai-runē simply nodded and raised her sword, flames roaring to life along its edge, turning the blade into a searing line of light in the darkness. Shit. I'd forgotten she could wield fire. She'd been the one to give the Eldhon-rhā the element of fire to help power it. The Aetherian lunged at the closest wraith, slicing through its shadowy form. The creature screamed, a sound reminiscent of nails dragged over stone, but the fire worked. The wraith retreated, writhing in the air as its dark, misty form began to collapse.

Kelsey shot a glance over her shoulder, her eyes wide. "We're under attack by ruhadim?"

"Stay on the wards," I snapped at her. "We'll take care of the wraiths."

Hank bristled next to her, hackles raised, his low growl a warning to the creatures.

I took aim with my crossbow, my heart hammering in my chest, and fired at the second wraith. The bolt tore through its center, a burst of golden light flaring as the empyrean energy collided with the dark magic holding it together. The wraith screeched and twisted, its body unraveling into a cloud of smoke before disintegrating into nothing.

One bolt left.

The third wraith surged toward me, faster than I expected. My empyrean arm shot up instinctively, the metal gleaming as it caught the creature's ghostly limb. Cold shot through my entire body as the wraith's touch grazed the empyrean alloy, but the arm held. The wraith let out a frustrated hiss, and I swung with all my might, knocking it backward.

Before I could get another shot off, Khai-runē was there, her sword a blaze of fire as it carved through the wraith's chest. It screamed before dissolving into the darkness, leaving behind nothing but the lingering stench of decay.

I exhaled hard, lowering the crossbow, the last bolt still loaded. "You alright?" I asked the rider.

Another nod. Guess that's how we were communicating.

I rushed to Kelsey, my pulse racing, sweat soaking through my shirt.

Kelsey didn't respond right away. She was still kneeling, perspiration dripping down her temple. "Almost… there…" she muttered through clenched teeth, her fingers moving faster, brushing over the invisible wards like they were an unsolvable puzzle.

Something was making the ground rumble, like people

running or stomping their feet. And then, like the snap of a whip, the wards fell and the air around us shifted.

Kelsey slumped, panting. "Got it."

We stood there, frozen like icebergs, listening. The sound that met our ears—a rhythmic pounding, like a heartbeat, but deeper, more sinister—sent a shiver down my spine. And underneath it, chants. Dozens of voices, maybe more, all rising in unison.

The thumping behind the door grew louder, more urgent. The chants intensified, like the walls themselves were breathing with it. Kelsey rose to her feet with my help, her body shaking, her face a canvass of pure terror.

"What is it?" I asked her as the Aetherian rider joined us at the entrance right outside the door.

"The rebirthing… it's already started."

"Shit. We need to do something."

She put a hand over my arm. "We can't just barge in there, Clint. We need to think first. There are armed guards in there. Not to mention they've probably already summoned The Four Horsemen—"

"That's not possible. Kate killed Astaroth and Malphas back in New York, and Mikha'el dispatched Chemoth and Beleth back to Hell."

"To open the Gates, Samael needs Four Horsemen to wear the Creation Stones, it's the only way the portal will allow him through. Astaroth and Malphas were part of his court, yes, but they weren't his only lieutenants. Any high order demon can be given the honor. And if Beleth and Chemoth weren't killed but banished back to Hell, then they can take new vessels."

I felt my stomach bottom out. How the fuck were we supposed to fight off Four Horsemen? All I had were the two bolts I'd used to kill off the wraiths and my arm. Kelsey had a handgun, and Khai-runē… I looked at the Aetherian and she curved a subtle smile. From a small satchel, she retrieved four golf ball-sized metallic spheres. The insides of the spheres were a cluster of gears and pulsing light. She gestured with her other hand, mimicking throwing the spheres into the air, there being an explosion of some sort, then shielding her eyes.

Grenades? God, I love alien tech.

The chants intensified and I swore I could almost see the door vibrate with the sound. "What are they chanting in there?"

"Shlama l'Samael. Shlama l'malka didan."

"What does it mean?"

She lifted her chin, and everything within me went completely still. It was almost like she was afraid to translate the words, to utter them out loud. Breathing deeply, she finally whispered, her voice shaking, "Hail Samael. Hail our true king."

"That's gotta mean he's either out of Hell or about to come out. It's now or never."

She grabbed my arm again, tighter this time. "Wait. *Wait.* If we do this, we can't go in blasting through these doors. The coterie functions as a collective consciousness, and they really do take it to the next level during rituals. The chants act like a cognitive adhesive, holding their minds together as one.

"They are all practically trapped in a trance web. This is actually when they are at their weakest; it's why they ward everything off right before a ritual. If we stay quiet, and gently slide in through a crack in the doors, they might not even notice. We stick to the shadows and assess before we make a move."

If this was our best option, we were fucked. But then again, it wasn't like I had a different plan. Not when Samael was *literally* being summoned and we had *literally* run out of time. Puffing out a breath, I gently cracked the door open and a gush of deathly cold air brushed over us, and an uncomfortable shiver ran over my entire body.

I didn't have a good feeling about this, but this was why we'd come here, and there was no turning back now.

The chanting beyond the threshold was even more oppressive. "Shlama l'Samael. Shlama l'malka didan," they chanted. The entire chamber seemed to pulse with it, the vibration sinking into my bones.

We crouched in the shadows, barely moving. The amphitheater stretched out before us, tiered seating circling a stone altar at the center. Every seat was filled with worshippers, faces obscured by hooded robes, all of them staring down at the ritual taking place in the pit. They were, as Kelsey had said, trapped in a trance web.

No one looked in our direction as they hummed and chanted.

I took the opportunity to stalk closer and nearly choked on my own saliva when I spotted Kate bound to the black stone altar, iron chains holding her down. My gut twisted, every instinct in me screaming to run to her, but we couldn't. Not yet, at least. Hank shook next to me. He must have seen or scented Kate as well, but he waited patiently at my heel. All those months working with him during our trip in search of the sanctuary had paid off. He now saw me as a second handler.

I padded him on the neck, reassuring him he was doing a good job.

An old man faced the audience, his tall, lanky frame shrouded in dark robes, muttering incantations I couldn't understand. And next to him…

Shit. It was Jax, his eyes glowing bright red. And in his arms… a baby.

He was clearly possessed by something dark and twisted. My blood iced. Last time I'd seen him possessed, he'd been struggling for control, but I could still see *him.* This was different; it was as if all traces of the man I knew were gone.

Kelsey grabbed my arm, yanking me back to the present. "The Horsemen… they're here."

I scanned the pit, spotting the four men standing at each point of a massive five-pointed star etched into the floor. Each wore one of the four Creation Stones, and their bodies trembled as some type of black-as-night smoke entered their bodies through their mouths. One by one, each man transformed from demonic being to angels made flesh.

Holy fuck. I'd forgotten how huge and imposing they were.

Just then, I spotted more movement in a corner behind the altar. I risked a couple more steps to get a closer look and a wave a relief washed over me. Chaz and Ta'herah had been dragged off the circle and placed on their knees, hands bound behind their backs. The guards in charge of them seemed to have lost themselves to the ritual and were just as entranced as the rest.

Kelsey pulled us all back into the shadows where we all crouched again. I lowered my voice as much as possible. "I saw Chaz and Ta'herah."

"What about my brother?"

I shook my head, and my chest tightened when her gaze clouded with worry. "I'm sure he's down there, too."

My words didn't seem to offer much comfort, but she nodded and sucked in a deep breath, collecting herself. This was the Kelsey I knew, focused and battle ready. "Okay, look, from what I learned growing up here, the gates must remain fully open during the entire rebirthing ritual for Samael to come through and be able to stay in our realm long enough to take over his vessel. Which means the Horsemen must remain anchored to the pentagram the whole time. That gives us a window of opportunity to strike when they are at their most vulnerable, because once Samael takes his vessel, it's game over."

"But wouldn't he be an infant?"

"Obviously, this has never been done before, but my understanding is that once he takes the vessel, whatever dark powers he possesses will allow him to warp time. He'll become a fully-fledged Nephilim before our eyes—and once that happens, there won't be any stopping him, especially with all Four Horsemen at full strength."

"So, our only option is to strike before the rebirth."

She cocked her head in agreement. "Even down here, where the veil is thinnest and with the full moon looming, if one single stone is removed from the circle, the gates will be too unstable. Either Samael won't be able to get through or he'll simply get sucked back into Hell."

"Okay. Then all we need to do to stop Samael is kill at least one Horsemen and re-take his stone."

"That's a lot harder than it looks, Clint."

I raised a brow. No kidding, but at least we had some type of plan. "We split up. Kelsey, you and Khai take the left. Hank and I will go right. We're gonna disrupt the ritual, but we need to time it just right."

Khai-rune caught my gaze and gave me a tight nod, padding her satchel. Thank God for alien tech. In this place, it was probably the only thing that could level the playing field.

"Khai, wait for my signal to detonate those spheres. We only get one chance at this, and I need to make sure we have all our game pieces in play."

Kelsey grimaced. "What are you gonna do?

I patted Hank on the neck. "We're gonna play a little game of search and rescue. I'll flick my flashlight, that will be my signal. Khai will set off the spheres, and you will take cover while the rest of us figure out how to take down one of the Horsemen."

"Clint, I'm not going to just hide this out. My brother is down there."

"Kels, you can barely walk. You're only going to get yourself killed. If you want to help your brother, then don't make yourself a liability."

"I'm already a liability, what difference does it make?"

I took her face in my hands. "A hell of a lot. Kels, please. If not for him, do it for me. Promise me you won't do anything stupid. Promise me."

She blinked, lips trembling. It wasn't an answer, but it was all she would give me. Deep down, I knew she wasn't going to listen, so I did the only thing I could. I kissed her.

For a brief moment, the hell being raised around us didn't exist anymore. The chants faded, the rumble under out feet subsided. All that existed was me and her and this kiss. Her soft lips melded with mine, and I inhaled her breath until I felt her in my lungs, until I'd made her a part of me. If this was the last time I'd ever see her again, then I wanted her to know I'd forgiven her.

She ran her fingers through my hair. "Clint…"

"I'm sorry, Kels. Sorry that we didn't meet in a different world. Sorry that we didn't have more time. That I couldn't make you my girl."

She shook her head. "Don't you dare talk like that. We're gonna make it out of this."

I wrapped a beautiful golden curl around my finger and gazed upon every inch of her face, etching her to memory. "When this is all over, I'm taking you out on a proper date."

With misty eyes, she smiled. "Deal." Pistol in hand, she climbed to her feet and blew me a kiss before limping after Khai-runē.

A weight pressed on my chest, like someone had placed a boulder over my heart. Watching her disappear into the darkness was one of the hardest things I'd ever had to endure, but being heartsick wasn't going to save our asses.

Hank and I moved quietly, slipping along the edges of the amphitheater, keeping low and out of sight as the chants grew louder, more frantic. I peered down into the pit one more time, and this time, Jax was standing over Kate's body, writing sigils over her skin with what seemed like blood.

What the hell?

I froze in place, almost entranced like the rest of the fifty or so gathered Devil's Army members. A swirling vortex of dark smoke churned behind the altar, causing the air in the chamber to ripple in waves. Unable to peel my eyes away from the sight, I stared in paralyzing awe, hair spinning widely over my head.

A creature emerged from the black portal. Standing about eight feet tall, he towered over everyone. Charred flesh covered most of his face and extremities, and atop his head was a crown of bones fused right into his skull. Sickly looking wings hung off his naked back, dragging on the floor behind him as he walked bare-chested toward the altar. What were likely once beautiful white feathers were now covered in a black, oil-like substance.

Despite his terrifying presence, the creature's twilight eyes gleamed brightly, like a winter sunset over the ocean.

I must have forgotten how to breathe. From the way Kate had described him, this had to be Samael. Which meant we were now beyond the point of no return. If we didn't stop him now, all mankind was doomed.

In all my wildest dreams, I never thought I'd ever see the Devil in person—at least, I'd hoped I'd never have to. I couldn't deny that a part of me was stunned cold. He was hideous but also unbearably beautiful in the most unnatural and unholy way.

The temperature suddenly dropped drastically, as if an arctic winter had blown in out of nowhere. Hoar frost spread throughout the entire chamber, covering every surface in feathery ice crystals. I shivered violently. The air wasn't just brutally cold; the chill that took a hold of my body felt like it had been dragged from the coldest corners in the universe and was now seeping down into my marrow, splintering through it like an ice breaker.

Tiny ice crystals coated Hank's fur, and a part of me worried this cold might be too much for him, but the shepherd didn't seem phased.

A puff of cold breath billowed from my mouth as I continued to stare at the angel-turned-demon. My mind couldn't wrap itself around it. *This* was Samael, the angel who rebelled. The angel who was cast down from Heaven and thrown into Hell. The angel who hated my people with such ferocity, he'd staged an Armageddon and was now on the brink of ridding the earth of all mankind.

He was so frighteningly atrocious, yet at the same time, so earth-shatteringly majestic, that I almost wept imagining how glorious he must have been before he Fell.

Something darker than fear vice-gripped my spine.

This world stood no chance against him if he took God's throne. No chance at all.

He drew closer to Kate, whispering something to her I couldn't make out, but the horror tracing over her features was indication enough that his words were pulling her apart bit by bit. He placed a hand over her heart and Kate thrashed, hurtling words at him that sounded incoherent from where I stood.

Fuck. What the hell was happening?

Suddenly, the worshippers all fell to their knees in praise. I had to crouch lower to keep from being seen as the old man— or priest, whatever the fuck he was—took Luke into his arms and raised him high above, like some offering. The baby wailed; his shrieking cries a sordid reminder of what these people planned to do here.

Someone held a large, opened book before him, some-thing reminiscent of a Bible, except this one looked like it had been pulled from a gruesome nightmare. "Behold, brothers and sisters," he began, his voice resonating over the crowd as he looked down at the book and read from the pages. "In my hands, I cradle the answered prayer of our salvation—the child of prophecy, whose body will become the holy vessel for our Dark Lord, the ruler of all realms, and our one true king. Samael."

Samael took a step away from Kate, more hoar frost spreading from his body as he took in the crowd of worshipping sheep. Jax drew closer to Kate, hovering his hand over her heart as if he meant to rip it right out of her ribcage. Kate began thrashing again, her screams almost muffled by the growing chants that had grown into a rumbling crescendo of voices and stomps.

The priest lifted Luke higher, his voice booming as the congregation pounded their feet in unison. "For centuries, we have been the faithful, the chosen, bound by a sacred oath to deliver Samael's rebirth. And tonight, we stand at the brink of eternity, ready to tear the veil between worlds once and for all. Samael, our dark father, who was cast down in chains, shall rise again in all his terrible glory!"

The chants of the congregation throbbed like a living organism, all while Jax seemed to mumble his own words over Kate's body. My stomach churned with acid watching her scream, watching her pull at her restraints to the point she was ripping her skin, blood leaking from her wrists and soaking the altar.

"The time has come for the reckoning!" the priest went on. "This woman's heart—the lamb's heart—will be the key that unlocks the gates forever. And with his mortal and angelic bloodline, this Nephilim child will forge the holy bond between Heaven and Earth that not even God can undo."

The priest swiveled toward Samael. "My Lord. My king of kings. I, your faithful servant, offer you this child, this anointed vessel, as the gateway by which you shall be reborn and made flesh again."

Jax's fingers were pressing harder now, and I could see

Kate's flesh sizzle where his skin met hers. "From the lamb, the blood of life shall flow. And from that life, a new world reborn."

Despite the boisterous chants, Kate's screams could have shattered stone; her pain was so intense.

Luke wailed and wailed, but the priest simply held him up by the arms. "Tonight, brothers and sisters, we shall be witnesses to the unmaking of creation. We shall be Samael's instruments of wrath and destruction. Samael shall embody his new Nephilim form, and with the stones of Creation, he shall call forth the rest of his court and take over all the realms of the universe."

I clenched my jaw, my heart thundering. We had to stop this. We had to stop this now.

I reached into my jacket and pulled out a switch blade and placed it between Hank's jaws, then I pointed down to where Chaz and Ta'herah were still on their knees.

Hank panted hard, ears pinned back, body primed for the run as soon as I was ready to give the command.

From across the way, I caught sight of Kelsey and Khai-runē. They, too, seemed entranced by the rite. I pulled out a pen flashlight from my backpack and prayed everyone was too focused on the scene splayed out before them to notice as I flicked the flashlight on and off a couple of times. Kelsey tracked it to me immediately.

When our gazes met, I nodded.

Time to bring the rain.

Everything happened at once— Khai-runē's grenades went off, filling the amphitheater with brilliant flashes of light and fire. The coterie screamed, breaking from their trance as the dark magic faltered. Hank was already charging toward Chaz and Ta'herah, tearing through the chamber to deliver the switch blade to Chaz.

And I... I watched as everything plunged into utter chaos.

Chapter Twenty-Seven

KATE

Oh, God. The cold that blasted from the gates as Samael stepped through stabbed at my skin like sharp needles forged of fire and ice. My eyes stung from the biting cold, watering as I tried to blink, but I was still able to make out the sharp edges of the crown made of bones fused to his skull and the charred, crusted skin covering his features. I shuddered at the memory of my nightmare, of my visit to the Wastes when he'd shown me his true face—the one he wore now.

As a seraph of the first sphere, he was larger than any other angel of the lower spheres, taller than Mikha'el, though the archangel was more muscular and carved like a warrior than a pampered prince. Yet, despite the angelic beauty that had been stolen from him, Samael was still a sight to behold. There was no denying he'd been an angel once, if not the most beautiful of them all.

Seeing him here, though, in my world, felt wrong, as if his mere presence went against the natural order of things, because it *did*. Samael didn't belong here, and he knew it. He'd *always* known it, and it had been that knowledge, that truth—that God hadn't created this world for *him*—that had grated him since humans came into existence, had cut him like rusted blades against his once luminous, unmarred skin.

"Katherine…" My name on his lips sounded like a curse, and I recoiled at the sound. I hated that he was seeing me like this, chained to this altar. To him, I was likely nothing more than a broken, defeated woman, a weak and defenseless human.

He stalked closer to the altar, as if gliding on air, his diseased wings dragging behind him like a cloak sewn from the scorched flesh of rotting sinners. His bare chest was partially charred, some areas still smoldering under the surface, as if Hell's fires had never stopped consuming him. Yet, his chiseled form could not be obscured under all that burned skin—more proof of his lost perfection.

"Do you feel it, Daughter of Eve? The pull of destiny?" His was a voice that rumbled like boulders cascading down a mountain, yet chimed like ethereal bells on a soft billowing wind—the kind of voice that reminded you monsters were real, and *he* was their king. His breath blew like a wintry gale that sent hoar frost crusting over every surface, making the slab of stone beneath me a bed of burning ice that was even more impossible to bear.

I fought from screaming, but the way my lips trembled, the way I set my jaw tight, couldn't hide the sheer agony I was in. The corners of his mouth curled as he took in the chains bound around my wrists and ankles, as he delighted at the sight of my quaking limbs, knowing full well that simply laying on that altar, defenseless, unable to protect my son, was worse than if he'd skewered me with the jagged edges of his crown.

Sick, sadistic prick.

He laughed, and I remembered how adept these fucking angelic creatures were at reading minds. He walked with his head held high, shoulders back, with the kind of pride that could only be exuded by the Prince of Darkness. I boiled at the way he looked at me with those damn shimmering, dusky-colored eyes —eyes that reminded me of fading daylight welcoming the night sky. It was like he knew their juxtaposing beauty infuriated me.

Like he knew he'd won—that no matter what I'd done, no matter what any of us *could've* accomplished to thwart his efforts, in the end, he had always been destined to win this war.

He smiled again, slow and cruel. "No one can escape their fate, Katherine. Not you, not even me. You are chained to a sacrificial altar, but your destiny is not to be the lamb that washes away the sins of your people; it is to be the chalice from which I'll drink, to become the sacrifice that will herald the end of your world." His words raked over me like a razor pressing against my throat. Those perturbingly arresting eyes narrowed, but even their beauty couldn't mask the horrors lurking inside his mind, the heartless cunning seething at his core—that corrupt and decrepit black soul that churned like an unforgiving blackhole.

He placed a large hand on my chest, right above where my heart pounded like a stampede. His skin felt glacial as his fingers curled into me, pressing down hard as if he wanted to rip out my heart with his bare hand.

I thrashed, teeth gritting. "My destiny is to end your existence."

Eyes burning brighter, he growled, "*Your* destiny, Daughter of Eve, like that of every human, is to *die*." As if it hurt him to tear his hand away from my heart, he clenched his fingers into a fist, then leaned closer to my face, where his gaze dropped into mine like an anchor sinking into the depths of the sea. "When Jax rips out your heart, I will gulp every ounce of blood that drips from its still-beating flesh. And once I take your son as my vessel, Jax will offer up his own life to seal the rite. I will be free to take the seat at my Father's throne and will finally lay waste to what remains of your disgraceful kind."

Words could not describe the sheer horror that raked through my body—not at his words, but at the wailing cry that pierced through the incessant chants.

Luke. Luke. Luke.

What were they doing to my son?

Ignoring Samael, I twisted on the altar, trying to get a better look at what was happening up front, and that's when I spotted the fucking priest lifting Luke high above as he began reciting some nonsense from a book. I couldn't even focus on what he was saying.

My baby was crying, and my heart shattered a million times over.

"Let me go! My baby needs me!" But my screams went unanswered as the priest went on with his sermon, with his praises for Samael. The damn demon simply looked over the sea of chanting worshippers.

Fucking idiots. They thought Samael cared about them, that they were his children. They had no idea that, to Samael and his court, they were nothing more than maggots needing to be stomped on. Samael couldn't give two shits about them, about the sacrifices they'd made for his cause. Soon they would all be dead, and it didn't matter to Samael if the people in this room had pledged their fealty to him or not.

To Samael, we were all unworthy humans. All deserving of death.

Jax shifted his attention to me, and my insides grew colder than the frost nipping at my skin as I took in the dead look in his eyes. Placing his hand over my heart, he started mumbling words I couldn't understand, and suddenly, my skin began to throb, as if he was burning me with his mere touch. Breaths burst from my lungs in frantic gasps, panic surging from my gut and up my throat. "Jax, please. Stop this. You need to wake up. You need to wake up."

Nothing. The words spilled faster from his lips, the chant more fervent, the words now in our own tongue. "From the lamb, the blood of life shall flow. And from that life, a new world reborn. From the lamb, the blood of life shall flow. And from that life, a new world reborn."

"Jax!" I screamed so loud I thought I might shatter my eardrums, but his eyes never met mine.

I whimpered, hot tears bubbling in my eyes. "Please… Jax. Baby, please. Open your ears if you won't open your eyes. Luke is crying, Jax. He's crying for us. Our son needs us."

His eyes finally snapped to mine, flickering between blood red and ocean blue.

"Jax!"

He shook his head in frustration, fighting the demon from taking back control over his body. Jax's hand trembled over my chest. He tried to yank it away but couldn't. "K… Kate."

A flash caught my eye, something flicking on and off in the crowd. I squinted, trying to figure out what the hell the flash was when I spotted Clint's empyrean arm glinting under the light of a torch, a flashlight in his hand, going on and off a couple of times.

But before I could even figure out what he was up to, the chamber erupted into utter pandemonium.

Explosions tore through the chamber like thunder, a deafening crash that shook the very foundation of the pit as a blue electric fire rained down over us. The crowd screamed in unison, their chants breaking into chaos as the shockwaves rippled through the amphitheater. My heart raced as the frenzy of panicked bodies surged forward, dark robes billowing. All I could think of was Luke. I needed to know he was okay.

The smell of burning flesh stung my nose and I retched. Heavens. What was going on?

"Don't stop the ritual, Barbatos! Don't stop!" I heard the priest yell over the crowd, accompanied by Luke's unending cries. They hit me like daggers straight through my chest, but at least I knew he was alive. Still, I couldn't see the priest, couldn't see my baby, and panic steamrolled right through me again.

Frantically, I searched the crowd for Clint, looking for the glimmer of his arm, but smoke clogged the air and I lost sight of him. Shit. I needed him to find Luke.

Still pinned to the altar, I gritted my teeth as a searing burn yanked my attention away from trying to find Clint. Jax was continuing to push his fingers into my flesh, right over my heart, and I didn't know how much longer I could endure the pain.

I searched his face for any signs he was still fighting the demon, but even though I could see his eyes flicking back and forth between red and blue, it was clear the demon was winning the battle. "Kate..." he whispered, his voice trembling.

"Jax," I hissed, my voice hoarse, my skin raw as it continued to burn. "Come back to me, baby. Come back."

Blue eyes, bright with fear, he managed to lift his hand off my chest an inch, enough to give me some relief, but the compulsion was too strong, and suddenly, Samael broke through the smoke and gripped Jax by the neck. "You indolent fool. You were chosen for one task. What's taking you so long?"

"The human keeps... fighting my compulsion... He is stronger than we thought..." he croaked as Samael squeezed his fingers tighter around the demon's throat.

Seething, Samael peered deep into the demon's eyes, as if searching for Jax himself, and when he seemed to find him, his mouth frothed. "If it wasn't for the fucking bargain you forced me to make, I'd rip out her beating heart myself. I might still, consequences be damned." Then he put a palm against Jax's forehead, causing him to convulse before he went completely still, eyes locked on Samael. "Now, Barbatos, finish the fucking ritual or I'll see to it you never leave Abaddon."

The demon spun toward me again, ready to restart the ritual.

Fuck. Fuck. Fuck.

I yanked on my chains, tried to summon my sigils, my wings, but nothing worked. The fucking iron had neutralized me completely. Then, there was another flash of gold and Clint's face came into view. He'd moved down the tiers and was closer now.

Close enough he could…

"Clint!" I screamed, my voice barely carrying above the din of Jax's demonic chant. "Clint, shoot Jax!"

The kid couldn't hear me. Damn this.

"Clint!" I roared again, this time with everything in me, and was finally able to lock gazes with him again. "The bolt… use the bolt! It's the only way!"

For a heartbeat, I saw the conflict in the kid's eyes. We had no other choice, though. Jax wasn't going to win this battle; the demon was too strong, and Samael had somehow just sent Jax deeper into his subconscious. Empyrean steel had been the only way I'd been able to expunge Astaroth from his body back in New York. Clint's empyrean bolt would have to work the same way. *This* was our Hail Mary.

"Take the fucking shot, Clint!"

Face hardening, Clint raised the crossbow, and without further hesitation, he fired the bolt. The air snapped as the empyrean arrow flew through the smoke-filled room, ringing with a high-pitched chime. It was too late by the time the demon realized what happened. He was struck in the upper shoulder and was thrown backward, body sprawling as it hit the ground hard, a wail of pain bursting from the demon's lungs.

Samael roared in fevered anger and rushed toward me. I closed my eyes, expecting him to punch his hand right through my rib cage, but a female war-cry erupted from out of nowhere, and suddenly, Ta'herah's body leapt from the shadows, flying over the altar and barreling into Samael, sending him tumbling backward.

I barely had a second to catch my breath before I noticed Chaz running toward me, Zadkiel's sword in his hand. Seeing the big guy wielding that sword was like someone had poured a cool salve over my burns. The Marine looked like a holy warrior, as if the blade had always been meant for him. He hacked down on my chains until they broke off and I was free, though I struggled to lift myself off the stone slab. "God, I'm so happy to see you. How the heck did you and Ta'herah get free?"

"Hank. Now get up, Kate," Chaz barked, pulling me to a sitting position. He handed me Emrandael, its cool, familiar weight grounding me in the madness. I felt weak, but now that I wasn't lying flat on the stone, I felt my power return to me.

I tried unfurling my wings, but Samael's enraged roar echoed through the pit, making the ground rumble. His massive form gunned for me, eyes burning with unholy fire. He swung his charred fist, and I barely had time to leap off before he pummeled the altar to the ground, the stone crumbling under his fury.

I stumbled backward, shielding my eyes from the exploding stone debris.

"We have to kill the Horsemen!" Clint shouted from somewhere in the crowd. "It's the only way to close the gates and send Samael back!"

Through the smoke and debris, I saw the Four Horsemen still standing at the points of the pentagram. Ta'herah and Khai-runē rushed toward them, their weapons blazing with the power of their elements, but shields had been raised around the Fallen angels, protecting them from an attack. A vibrating current of light connected them, the power from the Creation Stones pouring into the beam, the energy tracing over the carved lines of the pentagram and feeding the main vein that ran to the gate.

As long as they remained inside those shields, the gates would remain wide open.

Samael unsheathed a ginormous black steel sword from a scabbard at his back, that same oily, tarlike substance from the Wastes slithering along the blade's massive edge.

I took a few more steps away from the iron shards littering the floor until I was far enough and no longer felt the drain of my power. "Chaz," I said, "you need to find Kyle and have him take down the wards shielding the Horsemen."

Samael stalked closer, seemingly unaffected by the iron.

Chaz gripped the angelic sword tighter and cocked his short shotgun in his other hand. "I'm not leaving you here to battle this beast alone."

Gently unfurling my wings, I let them spread wide, let them shimmer with brightness, obliterating the shadows that clung around me. I spun Emrandael once over my wrist, then aimed the empyrean blade at Hell's angel. "Mikha'el's power burns within me. I'm not alone. Go, now. The only way to win this is to close the gates."

The Marine grunted in displeasure, but he nodded and took off in search of Kyle.

Samael sneered. "You can hide behind Mikha'el's sword, but it won't protect you from me."

I wasn't deluded; I knew Samael was unlike any demon I'd ever faced. Not even the Horsemen I'd battled or the sicarii I'd killed compared to this opponent. But I needed him focused on me. "Why don't you come closer and find out…"

From the corner of my eye, I spotted the slimy High Priest trying to make a run for it, Luke still in his arms. But Clint spotted him and he winked at me as he took off in a sprint after the priest, Hank at his heel.

Every instinct in my body wailed at me to run after that priest myself, to take my son back and gut the son of a bitch for attempting to offer him up to the vile creature standing before me.

But I knew I could trust Clint. *I* needed to deal with the Prince of Hell.

Samael's monstrous form towered over me, his wings dragging like dead weight off his shoulders, his eyes locked onto mine with such feral hunger for my death that it chilled me to the bone.

"Come and get me, you bastard," I whispered, tightening my grip on Mikha'el's sword.

And with a roar, Samael charged.

Chapter Twenty-Eight

JAX

Laying on my back, I woke in a haze, the world a blur of movement and sound. I tried to blink the fog from my eyes, but everything around me was a kaleidoscope of people running, screaming, erupting gunfire, and clashing metal. Felt like I was crawling out of the depths of a nightmare, only to find myself waking in the middle of another.

The instant I went to move my arm, a sharp jolt of pain shot across my shoulder blades. *What the fuck?* I gritted my teeth, trying not to scream, but the agony was too intense.

What the hell happened?

There was something different about me, though… as if the air had finally cleared after a storm, as if something dark and heavy had lifted from my chest.

My eyes snapped wide open. Barbatos… I couldn't feel the demon inside me anymore. But how?

Disoriented, I staggered to my feet, and that's when I realized I had an empyrean bolt lodged in my shoulder. Fuck. Well, that explained why the demon had been exorcised from me. The wound pulsed with a deep cold burn that had my head swimming. I almost stumbled off my feet again, but I managed to stay upright. My thoughts were such a scattered mess, I could barely remember my name or where I was.

A thunderous roar drew my attention, and my insides turned to ice when I took in the battle raging a few yards from me. Was I still stuck in a dream? I blinked several times, swaying in place. My arm felt wet and warm, which meant I was probably losing a lot of blood, but none of that mattered because all I could think about was Kate…

Kate, with wings, locked in combat with Samael.

What the actual fuck? I tried to walk toward her, but I stumbled and fell to my knees. "Kate…" I whispered, but her name was lost in the chaos. My heart pounded slowly but hard as I took in the absurd scene before me. She was taking blow after brutal blow, but she fought back with a ferocity that made my heart lurch. She was holding her own, but I still couldn't wrap my mind around the fact she had wings.

Kate had fucking *wings. And* she was wielding Emrandael? Somehow that didn't feel like good news.

"Jax!"

I whipped my head toward the voice. Chaz. He was running toward me, his face a mixture of relief and concern as he cut through the crowd. Behind him, figures I didn't recognize, female warriors, alien-looking and with strange weapons, were fighting against Devil's Army soldiers. My mind swirled again, trying to make sense of the madness.

Clint… Where the hell was Clint?

Chaz pointed his shotgun at my head. "Is it you in there, Cap?"

I blinked, stunned, my eyes trained on the barrel. "It's me, big guy."

"Yeah, how do I know it's *really* you?"

My breaths came out ragged. "You don't. But it's me, I swear." I nodded to the bolt still sticking out of my shoulder.

"Clint must have shot me with his crossbow. Empyrean steel. Demon is gone."

The Marine narrowed his eyes, his fingers tightening over his shotgun. This time the dizziness won out, and I fell onto my back.

"Fuck, man." Chaz scurried to my side. "Cap, you okay?"

"You need to pull the bolt out. I'm losing too much blood."

"If I pull that out, you're gonna bleed out faster. I need to tie a tourniquet first."

"Hurry." Blood kept seeping out, each breath I took making the wound pulse hotter.

Like a seasoned Marine, Chaz got to work. He tore off a piece of fabric from his shirt and folded the material into a makeshift band and tied it tightly around my upper arm, just above the wound. "This is gonna cut off circulation to your arm, but it'll keep the blood from gushing when I pull this thing out."

I nodded, feeling tension build in the pit of my stomach. My head kept spiraling, the blood loss making me lightheaded, but I trusted Chaz knew what he was doing.

He tugged the fabric tight, using a folded switchblade to twist the cloth, making the tourniquet even tighter. Pain shot up my arm as he twisted the blade like a lever, cutting off the blood flow. "Hold still," he muttered. "This'll be over quick."

With one hand holding the tourniquet in place, Chaz reached for the bolt. "Ready?"

I sucked in a breath, biting down hard. "Do it."

In one quick, brusk motion, Chaz yanked the bolt free. I screamed through clenched teeth, the pain blinding for a moment, but it was over almost as quickly as it began. He didn't waste time. As soon as the bolt was out, he tore another piece of cloth from his shirt, pressing it hard against the wound to slow the bleeding.

"You're gonna be okay," he muttered, tightening the

tourniquet one last time. "We just need to keep this in place until we…" He looked around. "Well, until we can get out of this shit hole."

"Copy that. W-where's Clint?" I stammered.

"I don't know," Chaz said, shaking his head. "Last I saw him, Kate had sent him after the priest who took Luke."

"Luke's missing? Fuck. We can't let that fucking priest get away with my son."

"I tried looking for Clint, but I couldn't find him or Kyle."

Kyle? The name didn't register, and I frowned, trying to shake the mist from my thoughts. "Who the hell is Kyle?"

Chaz shot me a quick look as if just remembering I'd been MIA for the last… who knew how long. "Doesn't matter. Listen, Clint's got this. He's with Hank. He'll find Luke. We've got other problems. We need to take down the shields protecting the Horsemen. If we don't, we can't stop the bastards, and apparently, that's the only way to send Samael back to his fucking hiding hole."

I looked up and my throat went dry when I saw Beleth, Chemoth, and two other Seraphim I didn't recognize; they'd completed their rebirths but were now standing inside red pulsing shields at four of the five points of the star, dark energy coiling around them like serpents. The Creation Stones hung from their necks, glowing like molten embers, power rippling off them and feeding the magic that was keeping the gates open.

"Yeah, we need to break the connection between the stones. Once the gates are unstable, Samael will be sucked right back into Abaddon. Give me a hand," I said, but as he helped me stand, my gaze shot to where Kate continued to swap blows with Samael.

Chaz squeezed my good shoulder. "Kate can handle herself for now, but if we don't kill the Horsemen, we're all screwed. Without Kyle, you're the only one who knows how to break down these damn shields."

As much as it killed me to do so, I tore my eyes away from Kate. Chaz was right. I couldn't help her, not in my condition. The best I could do was take down the pentagram's shields. I dropped to my knees in the center of the star, my vision going in and out of focus as I stared down at the intricate runes etched into the floor. The symbols shifted and pulsed with a life of their own, twisting my mind as I tried to decipher them.

"Chaz," I rasped. "There's a grimoire. The priest… had to be using it. I need you to find it. Large book. Looks like an ancient Bible, but demonic."

Chaz cursed under his breath as he searched the pit. "Demonic Bible? That doesn't sound like something I want to find."

"Man, just look for it. I need it to break the spell holding up the shields."

The two alien-looking females raged against more soldiers, their weapons slashing through the bodies like the worshippers were nothing but meat sacks. Then, growls broke through the sounds of battle and my spine went rigid.

Hellhounds.

"Chaz, you better hurry the fuck up, man!"

One of the alien warriors, the one with the long, braided raven hair, raised her sword, shouting something in a language I didn't understand, and the blade burst into flames. Shit. She charged at a hellhound that had stalked through the shadows, and the creature let out a hellish screech as the warrior speared it through the heart, its hide smoldering.

"Who the hell are *they*?" I asked, nodding toward the alien riders, my breath coming in ragged gasps as I tried gathering my strength.

Chaz's lips curled slightly upward. "Space warriors sent by Mikha'el. That's all you need to know. Just worry about breaking the damn shields."

"Yeah, well, I need that damn book first."

"Working on it." Chaz went back to searching. I clenched

my jaw, my focus narrowing on the runes beneath me—they looked familiar but not, like they were an ancient branch of the angels' language. My energy was draining fast, the blood loss making everything hazy. My fingers trembled as I tried to decipher the spell.

"Jax!" Chaz's shout jolted me. I turned to see him yanking the grimoire from the dead hands of a worshipper, ripping it free from the lifeless grip. He sprinted back to me, tossing the bloodstained book into my hands.

I fumbled with the pages, my vision blurring as I flipped through the dense text, the symbols swirling on the page like snakes. My hands shook, each movement more labored than the last as I struggled to find the right incantation.

A blur of motion appeared in my peripheral, but Chaz was on it immediately. He spun and shot the Devil's Army guard square in the chest as the man barreled toward us. Blood sprayed everywhere as the guy went flying. "Not to rush you or anything, Cap, but I'm officially out of slugs!"

"Copy that. Doing my best here."

Those alien warriors spun past us again, taking out guards left and right, keeping the pit clear so I could focus on breaking the shields. But the fight was intensifying—more hellhounds emerged from the shadows, circling like vultures around the ceremonial ring.

"We've got company, Cap!"

"I know, I know! I need another minute," I growled through gritted teeth, my breath shallow as I finally found the spell I needed. I scanned the page, reading the incantation, my heart pounding. "This is it. This has to be it."

I smeared my hand with the blood coating my arm and pressed it against the floor as I began chanting, each word scraping my throat raw. The runes glowed brighter, resisting me with a force that nearly knocked me backward. The energy required to break the spell was immense, and I was already teetering on the edge of collapse. Blood dripped from my shoulder, soaking the ground beneath me.

"Come on, come on…" I muttered, pushing harder, forcing my will into the spell.

Through the corner of my eye, I could see Kate still battling Samael. He roared as he swung his massive black sword, clashing with Emrandael and sending Kate crashing into the wall of the underground chamber. My heart clenched at the sight—she was giving everything she had, but Samael was relentless, his blows punishing, inhuman.

"I have to help her," I gasped, panic rising in my chest.

Chaz cut down another hellhound. "The shields, Jax. The only way you help her is by breaking the shields!"

I bit down on the panic, forcing myself to keep chanting. Each word was like a knife twisting in my gut, the power of the spell draining me. The wards fought back, resisting with every ounce of magic woven into the pentagram. My vision blurred, darkness creeping in at the edges.

And then—finally—the runes cracked, and the air around me exploded as the shields shattered. I collapsed to the ground, gasping for breath, my body trembling from the effort. "The Horsemen, Chaz. They're free."

But the fight was far from over.

Chapter Twenty-Nine

CLINT

The corridor was dim, shadows creeping up the walls like twisted fingers. I kept my footsteps light, the silence stretching between each breath I took. Hank was by my side, ears perked, every muscle coiled like a spring. We'd been tracking the priest for about five or ten minutes when he picked up Luke's scent.

We rounded a corner and that's when I saw them.

Kelsey stood a few feet ahead, gun drawn, her arm unwavering but her body trembling like a taut wire ready to snap. The High Priest was holding Luke, his bony fingers wrapped around the baby like a vice. Luke whimpered, his small body squirming in the priest's arms. Even with her rolled ankle, Kelsey had caught up to him first, and she'd intercepted him right before he'd made a run for it to the upper floors.

Kelsey's voice cut through the stale air. "Put the baby down," she growled, her finger tight on the trigger. But there was something else in her voice—a bitterness, a deep-rooted venom I hadn't heard before.

The priest's smile was cold, empty. "You don't have it in

you," he hissed, his voice dripping with arrogance. "You were always such a spineless child. You never fought. And you won't fight me this time, either."

I crept forward, Hank lowering his head as he padded beside me. My heart stormed inside my chest. Something wasn't right. This wasn't just about protecting Luke. Her gaze was locked on the priest with a burning hatred that felt like it had been festering for years.

"Kelsey," I said quietly, trying not to startle her, to keep this from spiraling out of control. "Don't listen to him. He's just trying to get under your skin. I'll find another way to get Luke."

She didn't even look at me. Her eyes were still on the priest, and her voice cracked with something raw, something I hadn't expected. "This isn't just about Luke, Clint," she whispered, the words tumbling out like they'd been trapped in her throat for too long. "This man… he's the one. He's the one who hurt us. Me. All those children…"

I froze.

"He's the one who—" Her voice faltered for a moment, then hardened into steel. "He's the one who did *it*. I can't let him walk away. I can't let him do this to anyone else. Not ever again."

A sickness curled in my stomach. The priest's smirk widened, and he pulled Luke tighter against him, as though sensing the power he had over Kelsey. He'd been the sick fuck who'd raped her when she was just a girl. The need to rip him to shreds raged inside my veins. Adrenalin fed my muscles, and I felt my limbs prime for the fight, because there was no way I was going to let this asshole walk out of here alive.

But a flicker of movement in the shadows stopped me in my tracks. A death wraith, skulking near the ceiling, its formless body drifting closer. The priest didn't notice, too focused on Kelsey, too drunk on his own power. But I saw it, and Hank saw it, too. His growl rumbled low in his throat, just enough to let me know he was ready.

"Kelsey," I said, keeping my voice low and steady. "Lower your gun. I'll find another way."

The priest's eyes snapped to mine, his smirk faltering just a bit. "Do you really think I'm scared of *you*?"

I shook my head slowly. "It's not me you should be worried about." I subtly gestured toward the wraith creeping closer, its hollow eyes fixed on the priest. "That thing… it doesn't care who you are. It doesn't care if you're in Samael's army or not. It's here for blood. And the baby in your arms? That's a nice morsel of pure, innocent life. More than enough to make it turn on you."

His smirk vanished, replaced by uncertainty as he glanced over his shoulder, seeing the wraith for the first time. The color drained from his face.

"Hand over the baby," I said, taking another step closer, my voice calm but firm. "And I'll give you my crossbow. It's made of empyrean metal. The wraiths won't come near you as long as you have it."

Kelsey clenched her teeth. "What are you doing? You're just going to let him get away?"

I gently put a hand over hers, trying to get her to lower her gun. "Remember what I told you after I kissed you for the first time?"

She eyed me, her mind working to remember, then one of her brows lifted slowly.

I never enter a game I don't think I can win.

I winked, and the tense energy that had wrapped itself around her spine released its hold and she seemed to breathe easier. She lowered her arm and gave me the gun.

Weighing his options, the priest's eyes darted between me, Kelsey, and the wraith. I could see the gears turning in his head. He knew he couldn't fight the wraith alone. He might have cared about preserving Samael's vessel, but he sure as fuck seemed to care about his own life more. His allegiance to his dark lord was slowly crumbling with each passing second.

"I don't believe you," he spat, his grip on Luke tightening. "You'll kill me the second I hand him over."

I held up my last empyrean bolt. "One arrow. That's all I've got left. And I'll give you the crossbow in exchange for Luke. It's your best shot at getting out of here alive."

The priest's gaze flickered to the glowing bolt, then back at the wraith that was now nearly upon him. Sweat beaded on the old man's forehead.

"Put him down on the floor and I'll throw you the crossbow," I said, my voice steady. "Or the wraith takes him—and you."

The priest's resolve cracked. With a growl of frustration, he put Luke on the floor, but he unsheathed a blade and held it out, threatening him if I made a wrong move. I gave Hank a quick command and the shepherd skulked forward. "He's just gonna grab the blanket to drag him to me. As soon as he's got the baby, I'll throw you the crossbow."

Hank did as he was told, and I nocked the bolt and tossed the crossbow to the priest, watching as he fumbled to catch it, his hands shaking. "There. Now get the hell out of here."

I scooped Luke into my arms, and whispered to Kelsey, "Whatever you do, stay very still."

Her gaze brimmed with confusion.

"Just do as I say," I mumbled under my breath.

Hank growled, his gaze fixing on something in the dark—something the priest hadn't accounted for. Low, guttural snarls suddenly filled the hallway. I knew what had been hiding in the shadows the whole time, and Hank had known it, too. The way his hackles had raised earlier had been the telltale sign.

The card I hadn't shown the priest.

Kelsey's body tensed beside me. I gripped her hand tightly, but I didn't move. The instant we took off running, the beasts would go on the chase. I needed to time this just right or we were all dead.

The priest's eyes widened as the wraith drew closer, but he didn't' seem to notice—or didn't care—about the three hell-hounds clawing at the ground, an alpha between them.

His mistake.

He was wholly focused on the death wraith. The creature barely moved forward when the priest panicked, his fingers fumbling with the crossbow as he raised it, but the idiot had no clue how to use it properly, and he fired without aiming. Luckily for him, it shot through the wraith, dissolving the creature into the shadows.

I puffed out a breath. "Trouble with those wraiths is the bolts go right through them."

The priest didn't seem to catch my meaning until it was too late. The bolt had killed the wraith, but it had flown right through its body and continued through the air, nicking the alpha hellhound across its face, narrowly missing its eye.

The alpha roared in fury, and that was my cue to go. The creature came charging at the priest with the force of a freight train. Grabbing Kelsey, I threw her over my shoulder, holding Luke tight in my other arm. We bolted down the hallway, Hank right on our heels, his growls echoing through the chaos.

Behind us, the priest screamed as the hellhounds tore into him, their claws ripping through flesh and bone. Kelsey twisted in my grasp, a low hum emanating from her as she chanted something I didn't understand. The words seemed to thicken the air around us, and suddenly, I felt a barrier form— a shield that sealed the priest inside the corridor with the monsters he'd once commanded.

The sounds of his dying screams were muffled once the shield went up, and I felt Kelsey's body shudder against mine. I slowed, gently setting her down, away from where we could see the priest dying, though we didn't need to see to know he was probably a mangled corpse by now. Her face crumpled, tears spilling down her cheeks as she let out a sob, the weight of her past—the torment, the abuse, the years of pain—finally catching up to her.

"It's over," I whispered, wrapping my arm around her as she cried. "He can never hurt you again. He can't hurt another child *ever* again."

For a moment, she stayed there, pressed against me, clutching my shirt. This… Her… Us… It felt right, and I never wanted to let go of this feeling. It both filled me with joy and utter dread.

Chaz's words rang in my head. *No attachments…*

Fuck that. I was done with just surviving. This, what I was feeling for Kelsey, was what *kept* me fighting. She made me feel fucking alive and there was no way I was giving up on that… provided we made it out of this mess.

Luke's little whimper was a reminder of just that—this battle was still raging, and we needed to get back to the chamber and close those gates.

"Warding is not my strength. The shield won't hold for much longer," Kelsey said, wiping the tears from her eyes. "Those hellhounds are gonna break through as soon as they sense a weak spot."

A thundering clash echoed down the hall, punctuating what Kelsey had just said. Those beasts were going to push themselves through her wards. I extended a hand to her and helped her to her feet. "Come on, I'll carry you."

"No. I can walk." But when she tried to take a step, she practically fell into my arms. All this walking had made it worse. I bent down and lifted her pant leg, and even through the ace bandage I could see her ankle was severely swollen.

"Kels, what he said about you not being a fighter, you know that's not true, right? You were just a little girl; you were scared. You can't let his words make you feel like you're to blame for what he did to you. What matters is that you're not defenseless anymore. You can fight back, and you did," I said, nodding toward the hallway where the priest had gotten what he'd deserved. "You don't have to push yourself to walk on an injured ankle to prove you're not weak, to prove you're a fighter."

Lips trembling, she looked up at me. God, I hated that she felt she needed to be this super strong, bad ass chick all the time. As if she wasn't allowed to be vulnerable. As if she wasn't allowed to ask for help. Caressing her cheek, I said, "It's okay to let me fight your demons, Goldilocks. And what's the point of having a friend with an empyrean arm if you're not gonna let me use it, anyway?"

She swallowed deeply. "You wouldn't understand. This is not a demon, Clint. This is different."

"Of course. I know it's different, but not all demons have claws and fangs, Kels. Me carrying you doesn't mean you're not strong and not able to kick ass. It just means you have a busted ankle right now, and I need to get us someplace safe fast before those nightcrawlers bust through those shields and shred us to ribbons. It's what it means to have friends who care about you."

She sighed, trying to collect herself. "It's not easy to just drop my walls, to forget the things that made me who I am."

I leaned in closer, my lips almost brushing hers. "I didn't say it would be easy, but at least let me help ease the burden. You can lean on me, Kels. I'm here for you."

She pursed her lips. "You're so persistent."

"When it's regarding someone I care about, you bet I am."

She offered me a reluctant smile.

I tugged on one of her curls. "Come on, Goldie. You can give me a bigger smile than that."

"Hellhounds are trying to break through my measly shields to get at us, it's hardly the time for smiling."

"Precisely why we need to try to find something to smile about in all this nonsense." Without warning, I slung her over my shoulder fireman style, and she squealed, a real genuine giggle rumbling through her. The sound made something warm kindle deep in my gut, and the smile that stretched across my cheeks made my face hurt so bad. I must've looked like a mad man running down an abandoned mental hospital, a woman draped over my shoulder, a baby in my other arm, and a dog at my heel.

No one would've guessed we were headed into the heart of a maelstrom about to battle Satan and his minions.

Chapter Thirty

JAX

Though the shields around the Horsemen shattered, they stood motionless, locked in some kind of trance induced by the Creation Stones. It was as if the stones kept them connected to the portal, stopping them from breaking the chain that kept the gate open. But even immobilized, their mere presence was devastating, in a perturbed kind of way.

With their seraphim forms restored—their wings shimmering like molten rivers of silver cascading down their backs, their bodies cloaked in golden light—the four angels were too beautiful to look at without feeling your soul shrink.

But these beings weren't typical angels. They were the worst kind of Fallen—twisted versions of what they had once been, their very existence corrupted beyond redemption. But it wasn't their grotesque beauty that sent a sheet of ice crusting over my skin, it was the golden diadems around their heads.

Fucking halos.

Chaz was already on his feet and charging toward Beleth, Zadkiel's sword in hand, before I had a chance to warn him.

The instant he swung the sword and tried to slash Beleth across the chest, a booming sound exploded, and Chaz went flying. He'd ricochetted right off the angel.

"Don't attack, don't attack. They're wearing halos!" I didn't know if the alien fighters understood me, but it seemed my staggering body and flailing arms were universal, because they halted their advance.

Clint ran in out of nowhere, a pistol pointed at my head.

I sagged. "Not you, too."

"Gotta know it's you in there, man."

I wiped sweat off my face. "It's me. I swear. Did you find Luke?"

He paused for a beat, his face not showing signs he believed me.

"Ask Chaz, kid. It's me. The bolt you shot me with purged Barbatos from my body."

He grimaced and lowered the gun. "Sorry about that. It was our last option."

"No need to apologize, kid. Thank you. So, what about Luke?"

"He's with Kelsey and Hank. He's safe."

I had no clue who Kelsey was, but if Hank was with him, then that was the most I could hope for. I wasn't even able to sigh in relief, though, before the air shifted, and a wave of blistering cold hit me just as Samael backhanded Kate with bone-crushing force, flinging her across the chamber. She hit the far wall with a sickening crack, her body crumpling before she pulled herself up, jaw clenched, eyes narrowed into slits of fire.

My entire body shuddered. "Kate!"

"I'm… okay," she croaked, but she looked a bit woozy as she climbed back to her feet.

Samael dropped into the pit like a thunderclap, unleashing a torrent of dark energy, a wave that rocked all of us back on our heels. His eyes blazed, his wings drooping behind him, each feather dripping with the sickness that ate at Abaddon. Every gaze turned to him as the angel took in the scene before him, at us trying to tear down his Horsemen and close the gates. Fury rolled off his shoulders and he pointed his sword straight at my face. "Your world ends tonight, Son of Adam."

I fell to my knees and pressed a bloody hand against the ground, over the runes on the floor, hoping to channel a shield. The runes responded, sparking into a wall of energy—only for Samael to punch right through it as if it were nothing more than smoke. He closed in, fists pummeling down. I barely had time to dodge.

Chaz charged forward and slashed at Samael with Zadkiel's sword, the blade flashing with holy fire, but Samael deflected the blow with a contemptuous roar, striking Chaz and sending him hurtling to the ground. The big guy hollered, and I knew he must have broken something.

Wind whipped my hair out of nowhere as the dark-skinned alien warrior used her staff to summon a cyclone, entrapping Samael and her fellow warrior within.

Shit. She could wield elemental magic.

She spun around Samael, trying to bind him inside the swirling storm of air, while the other warrior summoned a blazing fireball, flames coiling around her blade as she tried to strike at the angel. But even they struggled, their powers barely managing to slow him down.

The halos began to shimmer brighter, the light cast off by the rare metal illuminating the pit. Fuck.

Clint drew closer, swiping dust and debris off himself. "What's happening to them?"

"The halos are feeding off the energy created by the stones, reinforcing them. There's no way we can break through the magnetic barriers created by those diadems. They were gifted by God to the most elite—Samael and his court were stripped of theirs. I have no clue how the Horsemen reacquired them, though if I had to guess, Khama'el likely had something to do with it."

"So, what do we do? How are we supposed to close the gates?"

A loud crash sounded as the fire-wielding warrior got slammed into the wall of wind. Samael was relentless; he seemed to shrug off everything we threw at him. If we were going to win this, it wasn't going to be through brute force alone.

My mind raced, desperation clawing at me. To defeat the Horsemen, we needed to try something different, some other way to strip them of their power. We couldn't use empyrean steel due to the halos, but there was another way to tear an angel's essence from a possessed vessel.

A good old-fashioned exorcism. It would be a long shot given the Horsemen had completed their rebirth, but at the end of the day, they'd taken possession of human bodies to regain their angelic forms. Those human bodies had to exist inside them still… I could only hope.

There was only one way to find out.

Kate limped toward the center of the pit, and in that second, I didn't give a shit about the chaos going on around us. Didn't care about having to take down the Horsemen and needing to close the gates. Everything ceased to exist the instant I saw her. I fucking dashed toward her and took her into my arms, my injured shoulder be damned. She hugged me back, and it was like two oceans clashing against each other. I drowned in the feel of her body, the smell of her skin.

"Fuck. You're real, angel. You're fucking real. No more dreams."

She pulled back, her eyes bright with an internal fire as she took in my condition, but I knew she wasn't just concerned about my shoulder. I looked like hell after the torture I'd been put through the last few days. "I'm sorry Clint shot you. Sorry I couldn't get to you faster."

I grabbed her face and kissed her. "Don't you apologize for any of that. You're alive. Luke's safe…"

"He's safe?"

"He's with Kelsey and Hank," Clint replied.

Kate's eyes widened in horror.

"He's safe. I promise. Kelsey is alright."

She sighed and thanked the kid, then she looked up at me and tears rolled down her face. I dabbed at each one with my blood-smeared fingers. "Save those tears for later, angel. This fight ain't over."

Clint checked his gun for ammo. "How exactly do we defeat this asshole? I don't have my crossbow anymore."

Kate stiffened. "What do you mean?"

The kid shrugged off her question. "Long story. But regardless, this handgun won't do shit against him."

I nodded toward the portal. "Sending him back to Abaddon is our safest bet."

Kate tightened her grip on Mikha'el's sword. "But how? We need to take out the Horsemen for that."

I steeled myself, setting my sights on the Horseman of Death. "Empyrean steel won't help here. That's why I'm gonna rip Beleth right out of his skin instead."

"How?" she asked.

I hated having to pull away from her, but we had no time left and I had to do this right. One mistake, and it was over. "We only get one chance at this."

"What do you need us to do?" Clint asked as Chaz joined the circle. He held his side, grimacing as he walked, but the big guy looked like he still had a fight left in him.

"Yeah, cap. How can we help?"

"Keep Samael away from me and the Horsemen."

My words were punctuated by another loud clash inside the cyclone.

"Khai-runē is getting destroyed in there," Clint said. "We need to help her."

"Let's go," Kate said, but I grabbed her by the arm and pulled her toward me, my lips hovering over hers.

"Don't you die on me, angel."

She kissed me. "You, too." She looked over her shoulder as she joined Chaz and Clint. "What, no corny movie quotes this time?"

I couldn't think of any. "Just get back to me in one piece."

"Oh, don't worry, baby. *I'll be back…*" Her wide grin made my insides twist. I realized then how much I truly loved that woman. My whole existence revolved around her, and if something happened to her…

God, if something happened to her, I… I didn't know what I'd do, but it probably included burning down worlds.

I shook the uneasy thoughts from my head and knelt in front of Beleth. This was the asshole who had taken my best friend's body and extinguished the life out of him to initially open the gates all those many months ago. So, he would be the one I would try to exorcise first.

With my own blood, I drew the sign of the cross, the one sigil demons detested the most, over my forehead, and recited the words long used by priests to rid a demon from a human vessel. I was no anointed priest, but I knew the ritual well. "Exorcizo te, omnis immunde spiritus, omnis satanica potestas, omnis incursio infernalis adversarii…"

My voice trembled and doubt began to creep in as nothing seemed to be happening. I repeated the words, but Beleth's body appeared unperturbed. Shit. I retraced the cross over my forehead and began chanting the words one more time, all while the battle against Samael raged behind me.

Just when I was about to give up, Beleth's body convulsed, the halo flickering, his face twisting as the exorcism began to take hold. I kept going, the ancient Latin pouring from me like a lifeline, binding him, stripping his power.

Samael roared, and I shot a glance over my shoulder. The beast broke free from the whirlwind, turning to me with murder in his eyes. Chaz hurled himself between us, Zadkiel's sword flashing as he blocked Samael's advance.

"Finish it, Jax!" Chaz shouted, his voice hoarse as he clung to his side.

The fire-wielding warrior leaped forward, her blade blazing as she swung at Samael, trying to force him back. The wind-wielding one shot another ribbon of wind around him, momentarily holding him in place. Their combined powers crackled through the air, attempting to buy me precious minutes. I wouldn't let the opportunity go to waste.

"Ergo, draco maledicte et omnis legio diabolica…" I continued, my voice rising over the chaos. Beleth writhed, his vessel buckling under the strain, the Creation Stone hanging from his neck, flickering.

Samael let out another enraged bellow that knocked me off balance, his strength surging as he broke free of the elemental bindings. I tried finding Kate amongst the craziness, but I was suddenly rooted to the ground when, with a brutal punch, Samael's fist plunged into the fire-wielding warrior's chest. She gasped, a horrible, gurgling sound. His hand emerged with her heart clenched in his fist, her life snuffed out in a single, merciless blow. Her body crumpled, and her partner screamed, a sound of pure, unrestrained rage.

The alien warrior's eyes blazed, her grief turning into a violent storm of wind, pressing against Samael with enough force to crack stone. Her winds converged, pushing Samael toward the portal, her elemental magic thrumming around the entire room.

Beleth's form convulsed again. "I think it's working," Clint shouted over the sound of the churning wind. "Look at the portal!"

He was right. Whatever disruption the exorcism was causing, it was making the gates unstable. My chest tightened at the loss of the warrior, but there was nothing we could do for her now. I faced Beleth and traced the cross again, chanting the words with every ounce of hate in my heart.

The demon finally wrenched free of the vessel, hovering before me, a twisted smoke-colored figure, an unholy red gleam in his eyes.

Before he could attack, Chaz's voice rang out, "Jax, catch!"

He tossed Zadkiel's sword, the blade arcing through the air. I caught it just as Beleth lunged toward me. My hand burned as my skin touched the empyrean metal, but I didn't give a shit. With every ounce of strength I had, I drove the blade forward, burying it in Beleth's chest. He let out a bone-chilling scream as the sword pierced him, his form unraveling into tendrils of darkness that were sucked into the portal, severing the connection to his Creation Stone.

I chucked the sword back to Chaz and the ground beneath us trembled, the portal churning violently. The other Horsemen seemed to awaken, the magnetic field around them dissipating as the stones lost their power. Samael snarled, real-izing too late what was happening as the force of the collapsing gate began to pull at him, dragging him back to Abaddon.

But the asshole refused to go.

Samael raised his black sword, lunging toward me, but Kate appeared beside me and my heart dropped into my stomach. She raised her hands, her angelic power surging, creating a force of light that pushed against Samael, pressing him toward the gate. The wind-wielding warrior joined her, her power fanning Kate's, amplifying it.

Samael screamed, his body contorting as he was dragged inch by inch toward the portal. He slashed out wildly with his sword, catching Kate across the shoulder, the blade slicing deep.

"Kate!" I cried, but she held her ground, teeth clenched, eyes blazing as she continued to push him back.

With a final, furious scream, Samael was sucked into the portal, his form disappearing into the darkness. The Horsemen followed, their forms dissolving as the connection to the stones was severed, the gate consuming them one by one, the Creation Stones crashing to the ground as they hit the entrance to the gates.

Then the portal collapsed with a thunderous boom.

Kate swayed, her face pale, her hand pressed to her wound. The gash Samael had left was deep, dark veins spreading out from the wound, the angelic sigils alight in her arms dimmed and died.

"No, no," I whispered, rushing to her side, my hands trembling as I tried to help her. But her body wasn't healing. The wound was too deep, too poisoned with the Sickness.

Clint appeared beside us, pulling a vial from his pocket. "I have serum. It helped her back at the church when she was almost scorched to death. It can probably help her now."

Chaz knelt beside us. "I thought you told us back at the diner that none of the vials had survived. That they'd all broken."

Clint offered the big guy an unapologetic grunt. "I lied. I know. Not very noble, but I kept it just in case of something like this."

Chaz's jaw worked.

"Look, I made a choice to not use the serum to heal that Guardian, but his brother was infected. I couldn't save them both. Even if I'd healed him, he would've stayed behind with his brother."

"I'm not judging you, kid."

"Good, because I'm not accepting any criticism." The kid tapped the syringe, then plunged the needle into her arm. "Here goes nothing."

For a heart-stopping moment, nothing happened, and then, slowly, the darkness began to fade, the wound knitting itself closed as her body accepted the serum. Kate's eyes fluttered open, a small, grateful smile touching her lips, and Hank appeared out of nowhere and began licking her face. She laughed, and I never heard a more beautiful sound.

I kissed her forehead. "You scared the living shit out of me."

"That asshole can't kill me that easily."

"I'm sure, but let's stop tempting fate."

A young woman knelt beside us, Luke in her arms. "I believe this little bundle belongs to you."

Kate quickly pushed herself up to sit and took our baby into her arms, her eyes already misted over. "Thank you so much, Kelsey. Thank you."

The girl walked away, as did the rest of the crew, giving us a few moments to be alone with Luke.

"Everyone, listen up," Clint piped up. Look through the debris. Kyle is still missing."

As everyone got to work, I couldn't help but drink in every ounce of Kate holding on to our baby. I couldn't believe this was real. So many times, I'd been stuck in a dream loop where every time I found her, she'd simply dissolve into oblivion, only to relive the moment over and over and over again.

I wanted to cry, but all I could do was tremble. Fear as cold as the arctic crept into my bones. Fear of losing her and Luke all over again. Fear of being a trapped in a world where they didn't exist.

She let Luke wrap his little fingers around her pinky. "You're safe now," she whispered to him. "You're safe."

My heart ached so badly, I wanted to scoop both up into my arms and whisk them away somewhere no one could ever hurt us again. Looking down at the ground below us, at the runes, the pentagram, the spokes where The Horsemen had stood, I realized just how badly I wanted to get out of this place. This decrepit hospital was the epitome of everything that was wrong and awful about the people who ran the Devil's Army.

As I helped Kate to her feet, a sharp cry shot through the chamber. The girl who'd handed Luke to Kate knelt beside a pile of rubble; her body wracked with grief. I followed her gaze and felt my heart sink. A man lay beneath the debris, his body shielding the small, fragile form of a little girl.

"Kels!" Clint hollered from across the chamber, running toward her.

She clutched the man's hand, her shoulders shaking as she whispered his name, "Kyle…"

Clint grabbed her by the shoulders and hauled her up. "Oh, Christ. Kelsey. I'm so sorry." The young woman was inconsolable, clutching Clint's shirt and sobbing into his chest.

"Her brother, he's the one who gave the Devil's Army the location of the stones," Kate said, nodding toward where Clint held her in his arms. "But he also tried to help us. He died trying to protect his daughter. He wasn't any different than the rest of us."

"She's alive," Chaz shouted. "The kid is alive. Come, give me a hand." Clint, Kelsey, Chaz, and the warrior all helped lift the large chunks of stone that had fallen on Kyle. Underneath him, a small hand opened and closed, fingers wiggling slowly.

"Oh my God, Payton," Kelsey sobbed as she helped dig the little girl out from under her dead father. Covered in dust and blood, the little girl looked confused, but she recognized her aunt and immediately fell into her arms.

More debris rained from above and we had to dodge getting smashed by falling rock. "We need to get out of here," I said. "This place is going to collapse."

Kate stood in front of where the portal had closed and picked up the Creation Stones that had fallen when the Horsemen were pulled through. Wings suddenly materialized at her back, unfurling majestically to their full wingspan. I stood breathless, stunned. She looked like a divine being—a true hybrid of Heaven and Earth.

I slowly walked up to her. "Kate, your wings… When did this happen?"

With Luke still in her arms, Kate kept her gaze trained on the space where the gates of Hell had churned with depthless darkness. "Before he was taken to Abaddon by Khama'el through a portal just like this one, Mikha'el gave me his essence. He gave me these wings."

I gently caressed one of her feathers and she shivered. "I'm sorry, I should've asked if it was okay to touch them."

She turned over her shoulder and offered me a gentle smile. "It's okay. I'm still learning to get used to them."

"Kate, an angel can't give you wings. Regardless of what Mikha'el might have imbued you with, he doesn't have the authority to grant a human angel wings. It is the essence of who they are; humans are not built the same way."

"Then how do you explain it then?"

"His power likely awakened something within you… something that was already there."

She faced me completely. "What are you saying?"

"The only creatures able to have angel wings besides angels are Nephilim. It explains everything."

"Explains what?"

"Don't you see? When Zadkiel anointed you, he didn't give you angelic abilities; he awakened them. He knew you by name because he'd already known *of* you. Nephilim were hunted down to extinction because of the threat they posed not just to angelkind, but to humans. Their power rivaled that of a full-blooded angel. But stories tell of sanctions of angels who didn't believe all Nephilim were to be feared, and they fought to protect the bloodlines. They hid those who they believed would one day rise to redeem both races."

"My parents… they were human, Jax. What you're saying is insane."

"One of your parents, if not both, were Nephilim, their

angelic abilities probably dormant like yours. It also explains him…" I said, nodding down to Luke.

Kate looked at me with puzzlement etched across her face.

"He is a Nephilim because of you," I said.

"No. It was Astaroth."

"We guessed wrong, Kate. Astaroth was still a demon when he was inside me." I drew in closer to her, so no one could hear my next words. "*I* came inside you, Kate. Me, not Astaroth. He might have been trapped inside me, but it was my human body that made love to you that night. It was you who passed down your Nephilim heritage to Luke. It explains your growing strength, the magical properties of your blood— blood that shimmers with specs of gold. Your telepathic ability, your wings. It all makes perfect sense."

"Are you saying Mikha'el knew? Why would he keep that from me?"

"You'll need to ask him that."

Her face drooped and I realized my mistake. Kate turned to where the portal had churned. "He's in Abaddon, likely being tortured by Samael."

"There's nothing we can do for him, Kate. We can't follow him into Hell."

She spun toward me. "We've both traveled to the Wastes. We can travel there, figure out a way to get him out."

"Our consciousness traveled into the Wastes, not our bodies. And the Wastes are a realm all their own that exists within Abaddon. Even our consciousness can't travel into Abaddon itself. Only angels, demons, and the souls of the dead can enter that world."

"We can't just leave him in there. He sacrificed so much for us."

By now the rest of our companions had gathered around us. "I didn't mean to eavesdrop," Clint said, "but did you just say Kate is part angel?"

"I believe she is Nephilim."

"It would explain a lot," Kelsey added, stepping closer. "I've seen the way you fight, Kate. The way you use the angel's star power—that's something that can't be gifted. I saw you battle against Samael, watched you from a corner while I held your baby. No mortal could've fought him like that and survived, despite being anointed by two angels."

The alien warrior retracted her staff and holstered it to her belt. "I've fought alongside angels, Kate. I believe what he and Kelsey say to be true. You are no ordinary human."

"So, what are we supposed to do now?" Kate asked, looking at all our faces.

"Samael and the Horsemen are back in Hell," Clint said. "We stopped the rebirth. We won."

"No," Kate uttered. "We haven't won. We've just delayed the inevitable yet again. You think the Devil's Army are just going to stop coming for the stones? That they aren't going to try to bring the Horsemen back, that they won't try to reopen the gates? As long as my son lives, they will never stop looking for him. What about Khama'el and the sicarii? Are we supposed to just keep running from them, while our world continues to be consumed by this sickness. The gates might not be stable enough to let Samael through, but the gates aren't truly closed. Demons can still get through."

I gestured to the pendants she still held in her hand, plus the one I'd taken from Beleth. "We have all four Creation Stones, Kate. *We* can ensure no one gets a handle on them ever again."

"As long as the stones exist, the Devil's Army will never stop looking for them. We have to destroy them."

"They can't be destroyed," Kelsey added. "They were created by God."

Kate looked at the alien warrior. "Does your orb still work?"

The female nodded.

I swallowed thickly. "Kate, what are you thinking?"

"We will never reclaim our world or be able to heal from this sickness so long as Samael still breathes. Our son, our friends… no one in our realm or the rest of the universe will ever be able to live in peace knowing that beast still lives. Even if we find a way to hide the stones somewhere no one could ever find them, as long as that demon remains in Abaddon, I will never be free of his threat. None of us will."

"And how exactly do you plan to kill him? We have no way of getting to him," I said.

"*You* don't," she said, looking at all our weathered faces, "but *I* can."

My back tensed and a pit opened inside my stomach. "What are you talking about?"

"You said only angels, demons, and the souls of the dead can enter Abaddon. Well, according to you, I'm part angel."

I turned from her and paced. "No. I won't allow it."

Clint holstered his gun and ran an agitated hand through his hair. "Kate, I don't think this is a wise idea. How are we even supposed to get you into Abaddon? If we try to use the stones to open the gates, we risk Samael breaking through."

"We don't use the stones. We use the Eldhon-rā. Ta'herah, do you think you can use the orb to open a wormhole into Abaddon?"

"In theory, yes. But I'd need to know it's exact location."

Kate looked around the chamber. "The Devil's Army chose this hospital to open the gates because of its connection to Abaddon. Because the horrors here were so intense, it created some type of entanglement between the realms, or some shit I don't really care to understand. But what I do know is that if there's a way to open a portal to Abaddon that doesn't include using the Creation Stones, this place has to be it."

Ta'herah looked intrigued. "What's your plan, Kate?"

"I want you to use the energies in this chamber and see if

you have a way to use your orb to pinpoint some type of location for Abaddon. Once I go through the portal—"

"No," I said, cutting her off. "It's too dangerous. We won't even know if it works. What if Abaddon doesn't accept you? What if you end up someplace else, or worse, dead?"

"Not to mention, none of us can accompany you," Chaz added. "You'll be by yourself in a realm you don't know. Kate, not even the lot of us were able to defeat him. How are you going to do it alone?"

"There's only one way to find out."

I blew out a rankled breath and closed the distance between us, trying to reign in my frustration. "Kate, what you're asking of me… to just let you go into Abaddon to face Samael on your own… Do you even have an idea what Hell truly is? It is an unforgiving world. If Samael won't kill you, the place itself will."

"It's a risk we have to take, Jax. Samael has to die; it's the only way we can start to rebuild. The only way we can offer our son the life he deserves. Free of all this violence, this hatred. This evil."

I put my forehead against hers. "Angel, time works differently in these realms, specifically Abaddon. One day in that realm could be days, weeks, in ours. God knows how long you could be lost in there."

"It kills me to think about being separated from you and Luke again, but until Samael is gone for good and not just locked away, we will never have peace."

"Let's take time to think about this, to regroup. There's gotta be another way."

She palmed my cheek while she rocked Luke in her arm. I looked down at him, at his peaceful little face. God, I loved him so much and I'd barely been his father. "Jax, look at me."

I did as she asked and nearly broke at the resolve I saw in her eyes. She was gonna do this; no matter what any one of us said, she'd already made up her mind. "Kate, I already lost you once… I don't think I can lose you again."

"Baby, I'm coming back. I promise you, I *will* come back. And I will not only kill Samael, but I will rescue Mikha'el and find a way to close the portal for good so no other demon can ever escape Hell ever again."

Another rumble shook the foundation, and more debris fell into the chamber. Chaz stood by the entrance. "From the sounds I hear echoing down the hallways, the Devil's Army is making a run for it. Which means, whatever it is you all plan to do, we gotta do it pronto, or this hospital is gonna crush us like pancakes."

Chapter Thirty-One

KATE

The chamber creaked and groaned like stone grinding against stone. Chaz was right. We needed to act fast, or this building was going to crush us beneath its weight.

I peered down at Luke cradled in my arms, his blanket covering us both as I breastfed him. I'd hoped my breastmilk hadn't dried out since it had been several days since I'd given birth and I hadn't been breastfeeding, but it seemed I wasn't completely dry, and he took to the breast right away, gorging himself as if he knew it would be long before his next feeding.

Hopefully not too long.

After I finished feeding him, I handed him to Jax while I went to talk to Ta'herah, who was kneeling beside Khai-runē's body. She had covered her sister-in-arms with stones, placing them with reverence and silent grief.

I knelt beside her. "I'm sorry," I whispered, though the words felt too small. "She was brave. Her sacrifice won't ever be forgotten."

Streaked with grime and blood, Ta'herah's face was grim,

but it softened for just a moment as she looked at me. She dipped her head and nodded faintly. "She was a celebrated warrior in our world. She will be greatly missed."

I hated having to ask her for another favor, for one more sacrifice, but I had no choice. I knew the Eldhon-rā was already severely depleted of energy, that after this there was a poor chance she could use it to get back to Aetheria.

As if she'd heard my thoughts, she said, "I will do everything in my power to get you to Abaddon, Kate. But you must promise me this: you will kill Samael and claim his head in her name."

"I will claim it in all of our names."

Kelsey was nearby, her niece at her side, their eyes rimmed red from crying. Kyle's body had been covered with a discarded robe, but it didn't make the pain of his death any easier on them. I moved toward her, placing a hand on her shoulder. "Kelsey, I... I know words won't change anything, but I'm sorry about Kyle. He... he gave his life to protect his daughter, and I know what it means to be willing to do anything for your child."

She looked up at me, her expression unreadable at first, then she let out a sigh that seemed to carry a lifetime of regrets. "He did many awful things under the rule of the Army. It doesn't excuse anything, I know I'm guilty of the same shit. But of one thing I'm certain. He wasn't just my brother, Kate. Deep down, he was a good man—a man trying to do good by his family. I just hope people will remember that part of him, too."

"We will. We all will." The ground trembled again, and we all looked to the ceiling. "And I hope you and Clint can repair your relationship going forward. He's gonna need someone to keep him in line."

"I heard that," he shouted from one of the tiered seats. He'd gone back into the halls and had found his crossbow discarded alongside the high priest's mangled body, or whatever was left of him, which apparently hadn't been much. He'd recovered the two bolts he'd lost as well, and was now tending to his weapon.

"You were meant to," I shouted back at him.

Ta'herah retrieved the Eldhon-rā from her satchel, its mechanical, otherworldly gears shifting under her fingers. She walked to the center of the pit and began the activation process. Her hands shook, and I saw the pain in her eyes. Opening a portal to Abaddon would require a lot more energy than she believed she had, but the Aetherian was determined, if not for my people, then for hers.

Jax caught my gaze from across the chamber, his jaw tight, worry etched into every line of his face. We didn't have much time. I knew what I had to say, but the words sat lodged in my throat like stones. I forced myself to smile, even as the weight of it all pressed down on me. Jax stepped closer, his voice low. "You don't have to do this alone. You don't even know if you can come back."

My heart twisted, but I kept my voice calm. "I'll find a way. Either I'll rift, or Mikha'el will bring me back. But I have to try, Jax."

He closed his eyes, shaking his head as though trying to banish the thought. "But if you don't—"

"Then you'll have to finish this," I interrupted. "You'll protect the stones. You'll make sure the sanctuary remains safe. And you'll do it for Luke, for everyone we've lost."

Raw pain flickered across his features before he swallowed it down. "Kate…"

I leaned in, cupping his cheek. The heat of his skin was grounding, and for a moment, everything else faded away—the demons, the chaos, the weight of our losses. There was just us. "Hey," I whispered, trying to steady him, to steady myself. "Do you really think I'd leave you here all by yourself?

Who else is gonna call you out when you make stupid movie references, huh?"

He managed a small, broken laugh, and before I could step away, he pulled me into a fierce kiss. It was the kind of kiss that claimed me as his, not just my lips, but all of me. He inhaled my breath, as if in doing so he could somehow ensure he'd keep me here, keep me with him.

And the moan that rumbled through him… it was a promise. A promise that there was still too much left between us, too much we still needed to explore, to live. The kiss wasn't just a plea to return to him; it was also the tether that would keep us anchored. No matter where I ended up in this universe, I would tug on that tether, and it would bring me back to him.

When we broke apart, his eyes were blazing, a fire I knew he'd hold on to and never let burn out.

A surge of power flickered from Ta'herah's hands, and I felt the energy shifting as the Eldhon-rā hummed to life. She took a slow breath, her fingers flying over the device, but I could see the exhaustion in her face. She was struggling, the depletion of elemental magic slowing her movements, but she wouldn't let it stop her. With a final twist, the device clicked, and the air before us split open, the portal crackling into existence. It was dimmer, smaller than the last portal it had created, the edges wavering, unstable. I knew it wouldn't last long.

Jax grabbed my hand, his grip tight, and pulled me in for a strong hug with Luke cradled between us. "This is crazy," he said, "but I wouldn't expect anything else from you. This is who you are, Kate. Why you were chosen for this. Only a woman with such fierce love in her heart would risk it all for a world that maybe doesn't deserve it."

"You and Luke deserve it, and so do our friends. I do this for you, for them." I squeezed him tight, then I took Luke into my arms and kissed his forehead and gently whispered all the things I wished for him. How I would always carry him in my heart. How I would always find my way back to him and his father.

I handed him back to Jax and clenched my jaw, trying to keep myself from crying or I might lose my resolve. "Once I'm through the portal, you high tail it out of here. There's a nursery in the main building; I saw it when we were dragged down here. Probably where they were keeping Luke. I'm sure there's baby supplies in there. Raid everything. You're going to need it. Diapers, formula, clothes, whatever you can find. And find the sanctuary."

The chamber groaned again, rocks tumbling from above. There was no more time.

"Jax," I said, "promise me you'll keep him safe."

He swallowed hard, his hand trembling against mine. "I… I promise."

Hank nudged my leg, his brown eyes begging me to let him come. I knelt to scratch behind his ears, murmuring a quiet goodbye, wishing I *could* take him with me, but knowing he'd be safer here, protecting the others.

I stood, my hand brushing Jax's one last time, and then I took a step back, feeling the pull of the portal behind me. "Take care of each other," I said to the group.

Ta'herah's shoulders tensed. "It will close fast. Be swift or be lost."

Clint ran to me, putting his arms around me. "Come back to us."

I smiled and squeezed him back. It was the best I could do without breaking down.

"Take care of yourself, boss lady," Chaz said. "I'll keep your sword safe until you return."

The portal swirled like the maw of some ancient beast. I took a breath, the weight of everything settling over me. I didn't know what waited on the other side, but I knew one thing…

I was ready.

With one last look toward Jax, I whispered, "Our love will lead me back to you." And gripping Emrandael, I stepped through the portal, the world dissolving around me, leaving only darkness and the faint glimmer of light as I was swallowed whole.

Chapter Thirty-Two

KATE

The portal tore through the dark, yanking me forward, my entire body pulled through layers of reality that seemed to fold and ripple around me like thin sheets of ice. A wrenching, blistering cold surged over me, far worse than I could have ever prepared for. It wasn't just a chill; it was a profound, freezing emptiness that cut straight to the marrow of my bones.

Then, with a brutal lurch, I was through, my feet hitting hard stone as I staggered to a stop. My wings unfurled instinctively, and still shivering, I straightened and pulled myself upright, gathering my senses. I blinked several times, adjusting my vision.

It didn't take me long to realize that the Eldhon-rā had worked. I was both relieved and terrified as I took in the rough-hewn black stone that rose high, towering all around me. In the dim light, I could make out hundreds of twisted figures lined along the walls, their forms obscured by an impossible shade of darkness. And in the center of this great hall, flanked by three monstrous beings, was Samael—seated on a throne forged of interlocking bones and skulls.

He looked… pleased. Not the cruel, angry shock I'd expected, but a mocking satisfaction, as if he had been expecting *me* all along. That twisted smirk, the air of casual arrogance—it was all there, only sharper, darker, as if the power of Abaddon itself made him more whole here.

My skin burned from the biting cold, especially when I tightened my fingers around the icy condensation on Emrandael's hilt. The sword vibrated in my hand, as if the power within it wanted to break free of the metal. As if it shook with anger at being contained.

Then I realized why.

Mikha'el's limp and brutalized naked form loomed over the great hall, hanging above the dais, right behind Samael. His once brilliant brass-colored wings were nothing but frayed, bloodied feathers and exposed bone. They'd been nailed to a beam along with his arms. If it weren't for the fact that I knew angels turned to dust when they died, I would've thought he was dead. Which meant he'd been enduring this torture for who knew how long.

My body trembled, rage building in my blood. I wanted to look away from the horror, from the indecent and volatile display of his body, but that was exactly what Samael wanted. To terrorize and intimidate me.

I would not let him cower me into submission. And I would not let him get away with what he'd done to Mikha'el. I fanned my wings and aimed my sword at the vile king. "Release him, Samael."

He leaned back in his bone throne, relaxed his shoulders, and splayed his legs. He was dressed in some type of black armor that looked forged of the same rock that made up the interior of his castle. A cloak that looked like it was made of animal hide draped around him. He'd glamoured away his burns and chosen to show me his pre-Fall face. His long, platinum hair cascaded over his shoulders, though he left his bone crown on display. Always so prideful.

Samael cocked his head slightly. "Did you truly believe it would be that easy? That you could waltz into my kingdom, make demands, and I would so freely bow my head to *you*?"

I took in a deep breath, my lungs aching from the deep chill. "You don't seem surprised to see me."

"I'm not."

"You know what I am, then?"

"I suspected for a time, but it was confirmed when you displayed *those*." He gestured toward my wings, and the contempt in his eyes made my insides quiver. His hatred for me, for what I was, was so palpable, I felt it in the air particles that touched my skin. "What surprises me is how long it took you to pay me a visit."

The calmness in his voice, the stillness, was like a finely sharpened butcher knife. The type of knife that could cut through flesh with barely any assistance. "I was busy saving my world, as you know." I winked.

"Is this why you came here, Daughter of Eve? To mock me?" His twilight gaze darkened, and he leaned forward, hands gripping the armrests of his throne. "I do not suffer fools."

Any creature would wither and die under the weight of those terrifyingly beautiful eyes. I might've in a former life, but not this time, not after all the shit I'd been through. I took a step forward, my wings bristling, and the beings lining the walls, the creatures hiding in the shadows, shifted, making me keenly aware that I was severely outnumbered here.

"I came to offer you a deal." The room grew so quiet, my voice echoed off the stone walls for far too long.

After the awkward silence, one where Samael looked like he'd been cut out of marble, his steel façade finally broke. A laugh rumbled from his chest, a deep, almost mirthful laugh that made my bones rattle. His three lieutenants followed suit, accompanied by the rest of his court—those unseen creatures still hiding in the shadows cackling like hyenas.

I didn't think I'd said anything particularly amusing, but if Samael had wanted me off kilter, he may have just succeeded. I shifted on my feet, eyes carefully scanning the room. I couldn't see a threat, but an unexpected whisp of wind brushed against the back of my neck, like the intimate touch of a lover's breath, except the shiver that rippled down my back felt like rusted nails scraping over my skin.

Samael pushed up from his chair, his movements a liquid dance of muscle and armor as he stepped down from the dais and ambled toward me. His court quieted to an eerie silence, making every clang of the metal decorating his body that much more pronounced.

His cloak swayed, showing those sickly wings hidden beneath the heavy material. It wasn't until he stood a mere foot from me that I realized the cloak was made of night-crawler hide. I wanted to retch.

Samael wasn't just enormous; he was a mountain. I'd not been able to appreciate the sheer size of him when I'd fought him in that chamber, but standing in front of him now had me questioning my decision to come here, even if just for a millisecond. I remained motionless, my wings still fanned, Emrandael gripped tightly in my hand, ready to strike.

With an amor-plated finger, he tipped my chin up to meet his fiery gaze. His starkly white teeth glimmered with a predatory gleam. "You wish to bargain with the Devil, Daughter of Eve?"

The brutality of his angelic splendor had me wanting to drop to my knees. I didn't, though. It was his utter perfection that had made him the most flawed of us all, angel and humankind alike. I didn't recoil from his touch and met his gaze with equal fury, feeling the angelic blood in my veins flare, the sigils on my arms sparking to life. "My *name* is Katherine Elizabeth Jones, a citizen of Earth and Guardian of its people. And you will not take our home away from us."

He leaned in closer, the death chill of his breath crusting over my face. "Name. Your Bargain. Kate."

I took a quick step back and aimed my sword right at his chest. "A duel. To the death." I'll admit. I'd not stepped through that portal with a solid plan other than to find Samael and cut his head off. But if I was being honest with myself, I'd not had a solid plan since I was thrust into this battle between Heaven and Hell. It was more like some angel had shoved a sword in my hands, done the sign of the cross, and said… *go, fight the forces of evil.*

So, here I was.

Samael looked puzzled, as if that had been the last thing he'd expected. "You wish to battle me to the death?"

"If I kill you, your demons release Mikha'el and Cassael to me. And they will never cross over into Earth ever again, or any other realm for that matter. This will be their eternal prison, as it was always meant to be. With no king, no master."

"And *when* I kill you?"

"Earth will be yours."

He laughed again, spinning in place. "Brothers and sisters," he said, addressing his court. "This hybrid filth, this human born of tarnished angel blood, has the arrogance, the *audacity* to believe she alone holds the authority to gift me what is already *mine.*" He approached me again, teeth grinding, that grin he'd worn earlier morphing into snarling venom. "Earth was promised to me lifetimes before your line ever came into existence, *human.*"

"*Nephilim,*" I corrected him, the hubris in my voice sharp and piercing. I may have been smaller in stature and an infant compared to his eternal age, but I was done with his intimidation tactics. Jax had said Nephilim were almost hunted down to extinction because they were deemed too dangerous, possibly even stronger than angels. It was time someone gave this monster something to fear.

"If my blood is so tarnished, then why did you wish to take my son as your vessel? Seems to me that without my so-called filthy hybrid blood, you are nothing but another inmate serving a life sentence in this frozen cesspool."

His court took a collective gasp. Had they not known their master wished to not only escape Abaddon, but to also become one, if not the most powerful being in the universe? A god no one would be able to challenge.

The beast stared at me with the dark fury of his rage. "Foolish woman. You wish to challenge a Seraphim of the First Sphere to the death, then so be it." One of his lieutenants took his cloak and handed Samael a war helmet that looked like it'd been forged in the depths of Moria. Then he handed him a shield and that abominable, black steel sword that made the entire throne room shudder at the sheer raw power it exuded.

I looked at Mikha'el's ravaged body, and my heart banged against my ribcage like a feral lion hungry for vengeance. What he'd done to the archangel was unconscionable. Samael had to pay for what he'd done to him, and for every evil atrocity he'd committed against my kind. All I could do was pray that Zadkiel hadn't been wrong about me; that Gavri'el hadn't been mistaken about her prophecy, and that Mikha'el hadn't foolishly placed his faith in me.

I had no armor, no shield, no nightmarish-looking helmet, but I had Mikha'el's sword. But most importantly, I had a heart full of love.

The one thing this beast would never have.

Tightly gripping Emrandael with both hands, I took my position, my wings taut and ready for battle. "Let us begin."

Chapter Thirty-Three

KATE

His court erupted in a ravenous cheer. Shadows twisted in excitement, eyes gleaming from the void, drinking in the spectacle before them like starving beasts. I pushed down the surge of adrenaline, honing every thread of focus on the creature standing before me.

Samael's gaze lingered on me as he fitted his helmet and raised his massive, bone-carved shield, his dark sword flashing as he raised it to the towering ceiling. Every fiber of his being radiated with the shadowed grace of an ancient predator; a hellish creature sculpted for brutality, yet gifted with an angelic allure that somehow amplified the horror. But beneath that glamour lay rot, a festering hunger that devoured anything within reach.

And now, I was in his sights.

He didn't rush; instead, he moved toward me with the deliberate pace of someone who already saw his victory, who was ready to savor the slow death of his prey. Emrandael hummed in response, the power within the blade desperate, burning, wanting to be unleashed.

When Samael finally lunged, it was as if darkness itself came to life. He struck with terrifying speed, his sword arcing down toward me with an unholy strength. I brought Emrandael up just in time, feeling the clash reverberate through my bones, the force of his blow sending me skidding backward across the stone floor.

I barely had a moment to catch my breath before he was on me again, his strikes relentless, each one hammering down with an intent to shatter. I dodged to the left, parried, ducked, feeling his strikes chip away at my stamina as he forced me into a corner.

Panic surged within me, remembering the fight inside the pit. Had Jax not been able to break the connection between the stones and sent Samael back here, I don't think we would've won that battle. Doubt crept into my soul. What the fuck had I been thinking, believing myself capable of defeating Samael, the first-born angel, all on my own?

I shook the intrusive thoughts from my head. I refused to break. The fight had just started. Anger fueled my every move, an unyielding ire burning inside me as I met him blow for blow. And when I felt my strength waning, something else surged to the surface—a flash of energy, raw and instinctive.

Suddenly, I was no longer in front of him, but behind him, as if I'd blinked through space itself. Fuck, had I just rifted? I froze, shocked, but only for a second. Samael spun, his eyes flaring when he realized what I'd done. A smirk tugged at his lips, but there was a flicker of something else—surprise, maybe even doubt. He hadn't expected me to be able to rift.

I tightened my grip on Emrandael and lunged, my blade grazing his arm, cutting through the dark armor. He roared, the sound shaking the very walls as I twisted away, rifting once more just as his sword came crashing down where I'd been standing. The effort sapped me, though, a wave of weakness rolling through my limbs, but I ignored it, refusing to show him even a sliver of vulnerability.

Samael raised his head, eyes darkening. "Impressive, but hardly astonishing. Rifting comes at a cost, Katherine."

The room blurred, and suddenly, I was no longer in his hall but back in my old apartment in Brooklyn, the air cold and stale. I sat up in bed, my body drenched in sweat. Then I heard a distant wail. *Isabella.* The sound tore through me, and I knew…

Oh, God. I knew.

I jumped from under the covers and yanked the bedroom door open.

"No…" I whispered, shaking my head as the scene blurred again.

Roger's face was a twisted mess of blackened teeth and blood. "You could have saved us," he rasped, his voice echoing, taunting, Isabella's dead body laying limp in his arms.

A fierce tremor ripped through me, and I shook my head. This wasn't real. I tightened my grip on Emrandael, feeling the blade's power anchor me. This was Samael's game—his sick attempt to break my spirit—but I wouldn't fall for it. I forced my mind to snap back to the present, tearing through the illusion as I met his cold gaze once more.

"I won't play your games, Samael," I spat, feeling my wrath build like an inferno. "You can twist memories, you can taunt me, but you won't break me."

He let out a growl and lunged forward again, and I rifted away just before his blade could find me. This time, I reappeared above him, wings flared, plunging Emrandael toward the vulnerable joint in his shoulder armor. The blade struck true, slicing through the metal as dark blood spilled forth, and he staggered, his control faltering for the first time.

"*You miserable creature!*" he bellowed, and a wave of cold darkness exploded from him, crashing into me like an iceberg. It hurled me back against the stone wall, knocking the air from my lungs. I fell hard, but I was able to jump back to my feet, though a bit woozy from the hit.

Bastard. A cut from an Empyrean weapon hadn't been enough to crucially wound him, but it had clearly hurt him enough to send him into a rage. He charged, unrelenting, and this time I met him head-on, our blades clashing in a maelstrom of light and dark. His shield slammed into my ribs, sending pain lancing through my side, but I pushed through, twisting around to slash Emrandael down his back. His armor cracked, a jagged line splintering across it, and I continued my onslaught, every blow pushing him back.

Samael seethed, a shadow of worry breaking through the anger carved into his chiseled face. He finally realized he wasn't so invincible. His twilight eyes burned, and he roared, coming at me with renewed strength. Our battle cracked the stone beneath us, sending debris flying as our strikes rang out like thunder.

I stumbled, pain shooting up the side of my body. Broken ribs, for sure. My vision blurred, streaked by wetness. I had to use Emrandael for balance as I caught my breath. Samael was apparently doing the same, his breaths sawing out of him in sharp plumes of icy smoke.

He grinned, his lips smeared with black blood. "You are a worthy opponent, Katherine Elizabeth Jones. The angel whose blood you carry lives up to his legend. It's a pity his gift was wasted on you."

"What the fuck do you know about the angel blood in me?"

"A great deal, *hybrid*. Sadly, for you, you won't live long enough to know your angelic lineage." He charged at me once more with speed I had not been prepared for, using his shoulder to tackle me. The hit felt like a Mack truck had crashed into me, sending me spinning through the air until I hit a stone pillar. I landed like crumbling bricks, my entire body feeling like all my bones had splintered.

Breathing was too painful, each breath coming out in tiny

gasps. I tried to get on all fours, but every move I made felt like my ribs were stabbing me from the inside.

"You thought yourself mightier than me. You believed yourself capable of defeating the King of Hell." He stood over my broken body, his gaze promising death. "You were nothing but a blink in the span of eternity. Inconsequential." He smiled, cold and cruel, the kind of wicked that could only exist in a rotted soul.

"Fuck you."

He raised his sword, ready to strike me down, but I sunk deep into my soul, into that well of infinite love. All I saw before me were the faces of my family, of Luke and Jax and Hank[SC1]. [SP2] , of Clint and Chaz. Of all the people who fought with their life to protect those they loved. Of the Guardians who sacrificed themselves to save others.

A flower of strength bloomed in my heart, funneling the last of my energy into all my muscles. I channeled that energy and rifted once more, appearing behind him just as he slashed downward. He stumbled when he was met with stone, but when he spun around quickly, he found himself face to face with a filthy hybrid hovering above him—the Nephilim who would claim his life.

Without hesitation, I plunged Emrandael into his chest, pushing with every ounce of force I had left. He dropped his sword, his face contorting in shock, his armor now shattered and his flesh vulnerable beneath it.

He fell onto his knees, then his back, a hand grasping my blade as I pushed it deeper. I continued to hover over him, wings whipping, breath heaving. Emrandael glowed with an ethereal light, and all the demon could do was gurgle as black blood dribbled from his mouth.

There was something in his eyes, a flicker of recognition—of strange acceptance, maybe even gratitude. He tore off his helmet and blood seeped from the protruding bones of his crown. He raised his head, but I placed my boot against his face and pinned him to the ground. "It was you, Katherine. This moment..." He closed his eyes, and taking a deep, cleansing breath as if he knew it would be his last, he whispered, "It was *always* you."

I didn't understand his cryptic last words, but I didn't give a shit. A strange calm washed over me, and I tightened my grip on Emrandael, pulling it free from his chest. Then, with a single, decisive swing, I severed his head from his body.

It was a quiet, serene death—his flesh dissolving into a plume of black dust that scattered across the hall, then vanished. The ageless evil that had tormented humanity since its birth was... gone. The scene was too surreal. Incredulity weaved through my mind, my heart.

Had *I* dispatched Samael to oblivion?

Watching him simply turn to dust was too anticlimactic. As if his punishment for what he'd done to humanity had been too infinitesimal for it to be true, because not even the countless lifetimes he'd spent in this place had been enough to pay for his sins. And now his death had also been too short, too swift.

For all the misery he'd caused, he'd gotten away too easily. It felt unjust. Perhaps I would've enjoyed watching him agonize in pain, watching him beg for his life.

But the monster had just accepted his fate, then turned into a puff of ash. Meanwhile, the people I'd loved had suffered innumerably before they met their deaths.

Maybe I'd expected his stone castle to crumble upon his death, or that Abaddon's sky would roar with anger and sorrow. Maybe I'd hoped God would appear out of nowhere to mourn the death of His son, and I could take pleasure in knowing *I'd* done this...

A breath shuddered from me as I tucked my wings and gently lowered my feet to the ground. The Devil was dead—by my hand. But I felt no joy, no satisfaction.

Not even a sigh of relief trickled from my lips. All I *could* feel was utter sadness. Sadness for all the pain that drove Samael to hate my kind. Sadness for all the unnecessary death and suffering inflicted on humanity. Sadness for everything we had lost to get to this moment.

We had won, but at what cost?

Sapped of all my energy, I dropped to my knees on the stone floor and stared at the ocean of demons no longer hiding in the shadows. Even his lieutenants seemed speechless. No one moved, no one said anything. The only sound in the room was that of my ragged breaths. Teeth clenching from the piercing agony of my broken ribs, I lifted my gaze to where Mikha'el hung suspended over the dais.

My heart squeezed as I once again took in the gruesome sight of his broken form nailed to a beam. His wings were outstretched in agonizing suspension, a cruel mockery of his angelic grace now mangled, every feather caked with blood and bone.

I raised Emrandael and pointed it at the three lieutenants, the remaining Horsemen. "I've claimed your dark lord's death. Release the archangel or you, too, will suffer the blade of my vengeance."

Chapter Thirty-Four

KATE

The demons flanking the room lowered their heads, their sneering contempt replaced by an eerie, quiet compliance as who I believed to be Chemoth ordered them to bring Mikha'el down. They scattered to obey, and the *clang* of rolling chains echoed through the hall as the beam was lowered to the ground.

Legs trembling, I limped toward the dais and nearly buckled to my knees when I saw the totality of his ruined body. His once-bronzed skin was dulled and flayed, bruises casting shadows on every sinew. An iron collar gripped his neck, a strange hum emanating from it—probably the magic meant to bind and nullify every ounce of his strength.

It had left him indefensible, utterly broken.

I lowered to my knees beside him, and I couldn't hold back the sob that tore through me. His chest barely rose and fell, breaths so faint I feared they would stop at any moment. His eyes remained closed, the lines of his face drawn tight, etched with the horror he'd endured for what must've felt like an eternity in this place.

"Take off the collar. And remove the nails," I ordered, and the wretched demons simply obeyed. I wanted to scream at them, to condemn every single one that had stood by and watched this atrocity, but I didn't have the will in my heart, not when Mikha'el was dying before my eyes.

Noticing Samael's cloak hanging off his throne, I yanked it down and draped it over Mikha'el's nakedness. As I leaned over him, I pressed my hand over his chest and reached for the faintest spark of power left within me, but it barely flickered, only enough to close the smallest of his wounds. Mikha'el's eyes fluttered open, and he looked up at me. "Kate..." His voice was little more than a whisper, his chapped lips barely able to move. "You came."

A sob broke from my throat. "You thought I'd leave you to rot in this place?"

His pained gaze seemed to soften as he took in my wings, their faint glow illuminating his face. "I always knew... you would become this. A force of light... of justice." His eyes searched mine, pride shining through his exhaustion, but there was a depth of sadness there I couldn't bear.

"Did you always know I was Nephilim?" I asked, feeling as if the question clawed its way out of me.

He took a labored breath, his chest hitching, but he managed to raise trembling fingers to my face and brushed a strand of hair behind my ear. "Even the mighty shall Fall..."

"I don't understand."

"You are of my bloodline, Kate." He swallowed, grimacing in pain, his voice raw and low. "I am not your sire. But you *are* my descendant... of a mistake I made long ago." A hint of sorrow clouded his face as he remembered. "An error... but not a regret."

My chest tightened, and the tears flowed freely now. "Why didn't you tell me?"

"Because," he whispered, "a Nephilim must... earn their wings. Discover their destiny through... their own crucible."

The spark I'd given him was fading, and I pressed down on his chest again, trying to give him every drop of power I had left, the golden rivers of magic draining from me and into his heart, but it was as if he resisted it, his hand coming up to stop me.

"I've lived long, Kate," he said, voice weak. "It's my time. My purpose has been fulfilled. *You* were that purpose. I held on only for you. Now I can go."

"No," I choked out, shaking my head. "I need you. I don't know what comes next. What I'm supposed to do. How to rebuild from this. I can't do this without you."

A tender smile curved over his lips, as if he had known this moment would come, as if he had foreseen it. "You defeated Samael. *You* did that… without me."

My fingers tightened around his hand, unwilling to let him go. I'd lost so much, and now him? No, it wasn't fair. I couldn't lose him, too.

His hand brushed against my cheek again, and he looked at me with a sorrowful kind of peace. "You are my greatest gift… my redemption." His breath caught, the strength finally leaving him as his eyelids drifted shut. "Live for Luke. Live for your people. You all deserve the truth."

"Mikha'el…" I whispered, my voice breaking, but his eyes closed, his body sinking back into stillness, the last remnants of his light slipping away.

A hollow emptiness consumed me as I watched his spirit depart, as his body became nothing but golden pixie dust. A scream lodged itself in my throat that couldn't find release. I could barely hear Cassael's footsteps as she was brought to me, her face streaked with grief and exhaustion. She fell to her knees beside me, her shoulders shaking, and together, we mourned Mikha'el in the silence of that vast, empty hall.

But beneath the sorrow, a volcano churned within me, growing hotter and hotter until it erupted into full rage. My fists clenched, and I looked up at Cassael, my voice raw, my heart brimming with a need for retribution I could no longer contain.

"Take me to Him," I demanded, the words harsh and unyielding. "God needs to answer for this."

Cassael recoiled slightly, her wings folding behind her. "Kate… He has been gone for a long time. Elysium has remained empty for… years in your time, longer in ours."

I took her hand, my grip fierce. "I don't care what it takes, if I have to prostrate myself at the foot of His throne for eons, or if I have to travel to every realm to find Him, but He will answer for His crimes."

Cassael looked at me, her gaze flickering with apprehension. "Kate, none but angelkind are allowed entrance into Elysium." She took note of my wings, gently caressing a feather. "Even as a half-blooded angel, the gates might reject and kill you upon entry."

"The same was said when I chose to come here, and now Samael is dead. I will take my chances with Heaven's gates. And if I die, I die."

Taking a deep, resigned breath, she nodded. There was no changing my mind about this. I didn't bother addressing the horde of demons or the Horsemen who would be left behind. Their king had bargained with their lives, and he'd lost, condemning them forever. Their fates were now sealed, and after the havoc, pain, destruction, and death they'd unleashed upon my world, they could rot for eternity and then some for all I cared.

Cassael unfurled her wings and wrapped them around me. I prepared myself as she began to chant a song in her angelic tongue, steeling every broken piece within me. I gripped Emrandael as if I was gripping Mikha'el's hand and held on to his final words. Tears streamed down my face as I struggled to accept that Mikha'el, archangel of the Third Sphere, Commander of God's Heavenly Host, Guardian of Earth's People… my sworn protector… my *friend*, was gone.

Chapter Thirty-Five

KATE

Rifting across realms was significantly different than rifting for short distances. It felt more chaotic, like being swept up into a churning tornado, then being spat out into a void. I doubted I'd ever get used to it. Just as my stomach was about to give out, we were thrust out of the wormhole, and I landed on hands and knees on a pristine floor made of shiny stone that swirled with a prism of colors I'd never seen before.

It took me several breaths to gather my bearings, especially as it appeared my skin was burning. Plumes of steam billowed from me as if my body was too hot for this place. "What is happening to me?" I asked Cassael.

"I can't be certain," she said, helping me to my feet. "But you're the first Nephilim to step foot in Elysium, Heaven's capital city, and inside God's throne room. You've been allowed to enter, but the magic that shields our world from intruders of a different race detects that there is something different about you. I think it tried to incinerate you, but your angelic blood protected you."

"That's… comforting." The steam coming off my skin finally subsided, and I was able to focus on my surroundings. Cassael had said this was God's throne room, and even thinking the words felt unreal, impossible. As if this was all just a dream. My brain struggled to process what my eyes were seeing. The room was a marvel of glass and gold that stretched toward what appeared to be the endless ceiling. I stared upward, completely baffled at the impossibility of the place.

Cassael's wings trembled beside me, her eyes darting across the room. "Kate," she whispered, "this isn't allowed. Rifting into the city is forbidden by cardinal law."

But her worry barely reached me. I was spellbound by what lay before us. The throne room was an expanse of light refracted through crystal and gold, casting rainbows that danced over every surface. Intricate carvings adorned the walls, each curve and line too perfect not to have been crafted by magic of some sort.

It was too beautiful to be real.

And yet, despite all the unimaginable beauty, at the room's heart, where I expected grandeur beyond my mortal imagining, sat a simple wooden throne, worn but timeless. No splendor, no shiny metals or glimmering jewels, not a single embellishment adorned it.

Even if I could've ever imagined myself standing before God's throne, I would've expected a seat of unbridled authority and power, gleaming with divine radiance. But the reality of the humility of God's throne struck me like a slap across the face. It almost made me angry. I'd wanted to hate everything about this place.

But I couldn't. And I couldn't unleash the torrent of pain festering in my heart because the fucking seat was empty.

Disappointment pummeled through me like a mudslide. The Throne of God—the world's answer to divinity, what was supposed to be the seat of all justice and mercy—was barren, silent. My fists clenched, and I heard my breaths, heavy and echoing.

"I'm so sorry, Kate," Cassael murmured, placing a hand on my shoulder. "I knew this was all we would find."

"I don't accept this," I gritted. "God knows I'm here. Knows that I want answers, and I'm not leaving until I get what I came for."

The heavy doors of the throne room swung open behind us with a resounding crash. Instinctively, I flared my wings and drew Emrandael. I narrowed my eyes to sharp slits over the individual who strode in, my heart hammering with the need to drive my sword straight through his fucking heart.

Dressed like the slimy courtier he was, Khama'el paused at the entrance, as if he'd been stunned frozen. His silvery hair was neatly combed back, not a single strand was out of place. He looked refreshed, as if he'd been strolling through the sunny streets of Elysium, enjoying a perfect day before he was so rudely summoned to attend to this untimely intrusion.

He'd been delighting in the fruits of his labor while Mikha'el had hung like a butchered animal in the great hall of Samael's castle.

I clenched my teeth, tightening my fingers around Emrandael's hilt. "I am going to cut you to shreds for what you did to Mikha'el, you despicable worm."

The three sicarii flanking his back raised their crossbows and aimed them at my head, their impeccable armor glinting as the light beaming through the stained-glass windows danced over the silver plates covering their bodies. They sneered like wolves cornering prey, mouths practically frothing.

Khama'el put a hand up, pacifying his dogs. Ignoring me as if I was nothing but a speck of dust, he trained his silver-rimmed gaze on Cassael. "You are an exiled criminal, lieutenant. Sent to Abaddon to serve a sentence for your treasonous acts against our kingdom. For aligning yourself with the traitorous archangel, Mikha'el Bar Elah…"

I stepped forward, causing the sicarii to cock their crossbows. "You keep his name off your filthy tongue, you conniving piece of shit. Don't you ever speak his name. *Ever*," I gritted.

Cassael put a hand out, gently placing it over my sword. Her eyes met mine, her silent plea begging me to lower my hackles. Pressing my lips into a fine line, I relented, hoping she had a plan, and dropped my arm. My grip on the hilt didn't loosen, though.

She spirited her wings away, an act of submission. I did no such thing and stretched mine wider.

"Most Venerable Counsel…" she began, her voice raked with sorrow. "I stand before you, not with contempt or ill intent in my heart, but with an inconsolable sadness that can never be remedied."

Khama'el's breaths deepened, but he raised his chin and puffed his chest. He swallowed deeply, and it was clear he already knew what Cassael's words weren't saying. "There are consequences for every action, lieutenant. The *commander,*" he said, eyeing me, "knew the punishment for his crimes."

That was it. I was done with this nonsense. I rifted so fast, the shift in the air blew over Khama'el's face, knocking a perfect lock of hair loose. I stood mere inches from him and stared up at his disgustingly refined nose. "You can't help yourself, can you? She just told you Mikha'el is dead, and all you can say is he knew the punishment for his crimes? He was *Mikha'el.* A name known by all. Can you say the same about yourself? Of course not. Because you are nothing but a sniveling coward. A plotting rat.

"Is that why you did it? Is that why you betrayed him? Because you were jealous of him? Because he was revered throughout the universe, something you could never boast about? Because he was loved by his warriors, so much so that their loyalty to him was greater than their loyalty to God. Or was it the adoration from your Father? Because he was the virtuous angel who always aimed to do what was right. Or maybe you just wanted a chance to feel grand yourself; you wanted a slice of the glory you could never have."

He scowled but said nothing.

"But you know who *did* deserve to die? Samael. And I want you to know that I reveled, watching as his flesh turned to ash right after I cut his fucking head off."

His eyes widened in horror, and he shifted uncomfortably on his feet. His sicarii exchanged glances, and suddenly, they all looked like they wanted to bolt out of that room.

"Whatever he promised you, good luck with that."

Khama'el's expression twisted into something dark—a revulsion so deep, it almost felt like physical heat radiating from him. "You speak with such authority, but I think you've forgotten who you are, Katherine. Rather, *what* you are."

"Remind me, since you seem so inclined."

His brows dipped, eyes narrowing. "You are an abomination. A hybrid creature that sullies the very heart of Elysium, of what we are. You are the product of Fallen angels, the scourge of our people, the representation of everything that is unholy. Your wretched kind was eradicated ages ago by God Himself because you were deemed an error, a byproduct of a mistake. You shouldn't even exist."

"Not all of us were eradicated," I said with a snarling smile.

His lips curved in disgust. "Your presence here is blasphemous, and I will not have you defile the Throne of God any longer. Seize her!"

I met the eyes of all three assassins, letting my angelic blood blaze, the sigils on my arms flaring bright, my wings glimmering, and my eyes... I willed them to swirl like liquid sunlight. Terror seeped into their bones. "Do you know whose blood runs in these blasphemous veins? The blood of the archangel you wrongfully sentenced to Abaddon for a crime he did not commit." I fixed my gaze on Khama'el. "A crime *you* knew he did not commit."

"You reprehensible woman," he seethed. "I will tear off those wings with my own hands for the disgrace you've brought my people. I will—"

"Silence, Khama'el." The voice cut through the air like a blade, resonant and absolute, reaching into my core and pulling something taut, something primal. It was neither male nor female, yet it held an authority that went beyond human comprehension. "I've heard enough of your vitriol."

Khama'el froze, his mouth sealing shut as he and his guards fell to their knees, their heads bowed in reverence. Beside me, Cassael turned toward the throne and dropped to her knees as well, her face stricken with awe and a fear she hadn't even shown in the depths of Abaddon.

For a moment's breath, I stood with my back to the voice. I knew who owned that voice, but perhaps I'd not wanted to accept it. Maybe I wasn't as ready as I thought I was to face God.

"Mikha'el believed you were."

The sound of his name spoken by that otherworldly voice sent a shiver skidding over my skin. The wound of his death still felt too raw. It was almost as if I didn't want anyone uttering his name. No one deserved to… not even his creator.

I turned around, but I would not kneel, not to this God, not to the God who had abandoned my people and allowed such savagery to be committed, not just on humankind but angelkind as well.

The figure seated on the throne was made of pure light. It was borderline painful to stare directly at it. Perhaps this was why the angels around me had kept their heads bowed. I didn't care if the light would burn my retinas right off. God needed to look me straight in my eyes.

As if sensing my thoughts, I felt its piercing stare, as

though it could see every scar etched into my soul, every decision that had led me here.

"You have journeyed far, Katherine," the voice intoned, holding no trace of judgment, only a knowing that stretched beyond words. "And yet you do not kneel."

I straightened my spine, meeting the blinding light of its aura, even as my heart threatened to punch out of my chest. "I didn't come all this way to kneel at your feet. I came to order you to bring Mikha'el back."

There was a silence, weighty and endless, as if the throne room held its breath.

The figure inclined its head ever so slightly. "Mikha'el's fate has been fulfilled. His death cannot be undone."

A ribbon of anger coiled in my gut, and I took a step closer to the dais. "You are God, are you not? Then you *can* bring him back. You created him once. Create him again. Prove your power is as mighty as the universe believes it is and bring him back. I demand it."

"Light cannot exist without dark. Good without evil. Life without death. It is a cruel truth not even I can control. Fate is an inevitability that comes for us all."

"So Mikha'el's fate was simply to die like a discarded animal? Beaten and dishonored? After everything he did for you?"

"Mikha'el's fate was to bring you to me."

I straightened my back and flared my wings. "And what's my fate, then? Why did the almighty God go through such lengths to bring a lowly half-breed to his throne?"

"To correct my mistakes."

"Correct your mistakes? Do you mean kill your evil progeny? Because you lacked the balls to do it yourself?"

"I am not proud of the creator I was to him. Samael was meant to be the embodiment of all perfection, but perfection cannot exist without flaws. As I poured all the light of creation into him, so did my own darkness follow. My hubris, above all, corrupted his soul beyond measure. In my attempt to create the most unblemished being to ever exist, I gave life to the unholy. I failed, Katherine. I know I cannot undo the harm he caused."

"Harm? He didn't just harm my world. He killed millions of my people because of a feud he had with *you*. People who didn't deserve to die. Children… How can you sit there so calmly and talk about this as if all he did was beat his chest and try to take over."

"I understand your pain, Katherine. The pain of all those who have suffered sits on my heart. But the time of sorrow has come to an end. Samael's fate has been fulfilled."

"Fulfilled? You gave that unholy being reign over my world, abandoning us to his darkness, his depravity. How can you expect us to accept that our suffering was on purpose—a purpose you predestined—and that now we should just be okay with it because he's finally dead?"

The light emanating from the figure dimmed, but that otherworldly voice grew stronger. "His purpose was to test humanity. You may not agree with my methods, but privilege to the knowledge of the universe comes at a cost, and not all are worthy to sit at my table. His fate was to show the imperfections of the human soul, to prove that none were worthy to stand before the throne of God, and in doing so, he revealed the true beauty of the human spirit. But the paths of suffering and joy, of loss and victory, are bound to the will of each soul. The struggle is woven into the fabric of existence. It was my love for your people that gave birth to that challenge. I never turned away from humanity; quite the opposite. I've been with you all along, championing the rebirth of a new, brighter future for your people."

My fists clenched, rage boiling to the surface. "That's an excuse and a complete lie," I bit out. "You left all of us to rot, to fight alone. And you have the gall to sit on this… this throne, inside a castle made of glass and gold, speaking of fate and struggle as if it justifies the pain. Not all who suffered were unworthy. Roger and Isabella? Did they deserve to die like they did? Where were you then? Where were you when all the people of Earth were dying from war and disease and hunger?"

The figure's light flickered, as if my words struck it like a blow. It took a long, quiet breath—a soundless movement that brushed within me. "I was where I have always been, Katherine. In the fire of your spirit, in the courage of those who stood by you as you fought to uncover the truth, as you fought to protect those you loved, as you fought to defend all of humanity against the Devil… and even against me."

"That's it? That's your grand explanation? You weren't there to save us, but to give us the strength to save ourselves?"

"Even the most destructive of storms serve a purpose. Consider the mighty trees of the forest. They do not grow strong in the calm, gentle breezes, nor do they sink their roots deep in the unchallenged soil. It is the storms that test them, the fierce winds that force their roots to burrow deeper into the earth. The rain that batters their branches feeds the soil that nourishes them. Without the trial of the storm, the tree would be weak, shallow-rooted and fragile."

"You're the storm, is that it? All our suffering, that was to make us stronger? What for? What if we never wanted this burden? Shouldn't we get a say in what happens to our life?"

"You didn't have to descend into Hell or traverse the universe to stand where you stand. Those were your choices, Katherine. You may not believe in yourself, but Mikha'el believed in you, in the strength you'd one day find. You are his legacy. And it is through this legacy that his light continues. And it is through that light that you shall bring your people out of darkness. The truth has a cost, and only those willing to put their lives on the line, only those willing to fight for it, will survive. Darkness is death. You chose to fight for the light. That is why you stand before me. That is why you will shepherd your people out of the tunnel and into the truth."

The words twisted painfully within me. I wanted to shout, to rail against its serene and calming force, to scream until it felt the rage burning in my heart. But I couldn't, because part of me knew the ugly truth it spoke of. Mikha'el had believed in me, had held on through unspeakable suffering because he had faith in who I would become. *That* faith was the anchor that had kept him alive.

"You want *me* to be the one who brings my people out of the darkness? A darkness *you* created? We never chose to be kept in the shadows. You never even gave us a real choice. And now you want me to shoulder that task? I am but a woman. A woman who is beaten and tired. How am I the one to bring all of humanity out of the dark?"

"The answer to all your questions lies in your blood. How do you think Mikha'el's bloodline on Earth was preserved? Who gave the order to purge the unworthy but to protect the descendants of the one who one day would rise to bring their people out of the nebula and into enlightenment? It was me. Many rose to the challenge, but all of them faltered. But you… you found the way. In the middle of all the darkness, of all the pain, of all the death and destruction, you found the light within you. You found your wings, child. You ask how it is that a simple woman can be the bridge for her people? Fate is fate, Katherine. But this choice… *this* choice is yours."

My head spun, trying to make sense of everything God said. Who were the many that rose and faltered? The prophets? Were they all descendants of Mikha'el? Was I a descendant of them? This was too much, but it absurdly made sense. It made sense why Mikha'el had always been there. Fighting for humanity, fighting for hope.

"I'm not a prophet. Nor do I want to be."

"And that's why *you* are the one worthy of Mikha'el's

blood. Power corrodes the heart, Katherine. To refuse it is a sign of strength and not weakness."

"The only thing I want is for the people of Earth to have an equal seat at the table. To be regarded amongst the peoples of the universe as worthy to exist. What I want is for my people to be free of nonsensical rules and simply be given a chance to believe without the blindfold over our eyes."

"Then you wish to see beyond the veil. Do you not want to lead your people to the truth as well?"

My shoulders sagged, and I took a deep and prolonged breath. This was it. This was the crossroads. This was the moment of choice. The truth. It was what I always wanted. And now, standing before God, I wondered if it all had all been worth it. The trail of blood I'd left in my wake to get here.

"I think… I think I've seen plenty. What I want… what I *wish* is to live in peace with my family. I wish to watch a sunset without worrying about monsters lurking in the shadows. I want to live knowing that life is not a test, but simply an experience, an opportunity to live to the fullest and find happiness."

God descended from the dais, light glimmering off its body like diamonds, gently revealing a being not of angel or humankind, but something in between. Something indescribable yet magnificent. The warmth that radiated from that light was soothing, a blanket that beckoned me to fall into it and sleep.

I'd never felt so tired as I did that moment, when God stood before me, as if granting me the permission to allow myself to finally let go of all the weight I'd been carrying. The temptation to let myself be healed by that light, that warmth, was almost too much to bear.

We stood like that for a minute or for a hundred years, time had no bearing here. And in those moments of utter silence and tranquility, I knew that if I let myself fall into those loving arms, God could absorb all my pain and mend all the shattered pieces of my soul. This being was my Creator. The beginning and end of all things. My spirit recognized it before I did and accepted it. God could lift all my grief from my heart with one breath if I allowed myself to relinquish my pride.

But why should I be free of my pain? If God's all-powerful love couldn't bring back all the people who had died or erase from the heart of every survivor the horror they endured, how could I allow *my* wounds to be erased? No. My pain had brought me here. My pain had made me understand. My pain had been my path, and I couldn't un-walk it.

A smile traced over God's lips, but there was a touch of sadness tugging at the corners, as if there had been hope that after revealing the truth to me, my faith had been restored.

Which meant, despite fate, my will could still be mine.

"Healing takes time," I said. "Knowing the truth does not mean I accept it. You might be The Creator, but that doesn't mean humanity can forget what they suffered—because of everything that you kept from them, because of a game you chose play. *I* can't forget."

"I never believed you would. But the time of reckoning has passed, Katherine. There is much left to be done if humanity is to rise from the ashes. Your triumph over the darkness is just the beginning. Still, I understand your need to distance yourself. You're not ready, nor do I expect you to be, but when you *are* ready to rebuild, to bring forth the awakening, I will be here."

"I don't know if I'll ever be… I found my wings because of Mikha'el. He wasn't just my guardian; he was my friend. *He* guided me here. Without him… I'm lost."

"Mikha'el loved you, Katherine. Love you like he loved a daughter. And he believed in you and what you would be capable of. He was what Samael could never be, and that was both my greatest achievement and greatest downfall. But he is fulfilled—in you. Which means wherever you go, he will always be there with you. To guide you. To show you the way. You need only look inside your heart, and he will answer."

"What about the stones? The gates? How do we make sure this never happens again?"

"There is no need for the stones. With your bargain, you made certain no demon will ever escape Abaddon. Such are the nonsensical rules of the universe." There was a bit of amusement in that powerful voice. "The only power that exists, is the power we put faith in, Katherine. Without faith in them, the stones are but stones."

"So, the stones, they only worked because we believed they would, because Samael believed they kept him locked up."

God simply smiled. "On your knees, Nephilim. And hand me your sword."

This time, I did not rebel and did as I was asked.

Gid placed Emrandael on each of my shoulders. "Katherine Elizabeth Jones, you will return to your people, and you will bring with you a symbol of hope and peace—my promise to them from this day forward. The storm has subsided. It is now time for humanity to open their eyes. This sword shall be the beacon for the citizens of Earth... The reminder that you and your son are now the only living descendants of Mikha'el Bar Elah. You are the bridge that will forge the bond between Earth and the rest of the universe. When the time comes, I will call upon your bloodline and should they deem themselves ready, they shall take their rightful seat at my table and usher humanity into their awakening. Stand now."

I was unsure what to do. I'd come here with such rage in my heart and now all of it was gone. I looked around the throne room and wondered what Heaven looked like outside those windows. How it would feel to soar through its skies. So many questions remained, but I wasn't ready to ask them. Not yet.

"The kingdom of Heaven will always welcome you with open arms. But now you must return home. Rest. Enjoy your family. Be merry and fruitful. Elysium will still be here when it is time for your return."

I nodded, oddly feeling nothing but peace in my heart.

Cassael rose to her feet and touched my shoulder. "It's time, Kate."

I looked to God once more. "There is something else. Roger and Isabella… Are they…?"

He smiled. "They are where they are meant to be."

It wasn't the answer I'd hoped for, but it was enough. Cassael went to wrap her wings around me to rift me back, but I stepped away. "No. Let me. I need to do this on my own." "Kate, rifting between worlds is difficult. It also requires a lot of energy. You've been through a lot."

"I'll manage."

"But you don't even know how to get back to Earth."

"My heart knows. Trust me, I'll be fine."

"Kate…"

"Cassael," God said, "some journeys must be traveled alone."

The lieutenant nodded and stepped back. "Safe journey, Katherine. Until we meet again."

"And Katherine…" God said.

"Yes?"

"There will be retribution for Mikha'el's unjust imprisonment and death." God's fiery gaze shot to the back of the throne room, where Khama'el and his sicarii were already bound by golden shackles. I hadn't even noticed when other angels had stormed in and bound them. I fixed my gaze on Khama'el. His burned with rage, but all I offered him was a short smile.

I closed my eyes and sank deep within myself and found that string… the one that tethered me to Jax. I tugged, then I was gone.

Chapter Thirty-Six

JAX

The scent of warm batter and melting butter filled the small kitchen at the house the sanctuary—now called *Los Guardianes Sanctuary*—had offered to our crew of eight, which included me, Luke, Clint and Kelsey, Chaz and Ta'herah, plus Liling and Camila. It was a modest home, and we all had to figure out how to squeeze in, but it had running water and electricity, but most importantly, it was safe.

We loved it. It was the closest thing any of us had experienced in a long time that felt like a real home. And I guess at this point, it *was* home. Except for the fact that not a day went by where I didn't think about Kate. No place would ever truly feel like home to me without her.

Still, even after the three years since Kate had traveled to Hell, I hadn't given up hope that she would return to me one day. Especially since, not long after she left, and we arrived at the sanctuary—thanks to Clint's maps and Ta'herah's alien compass—we noticed the sudden disappearance of not just shaitan, but the undead. It was like the demons got summoned back to Hell and the zombies all just dropped dead —for real this time.

I was convinced she'd killed Samael and had figured a way to trap all the demons back in Abaddon. I mean, it was Kate. If there was someone with the will and might to do it, it was my angel. There was no way to be certain, of course, but I felt it in my heart. And I felt it in the air we breathed. It was like the sickness that had plagued the earth, the darkness that had hovered over us, heavy and oppressive, had suddenly lifted and we were able to breathe the clean air again.

Where she'd gone after that, I had no idea. I had to believe she'd simply taken the long way back home and had gotten caught up in the rift between realms. No clue what had happened to Mikha'el, either. I imagined they were together. It was the only thing that made sense, and that was not just me trying to make myself feel better by building false narratives. All I knew was that both Hell's demons and the sickness had vanished, and that was as good a sign as we could get.

I wasn't naïve, though. There were days that not knowing her fate or that of the archangel's filled me with dread. What if they'd succeeded at killing Samael, but they'd never managed to get out of Abaddon?

But whenever those thoughts crept in, I just looked at my son, like right now, when his little feet were swinging back and forth beneath his chair as he sat at the small wooden table, his chubby fingers drumming an impatient beat as he waited for more pancakes. Moments like these reminded me that there was no room for fear in my life anymore. Only hope.

His bright blue eyes watched me with a gleam that made my heart swell. If only Kate could see the beautiful little angel she'd created. I flipped another pancake. "Almost ready, little man," I said, casting Luke a wink over my shoulder. He clapped his hands, an impatient giggle escaping as he wiggled in his chair.

Outside, the sun stretched across the garden, dappling the

blades of dew-kissed grass with a diamond-like shimmer. Hank was sprawled in a patch of sunlight on the linoleum floor, his thick fur glistening, ears twitching with contentment.

Liling walked in through the back door, humming softly as she showed me the strawberries she'd picked. "We have a good batch this year. They are so fat and juicy," she said, taking a bite of one.

"They do look fat and juicy. I'll cut them up and mix them with blueberries. What do you say, Luke? Want a berry salad?"

His eyes rounded and he offered me the hugest smile ever. I took the strawberries from Liling and began washing them when a sudden, deafening *boom* cracked the air. The three of us flinched as if the explosion had come from somewhere right outside the house. Hank jumped to all fours and immediately rushed to where Luke was sitting, vigilantly standing guard at Luke's feet.

"What the heck was that?" Liling asked, looking out the kitchen window. "Sounded like a thunderclap."

"That wasn't thunder." Ice dripped down my back and I looked at Luke. He'd seemed startled. "You okay, buddy?" He nodded, playing with Hank's perked ears.

"Everyone is going outside…" Liling said as she continued to peek out the window. "What do you think that was?"

Before I could answer, Clint burst into the kitchen, eyes wide, a sheen of sweat glistening on his brow. He looked like he'd sprinted across the sanctuary. "It's Kate…" he said, breathless, his voice rough with urgency.

The room spun, reality tilting on its axis. I didn't need to ask for clarification. The tone in Clint's voice, the way he stood there, chest heaving, was enough. I turned to Liling, who had already stepped forward, eyes wide and expectant.

"Stay with Luke," I said, voice sharper than I intended. She nodded, scooping him up as he started to protest.

"Daddy, what's happening?" Luke's voice quivered, tiny

hands reaching for me, and the weight of his fear nearly rooted me to the spot.

"I'll be right back, buddy," I promised, forcing a smile that felt like glass shattering inside me. "Liling and Hank won't let anything happen to you."

I sprinted outside, heart hammering in my chest, my gut twisting into knots as my eyes landed on the crowd gathered in the middle of the courtyard. People murmured, faces pale with worry, parting as I pushed through.

And then I saw her.

Kate lay crumpled on the ground, her wings splayed out, steam curling up from her skin. She looked as if she had fallen from the sky, like a star yanked from the heavens. Chaz was there, his hand hovering near her as if afraid to touch, eyes flicking up to meet mine with a mixture of fear and relief.

"Make room," I said, my voice raw as I dropped to my knees beside her. The world narrowed until it was only her and the slight rise and fall of her chest, her flushed cheeks, and Mikha'el's sword gripped in her hands.

Without hesitation, I slipped my arms beneath her, lifting her as gently as I could. Her body was limp, terrifyingly so, and the heat radiating from her made my skin sting. But she was alive.

Heaven help me I thought I might break down, but I needed to keep myself together. Kate was alive. She was fucking alive, and she was here.

"Get back!" someone shouted as I stood, and I barely registered the crowd dispersing, making room as I started for the infirmary, each step faster than the last.

"She just appeared," Chaz said, trailing close behind me, his voice tight with unspoken questions. "One second the courtyard was empty, the next—"

"I know," I said, cutting him off. I couldn't listen, couldn't focus on anything other than the weight in my arms and the thrum of her heartbeat against my chest.

The door burst open as I shouldered my way into the small clinic, Chaz trailing behind me. The nurses inside seemed frozen in shock, eyes wide as they looked at the woman with wings cradled in my arms. "What happened?" one of them asked.

I quickly laid her on one of the gurneys. "I'm guessing she had a rough landing after rifting. Where's the doctor?"

Clint rushed in from outside. "Doc was on a house call. She's on her way now."

I clasped his shoulder as the nurses started taking vitals. "Thanks, kid."

"I'm gonna go update the others," Chaz said, rushing back out the door.

Clint raked anxious hands through his hair. "I just hope she's okay… I was helping Kelsey with the little kids at the rec center when I heard the *boom*. I tried to get to you as fast as I could."

"You did fine, Clint. She's breathing. That's what matters."

Doctor Grant stepped into the infirmary, her lab coat swaying as she rushed to the gurney. Kate was already hooked up to a monitor, which showed that her heart rate seemed stable, but I was no doctor.

"How she look, doc?"

Doctor Grant used her stethoscope to check her heart and pulse. Looking her over, she didn't seem concerned at all. "Well, I've never treated an… angel before, but her heart rate seems fine. Oxygen levels are normal. I mean, for a human."

"She's Nephilim."

"I've never treated one of those, either, but given her stable vitals, I'd say she's… Well, it's almost like she's just sleeping."

"Sleeping?" Clint asked, raking another hand through his hair.

"Very deeply," the doctor said. "We're gonna give her some fluids, but I think she just needs to rest."

A puff of relief blew from my chest. "What about the heat coming off her, though? The flushed skin? She looked like she was burning up when we found her."

"She doesn't have a fever, if that's what you're asking. Really, Jax, she's fine. She's cool to the touch now. Maybe something to do with the angelic properties in her blood?"

"Maybe? I'm gonna stay here until she wakes up."

"I'll have them wheel her into one of the private rooms."

"Thanks, doc."

"Don't mention it." She placed a hand on my shoulder. "I'm glad she's back, Jax."

After they brought her into the private room and the nurses walked out, leaving Clint and me alone with her, the kid sank into a chair in the corner. "I can't believe she's here. She found us, Jax. She found her way home."

Home... Kate was home. The words almost couldn't solidify in my mind. I'd dreamt of this moment every single day since the moment she disappeared into that portal. I stood at the foot of her bed, watching as her chest rose and fell, her face peaceful as if she was, in fact, just in a deep sleep. Her wings had spirited away, maybe a self-defense mechanism? Who knew.

All that mattered was she was home. Christ. Kate was home. I almost didn't want to say the words out loud, fearful this was all just a dream and somehow, I'd wake up. I walked beside her and took her hand in mine, the warmth of her skin seeping into my bones. I rubbed her knuckles gently. "Take all the time you need, angel. I'm not leaving your side."

Reckoning

THE REST of the day came and went. Chaz, Ta'herah, and the girls stopped by to see how Kate was doing, and to force me to take a break. To at least eat something, but when I refused, they took turns bringing me snacks. I needed to be there when Kate opened her eyes. Thankfully, Kelsey and Liling had paired up to babysit Luke. He kept asking for me, but I wasn't ready to tell him about Kate yet. I honestly didn't know how, but at minimum, I needed her awake before I broke the news to him.

I'd made sure to talk about her any chance I had. I hated not having a photograph to show him who his mommy was, but at least he knew about her and that she loved him so much. My worry now was how Kate would react when she woke up and realized she'd missed the last three years of his life. When she went into that portal, I'd warned her of the time warps when traveling to other realms, especially Abaddon, but she'd made the choice to leave anyway.

I didn't fault or resent her for it. She'd done what she'd needed to, and thanks to her, the world had begun to return to some semblance of normality. Still, I knew none of that would be enough to soften the blow that Luke was now three years old. But he was such a sweet and resilient boy, I was certain they would become close pals in no time. He'd had the girls spoiling him a million times over since we'd arrived at the sanctuary, and I was forever grateful for their help. Clint and Chaz, too. Not to mention Hank was the best guardian a kid could ever hope for. But nothing could replace a mother's love. As much as I knew the news would tear her apart, in the end, she would step into her role as mom as soon as she rose from the gurney.

Night fell and she still hadn't woken up. I tried not to panic, holding on to the hope that I knew had brought her back to me, but I couldn't help the heaviness that had begun to settle over my chest. I wanted to take her into my arms so badly. I wanted to see her eyes, hear her voice, kiss her lips.

God. I just wanted her to wake up so I could tell her how much I'd missed her and how much I loved her, probably more than ever.

Eventually, everybody went back home to get some sleep. I pulled a chair to her bedside and remained in the same spot, holding her hand until sunrise. Until, with a soft voice, Kate called my name and life returned to my body.

Chapter Thirty-Seven

KATE

The soft murmur of voices wove through my consciousness like a gentle breeze. I felt the warmth of sunlight brushing against my skin, the scent of clean linens mingling in the air. Blinking my eyes open, the world settled into focus—whitewashed walls, a tall window letting in slanted beams of golden light, and beside me, Jax's familiar profile. His dark hair was tousled, his long lashes framing closed eyes, and his face was etched with the weariness of someone who'd been waiting far too long.

"Jax…" My voice was barely a whisper as I ran my fingers through his hair. His eyes fluttered open and relief bloomed across his face, and in an instant, his arms were around me, holding me so tightly it was as if he feared I might disappear again.

"Kate," he said, voice cracking. "God, angel. I can't believe you're really here."

I exhaled shakily, the tension in my body unwinding with each heartbeat that matched his. I pulled back just enough to see him, to touch his face and trace the familiar lines. "I'm here," I said, my voice hoarse and splintered. "I'm home."

Jax's hands cupped my cheeks, searching my face as if he needed confirmation that this wasn't just a cruel illusion. "Are you okay? Do you feel alright?"

A soft, tired smile pulled at my lips. "I'm fine. Just… a bit disoriented. Rifting took everything out of me. I felt like I was spinning through a thousand realms, lost and weightless until I felt the tug—" My gaze locked onto his glittering blue eyes, and I pressed my palm over his heart. "The tug of your love. That's what brought me back."

He let out a shuddering breath, pulling me close again, forehead resting against mine. "I don't think I've breathed properly since you left."

"I'm here," I repeated, grounding both of us in that truth. But the memory of why I had left, of what had happened in Abaddon and at God's throne, pulled at me like a shadow that had followed me home. "I killed Samael," my voice was low, "but I couldn't save…" Sobs choked my throat.

"It's okay, angel." Jax wiped at my tears, the tears that wouldn't stop coming.

"Mikha'el, he… What Samael did to him. I couldn't save him. I tried, Jax. I tried. I even went to Elysium. I begged God, but I—" My words caught, too raw to touch.

Jax snapped his gaze to me, holding my face in his hands. "Did you say… God?"

I nodded, tears still streaming down my face in rivers, as if all the pain and devastation had finally caught up to me and I couldn't stop the onslaught of emotions.

Jax simply kept wiping them off my cheeks, his eyes glistening with tears. "Not right now, angel. We have plenty of time to talk about what happened to you while you were gone. You decide when you're ready." He brushed a stray lock of hair behind my ear, his thumb grazing my cheek.

I shifted, sitting up fully, taking in the quiet room, the slant of light cutting across the floor. "Where are we? How is every-one? Hank—oh God, and Luke, is he okay?"

He smiled softly, the corners of his eyes crinkling. "Every-one's safe. After the fight at the asylum, once you went through the portal, we managed to rescue the children. It took a week, but we made it to the sanctuary. Hank's fine, sunning himself outside as usual. We reunited with Liling and Camila—"

"Oh, my God. The girls! They're okay?" I interrupted, hope flaring in my chest.

"Yes, they are fine," Jax confirmed. "Alive and well. And Ta'herah stayed with us, too, though she's got her own story to tell."

Relief washed over me, an unexpected surge of warmth amid the chaos. But just as quickly, the lightness faded as I looked into Jax's eyes and saw something deeper, heavier.

Weariness clasped my heart. "What is it?"

He drew in a long breath, fingers tightening around mine. "Kate, there's something you need to know…" His hesitation was like a knife twisting in my gut. "Remember what I told you about the time warps when traveling through realms? Especially Abaddon?"

The way my heart had begun to crash against my chest made my hands tremble. My mind was already spinning with what I thought he was going to say, but I couldn't bring myself to utter it out loud. The repercussions of that reality… I shook my head.

"Kate, please. You need to listen."

I pulled away from him and regretted it the moment I saw the hurt in his eyes. But I couldn't focus on anything else, not until I knew. "How long?"

"Three years."

The words slammed into me, stealing the air from my lungs. I felt the room tilt, the ground shift beneath me. *Three years.* My heart pounded harder, a thundering echo of lost moments and laughter I would never get back. Luke. My baby. I blinked rapidly, trying to process the cruel passage of time, tears burning as they spilled over.

"Three years," I repeated, the reality of it pressing down on me like a weight. "That means… Luke's three now."

Jax's eyes shone with both grief and understanding, his voice gentle but firm. "He is. I know that's a lot to absorb; that it hurts, Kate. But you did this for him. For a chance at a life free from Samael's darkness."

A sob escaped me, raw and jagged. I felt the loss carve itself into my soul, each moment I'd missed, every milestone I'd never seen. Jax took me into his arms, and I let him hold me until my tears dried up, though I don't think I could ever stop mourning those lost three years. But amid that pain, I found the truth I'd been taught, the duality that held the world together—life balanced by death, joy tempered by sorrow, love strengthened by sacrifice.

God had told me many would reap the rewards of my sacrifices, though they would never know what I'd lost. I'd lost experiencing the last three years—the *first* three years—of my son's life, but I'd gained the rest of a lifetime with him. Free of the pain and sorrow Samael had caused.

After a long while, I wiped what remained of the tears and I met Jax's eyes, finding strength in his steady gaze. "I need to see him."

Jax leaned in and kissed my lips, a soft tender kiss, one laden with love and understanding. He was trying to soften his words. "I haven't had a chance to prepare him since you arrived yesterday. I want to talk to him first."

I lowered my chin and nodded, but it was hard masking the tears that threatened to crest once again. "I understand."

He tipped my chin up, those beautiful blue eyes sparkling in the daylight. "Angel, I've talked to him about you every day since you left. Not a single day has gone by, even when he was just an infant, that I didn't tell him how much you loved him and how fast I knew you were traveling across the galaxies to get to him."

"Does he know? About what I am… What *he* is?"

"He knows he's special and that you are special just like him, but his wings haven't manifested yet."

I sucked in a deep breath and settled my emotions. There was nothing I could do to change the loss of time, but I could control how I chose to live the rest of my life, starting with this moment, this opportunity to meet my son again, for the first time.

"I'm going to send Liling and Camila over with some clean clothes. They've been dying to see you. There's a shower through there," he said, pointing to a door in the room.

"Did you say… shower?"

He smiled. "Lots has changed since you left, angel. You killing Samael… it changed everything. The demons, the devoured… they're gone. People have started living again. Life has returned to Earth. We've begun to rebuild, to find meaning again. All because of you. You did that, Kate." He leaned in for another kiss. "God, I've missed you so much, you have no fucking idea. I want to hear about everything that happened, but we have the rest of our lives to catch up. Right now, I want you to shower, take some time to take this all in. Eat something. I'll come back for you when it's time."

I nodded, the hollow ache inside me still throbbing but steadied by his presence. "Okay," I whispered.

He stood, pressing a lingering kiss to my forehead before stepping away. As the door closed softly behind him, I sank back into the bed, eyes lifting to the ceiling as I clutched the sheets with trembling hands. *Three years.* Three years gone, in the blink of an eye.

But I was home. And soon, I would hold my son.

I stood in the silence of my infirmary bathroom, the steam from the hot shower still hanging in the air. I wiped at the mirror over the sink and took a deep breath. For the first time in what felt like eternity, I stared upon my own face, a face I barely recognized any more. There was a gauntness to my cheeks, a hollowness beneath my eyes. My hair, once dark and lustrous, now seemed streaked with whispers of silver that glinted like battle scars. They reminded me of my mother, who had gone gray young. But it was my eyes that caught me off guard the most; they looked haunted, older, as if I'd lived several lifetimes since I last gazed into them.

I unfurled my wings, the span catching the light and casting a shimmer across the walls. They seemed larger somehow, more brilliant than I remembered, the feathers edged in a deep gold, almost brassy color that spoke of Mikha'el's lineage. My heart squeezed and I wanted to cry, but I held back the tears.

Today was not about mourning. Today was about celebrating life. Family.

For a moment, I stared at the reflection, the weight of those three lost years pressing into my chest, as heavy and immovable as stone. The people I'd left behind—the people I loved—had continued to live, to grow, to change without me. The thought of stepping back into their world—a world that had moved on—left me feeling like an outsider in my own life.

A knock at the door pulled me from my thoughts. "Kate, you ready?" Jax asked.

Wings folding back against me, I dressed quickly. "Be right out." When I finally opened the door, his eyes shone with a mixture of anticipation and something tender. He reached out a hand, a silent invitation, and I took it, the warmth of his touch grounding me.

I decided to leave Emrandael behind until after I saw Luke. I wanted to go to him as his mother, not as a warrior. As we stepped out of the infirmary, the sunlight spilled over us, brighter and more vivid than I'd seen in years. The sanctuary was alive, bustling with people who paused in their work, their conversations, to watch us pass. Faces turned toward me, eyes wide with awe, reverence, and curiosity. I could hear whispers say… *'Kate, the Guardian, the one who slew the serpent.'*

A woman approached, her stride confident, shoulder-length blonde hair bouncing with every step. "Welcome home," she said, a warm smile spreading across her face. "I'm Rachel, the governor of *Los Guardianes Sanctuary*. We named it in honor of you and your crew when they arrived with your story."

Emotion caught in my throat, and all I could do was nod. "Thank you," I whispered, voice breaking. "Thank you for opening your home to them… to me."

Rachel's smile deepened and her eyes glistened as she placed a reassuring hand on my arm. "It was never a question. Your story, your sacrifice, has become a beacon here, a symbol of hope for our people and for the other sanctuaries in the area."

Before I could respond, another couple approached. The sight of them jolted my memory—an echo of the day we met them at the shore of the Hudson River, their boat a lifeline as they agreed to ferry us across the water. The woman's eyes, warm and knowing, crinkled at the edges as she took my hand. "I always knew you were something special, Kate. I told my husband that day that I knew you'd make your way back to us."

I smiled, the memory lifting some of the weight from my chest. "Thank you for trusting in me, for telling me about this place."

"Just glad you found us, hon."

As we moved farther, my gaze found Chaz standing beneath a tree, Ta'herah beside him, a small child cradled in his arms. Ta'herah's usually fierce eyes softened when they met mine. "Welcome back, Earth child."

Chaz grinned, the same roguish smile that could light up any room. "Took you long enough, boss lady," he teased, his eyes twinkling. He unsheathed Zadkiel's sword from a scabbard. "I told you I'd keep it safe until you returned."

"No. You earned that weapon, Guardian. Keep it."

He nodded in appreciation and Ta'herah's sighed as her gaze softened. "When the portal closed, the Eldhon-rā ceased to function, the elemental magic completely spent."

I laid a hand on her arm. "Oh, no. How are you supposed to return home?"

She smiled. "It is of no matter, for from the moment I saw this male," she gestured to Chaz, "I knew he would be a fine mate. That he would give me strong offspring. I do not wish to return to Aetheria. Earth is my home now."

Chaz's laughter rumbled, and he kissed the top of the child's head. "Glad I could oblige."

I almost broke into laughter again, but Clint pushed through the gathering, Kelsey by his side. He didn't give me a chance to say anything before he wrapped me in a fierce hug, murmuring, "I've missed you, Kate."

I hugged him back, the familiar strength of his embrace anchoring me. "I want to say I've miss you, too, but, in my timeline, I've barely been gone a day." He chuckled and I ruffle his hair. "But I sure am glad to see you, kid." When I pulled away, I noted the way he and Kelsey stood close, his empyrean metal fingers laced through hers. It was a testament to the time that had passed, to the changes that had taken place in my absence.

"Welcome home, Kate," Kelsey said.

Finally, we reached the front porch of a white house with

black shutters and a lemonade porch. It was simple, inviting, and there, behind the storm door, Hank waited, tail wagging so hard it looked like a propeller. The door creaked open, and he bolted out, nearly knocking me over as he jumped up, licking my face and whining with joy.

"Oh, Hank," I said, tears streaming down my face as I buried my hands in his fur. "So happy to see you, too, buddy." He looked the same, save for some gray hair around his snout and a rounder belly. Other than that, he was still my good boy.

The moment stretched, until the door opened wider, and Liling and Camila stepped out, a small boy holding their hands. The world stilled and I dropped to my knees, my breath catching somewhere in my chest as I took him in— dark hair like mine, eyes the exact shade of Jax's glimmering blue, and little freckles scattered across his cheeks and nose.

He looked at me, head tilting with a child's curiosity. "Are you… my mommy?" he asked, his voice small, yet clear.

A sob tore through me, and I nodded, unable to speak past the lump in my throat. "Yes, baby. I'm your mommy."

He hesitated only a moment before he ran into my open arms, and I held him as tightly as I dared, as if letting go would mean losing him all over again. I breathed in the scent of him, the warmth, and I knew that no matter how many years had passed, this moment was worth every battle, every sacrifice.

Jax knelt beside us and wrapped his arms around us both, cradling us in his strength. I was home. I was finally home, and I never planned to leave my family ever again.

Chapter Thirty-Eight

KATE

The warm, savory aroma of garlic and tomatoes filled the air as I sat at the dining table, surrounded by the people who had become my family. The low hum of conversation, punctuated by the clinking of silverware, blended with the occasional giggle from Luke as he played with his fork, waiting for dinner to be served with a mischievous gleam in his eyes. I sat between him and Jax, my heart swelling as I took in the scene before me, Hank at our feet beneath the table.

Liling and Camila shared a smile, some secret meaning passing between them. The girls had grown as close as sisters. Ta'herah sat with her back straight, her warrior's posture softened by the warmth in her eyes as she watched Chaz recount a story, his hands gesturing wildly to illustrate whatever tall tale he was spinning. She'd swapped her armor for normal human clothes, but the Aetherian rider would always be a presence to behold.

Clint and Kelsey emerged from the kitchen, Clint balancing a large pot of meatballs in one hand and a platter of baked bread in the other. Kelsey placed a large bowl of spaghetti in the middle of the table. Clint's grin was wide as he settled the rest of the food. "I thought it would be nice to cook up a Sunday dinner like my family used to make," he announced, a trace of nostalgia coloring his voice. "To welcome you back home to us, Kate. May we share many more meals like this."

The memory struck me with an unexpected sharpness. The image of another dinner, simpler and tense, just before the sicarii had attacked and everything had changed in an instant. Before I could be swept up by the tide of memories, Jax's hand brushed against mine under the table, anchoring me in the present. His touch was gentle, a silent reminder that we were here, together, and safe. For now.

Dinner was filled with stories and laughter, voices overlapping as everyone shared moments from their day or old memories that hadn't been spoken of in years. Luke leaned against me, his small hand clutching my sleeve as he giggled at one of Clint's jokes. I pressed a kiss to the top of his head, breathing in his sweet scent that made my heart ache with a fierce, protective love.

As plates emptied and yawns stretched across the table, one by one, everyone stood. Liling and Camila offered to clean up, and Clint walked out with Kelsey for a late-night stroll, their fingers intertwined. Ta'herah rose with Chaz, their daughter nestled sleepily in his arms as they departed to bed.

Jax stood and reached for Luke, lifting him up in his arms. We walked together to Luke's room, and I asked Jax if it would be okay for me to do the bedtime routine. He had no objection, and Luke was more than excited for me to give him his bath.

His room was cozy, filled with little details that spoke of Jax's love for him: a shelf of worn books, a stuffed bear with a patched-up ear, a small blanket with stars stitched along the edge. My heart swelled, both with melancholy for the things I'd missed, but also with anticipation for the memories and tokens I would be able to add to this little life Jax had preserved, like he'd been holding it in place for me until I returned.

I helped Luke into the tub, the warm water easing his sleepy muscles as he giggled and splashed. "Mommy, can we read the star book?" he asked, his voice barely a whisper as I wrapped him in a towel and lifted him onto the bed and dressed him in his PJs.

"Of course, sweetheart," I replied, brushing his damp hair from his forehead as I settled beside him.

Jax pulled the book from the shelf and handed it to me. "You'll probably have to read it to him like four times before he falls asleep. I'll be in the room across the way when you're ready." He leaned in and kissed Luke on the forehead. "Love you, buddy. Be good to Mommy, and don't make her read it too many times."

"Like ten times," Luke said, giggling.

"Wise guy," Jax said. "See you when you're ready, angel."

I read the book about ten times until his eyes fluttered closed, his little body curled against mine. I would've read it another ten times if he'd asked me to. The steady rise and fall of his breath was a lullaby I'd longed for in the darkest nights when the Devil's Army had taken him from me. Pressing one last kiss to his temple, I gently untangled myself and tucked him in, lingering for a moment to take in the soft glow of the moonlight spilling through the window, casting silver shadows across his peaceful face.

Hank had been lying on the floor next to Luke's bed. I padded my leg, a command to follow me, but he just perked up his head and stared at me, ears twitching. I smiled. "After three years, I guess I can't blame you if I'm no longer your favorite. As long as it's Luke, I don't mind. Sleep well, buddy."

When I finally made my way to the room across the way, Jax was there, standing by the window, bathed in the pale light of the moon. His silhouette was strong and steady, a guardian keeping watch. He didn't turn as I approached, but I could see the tension in his shoulders ease when I placed my hand on his back.

"It's a beautiful night," he said, his voice low, carrying the weight of everything unsaid.

"It is," I agreed, my fingers tracing idle patterns along the line of his spine, his back muscles flexing at the slide of my hand. God, I'd forgotten how good it felt to touch him. We stood in silence for a moment, the cool night air drifting through the open window, carrying with it the scent of jasmine and the distant sound of crickets.

He turned to face me, the moonlight catching the deep blue of his eyes, making them shimmer like the sea at dusk. There was something raw in his expression, a vulnerability he rarely let show. "I tried not letting fear get the best of me," he admitted, the words almost inaudible. "But there were days where not having you here… it became so unbearable, Kate, I wanted to rip open the gates somehow and go look for you in Hell. But then I thought… I couldn't abandon Luke. You'd probably kill me."

I smiled. "I definitely would've." Cupping his face with both hands, I whispered, voice trembling, "I was afraid, too. I knew I was leaving, but I didn't know how or when I'd be back. But I did, Jax. I came back to you. To both of you."

His arms wrapped around me, pulling me close until there was no space between us, the steady thrum of his heart a beat that echoed mine. We stood like that for what felt like forever, a moment suspended in time where the world outside our window ceased to exist.

Love and desire flared in my veins. In my mind, I hadn't been gone three years, but I had started to feel the weight of my absence, how it had impacted everyone, and I was ready to make up for every lost minute, starting with Jax, with the man who had stolen my heart and given me back hope. "I don't want to waste another second," I said, my voice stronger now, filled with certainty. "I want to be with you, Jax. Completely."

His breath caught, and for a moment, he just looked at me, as if trying to memorize every detail of my face. Then, with a gentle touch, he brushed his lips against mine, a kiss that was soft at first, tender. But it deepened, growing with a heat that chased away the chill of the cool night. When we finally broke apart, his forehead rested against mine, both of us breathless. "I love you," he whispered, the words a promise and a plea all at once.

"I love you, too."

"Are you sure you want this… right now?"

"Trust me. I want you now more than ever."

With those words, Jax lifted me into his arms and I wrapped my legs around his waist. He grabbed my ass and the thrill that raked through me reached every nerve ending, the star energy in my veins already igniting. "Christ, angel. Have you any idea how many times I've envisioned this moment? I've needed you so bad, baby. Your body. Your breath. Your heart pounding against mine…"

I kissed him harder, my tongue battling with his, the heat and wetness of his mouth driving me wild, the sensation making me so wet for him, my clothes felt too tight, too rough against my skin. I needed him to rip them off me. Needed my naked skin against his. Needed him to touch me in places only he could. To own me like only he knew how.

"Jax, please… It feels like it's been too long." Not just with him, but too long since I could be with someone and not worry that this might be the last time. Too long since I'd been able to completely leg go and not have a single ounce of fear in my heart.

He walked us over to the bed, where he sat me on the edge while he stood before me. My mouth watered at the sight of the ridge building in his jeans. He unbuckled his belt, and excitement bubbled up inside me, remembering how he'd used a belt on me once. That moment had been seared into my heart and into every inch of my body. What he'd done to me that night had been liberating, an intoxication beyond measure. As if seeing those thoughts in my eyes, he said, "I still fantasize about that night, angel. I've come to the image of you on your knees and that belt wrapped around your neck countless times while I waited for your return. But right now, I want you without games."

He tried unbuttoning his jeans, but I put my hand up. "Let me." I gasped when I pulled him free.

Stars have mercy. He was still as large and beautiful as I remembered. Jax shimmied off his pants and boxers and pulled off his shirt until he stood completely naked before me. "Put me in your mouth, angel. You've no fucking clue how badly I've been dying for the feel of your lips around my cock."

I lowered to my knees and stared up at the beauty of his body. His abdomen and chest rippled with muscle, and it was the evidence of all the hard work he'd been putting in helping rebuild this town. He looked so stunning, his hard cock jutting out, begging for me to take him into my mouth. Jax laced his fingers through my hair and gripped me tight at the base of my skull.

Shit. It reminded me about how rough he liked to fuck my mouth. Wrapping my hand around the base of his shaft, I guided him into my mouth slowly, which only made him grip my hair tighter, the tingly sensation reaching down between my legs. I was still dressed, but this was what he wanted. To torture me just a little.

I ran my tongue over the slit of the head, tasting the dewy

drop at the tip. He moaned as I licked it off him, a rumble that vibrated through my body. "Fuck, Kate…" He spread his legs wider and drove himself deeper into my mouth, taking over the pace, fucking my mouth just how he wanted, deep and hard, with abandon. It was punishing, especially as his grip on my hair tightened, making me see stars, but I didn't give a shit. I couldn't get enough of his cock ramming into my mouth, filling me until it hurt.

I ran my hands up his legs, caressing his muscular thighs, his backside. He made sure to hit the back of my throat with every thrust, with every throaty growl, until his entire body tightened. I knew he was close… so close, I salivated. I loved it when he turned feral for me. It made me want that salty taste in my mouth even more. Made me crave it like I'd been thirsting for him for ages. But he pulled free, panting, his chest rising and falling so fast I thought his heart was going to rip right out of his chest.

I licked my lips, silently begging him to give me what I wanted.

"Not yet, angel. I've not had you for far too long to rush through this meal."

He took my hand and guided me to stand, his lips meeting mine as he gently unbuttoned my pants and slid a hand down the front and under my panties. He moaned again, that throaty sound he made my undoing. He wasn't shocked to find me drenched, more like relieved. The feel of my slick center sent him into a frenzy, and he quickly stripped me of all my clothes and laid me on the bed.

"I made use of the trimmers this time," I said with a wink, and he burst into such a joyous laugh, I couldn't contain myself and joined him.

"Let's have a look then," he said as he spread my thighs open and took in the sight of me. "Fuck me, you're gorgeous."

I held my breath as he expertly found the tender spot right

at the top of my slit. My hips lifted off the bed. I couldn't have enough of his tongue as he licked me up and down, drenching me with his saliva. Images of that time we found the Oreos in that abandoned apartment and the way he showed me how expertly he could use his tongue on the cookie sent my orgasm into the stratosphere. "Come in my mouth, angel. I want to taste every drop of you."

I practically lost my mind at his words and savored the sweet torture between my legs before letting go. He lapped up my release until he felt satisfied that he'd licked it all up. He crawled over me, his cock impossibly hard. Instantly, my insides revved up again. He kissed my stomach and up my chest, licking and biting my nipples until I was writhing beneath him.

The muscles on his arms and shoulders were massive, rolling like boulders every time he moved. "Jax, please. I need you inside me."

He lowered his mouth to my neck, kissing his way up to my ear, nipping my earlobe as he gently pressed his hardness against me. But he didn't go inside; he simply teased, making me savage for him. "How much longer do you need me to beg?"

"Until I'm satisfied that you've paid for making me want you to the point of utter torture." He nibbled some more. "You have no idea what it's been like to not have you for the last three years. The torture of craving your touch, your fucking taste, angel…" He cupped a breast and moaned. "The feel of your body under my hands. The wetness between your legs." Lips hovering over mine, he met my gaze. "Baby…" he breathed, his pelvis pressing harder against me as I spread my legs for him. He smiled knowingly. "I want you, too. More than you can possibly imagine. My cock moving inside you, filling you until you can't take me anymore. It's all I've been thinking about." His breath brushed over me as he whispered those words over my lips, and I swore I would come with him just pushing the tip against me.

When he saw how close he'd gotten me to the finish line again, he crashed his lips into mine and drove himself deep inside me, painfully slow until he buried himself all the way to the hilt, until I felt every single inch of his length and my walls stretched to accommodate him. He started off slow, never breaking eye contact, savoring every second that our bodies were connected, every thrust, every moan. We couldn't get enough. Neither one of us.

But I wanted more… needed more. I needed him to purge me of my pain, of all the darkness that had tried to consume me. I wanted him to fill me with his love until nothing remained of me or him, and there was only *us*.

Our breaths grew shallow, and his pace intensified. We were past making love. I wanted him to fuck me.

His lids grew heavy, his jaw tense. "Fucking hell, angel. You feel so amazing." He got on his knees, put his palms on my thighs to spread my legs wider, and began hammering, relentlessly. His gaze was drunk on my body, on the image of his cock ramming into me, on my wetness coating his length, on the way my breasts bounced with every thrust. He couldn't get enough… He wanted more, more, more.

This… this moment when not only our bodies but our souls became one, was our communion with the divine. This was how we became whole, when our bodies met, when our breaths became one and he could take everything from me. And I wanted him to take it all, to take as much as he could. All my pain, all my sorrow, all the heaviness that sat on my shoulders after learning the truth of who and what I was. The implications it had for the entire world. The burden placed upon me was a mountain of jagged rock. But I would bear it. Damn me, I would fucking bear it, but right now, when it was just me and Jax, I would allow him to take it from me. To make me forget. To make me feel only him and his love.

And heavens, I fucking loved this version of him—so unhinged, so lost to the pleasure he was giving and taking from me all at the same time that it felt like rifting through worlds.

His eyes met mine, and I knew he saw it: my need to have him purge me of the events of the last years of our lives. There was no need for him to utter the words because they were etched in his lust-filled eyes… *I will make love to you every day and night if that's what you want, angel. If that's what you need. I'm yours.*

He slowed a little, trying to keep himself from coming, but he began that torturous circling motion with his thumb right over my clit until I lost it. "That's it. Come for me again. Let me be the one who heals your wounds, baby."

My screams must have been heard across the entire sanctuary, but I didn't give a damn. I rode the wave of pleasure that wracked through my body until I couldn't stop trembling. Jax licked his fingers, and I swore his eyes glowed red with wickedness. "It's my turn."

"I want to be on top."

He turned me over quickly, our bodies never losing that connection. And when I was finally on top, his cock buried deep inside me, my skin began to tingle, my sigils flaring to life all over my arms. Then my wings unfurled to their full span, illuminating the room in sparkling light.

Jax gasped, his hands on my hips as I rode him. His eyes skimmed up and down my entire body until he couldn't tear his gaze off my wings. "Fuck… you're a dream. You have to be a fucking dream."

"Touch them…" I moaned, bringing them closer so he could reach the flight feathers. His fingers were deft as he gently skimmed over the shafts, preening each feather. The sensation rippled all the way from the tip of the feathers to my spine, sending pulse after pulse of mind-blowing pleasure throughout my entire body, down to my clit.

"They are so soft..." he said, his voice trailing. "I don't know how much longer I can hold back..."

My sigils burned brighter than they ever had; I was almost glowing. Jax's throaty moans were uncontainable as I squeezed him hard with my inner walls. Every lift and drop felt excruciatingly delightful. I could do this forever, if only to see the way his entire body responded to me. His muscles strained, thick veins roping over his neck, his shoulders, his arms. He looked so beautiful splayed out below me, and I understood now why angels had Fallen. His fingers dug into my thighs as he met each drop with an equally forceful thrust.

"You're gonna make me come, angel..."

My wings whipped and whipped, a vortex of air churning everything loose in the room. It was like my wings were responding to the tension building in my groin, my moans rising in pitch, matching his as we both chased the finish line. Faster, harder. I'd never felt sex like this before; every single one of my senses was heightened and the sensations circulating over every feather, shaft, and bone of my wings was insane.

Jax reached for my neck and pulled me in closer until our gazes were locked in an epic battle. I wanted his release, he wanted mine. "I fucking love you so much," he growled. "If you ever leave me again..."

I placed a finger over his straining lips. "Hush... I'm never leaving you ever again. That's a promise." I put my forehead against his, our breaths sawing in and out of our chests, our hearts pounding so hard, it was almost as if they wanted to punch through our ribcages and touch each other.

With one final roar, Jax's body stiffened, and his cock expanded inside me, flooding me with his release. He came, wave after wave, until his cum spilled out of me, triggering my own release. A flash of light exploded from my body, star energy filling the entire room until I came down from the euphoria of my climax and collapsed on top of his chest, my wings draping over our bodies.

WE WENT three or four more times after that. There were so many moments of tenderness, where we both cried and held each other like we never wanted to part, and moments of absolute reckless fucking, where I let him do all sorts of filth that would certainly land me in Abaddon one day. I didn't care. My body was wholly his to do as he pleased. I could never belong to anyone else, not in this lifetime or the next—not after the way he owned me, mind, body, and soul.

Once we were spent beyond exhaustion, we put on PJs, or I was certain we'd end up fucking again, and we needed rest. The world looked different now, but rebuilding required work, and everyone in the sanctuary had a job. Tomorrow, I would get my duties assigned and begin the arduous task of catching up with the last three years. I would tell Jax and the group everything I learned about my angelic lineage and my conversation with God.

Even thinking about that made my head hurt.

I'd spoken to God…

I didn't want to think about that tonight, though. Tonight, we would sleep.

Jax wrapped an arm around my waist, and his warmth swallowed me whole. I breathed deeply, contently, as I snuggled in closer to him. "You are my compass. My true north," I whispered softly.

He smiled against my ear. "Quoting *The Mummy*? And here I thought I was the corny one."

I jabbed him playfully with my elbow.

He chuckled. "Ow."

"It was how I was able to find my way back to you, smart ass. Because you truly are my compass."

He kissed the back of my bare neck, sending ripples of sweet shivers down my spine. "And… you *complete* me, angel."

Joy lit up inside my veins. Jax had no clue Jerry Maguire had been one of my favorite movies of all time. It wasn't long before he was out cold, his deep breathing the most comforting sound I could imagine. Just as I began to fade, a small knock on the door startled me. The door creaked open, and a little head popped through, followed by Hank's snout poking in as well. "Daddy…" Luke whispered, rubbing his eyes, his voice groggy.

"Daddy is sleeping, honey. You having trouble going back to sleep?"

He nodded, and my heart melted watching him standing at the entrance, his canine guardian probably groggy himself, but I knew him well enough, and sleep would never keep Hank from doing his job.

"You want to come lay with us?"

"Yeah." His little voice tugged at every motherly fiber in my body. He scurried over to my side of the bed and snuggled in under the blankets, burying his body into mine. Hank hopped on also, and splayed his huge body at the bottom of the bed as if his humans didn't need to stretch out their legs. With one large huff, he closed his eyes and fell back to sleep. He'd definitely put on some weight in addition to gaining some gray whiskers. He'd probably been making up for all the missed treats. He deserved them; he deserved all the doggy treats in the world for what he'd done to save it.

I took in a deep breath and smiled, smiled so wide my cheeks hurt.

Jax's arm draped over my waist, Luke tucked into my side, Hank at my feet. This was my whole universe, all in one bed. I closed my eyes. There wasn't dread or worry in my heart. All I had was love so abounding, it threatened to overflow.

Inhaling Luke's scent, I took one last breath before falling asleep.

And for the first time since forever, I didn't fear the night or the new day the sunrise would bring.

The End

TRUTH IS THE MOTHER, THE FOUNDATION, AND THE ROOT OF ALL THINGS. IT IS SHE WHO DELIVERS THOSE WHO KNOW HER.

The Gospel of Truth

Epilogue

KATE

Two years had passed since I'd arrived back on Earth, but the memories of war still lingered like shadows on the edges of my mind. Yet, today, as we walked along the Observatory in Barcelona, those shadows seemed less daunting, more like reminders of what we had endured and why we were here now. The once-overgrown place, tangled with vines and swallowed by neglect, was now vibrant with life. The ancient stones had been washed clean by sun and rain, standing proud against a backdrop of blue sky and the glistening Mediterranean. The observatory overlooked the city sprawled below, bustling with the hum of restoration and renewal. The peaks of the Pyrenees stood like silent sentinels, their jagged forms softened by distance.

Mikha'el had brought me here once, after Luke and Jax were taken by the Devil's Army, when hope had been stolen from me and I wasn't sure I could recover. Back then, the visit to this place had served as a turning point. He'd shown me the boundless beauty of our world, urging me to remember what I was fighting for. I had promised him then that we would come back when the war was over, that we would share an ice cream under the open sky. And though he was not here in person, I was determined to keep that promise.

I sat on the same stone ledge I'd sat on with the archangel, letting the warm breeze push stray strands of hair from my face. The sea stretched out before me, a vast, unending sapphire that caught the sunlight and turned it into liquid jewels. Behind me, the city was alive with the sounds of hammering and laughter. *La Sagrada Familia* rose defiantly from its wounds, covered in scaffolding and the hopeful hands of builders who were piecing its shattered majesty back together.

Shortly after arriving at the sanctuary two years ago, I made sure to meet with Father Ortega as well as with the Guardians of the Eastern Headquarters. With Samael gone and the gates permanently closed, our duty to protect humanity had shifted. Our job now was to guide our world to the new awakening. Faith and religion as we knew it before the gates opened had ceased to exist. As much as those years of Hell on Earth were the worst years in humanity's history, it did usher in a new dawn. The whole world could now live under one truth.

Humans were now part of the Astral Concord, which made us eligible to receive assistance from the people of other worlds. Their technology and celestial powers were crucial in our rebuilding, and for the first time since humans came into existence, we finally knew and accepted we were not alone in the universe.

I could now look upon the streets below with renewed faith in my heart. Because it wasn't just Barcelona that had changed. Every city in the world now teemed with people who had learned to appreciate the simple joy of being alive. Life thrived, not in the same hurried rush as before, but at a pace that spoke of gratitude and resilience.

A sudden gust of wind swept past, tugging at the loose

fabric of my dress. I glanced to my left just as a young boy scrambled onto the ledge beside me, his small fingers gripping the stone as he balanced himself. He turned his face upward, and my breath caught. His dark hair shimmered under the sun, but it was the flash of gold in his eyes—a fleeting, knowing glow—that sent a shiver racing down my spine. He smiled, a lopsided grin that was somehow both innocent and ancient.

"*Hola*," he said, his voice soft as the wind.

Before I could respond, a woman's voice called from the path behind us. "Miguel, *vamos!*"

The boy's smile widened before he turned and hopped down, running toward his mother. I watched him go, my pulse thundering in my ears. For a moment, I swore I felt the brush of a familiar presence, a whisper of wings on the breeze.

"Mikha'el," I whispered, the name slipping from my lips like a prayer. Was it a sign? A reminder that, even though he was gone, he was still watching, still here in some way? I let the thought settle in my chest, warm and bittersweet.

"Mommy!" Luke's voice pulled me from my thoughts. I turned to see Jax approach, holding Luke's hand as the boy skipped beside him, his bronze wings catching the sunlight in a way that made them gleam like molten metal. They were beautiful, strong, just like the wings of the archangel whose lineage lived on in my son's blood.

It had been the manifestation of his wings that prompted me to make this trip, to bring both Jax and Luke to the place Mikha'el had brought me. The place where I had vowed I would descend into the bowels of Hell to bring my family back.

Nephilim were supposed to earn their wings, so Mikha'el had said. Luke's appeared one day after he found an injured puppy that he brought to the barn at the sanctuary and began nursing back to health with the help of one of the older kids.

Shortly after that, finding injured animals and helping them recover became his mission.

I smiled, thinking about the way he lit up every time he helped an animal. He was such a gentle, old soul.

Jax grinned as he handed me an ice cream cone, the corners of his eyes crinkling with happiness. "Vanilla with chocolate chips, just how you like it."

I took the cone, my fingers brushing his, and smiled at him. "Thank you."

He settled beside me on the ledge, lifting Luke between us. Our son's laughter rang out as he took his first bite, smearing ice cream across his cheeks. I chuckled, using the edge of my thumb to wipe it away.

We sat in silence for a while, watching the world below. The sea whispered its secrets, the wind carried the scent of salt and lavender, and the sun painted the sky in hues of amber and rose. This was the world we'd fought for—not perfect, not untouched, but healing and alive. People had learned to live with the knowledge of God's existence, of realms beyond their own, with such tenacity, it was breathtaking. They had learned to cherish each day, each breath, in a way they hadn't before.

I let my gaze drift to Luke, who was now leaning against Jax's side, his eyes wide as he took in the city and the mountains and the sky. He looked up at me and smiled, and I knew then that whatever lay ahead, whatever choices still needed to be made, I could face them. I'd fought and bled and lost, but I had gained so much more.

"Look, Mommy," Luke said, pointing at a dove that soared high above, its wings spread wide, catching the wind as if it owned the sky.

"I see it, baby," I replied, my voice full of wonder. And as we sat there, together, with the world sprawling before us, I knew that this moment was enough. For now, it was enough.

And that was all I needed.

Reckoning

Acknowledgments

As this chapter of the Hell's Angel series draws to a close, I'm overwhelmed with gratitude for everyone who walked this path alongside me.

To my readers: Thank you for your passion and loyalty, for championing these characters and their stories. Your messages, reviews, and enthusiasm have been a guiding light, and I couldn't have imagined completing this series without you. I'm endlessly grateful for each of you and for the impact you've made on this journey.

To my family and friends: Your support through endless drafts and late-night edits has been the backbone of this series. Thank you for believing in me even when I doubted myself, for the laughter that grounded me, and for the love that fueled these stories.

To my team—editor, beta and ARC readers, and everyone who lent an eye, heart, or hand: You've helped shape this world in ways I could never have done alone. Your insight and dedication brought depth to this story, and I'm honored to have had you by my side.

And to the characters who sprang to life in these pages: Thank you for the journey, for revealing parts of myself I didn't know existed, and for showing me what true strength and sacrifice look like. You may be fictional, but your legacy lives on in the hearts of every reader who's turned these pages.

With this final book, I close a chapter of my own life, one

marked by grit, resilience, and wonder. Thank you, Hell's Angel family—for everything.

And for those of you who have asked if this is the last you'll ever see of these characters, I think for now we should let Kate and Jax enjoy their HEA, but I'm not closing the door to other possibilities just yet…

Meet the Author

REAL LOVE AS IT IS. MESSY. COMPLICATED. AND SINFULLY ADDICTIVE.

Born in Colombia and raised in New Jersey since the age of eight, Olivia always dreamed of becoming a storyteller. Now, she enjoys crafting novels with deep, layered plots because romance is not just about the first kiss and the happily ever after, it's about everything in between.

In addition to writing, Olivia loves reading across all genres, binge watching her favorite TV shows, and hanging out on Tuesday nights with her girlfriends for wine, snacks, and junk-TV therapy. Olivia lives in Northern New Jersey with her hubby, three boys, and a mini Aussie named Rosie.

READ MORE FROM OLIVIA
A Dream of Blood and Magic

*Underworld meets Kingdom of the Wicked in this forbidden love,
rivals to lovers, high stakes, slow-burn gothic contemporary
fantasy romance ~ Get it NOW*

www.ingramcontent.com/pod-product-compliance
Lightning Source LLC
Chambersburg PA
CBHW022016300726
48970CB00003B/906